This book is dedicated to El Shaddai, who knows the end from the beginning, makes a way when there seems to be none, and always knows what's best;

My husband, who loves me with a selfless, patient, sacrificial love, continually demonstrating to me the true meaning of the word;

And to my readers who have been waiting for the completion of this series for years while I had babies, raised kids, and got distracted. This one's for you.

Ann A. GOERING

To The Beat Of A
Fools' Drum

THE MOUNTAIN
REDEMPTION SERIES

Cover design copyright © 2025 by Ann Goering. All rights reserved.
Cover design by: Angela Weldin
Cover Photos: Canva.com, Shutterstock.com
Edited by: Rachel Garber
Narrated by: Amberly Stark

ISBN: 978-1-965499-17-7 - Ebook
ISBN: 978-1-965499-18-4 - Paperback
ISBN: 978-1-965499-19-1 - Audiobook

Library of Congress Control Number: 2024926299

www.coveredporchpublishing.com
www.anngoering.com

Requests for information should be addressed to:
Covered Porch Publishing, Ann Goering, PO Box 464, Branson MO 65615

Printed in the United States of America

29 28 27 26 25 A 8 7 6 5 4 3 2

FREE BONUS SHORT STORY

We know Mother Emaline from her role as Raya, Chenoa, and Nizhoni's beloved mother-in-law. But while we've seen her unwavering faith and the impact she's had on her daughters-in-law, where did her faith come from and what were her years like before tragedy struck?

There was a time when Emaline's own life was filled with the rosy hues of love and coming of age – yet even then, storm clouds were brewing on the horizon. A family secret, a desperate situation, and a stranger at a ball collide in a perfect storm that promises to solidify her faith and her future – or break her in the process.

To get Emaline's short story absolutely FREE and start reading today visit:
https://anngoering.com/mountain-redemption-series

One

One day. One hour. One accident. One fire.
Everything had been lost in an instant.

Colorado Territory, August 1874

N izhoni stood transfixed, her mind racing back across the months, her heart falling. She hadn't been back to the high mountain town since leaving for her people's winter camp last fall. The summer heat was pressing in around her, and the aspens' green leaves were dancing in the breeze. It had been nearly ten months since she'd visited town. Surely, she'd thought, enough time had passed. After so long, she would be able to come back with her sister and friend for supplies without thinking of the past. However, when she'd glanced over to reply to her sister's lighthearted comment as they walked by the small white church with the quiet cemetery spread out beside it, her eyes had fallen on the roughhewn cross that stood in remembrance of her late husband and son. Unable to speak or move, she froze mid-stride. Memories came crashing back one after another, sweeping her away to another time, another place.

Suddenly, she was again searching her mother-in-law's cabin, looking for the source of the smoke that laced the air. She was hearing her sister-in-law Raya's scream from the front porch and racing across the room, a sense of dread filling her heart. She was following her younger sister-in-law, Chenoa, out the front door,

1

seeing with her own eyes a sight that would be seared into her memory for the rest of her days. With painful clarity, she could again see, feel, and hear the tragedy of the mill door blocked by heavy logs that had tumbled down against it. Once more, she watched in horror as flames greedily consumed the mill—along with everything and everyone inside it.

She could hear Chenoa screaming out Will's name just before the girl had dissolved into sobs. The smell of burning wood filled the air, stinging her eyes. She could feel her unborn child moving under her hands as she pressed her palms to her swollen belly while she coughed and choked on the heavy, dark smoke. It was being whipped around the homestead by strong winds that had hit with the dry thunderstorm moving across the Rockies, and its presence made breathing difficult. Or was it simply the horrific sight that kept her lungs from being able to draw in a full breath? Frozen in place, she had simply watched as Raya sprinted toward the mill door, trying desperately to move the large, heavy logs that held it shut. But they hadn't moved an inch.

Raya had called for help, and she had forced herself into motion, her legs weak and shaky as she ran across the yard. As she ran, a horrific truth pounded through her consciousness over and over again like the beating of a drum: Alex was inside the fire. Her husband was inside the fire. The love of her life was inside the fire. Her stomach churned in response, but there was no time to be ill. She had to do everything she could to help.

Getting down on her hands and knees, she pulled with all her might to help move the log that blocked the door; Chenoa, Raya, and Mother Emaline beside her. It wasn't enough. Embers rained down around them. Enough had landed on the heavy log that it was starting to catch fire, and her hands throbbed from her frantic attempt to move it, big burn blisters already forming. Sweat was running down her face. The heat was blistering as she worked, the flames not nearly far enough away. The roar of the fire filled her ears, and suddenly, there was a loud crash as the last part of the roof fell in. Beside her, Chenoa screamed in fright. Sitting back on her heels, Niz looked up at the fiery mill and knew the truth she'd been trying to deny: Alex was gone.

"Girls, come away from the fire. It's no use. They're gone," Mother Emaline was wailing. She pulled on Nizhoni's arm. "Please, come away. Think of the baby," she begged.

Nizhoni knew her mother-in-law was right, but she didn't know how to give up. Her husband was in there. Even knowing he was gone, she couldn't stop. She had to keep trying. Maybe she was wrong. Maybe he was still alive. She had to cling to hope. She had to stay busy. Mostly, she was loath to quit, more afraid of the grief should she be still than she was of the heat and the flames.

"It's going to catch the trees!" Hearing the shout, she turned and saw the neighbor jumping off his horse, a bucket in one hand, a gunnysack in the other. Behind him were his wife and his half-grown son, and behind them, more neighbors. They were all there to make sure the fire in the mill didn't spread to the forest, moving this from a family tragedy to a tragedy for them all. Forest fires spread fast in the high mountains, and if they didn't get the blaze under control quickly, all their houses, their barns, their fields, their town—it could all go up in smoke.

Knowing there was nothing she could do for their men anymore, Nizhoni jumped into action to do what she could. Running to the barn to get their own buckets and sacks, her footsteps pounded as she ran toward the creek, the strong winds whipping at her dark hair. Her eyes moved up to the dark storm clouds overhead. She wished they would open and give them rain. But no rain came. Thankfully, more neighbors did, and little by little, working together, they subdued the flames.

After what felt like a hundred trips back and forth to the creek, she set down her bucket and began to beat at the flames with her wet gunnysack. They were winning the battle. They just had to continue on until the fire was out and there was no chance of the wind stirring it back up.

Her back ached. Her arms hurt. Her hands throbbed where she had burnt them early on. Her legs were tired. She was winded and panting for air, and yet she kept on. They had to get the fire out. They had to save their homes and the valley. She wouldn't let herself think beyond that.

It had been dark for hours when they finally put out the last of the embers, and Nizhoni was able to put down her bucket and sack. Every muscle in her body was in pain. She felt ready to collapse. Instinctively, she knew she should have listened when her family members and neighbors had begged her to sit down and let them fight the fire—it was senseless for an expecting woman to exert herself like she had, they reasoned. But she had pressed on, frightened to feel all the emotions that would come whenever she finally stopped. As it turned out, she shouldn't have worried. She was too exhausted to feel anything at all. She only felt numb with shock and denial.

Looking at the drooping shoulders of Mother Emaline, Raya, and Chenoa, she knew they were feeling just as dazed as she was. Their faces were black with smoke and soot, their hands were dirty and covered in burn blisters, and their clothes were soaked from both water and sweat. She knew the same could be said of her. But she didn't care. None of them did. Once the last of their neighbors finally left, they didn't wash their faces; they didn't bandage their hands; they didn't even speak. Walking wearily into Mother Emaline's cabin, no one bothered to light a candle. Chenoa and Mother Emaline simply collapsed on the older woman's bed, fully clothed, with even their shoes still on. Raya took a quilt off the back of the rocking chair and handed it to Nizhoni before taking another one for herself. They both laid down on the floor, too weary to care, too heartsick to feel. Physically, emotionally, and mentally exhausted, they slept.

The next morning, Niz woke to sobs. Mother Emaline was standing by the window, looking out at the ashes of their lives, her hands clasped over her mouth. The nightmare they had woken up to was many times worse than anything they had experienced in their dreams. However, the tragedy was not done.

Niz hadn't felt well when she awakened. There was a tightness in her belly—a dull ache in her lower abdomen. Still, she had followed Raya outside to the pile of blackened rubble and ashes, hoping against all hope that somehow, someway, it wasn't as bad as they had feared. She told herself that perhaps the men had sheltered under something and been spared; the family savings that were hidden under a floorboard hadn't burned, or even that the full cashbox Alex had been balancing had somehow survived the fire. But with the air still thick and hazy with smoke, and only a pile of smoldering ashes where their family sawmill had stood only the day before, she knew any hope she'd been clinging to was futile. In the light of day, she could see the truth—there was nothing left.

It was at that moment, cheeks wet with tears, her heart breaking, that a searing pain had ripped through her middle. Crying out in agony, she had sunk to the ground, clutching her belly. But she had been as helpless to save the little one inside of her as she had been to save her husband. An hour later, she had delivered a tiny son, perfectly formed and yet so very, very small. Too small to make it in the world. Though she had cradled him against her chest, and begged him to stay, he had lived only a few minutes. She still remembered with tragic clarity the excruciating agony she felt when he took his last breath, though she could no longer determine if the pain that filled her was of body or heart. It all ran together in her memory, and now, remembering, the pain seized her again. She felt as if she couldn't breathe.

Like a knife to her heart, the date came to mind, and she realized it was the one-year anniversary.

One whole year without her loving husband; one whole year without her beloved son.

Had he been born on time, her son would have been nearly crawling by now. She would have had him laced into a cradleboard for her trip to town, carrying him, safe and snug, on her back. He would have been smiling and playing and making sweet baby talk.

A picture formed in her imagination of what life should have looked like. She could see herself on the floor of the cabin she shared with Alex, playing with their son when he walked in the door after a day of work. She could imagine how his face would have lit up and how his eyes would have danced as he crossed the floor to kiss her hello before ruffling his son's hair. He would have picked up the child and given him a little toss in the air to elicit precious baby giggles before leaning in for another kiss from her. She would have dished up their dinner, and they would have eaten together in front of the fire, giving their son little bites from their bowls. Then she would have nursed their son to sleep, singing to him softly, before kissing his sweet face and laying him down for the night.

That's how it should have been. That's what August 1, 1874, should have looked like. Not this. Not a rough cross standing in remembrance of a father and his son, flanked by two more rough crosses standing in memory of the brothers who had fallen by his side.

"Nizhoni?"

Startled out of her painful thoughts, Nizhoni looked over at her friend, Soaring Eagle. The woman was watching her, a puzzled look on her face. "I . . . I'm sorry. What did you say?"

Nizhoni's younger sister, Ever Flowering, turned to see what she had been looking at, and when her sister turned back, Nizhoni could see deep compassion in her eyes. Ever Flowering knew, even if Soaring Eagle didn't. "Do you want to stay awhile? We could go on to the store and you could meet us there," she offered.

Nizhoni took a deep, staying breath and shook her head, propping up a smile. "Of course not. The sooner we get what we need at the store, the sooner we can return home," she said, looping her arm through her sister's. "Let's go."

Though she smiled and laughed with them as they walked away, Nizhoni's heart stayed at the cemetery. Unable to speak of the departed, according to the religion of her people, she could not share her pain, nor would it do any good to sit at the grave. She felt the loss, her grief, her guilt, as strongly walking to the store as she would have had she remained at the roughhewn cross. Just as she did every day. It didn't matter that grief had a heavy grip on her throat, making it hard to swallow, that her heart ached for her son, or that the way she missed her husband felt like a physical pain in her chest. They were gone. And life had moved on. She must as well.

So, as she had been for months, she rebuffed her pain, convinced herself that she was fine, pushed down the grief that threatened to overwhelm her, and carried on. It had been a year. She needed to be able to go to town without getting stuck in the past. She needed to be able to keep a lid on her loss and keep up the appearance that everything was okay. She had to convince everyone that she had moved on. Because if she didn't, if she admitted the truth—even to herself—she didn't know how she would survive the enormity of her grief.

She should be a mother, but her arms were empty. She should be the loving wife of Alex Applewood, but instead she was the wife of Fire Maker. She should be sewing quilts, sleeping in a log cabin, and making fried chicken on Sundays, but instead, she was back at home in her native village.

It wasn't that she didn't want to be there, she loved her village and her people. She'd always known she would one day go back. But this wasn't how it was supposed to happen. Alex had promised he would go with her after just a few more years of working with his brothers. He had said he would live among her people with her and help her to protect them from the government that was taking their lands. They were supposed to have gone together. He had promised. And now she was alone.

Alone, with a husband who was unkind and foolish, harsh and proud. She wished she could go back and undo what she had done the day she agreed to marry Fire Maker, but she could no more go back to erase her lapse of judgement than she could erase the day of the fire.

When Fire Maker had come to her mother's wickiup, where she was staying, just six weeks after the tragedy to ask her to be his wife, she'd been overwhelmed by her grief; she hadn't been thinking straight. She'd only been back in the village for a short time and was desperate for some comfort from her loss. Never before had she felt so alone, so empty. She hadn't thought of the man Fire Maker was or the reasons she had turned him down the first time he asked for her hand in marriage, long before she'd met Alex Applewood. She'd only thought that maybe, somehow, a new husband would help fill the void inside her.

She'd been wrong, and if only she would've thought it through, she would have known that. Fire Maker was strong, intelligent, and handsome, but even as a teenager, she had sensed that he wouldn't make her a good husband. He was proud and boastful, quick to act and slow to help. His actions were often selfish, and his words and judgements harsh. He wasn't like the other men in their village who were honest and devoted, strong of character, and brave. He thought only of himself and cared for no one else.

Yet, in her grief, she hadn't considered any of that. She had only been seeking comfort to fill the gaping hole in her heart, and so, when he asked, she had agreed. After they were married, it had taken only a matter of days to realize what a terrible mistake she had made, but by then, it had been too late. And so, she had pushed down her disillusionment and disappointment, burying them down deep alongside all her other hurts. She'd put a smile on her face and continued on with life.

Because if she didn't, what else was she to do?

She could only press on, caring for her family and her people. She kept herself going by finding comfort in the feel of the wind in her hair, the beauty of the rugged Colorado landscape, the work that kept her hands busy, the love of her mother, sisters, and friends, and the hope that somehow, someday, her heart would heal and life would get better.

How that would happen, she didn't know.

Stepping inside the general store, Nizhoni quickly recognized the storekeeper as she had often been the one to do the shopping for the Applewood family. She'd enjoyed the outing and the challenge of getting everything the family needed for the best price possible. Often bringing eggs from the hens or vegetables from their garden, bartering for supplies had been one of the highlights of her week. Now, whenever her tribe needed supplies, they sent her to do the same. They said no one could get as much as she could for so little. If there was one thing she knew how to do, it was how to make a good trade.

The storekeeper gave her something in between a grimace and a smile as she approached his counter. She knew the man loved to barter as much as she did, but he liked to keep up appearances that he didn't. He would look less than pleased to see her, but in the end, they would both feel content with the deal they would strike and the fun they'd had coming to it.

"Ah, Ms. Applewood. I haven't seen you in quite a spell."

"The hunting has been good," Nizhoni explained. Though she hadn't spoken the white man's language in many months, the words formed easily on her tongue. Her sister and friend watched her as if it were magic. She had been trying to encourage them to learn English, too, but they had no desire to learn, frightened by the very idea of it.

She watched the storekeeper's expression change, and he searched behind his counter before straightening with a stack of letters. "I almost forgot. These came for you."

Taking the letters, Nizhoni smoothed her hand over the front of the first, her heart constricting painfully. There were five envelopes. She could make out her name on the front, but nothing else. Despite Raya's frequent offers to teach her to read, she hadn't learned, as afraid of looking dim-witted as Soaring Eagle and Ever Flowering were of the English language. She was used to teaching, not being the student, and the very idea of it had repelled her. Now, she wished she had swallowed her pride and taken Raya up on her offer. She imagined all five letters were from her and Mother Emaline, and she desperately wanted to read them. She missed them terribly. After nearly a year apart, to hear how the beloved women were doing would indeed be like balm to her lacerated heart.

"Do you, uh, need me to read those to you?" the storekeeper asked, looking up at her over the rim of his spectacles.

Nizhoni raised her chin. "No," she answered quickly. She would never accept his help reading the letters. To do so would put her in his debt, and she'd come to do business. Besides, if he knew she couldn't read, then perhaps he would think less of her, lose respect for her, and see her as a less formidable opponent. That would certainly never do. She tucked the letters into the beaded leather bag she carried. She would have to figure them out later. "I came for supplies," she continued, getting down to business.

Half an hour later, she walked between Soaring Eagle and Ever Flowering on their way back out of town. Under a grove of aspens just past the outskirts, they found Ever Flowering's husband, Walks With Power, right where they had left him. Uncomfortable among settlers, he had elected to stay with the horses, trusting Niz to do the trading.

Sheathing the knife he had been sharpening, he looked over their purchases approvingly. "You were able to get a good amount of ammunition and tobacco in exchange for the hides and dried meat we sent," Walks With Power praised. "Well done."

"Not only that, but we also got blankets, several new pots, and some sugar to sweeten the bitter teas with," Ever Flowering told her husband proudly, opening her pack to show off the goods. "And a pair of tweezers for mother to help with her beadwork."

"Our people will be happy. You made a good trade."

Nizhoni smiled as she began to lash her full pack onto the horse she had ridden. Their bags were full of provisions their people needed, and she was proud of the deal she'd been able to strike. It had been a good trip.

As they mounted up and started back toward their village, she glanced over her shoulder for one last look at the little white church that stood serenely on the edge of town. Giving herself a little shake, she turned forward again, refusing to dwell on the memory of the wooden cross that represented such a great loss in her life.

What was done was done. Her life as an Applewood was over. She simply had to keep moving forward. As on the day of the fire, she was afraid to be still, knowing that if she ever stopped moving, her grief would catch up with her. And if it ever did, she didn't know if it would be something she could survive.

Two

One week later . . .

Nizhoni sat beside the fire, listening to the happy sounds of camp as she continued to weave the willow bark she held into a coiled basket. It would only be a couple of months before her people began their journey to their wintering grounds at lower elevations, and having good, tight baskets to carry enough water for their journey was imperative.

She looked up and smiled as her mother approached and sat down beside her on the blanket she'd spread over the gravelly soil.

"Only another moon before the buffaloberries will be ready to gather," the woman said, looking pleased. "I checked them today, and they're growing well. The harvest will be plentiful this year."

Nizhoni's face brightened in anticipation. Though the small red berries were tart and sometimes bitter, they were something she looked forward to all year. She enjoyed gathering, drying, and grinding them for meals of Pemmican throughout the long, cold months when fresh food items were scarce. What she liked most, however, was mixing them with hot water and sugar from the store in town for a frothy dessert. The once-a-year treat always whispered of the coming fall when the aspen leaves would splash their vibrant golden hues over the mountainsides and the elks' haunting bugles would echo amongst the trees.

Not long after, the first snow would fall, and her people would make their way out of the high mountains. Settling in sheltered camps at lower elevations, they would gather with other bands of their people to spend the winter around their fires, resting, and preparing for the coming spring.

For the majority of the year, their people broke up into smaller groups to hunt and gather and live off the resources of the earth, but the winter was a time when they came back together. The land they lived on was vast. To the south, to the north, and to the west, their people would gather at central locations to winter with other small bands in their area. Together, they all made up one people. Tucked into their brush-covered wickiups, with hides hung over the walls to insulate them from the harsh Colorado winter, information would be shared, tools and weapons mended, stories told and passed down, and new clothing sewn and decorated.

Looking up at the bright green leaves that hung on the trees, Nizhoni knew that although it was not far off, there was still a little more summer to be had before fall set in. It would still be a month or more before the first frost would kiss the mountains and bring out the sweetness of the berries.

"Yes, the wait will not be long," she agreed, knowing the days would pass quickly. "Soon, the nights will turn cold, and the berries will be ready."

Though the buffaloberries could technically be gathered before the first frost, only one who didn't know any better would do so—and then usually only once. Nizhoni had been foolish enough to make that mistake when she was young, too eager to wait, and she'd never repeated her error. Her mouth puckered at the memory. The berries would be much sweeter if they waited.

"I look forward to the day," Shy Fawn told her, a twinkle in her gentle eyes. Nizhoni knew her mother looked forward to the small, red fruit as much as she did. Moving on, Shy Fawn reached over to feel Nizhoni's basket. "It's a good weave."

"Thank you," Nizhoni answered, pleased by her mother's praise. She'd been weaving baskets for years, but she still had much to learn.

Watertight baskets were the most difficult to make. In order to hold water, the weave had to be very tight. Once finished, the basket could be covered with the sap of the pinon pine, and if done correctly, it would hold the precious liquid that was their lifeblood in the arid plains and mountains her people called home. Leaking baskets could be life threatening during a migration, even if the journey only took four to five days as theirs did. In a dry landscape, it didn't take long for dehydration to kick in and become dangerous. Her mouth turned down. That was precisely why she had been so angry when Fire Maker carelessly tossed a perfectly good water basket into the fire while in a drunken rage.

"Once you cover it with sap, you won't lose a drop," her mother continued. "I wonder, though, where your old one went. I haven't seen it in some time. Did it spring a leak?"

Looking over into her mother's concerned face, Nizhoni shook her head. Though she didn't want to share about her husband's careless deed, she couldn't bear to let the woman think the basket she had expertly woven for her daughter with her own two hands had been faulty. "No, it never leaked, Mother," she answered.

"Then why do you make a new one?" Shy Fawn pressed gently.

For just a moment, Nizhoni let her thoughts return to the argument that had proved fatal for the basket. Fire Maker had been in a foul mood, which she had come to realize was his normal. Though his disposition was not uncommon, the amount of alcohol he had consumed was; it had taken an unpleasant situation and turned it dangerous. He had entered their wickiup looking for a fight and had not delayed in finding one. Several of her belongings had been tossed into the fire as a result, and she still carried the yellowing traces of his anger on her upper arms. She was thankful the short sleeves of her soft buckskin dress hid the bruises from her mother's eyes. Hiding the evidence seemed the best way to avoid the questions and worry she would undoubtedly see in Shy Fawn's gentle face should her mother know the truth.

It simply was how things were. Nizhoni had made a mistake in marrying Fire Maker. And now, she was paying the price.

But she wasn't going to say any of that. Not out loud. Not to her mother. Admitting it would make it too real. Her mind worked quickly.

"I want another for the trip," she offered. "One can never be too careful when it comes to having enough water."

Her mother nodded, satisfied. "I see my daughter is very wise. Ah, I almost forgot my errand. I came to tell you, White Bird and I have just returned from checking the amaranth patches, and tomorrow, we will gather the amaranth seeds."

Visions of the branched plants that often grew as tall as she could reach filled Nizhoni's mind. The plants' greenish-white, dense flower spikes weren't flashy, but thousands of tiny black seeds could often be found in each tassel-like spike. The spikes would be harvested from the plant and dried before being beaten to release the seeds. In the months ahead, their people would grind the dried seeds to make their traditional flatbread and thicken their stews.

Thinking of the work that would keep her hands busy for the next many days, a smile touched Nizhoni's lips. She enjoyed gathering the food sources of her people. It was something she had missed while at the Applewoods'. Whether it was berries, nuts, greens, or seeds, as the women went about their task of gathering, they talked and sang, told stories, and strengthened the bonds they shared. It was hard work, but good work, and she loved completing it alongside her mother and sisters, her friends, and the women of their tribe.

With her mother's declaration brightening her spirits and chasing away the shadowed memories of her home life with Fire Maker, Nizhoni fell into easy conversation with the woman. As time passed, their talk meandered ever further away from her reason for weaving a new basket, and Nizhoni enjoyed the simple pleasure of spending the afternoon conversing with a woman she loved so dearly and held such great respect for. No matter what loss and difficulty her life had held, she would be thankful for her family, her village, and the ways of her people. They brought purpose and beauty to her days and gave her something to wake up for each morning.

Nizhoni loved how her people's tasks followed the seasons, how connected they were to the earth, and the beautiful mountains they called home. She loved gathering berries, seeds, and roots. She enjoyed utilizing the resources of the land like the inner bark of the ponderosa, the yucca, and the willows. And she reveled in the excitement of the men returning from their hunts. Sometimes the men would be gone only a few days, sometimes a week or more, but the joy of processing their harvest, knowing their people had what they needed to survive, was always satisfying. She loved the fierceness of the thunderstorms that rolled over the mountains nearly every afternoon in the summer, the dazzling views of the high peaks that surrounded them, and the serenity of happening upon herds of elk grazing in the meadows.

Nizhoni tipped her face up to the sun as her mother talked and marveled again that so much love could share the space of her heart with such deep grief. It felt as if one shouldn't be able to exist with the other, but here she was living in the tension of both having residence within her. She was happy to be back with her people, adored their life as hunters, gatherers, and guardians of the land, and yet her heart was broken, her grief too deep to face, her mistake with Fire Maker keeping her in misery. Her heart began to ache, and she steeled herself to it, shutting the door of her mind on the painful thoughts, refocusing fully on the pleasant conversation she was engaged in and the basket she was weaving.

Later, once her mother had given her approval on the completed basket and left to return to her own wickiup, Nizhoni heated sap from the pinon pine and generously covered the new vessel. When she finished, she set it aside to dry, satisfied with her work. It had taken her several days to finish, and it wasn't as pretty as her mother's had been, but it would do its job sufficiently. If they suffered from dehydration on the trail, it wouldn't be the fault of her new basket. For that, she was thankful.

Turning, she began preparing an evening meal for herself and Fire Maker. Though many of the men were gone hunting, her husband had elected to stay in camp. From where she stood, she couldn't understand why as all he seemed to be doing was sleeping, caring for his prized horses, and wasting the days away drinking with his friends—nor had he been eager to explain when she'd asked. Regardless of that, she hurried to have his dinner ready. He didn't like to be kept waiting.

As she cooked, Nizhoni reflected on the man she'd married. He was very strong and very handsome. Last winter, he had been named the chief of their people, and she understood why. He had a quick mind, good aim, and was adept at collecting horses and accumulating wealth. It had been those attributes that had secured the position of chief for him once his father passed on. Their people thought he could lead them to continued success and prosperity amidst a world that was changing rapidly around them. Back then, she hadn't fully understood that his success was born of his selfishness. She was guessing the braves who appointed him hadn't either.

With her front row seat to his life, Niz had since learned that he didn't care who he hurt or who had to pay the price as long as it got him further ahead. The ways of honor and respect that governed their people seemed to be absent in him. He only appeared to care about himself.

In part, Niz had somehow seen it, sensed it, even from a very early age. But after the tragedy, she hadn't been thinking about that. She'd only been longing for comfort. Comfort and escape. She wanted to escape from her pain, her loss, her emptiness, her loneliness. Little did she know, she was only escaping to more of the same—her husband had no desire to comfort, love, or help her heart heal.

If only she would have stopped to think about why such a proud young man—the son of their chief—would be so eager to make her his wife, even after she'd refused him and married a white man instead. If she had, perhaps she would have seen that his proposal was nothing more than revenge meant to appease his stinging pride.

She had made a mistake the day she turned him down and an even bigger mistake when she'd married Alex Applewood. But now, the spirits had punished her, and she had proven to the village how wrong she had been by coming to her senses and becoming his wife. At least that was what he had told her on the night of their marriage ceremony.

In his mind, their matrimony had been her public confession of her folly, repentance of her wrongs, and acknowledgment that he was indeed the better choice. He had relished it. It would have been enough to convince him to marry her, but she knew he'd had other motives too. As much as he hungered for revenge, it was only half of it. His pride was equally ravenous. For better or worse, she was considered to be beautiful, fiery, and untamable. And what arrogant and prideful man didn't think he deserved the best, or could help being drawn by a challenge of wills? He'd done his best to break her spirit every day since, and she knew enough about him now to know he would not stop until he won.

She looked up as he ducked into their dwelling. Her stomach fell with dread. His handsome face was turned down in an unpleasant scowl. "Is it time to eat?"

"Nearly. Give me ten minutes, and I'll have it ready," she answered carefully, stirring the rabbit, wild onion, and acorn stew that was bubbling over the fire. Pivoting, she flipped the flat bread she'd made from grinding wild grass seeds.

He grunted. "You know I want to eat as soon as I come in. You should have started cooking earlier. I'm hungry now." His gaze was hard, his eyes narrowed, his displeasure obvious.

"I'll have it ready soon," Nizhoni promised, biting back all the retorts that came instantly to mind, reluctant to start a fight.

Fire Maker sat down near the fire and sharpened his knife while he waited. She watched him for a moment, wishing she could say something that would improve his mood. If love and warmth were out of the question, as they clearly were, perhaps they could at least find a way to make life together bearable. Despite everything she knew about him, she couldn't find it within herself to give up hope. She couldn't accept that this was how things would always be.

"How was your day?" she finally asked, hoping the question might stir a pleasant conversation.

Fire Maker didn't answer or even flinch. Thinking perhaps he hadn't heard her, she repeated her question. Nothing. She narrowed her eyes as she realized he didn't consider her worth the effort. He clearly had nothing to say, nor did he seem to hold any fondness for her. She knew from experience what he believed her place was, and companion had no part in it. Niz turned back to their dinner, her pride smarting.

Alex, on the other hand, had been full of merriment, his eyes twinkling with it, his thoughts constantly full of either mischief or fun. He had baited and teased her mercilessly, but it had all been rooted in goodwill and love. He had loved to rile her up. Truth be told, she had enjoyed it as well. She had appreciated his knack for interesting conversation, his willingness to talk about important things with her, and how he looked at her when she spoke—like her intelligence and wit made her a wonder that he found irresistible.

Her heart began to hurt, and she pressed a fist to it. It was only because she'd walked by the church last week. That's why it hurt so much. Soon, the memories would begin to fade again. She just needed to keep moving forward until they did.

"We're going to gather the amaranth seeds tomorrow," she said, trying again.

Though her husband didn't seem to need conversation, she desperately did. Their home and their marriage were lonely. The silence felt deafening. Though she'd been unsuccessful to date, she wanted to be her husband's friend and confidante. Even if their marriage was void of love, she wanted to share information, ideas, problems, and solutions. She wanted to discuss issues their people were facing with him and help plan for the future.

Niz wanted to ask when the warriors would return, to know what the latest news from the government was, and how the wild game numbers seemed that summer. Though she was married to the chief, she knew none of it. She nearly felt more ill-informed about what was going on with her people than she had while living with the Applewoods. Though she longed to be in the know, her husband didn't seem to wish to discuss any of it with her. From his own lips, he had shared that she was there to serve him in whatever capacity most improved his life. Outside of that, he had no use for her—or anyone, for that matter. She reminded herself of that again now. It wasn't just her.

A grunt was his only answer.

She should stop. She knew she should stop. He clearly wasn't eager for conversation. But Nizhoni couldn't help it. She counted up in her mind how many days the braves had been hunting and couldn't imagine they would be gone much longer. Surely, they would return soon, victorious and triumphant, with plenty of meat to distribute throughout the village and also dry and store away for later. "So, do you suppose we'll begin to look for the braves tomorrow?"

"Stop bothering me, woman!" he snapped, clearly annoyed. "You can't just talk and talk and talk anytime you want. I have a lot on my mind, and I don't want your constant jabbering making it worse." Fire Maker pinned her with his dark, stony eyes before standing up and going for his hand drum. Settling on his sleeping mat with the instrument between his legs, he began beating the top of it, ruling out any hope of a conversation with his loud music.

Nizhoni turned back to the fire, her heart sinking with every beat of his drum. Friendship and camaraderie were clearly not going to be achieved. She had known it for months now, and yet, for some reason, she continued to hope. She continued to try. Raising her chin, telling herself it didn't matter, she went about her work.

When it was ready, she served the stew and flat bread. Fire Maker ate, left his empty bowl on the floor where he had sat, and disappeared out the hide that covered their doorway, all without another word. She didn't know where he was going, nor would she even if she had asked. He would be back later. And she felt sure that whenever he was, she would wish he had stayed out longer.

Choosing to think about more pleasant things, Nizhoni turned her attention to her dinner. It tasted good. Cooking had always been one of her strengths, but her three years at the Applewoods' had expanded her abilities, giving her a chance to experiment with different ingredients and spices. She'd learned the white man's way of cooking, as well as a few dishes from her sister-in-law, Raya, who hailed from a foreign land across the sea. Combining her knowledge of all three cuisines improved her skills. Now, back at home in her village, she was enjoying taking the natural ingredients she foraged for with her people and a few spices she had traded for in town and using them together to create delicious meals.

Her thoughts settling on Raya, Nizhoni's gaze fell to the spot where her buckskin bag lay hidden between two elk hides. The bag was where she kept her most precious belongings, including the letters she'd gotten in town. She wouldn't take the chance of Fire Maker finding it and burning the contents.

In the loneliness of the wickiup, she desperately wanted to open the letters and hear news of her family that felt as much a part of her as the mountains and creeks and clouds. For three years, she had lived side by side with them, cooked with them, gardened with them, and sewed with them.

The Applewood family had spent nearly every evening during those three years sitting together in front of the fire, listening to Raya read, dancing around the room as Alex played his fiddle, laughing, and telling stories. Niz had handled the majority of the cooking during those years, and she never remembered a meal being eaten when she was not thanked for and complimented on what she had prepared.

Running her finger around the rim of her turtle shell bowl, she thought back to how it had all started.

Alex had struck up a friendship with her father and Chief Great Mountain when—under the guise of bringing goods to trade—he had first visited their village. As her father and Chief Great Mountain looked through the supplies he'd brought, he'd glanced around the camp with curious eyes. She remembered the exact moment his gaze had landed on her. Her heart had given a wild kick at his friendly smile, and though she hadn't understood it, she had felt inexplicably drawn to him. Luckily, Chief Great Mountain, who could make the white man's words, liked him too. He said Alex had a pure heart and invited him back.

On his way out that day, Alex had found her down by the river. She'd been waiting where she expected him to cross, hoping for a chance to speak with him before he left. Alex knew the simple signs used by the plains tribes, and she had picked up enough of it at their winter camp to communicate a little. He introduced himself, and she asked him to teach her English.

For some time, she had been desperately wanting to know the language of the people who were overtaking their lands. How could she communicate with their new neighbors, plead the case of her people, or understand what was going on if she couldn't speak the language? Despite Chief Great Mountain assuring her that it was unnecessary, she felt like she needed to know English. And she couldn't imagine a more intriguing teacher. She had offered to teach Alex her language in trade, and he'd quickly agreed. The teaching had begun that very day.

She'd soon learned that he was not a trader at all, simply a young man who craved adventure and was seeking to learn all he could about the world around him. He lived near town; his homestead was only seven miles away. With his best friend away working on the railroad while he had been summoned home to help his brothers run the family sawmill, her village was the closest thing to an adventure that Alex presently had. He'd been determined to build a good relationship with the tribe and learn their language in preparation for a trip south, deeper into the lands of her people, that he was planning to make once he could escape from the mill again.

The braves both young and old liked him, and he continued to come, no longer needing to bring goods to trade to ensure he would be welcome. He came to smoke pipes with them, visit with Chief Great Mountain, and see Niz. He frequently brought gifts for her people, and the village continued to be open to him. She was glad, because she was falling quickly. The weeks between his visits felt excruciatingly long. When he interlaced his fingers with hers one afternoon when they were sitting in a meadow practicing their respective languages, she'd seen the promise written in his eyes. She had made no objection when he leaned in for a kiss, nor when he told her he wanted to make her his bride.

When Alex asked her father for her hand in marriage a week later, her father simply dropped his head in resignation and gave his permission. Her mother, on the other hand, had argued fervently, wanting to keep her daughter close to home.

"We both know our daughter and how she feels about him, Shy Fawn. And if I haven't figured out how to bend her course in the past seventeen years, I don't know that I will now," her father had admitted to her mother in front of them all. Shy Fawn had glared and stalked away, her brown eyes swimming with tears. Nizhoni had felt too excited to be offended by her father's words or persuaded by her mother's objections.

Though she hated to leave her family, Alex had promised they would be back, and she was thrilled about the adventure they would have together in the meantime. They were married in a traditional ceremony only a few days later. Alex presented her father with the traditional gift of a horse, and she hadn't been able to stop smiling as she rode double behind him on their way home to the cabin he'd built for them on his family's homestead.

Shortly after she joined the Applewood family, Mother Emaline had grown gravely ill. Will had still been an overgrown kid. Luke was solemn, though kind, and hard working. Though she was head over heels for Alex, it was Raya—with her musical laughter and bright and ready smile—who had really welcomed her into the family and helped her adjust to life in the Applewood household.

With Alex busy in the mill, Raya helped her piece her first quilt and sew her new clothes, while telling her stories about the family she'd married into. They had become fast friends, and Nizhoni held her sister-in-law in her heart as deeply as she did her own sisters. Raya had been a bright ray of sunshine throughout her three years with the Applewoods, though Niz hadn't seen it so clearly then as she did looking back. After all, one never appreciated a sunbeam so much in the middle of the day as when reminiscing during the night.

In time, Mother Emaline recovered and regained her strength. The woman was so much like Nizhoni's own mother that she eased the ache in Niz's heart at being separated from Shy Fawn. Both women were highly maternal, continually teaching, training, and looking out for their young. Mother Emaline was every bit the mother to Nizhoni that she was to her own sons, and then some—after all, her daughters-in-law were the daughters she'd never had. Her pride and joy, she called them. She had their back in every situation, sided with them in every disagreement, and filled each day with cheerful encouragement. Just thinking of the dear woman brought a smile to Niz's lips. Oh, how she loved her.

Chenoa had joined the family the winter before the fire when Will, the youngest Applewood son, had taken a wife. Raya and Nizhoni welcomed her with open arms, instantly taken with the sweet and timid young woman. There was something about Chenoa that somehow made her seem as delicate as a porcelain teacup and as innocent as a child, and Raya and Niz were enamored. The whole family doted on her. She was with them only six short months before tragedy struck. But six months had proven to be plenty of time to form a deep love and connection.

Niz looked around her small wickiup—a dim, dome-shaped brush shelter with a diameter of about fifteen feet that kept her physically warm and dry—and missed all the sunshine that had flooded the Applewood cabins. They had always been full—full of people, full of laughter, full of conversation, full of love. Though she had no preference between a wickiup and a log cabin, her new home felt empty, void of light and love. It felt as empty as she did.

She spread her hands over her womb and wished again that she could be with child. Perhaps a child would bring her and Fire Maker together. Even if it didn't, she could throw all her love and energy into a baby of her own. They had constructed a wickiup big enough for a family and had been married nearly a year now, but her womb remained empty. She was no more full of light and love and hope than her shelter was.

Suddenly afraid of the grief she felt welling up within her, like the rumble of thunder coming over the flats, Nizhoni pushed herself to her feet. She grabbed her pot and hurried outside to wash it. Down at the banks of the river, she sat for a long time in the tall grasses, hidden from sight. She watched the fading light play across the rocky slopes of the mountains, observed the movement of the river as it splashed along, and studied the wildlife that inhabited the banks. From the water bugs that seemed to skate over the surface of the river to the small rabbit she saw hop out of the grasses to drink, the river was teaming with life. She breathed deeply of the musty aroma of damp earth mingled with the fishy scent of the river and the sweetness of the Evening Primrose growing wild on the banks. When the setting sun sent splashes of color across the sky, she watched in wonder. Finally, when the stars appeared overhead and the night noises of the forest began, she unfolded her legs from under her and made her way home.

With so much nature surrounding her, so much to watch and observe, she could turn her mind off to the thoughts that had plagued her in the shelter. She could pretend like nothing mattered outside of the world she could see and touch and feel. And thankfully, due to full days of hard work, she slept as soon as she curled up on her bed of furs, again avoiding the memories that pained her.

Three

The next morning Nizhoni talked and laughed with friends and family as they gathered the mature amaranth seeds. Cutting the large flower spikes from the plants with their knives, they were careful not to dislodge the tiny seeds, loathe to waste any of the nourishing grain. The seed heads were then laid out on buttery smooth hides to dry in the summer sun.

As they worked, the women snacked on seeds, eating them raw to keep up their energy. The raw seeds were nutty and herbal, chewy in texture, with a hint of a peppery flavor. Niz savored it, the familiar taste comforting. It tasted like the end of summer. Wiping the perspiration from her forehead, she sorted some of the seed heads into her satchel, as the others were doing, to be made into fresh amaranth flatbread that night. The bread was also a taste specific to late summer—it would have a slightly different flavor once the amaranth was dry. Nizhoni hoped the hunting party would be back with fresh meat to go along with it. That would truly make it an end of summer feast.

When the sun moved low on the western horizon, the women worked quickly and carefully to transfer the seed heads from the hides into large baskets. Back at the village, they would be laid out in their wickiups to continue drying where the wind couldn't reach them as the grain began to separate from the flower spikes. Once dried, the women would use their seed beaters to extract every last seed from the spikes before taking them out in a gentle wind and pouring them from one basket to another, allowing the breeze to blow away the lighter chaff while the heavier seeds

26

collected in the bottom. Finally, they would be taken back inside and laid out to dry once more before being stored away to eat during the winter.

They still had much work ahead of them before the amaranth would be ready to store, but it had been a good day. Tired but happy, Niz walked between Soaring Eagle and Ever Flowering as they made their way back to camp that evening. Her mother followed only a few steps behind with Nizhoni's youngest sister, Cloud Walking. As they approached the village, they heard a commotion. Excitement filling her, Niz broke into a run. The men must have returned from their hunt!

There would be fresh meat for supper, as well as much work to be done with processing the harvest. After her trip down memory lane the night before, Nizhoni was more than ready for the extra tasks that would keep her hands and mind busy. She mentally began making her to-do list. The animals would have to be cleaned and skinned, the hides tanned, and the meat sliced thin to dry. Much of the work would fall on the women, and they wouldn't mind at all. The men had worked hard to hunt the animals. Now they would rest, and the women would happily step in to do their part. Of course, it couldn't all be done that night, so she started weighing what they would need to see to right away and what could wait.

Making it to the outskirts of camp, Nizhoni stopped short, as did those who had been running with her. She instantly went cold as she took in the scene before her. The horses tied at the edge of camp wore saddles, and they all knew what saddles meant.

"Soldiers!" Ever Flowering whispered, her eyes wide. Niz nodded gravely.

Having soldiers come to the village was rarely good. She looked around to see if the hunting party's horses were there, too, but she didn't see them in the corrals. Trepidation filled her as she processed the fact that soldiers had come when most of the braves were out hunting. Only the elders, children, and women remained in camp.

And Fire Maker, she reminded herself quickly.

Even with his harsh disposition, his presence was some consolation, and Niz suddenly felt thankful he had stayed. If the soldiers were in camp, at least their chief was, too.

Though the rest of the women held back, quiet as they tried to determine if the soldiers had come in violence or peace, Nizhoni started toward her wickiup. As she hurried between dwellings, she noted that the few women who were still in camp were cooking over fires, children were running and playing, and Soaring Eagles' grandfather, Wise Hawk, was sitting outside his shelter napping. All seemed to be peaceful, and Nizhoni quickened her steps. Where were the soldiers? Where was Fire Maker? And what was going on?

As she drew near to her wickiup, all was quiet. Planning to drop off the baskets of seeds she carried before continuing with her search, she ducked inside. She paused near the door, giving her eyes time to adjust to the dim interior, and once they did, her heart leapt into her throat. There, in her shelter, were five soldiers seated around the fire with Fire Maker. The smell of tobacco smoke overwhelmed her, and she couldn't help but cough. Four of the soldiers were smoking with her husband. No one was speaking.

Lifting his hand, Fire Maker waved her over. His expression looked displeased, his handsome features turned down in a stony glare. "Where have you been?"

"Gathering the seeds of the amaranth," she answered quickly, keeping her voice quiet, surprised by his question. Surely he had known that—she had told him of her plans the night before. But what was most surprising was that he was inquiring about her whereabouts. She wouldn't have expected him to speak to her at all, especially in front of soldiers. If ever there was a time for him to ignore her, certainly it would be now.

"You should have been here," he told her, seeming irritated. "I have need of you."

Nizhoni glanced at her husband warily before shifting her attention through the smoke to the men dressed in dark blue uniforms. "What do you need?" she asked, fearing his answer.

Though she had planned to find out where Fire Maker and the soldiers were and see what she might overhear about their reason for visiting, she did not wish to be in the middle of whatever was going on. Nor did she trust her husband to protect her. She had only meant to be a bystander, not a participant.

Fire Maker glared at her. "Don't pretend you don't know."

Nizhoni turned back to consider him, both puzzled and worried. "Do you want me to cook a meal for you?" she finally ventured cautiously.

"I can't make the white man's words," he told her bluntly.

His declaration caught her off-guard. It had never occurred to her that when Fire Maker's father died during the time of many snows, that their village had been left without a man who spoke English. She had assumed Great Mountain had passed his knowledge of the white man's language down to his son. Without the luxury of conversing with her husband, her assumption had never been confirmed nor denied.

"What . . . what do you want me to do?" she asked hesitantly. Niz felt sure he wasn't asking her to help him speak to the soldiers. Women weren't included in important conversations; the politics of the village were handled by the men. She expected him to order her from the wickiup at any moment.

"Are you really going to make me say it?" He fixed her with his angry eyes. She stayed quiet, uncertain about what he was asking, afraid to guess wrong. His eyes narrowed at her. "Fine. Have it your way. If your ego needs to hear it, I'll say it. I need you to translate for me."

Nizhoni lifted her chin even as she felt the color draining from her face. Once again, he had misunderstood her. She took no satisfaction from him admitting that he needed her. In fact, she would much prefer he speak to the soldiers himself.

If she had to translate, she would be entering dangerous water. One misstep and she would face her husband's wrath. One wrong word and she could put her people in danger. Though she was known for being spirited and outspoken, she knew her place—and it wasn't here, in a conversation between the army and the leader of their tribe.

But she could tell by Fire Maker's expression that he wasn't asking. He was telling. If she refused, she had no doubt that he would not wait—nor care—to hear her explanation. Though fire burned in her heart, fear flickered in her mind. She did not wish to face his wrath. Besides, if no one else could make the white man's words or understand them, then she was her village's only hope to communicate with these men who now made the laws, set the boundaries, and controlled the lands her people called home. Succumbing to logic, she nodded.

Smoothing a hand over her beaded buckskin dress, she sat down between Fire Maker and the obvious leader of the small group of soldiers, as her husband directed. Taking a deep breath, she turned to face the soldier.

"I am Nizhoni, and I will translate for you," she said in English. She watched in alarm as the soldier's body language changed, recognition flickering across his demeanor.

"Niz? Niz Applewood?" he asked incredulously.

Fire Maker shifted beside her, and she flinched, knowing he recognized her first husband's last name. She would surely hear about that later. Searching the dark shadows cast by the soldier's hat, she tried to make out the man's features, hoping to place him. When he swept the cap off his head, eliminating the shadows it cast over his eyes, her breath caught. She felt faint as grief laid siege against her heart.

Why, with all the soldiers in the U.S. Army, would Alex's best friend show up in her wickiup? She hadn't seen him in years as he had joined the army shortly after she and Alex wed, but it was undeniably him. A hundred stories Alex had told her about the man sitting in front of her bounced around her swirling thoughts, and she fought to keep the past in the past.

Fire Maker roughly jerked her arm and nodded toward the soldier, clearly not appreciating her silence. Her mind hurried to formulate an answer.

"I am Nizhoni," she repeated firmly, steeling herself against the emotions. "Wife of Fire Maker, chief of our people."

Confusion and concern darkened the soldier's eyes as he considered her. "I . . . I apologize. I must have you confused with someone else."

She could see that he didn't believe the words he was speaking. He knew who she was, just as she knew him. He sent her a questioning look that pierced her. Niz gave a slight shake of her head. She didn't want to face his questions. They were sure to release the dam of memories, emotions, and grief that she was doing her very best to hold off. Additionally, anything about Alex or her life as an Applewood made her husband's anger blaze. No matter how innocent the conversation was, if anything more was said, she would undoubtedly pay for it later. So even if the man in front of her didn't understand, and even if the questions in his eyes were making it hard to breathe, she couldn't act like she knew him. She wasn't Nizhoni Applewood anymore. That girl he thought he recognized was gone.

"What is your name, sir?" she asked, trying to keep her expression free of emotion.

He cleared his throat. "Major Ezra Taylor of the United States Army," he answered. He put his cap back on his head, shrouding his face in shadows once more. "I have come to ask the chief if you have had any dealings with a group of Comanche? They stole many horses—even some from us—and are on the run. I have reason to believe that they might be in this area."

"Comanche?" Nizhoni echoed, stunned. Why would there be Comanche on their lands? The fierce tribe was known to live over the mountains on the Great Plains, and she remembered hearing talk just last winter that many of them had been forced onto reservations in Indian Territory. From maps of Alex's that she'd seen, she knew the distance between her village and Indian Territory was great—likely over seven hundred miles. How could they have ended up on the lands of her people? Her mind hummed. Maybe the greater question was what would happen if they stayed?

Her people had been living at peace with the settlers in the area for years. If there was a band of renegade Comanche raiding for horses, could it threaten the peace that Chief Great Mountain had worked so hard to establish? She certainly didn't want the soldiers thinking they were in league with the raiders; relations with the U.S. Army were precarious enough. "No, we haven't seen them," she answered quickly.

"Ask your husband," Major Taylor instructed, nodding at Fire Maker.

Color rising in her cheeks, embarrassed that she had dared to answer for Fire Maker, Nizhoni turned and quickly relayed the question to him. He was less forthright with his answer, and she couldn't help wondering why as she relayed it to the soldiers.

She had expected him to be honest and transparent, sharing that they hadn't seen a Comanche in as many years as they'd been alive, but instead, he was cryptic. As she translated back and forth between her husband and the soldiers, it became clear that Fire Maker wasn't interested in making friends or keeping peace. Apprehension and worry began to fill her. He wasn't a good husband, but she'd hoped he would at least follow in his father's footsteps and make a good chief.

Major Taylor watched Fire Maker through the haze of tobacco smoke, his eyes shadowed, his mouth grim. Finally, he spread his hands in the air in front of him. "I understand that you are wary of us, Fire Maker, but I assure you, we mean you and your people no harm. We live side by side. There is no good that will come of ill-will between us. We have come to you in good faith. We have not come to take, to raid, or to harm. A raiding band of Comanche is an enemy to us both. They take what is not theirs. I'm not asking for your help tracking them down. I'm only asking if you've had any run-ins with them, or if you know their whereabouts."

Nizhoni turned to her husband, carefully relaying the Major's words, silently willing him to take the olive branch and respond in kind. All he had to do was reply honestly and sincerely. But watching her husband's hard expression, she knew it was not to be. When she heard his answer, she closed her eyes for a moment, then turned and delivered it.

"You say they are an enemy to us both, but the only enemy I see is you," she repeated, keeping her expression blank. If she did not deliver Fire Maker's words as spoken, he would know when there was no reaction from the soldiers. He would see it as defiance and disrespect, and she would answer for it once the soldiers were gone. Besides, as the Major had made clear, the soldiers had come to talk to Fire Maker. Her only job was to translate what was said.

Niz watched the offense register in the faces of the soldiers. Backs straightened, eyes narrowed, faces turned red and angry as they turned to look at their leader. Major Taylor held Fire Maker's gaze for a long moment before giving a curt nod. "I see our business here is done."

The five soldiers stood and stiffly left the wickiup; Fire Maker watched them go. Nizhoni couldn't hide the frustration and fear she felt when she looked at him. "You had the chance to keep peace between us and the army," she accused, her temper flaring. "You know how hard those who've gone before you have worked to keep our people at peace! Would you really throw it all away so quickly?"

His glare was fearsome. "Don't you question me! Just because you translate between us doesn't make you an expert. I'm the chief, so don't interfere in my business, Nizhoni *Applewood*," he snarled back.

Her breath caught as his words hit their mark. He made something that had been so beautiful sound so ugly. Her throat began to ache, and she hurried to her feet before his hurtful words could become hurtful actions.

"Where are you going?" he demanded, narrowing his eyes.

She grabbed the pot. "I need to get water to start our supper," she told him, not waiting to hear his reply. She escaped out into the fresh air of the early evening, making her way quickly toward the river.

Glancing across camp, she saw the soldiers mounting their horses. For just a moment, she watched them longingly, wishing she could run after them. If only she could assure them that they hadn't seen the Comanche and settle the matter in their minds. She wished she could tell Major Taylor why she was back in her village with Fire Maker instead of at the Applewood homestead, as he had clearly expected her to be. And after apologizing for Fire Maker's bad behavior, she would tell them that her people would work with them to maintain peaceful relations. But what good would it do? She wasn't the chief.

Across the distance, her gaze met Major Taylor's, and he tipped his cap to her. Her heart hurting, her throat aching, Niz turned away, hurrying on to the river. If Fire Maker was watching, any further communication with the soldiers on her part would only make things worse. Besides, for her entire life, people had been telling her to learn her place. Interfering in tribal relations with the government was certainly not it.

At the river, she walked upstream for a while and then squatted down on the bank, watching the water carry along on its way. As she did, she took deep breaths, doing everything she could to push back the wave of sorrow that was rising up within her.

The sight of Ezra Taylor had brought up a myriad of memories that choked her with grief. The first few times she'd met him, he had come to her village with Alex after returning from working on the railroad. Later, he'd stood as Alex's best man at their wedding. A few weeks after they were married, he had joined the entire family for dinner at Mother Emaline's cabin. On each occasion, he and Alex had been full of fun and laughter as they shared about their expeditions exploring the mountains of Colorado Territory, but at dinner that night, they had kept the entire family on the edge of their seats, sharing stories that not even Mother Emaline had heard before.

Alex, Emaline's secondborn, had always been hungry for adventure. He'd tried mining, struck out on month-long explorations to see what there was to see throughout the territory, visited Denver, hunted buffalo, made contact with natives, helped lay the railroad across the Great Plains to Cheyenne, and tried his hand at ranching. That was all before the age of twenty-one; before he married Niz. And, as Alex told it, Ezra Taylor had been at his side through it all.

The duo had been in too many scrapes to count during their adventures together, and sitting around Mother Emaline's table, they had reminisced about many of them. Niz still remembered how pale poor Mother Emaline had been, and her heartfelt—and numerous—declarations of thanks be to God that they were both still alive to tell their tales. Will, who had always idolized his older brother, had been wide-eyed and enthralled by their stories, while Luke, the oldest, had suggested a little more time at the mill and a little less time galivanting around the territory would keep them from getting in so many close calls. Raya had listened with shining eyes, just as enthralled as Will, and Niz had only smiled, imagining Alex using the wild stories to entertain their children someday. In her mind, she suddenly saw again the wooden cross standing in a small cemetery and realized afresh that day would never come. Sorrow rose up to overtake her, but she willfully pushed it away.

Ezra Taylor had come over for supper again once more before she had accompanied Alex to town to see Ezra off when he left to join the army—his next grand adventure. With one hand holding Ezra's horse in place, Alex had tried one last time to convince his best friend to stay. But Ezra had only clapped him on the shoulder with a laugh and told him that though he'd miss him, he'd still take adventuring solo over the prospect of admitting defeat and settling down.

That had been nearly four years ago, but Niz still remembered exactly how she'd felt standing there watching Ezra ride away, feeling with every fiber of her being how much Alex longed to be riding off with him. She had felt like a chain that was holding him back. When Alex had expressed as much, though, with a mischievous twinkle in his eye, her distress had morphed into offense and then anger. He was the one who had chosen to get married! She certainly hadn't forced him. Upset, she had called him a choice name before turning and stalking off, yelling back that if he wanted to go so badly, to go! She could return home and carry on with her life, with or without him.

His big, jolly laugh had rung out through the empty street, encompassing her with its sound. Jogging after her, he had caught her up in his arms, ignoring her fiery protests, and slipped around the side of the general store, where he had promptly kissed her soundly. She touched her lips softly, remembering how his kiss had taken her breath away. With that one kiss, her resistance had faded, and she'd found herself melting in against him. In the privacy of the ally, he'd reminded her of all the reasons why he would rather be with her than anywhere else, especially on a dusty trail with only the likes of Ezra Taylor for company.

With a shuddering breath, Nizhoni leaned over and splashed cold water on her face, washing away the bittersweet memory and shocking herself back to the present. Reaching out, she filled her pot with water and stood. The past was over. Alex was gone. And she had supper to make.

~~~

When the sun rose, the women returned to the amaranth patch. Again, the work was hard, but the day was enjoyable. By midafternoon they had gathered all they would take from the patch—the rest of the flower spikes would be left to drop their seeds to replenish the plant for next year's harvest. Their workday ended earlier than it had the day before, and they talked and laughed together as they walked home. This time, when they arrived back at camp, the hunting party had returned. There was much rejoicing as the braves told their tales while the women processed the hunt.

That night there was feasting and celebrating, and Nizhoni's heart sang with happiness. She laughed with her mother and sisters, celebrated with her friends, danced to the beat of the drums, and filled her belly with the good late summer harvest. It was such a fun evening that even Fire Maker couldn't ruin it for her when he stumbled loudly into their wickiup in the middle of the night, having drunk too much again. With groggy eyes, she'd simply turned over on her sleeping mat, thankful he'd passed out upon making it to his stack of hides.

In the morning, she was up early with the other women to continue processing the braves' harvest. Though the elk had been skinned and gutted the night before, it was time to thinly slice and hang the meat. Once that was done, they would begin to scrape and finally tan the hides—something the women in their tribe were known for doing excellently. Nowhere else in Colorado Territory could you find hides so smooth, pliable, and uniform as you did in the villages of her people. The golden hue, faint smoky aroma, and luxuriant softness were things that could only be achieved by an expert craftsman, and they had been passing down their expertise for generations. Knowing that made her proud. Processing a hunt was physical work, though, and as the late summer sun rose high in the sky, she wiped the perspiration from her forehead.

"It's warm out," Ever Flowering said, stopping beside her.

"It is," Niz agreed. She paused for a drink of water and noticed the expression on her sister's face. The young woman seemed to be bursting with some sort of happy news. "What's got you smiling so big today?" she asked, a smile filling her own face, too. Ever Flowering's happiness always seemed to be contagious.

"Niz," Ever Flowering started, "how did you know you were with child?"

For just a moment, Niz stared at her sister in shock, then her shock dissolved into pure joy. "Ever Flowering!" she shrieked. "Do you think you might be?"

She'd been eagerly waiting for this day. Her sister, who was just a year younger than she was, had married Walks With Power just a month before Niz returned home to the village. Now, the twenty-year-old had been married a year, and Niz had been hoping she would have an announcement soon. Ever Flowering and Walks With Power were the sweetest couple; she couldn't wait to see them become parents. With her sister's big heart, bright smile, and gentle ways, Niz knew she was going to be a wonderful mother. Additionally, it had been a difficult few years for their own mother with their father dying, and Niz had desperately hoped that at least one of Shy Fawn's daughters would soon be able to lay a babe in her arms to help fill the void.

Thoughts of her own tiny infant began to rise, and Niz instantly silenced them. She would not let the past steal her joy. Nor would she allow her own unfulfilled hope to keep her from rejoicing with her sister. This moment was not about her; it was about Ever Flowering.

"I've suspected for a while but wasn't certain."

"Your monthly flow?" Niz questioned.

"Missing for just over four moons."

"Nausea?"

"Yes, often, sometime back. But then it went away—maybe a moon or two ago. At the time, I wondered if I hadn't dried our meat long enough."

Niz laughed. "I don't believe it had anything to do with your meat. Have you noticed any changes in your body? Any tenderness or thickening?"

Ever Flowering nodded shyly. "And then this morning, I felt something. Just a quickening, really. It was faint and brief, but . . . I felt it."

"I remember that feeling," Niz said, offering her sister a brilliant smile. She reached out and laid her hand against Ever Flowering's cheek. "I think all the signs are there, sister. It seems you're going to have a baby!"

"Do you really think so?" Ever Flowering asked, pressing her hand over Niz's, her eyes full of light. "I've often wondered, but I haven't let myself hope. I've been so worried after . . . well . . . after your grief." The girl's eyes slid to the ground.

For the briefest instant, the memories, the sorrow, the grief tried to rise up and cast a shadow over Niz's joy. Again, she shut the door on it, relegating it to the back recesses of her heart. "This will not end the same way," she said confidently. "I exerted myself too much. It's as simple as that. You're not so foolish. And I am going to be right here, right at your side, to make sure you don't. You are going to have a healthy pregnancy and give birth to a healthy child. I'll make sure of it," Niz said, swearing to it in that moment.

She couldn't go back and undo what she had done. She couldn't go back and rest more, do less, and heed caution to save her child. But she could take care of her sister. She could be careful with the life of her unborn niece or nephew. That would be her single-minded mission. That would be what would give purpose to her days, her chance to right the wrongs of her past, her way of honoring her own dear son. That was something she could do.

Ever Flowering raised her dark eyes again, and Niz could see the joy shining in them. "I'm going to have a baby!" she said in awestruck wonder.

Niz could feel her own face blossoming into a beaming smile as she looked directly into her sister's brown eyes. "You are going to have a baby," she agreed.

Together, they hugged and rejoiced, laughing and crying all at once.

"What has you two so happy?"

Niz and Ever Flowering looked up to see their mother paused nearby, balancing a stick draped with thinly sliced elk meat in each hand.

Ever Flowering's cheeks were wet, but her eyes were shining. "I think you're going to be a grandmother," she said.

Nizhoni watched the tears pool in Shy Fawn's dark eyes. How long must the woman have waited to hear those very words? Niz gently took the sticks laden with sliced meat from her mother, continuing to the drying rack with it, leaving Shy Fawn free to celebrate the joyous news with her daughter.

When she returned, Nizhoni left Ever Flowering and Shy Fawn to continue celebrating while she started back to work. No matter how excited she was, the braves' hunt needed to be processed before the meat spoiled. When Ever Flowering was ready to work again, Niz fetched her sister's supplies, setting her workstation up beside her own so they could chat as they sliced. They discussed pregnancy, what to expect, and how Ever Flowering was feeling—with Shy Fawn and Cloud Walking popping in frequently to add to the conversation. Together, they calculated when to expect the child, made plans to start on a cradleboard, and dreamt about the year to come with a little one in the family.

The day passed in happy conversation, good work, and the rosy hues of a promising future. It was late in the afternoon when something Ever Flowering said stilled Nizhoni's hands.

"Ever Flowering, did you just say Walks With Power's horse was stolen on the hunt?" Niz questioned, looking up quickly, alarmed.

Her sister's expression revealed her surprise. "You hadn't heard?" Niz shook her head. "I'm surprised Fire Maker didn't tell you. But yes, the horses were stolen . . . but then the soldiers returned them."

Confused, Niz wiped at the dark hair that was sticking to her forehead with the back of her soiled hand. "Wait. Are you saying soldiers stole the horses?" Ever Flowering shook her head. "Start at the beginning," Niz instructed.

"Walks With Power said they came across some soldiers early on in the week when they'd first started their hunt. The soldiers had a scout with them who could communicate with signs, and he told them they were out looking for horse thieves. Walks With Power and the others assured them they were out hunting, that our people are peaceful, and both groups went on their way. He said the soldiers were decent and the leader even seemed friendly."

Niz pursed her lips, knowing instinctively that Ever Flowering was speaking of Major Taylor. He'd always been as friendly and open as Alex. They had often said that on the western frontier, a man never knew when he might need a friend.

"Well, when the hunting party woke up yesterday morning, the horses were gone. They found moccasin prints and knew it must be the horse thieves they'd heard about. They started tracking them on foot. They'd only gone a few miles when they came across the soldiers who had been looking for them. It turns out the soldiers had found a small band of Comanche not far from the brave's camp earlier that morning and recognized Stands Tall's horse."

Nizhoni didn't doubt that. The flashy black and white paint was hard to mistake. Thinking back to when the soldiers had visited, she realized they must have found the Comanche only the morning after coming to speak to Fire Maker. That sent a shiver down her spine—that could only mean the Comanche raiders had been close by. "They captured the Comanche and the horses?" she asked hopefully.

"No, Walks With Power said the Comanche saw them coming and made a run for it. They left the stolen horses behind—"

"They were probably worried they would slow them down," Niz reasoned.

"Probably so," Ever Flowering agreed. "Anyway, the soldiers rounded up the horses, and when they recognized Stands Tall's paint, they returned them. The scout wasn't with them anymore, so they couldn't communicate well, but they got across that they knew the braves would need their horses to transport their hunt back to camp."

"That was really nice of them," Nizhoni observed, stunned.

Her people had been mostly at peace with the newcomers to the area for as long as she could remember, able to simply avoid them for the most part in the vastness of the high mountains. Where there was contact, Chief Great Mountain had been adept at keeping the peace. The settlers nearby were mostly mountain men—or had been at one time—and had learned to live in relative harmony with the native inhabitants of the land. Thus, their people had not encountered the same kind of violent hostilities that their brothers on the plains and southern mountains brought word of. But still, even having had mostly peaceful interactions, the gesture was unheard of. The soldiers very well could have kept the horses for themselves since they had found them, leaving Walks With Power and the others to blame the Comanche. But they hadn't. They had returned them. Nizhoni mulled it over in her mind, trying to make sense of it.

Ever Flowering continued to chatter, as happy and talkative as the birds of the forest, soon pulling Nizhoni's thoughts to other things. The late afternoon sun continued to drop in the sky until it slipped behind the western mountains, and dusk began to settle. Finally, splitting ways as they went to their separate wickiups for the night, Nizhoni went inside feeling happy. With the setting of the sun, they were one day closer to welcoming Ever Flowering's new baby. That was something to look forward to.

Four

"Ever Flowering is with child."

Nizhoni glanced up quickly, surprised to see her husband standing inside their wickiup. She hadn't heard him come in.

"Yes," she answered, a smile lifting her full lips. It had been two days since her sister told her the news, and the hours that had passed had done little to diminish her joy. Instead, every parting day made it grow as she once again remembered she had something to look forward to.

"Walks With Power told me."

Niz considered her husband's expression. He didn't seem pleased. Did he think she should have been the one to share the happy news? It wasn't as if they conversed much. "I hope you congratulated him."

"I did. But what I don't understand is why your sister is with child, and you are not."

Nizhoni's chin jerked as she absorbed his accusatory words. She answered carefully. "These things take time, Fire Maker. They've been married longer."

He rolled his eyes. "Barely."

"Well, maybe by the time the winter snows fall, we'll be expecting our own baby," she reasoned. She could only hope. Though she regretted her choice of a husband, she longed for a child to ease the emptiness of her arms—and heart. She told herself it might improve the strained relationship between them,

43

too. Surely Fire Maker would be happier and kinder if she were carrying his child. Perhaps it would give them some common ground—something safe to connect over.

"Maybe," he scoffed as he walked further into their home. He didn't sound optimistic. "Do you know why I married you?" He stopped directly in front of her, towering over her as she knelt on the floor.

She kept her eyes on the seeds she was grinding with her metate and mano. Only a little more, and it would be fine enough to make the dough for their flatbread. She focused her attention on the rhythmic motions of her work rather than her husband. She could tell by the sound of his voice that he wasn't planning to lavish her with words of love and affection.

Undeterred, he continued, his voice hard. "I married you because of your beauty. There's no one else among our people whose looks even come close to comparing to yours."

When he stopped, the tension in her shoulders began to ease. That hadn't been as bad as she'd expected. In fact, it was as close as her husband got to paying her a compliment. She would ignore the fact that he had admitted to marrying her only for her appearance and choose to believe that, however ill formed, he was trying to say something nice.

"Thank y—"

"Even your own sisters pale in comparison—like drab, withered weeds next to a stunning wildflower," he continued with a sneer, interrupting.

"That's not true!" she argued, lifting her gaze to him, hurt by his cruel appraisal of her sisters. They were both beautiful girls.

Why couldn't he have left it as a compliment? While she would enjoy being called stunning and beautiful if there had been any love and emotion behind it, the lack of it, along with the mean-hearted slur to her sisters, robbed his words of any joy or meaning. Recognizing the anger burning in his eyes, she realized he had never meant to flatter, only to wound.

"It is true, and you know it!" he shot back, seeming triumphant.

Seeing how he took pleasure in knowing he had gotten to her, she suppressed her reaction. Swallowing her emotions and smoothing out her facial expression, she dropped her eyes and started back to work again. Pressing down, she rocked the stone mano around in a circular motion over the seeds scattered across the metate.

"No one else has your lips, your eyes, your figure," he continued pointedly.

She lifted her chin defiantly but kept her eyes on her work. If only he spoke such words tenderly with any ounce of kindness, emotion, or feeling. Instead, he spoke only approvingly, as if discussing a well-muscled horse.

Nizhoni flinched as Fire Maker suddenly squatted down right in front of her. Reaching out, he took her chin roughly in his hand and lifted it, forcing her to meet his eyes again. "But tell me, what good is a beautiful wife if she won't give you any children? What good is your beauty if you won't bear strong and handsome sons for me?"

Fire snapped and smoldered in her heart, and she glared at him. "It's not as if I'm intentionally not getting pregnant!"

"Are you sure about that, *Nizhoni*?" he asked, seeming to mock her with the meaning of her name. Only he could take a word that meant 'beautiful' and make it sound so ugly.

She jumped to her feet, feeling better able to take his insults standing up. "Yes, I'm sure about that!" she cried. "What do you think I'm doing, Fire Maker? Taking precautions to ensure I'm not with child? Would I dishonor us both in such a way? Do I not long for a child to hold in my arms? Do I not wish with everything within me that I was expecting a baby just as Ever Flowering is?" She turned away from him, covering her face with her hands, ashamed of the emotion she couldn't hide. She didn't want him seeing how his accusations hurt and angered her.

He grabbed her arm and jerked her back around. "Don't turn your back on me!" he exploded.

"Maybe it's just not going to happen for us," she told him, her voice low and angry, the fire within her clouding her reasoning. "But if it doesn't, then lay your blame elsewhere, because it's not me! I've carried a baby! I'm capable of growing a husband's seed . . . if there's any seed to be grown!"

His slap sent her to the ground, and she stayed there, looking up at him, her hand covering her cheek, her eyes smoldering. Lovely. Now she would have to apply a poultice of yarrow before bed and hope the skin wouldn't bruise. If it did, she would have to paint her face in the morning to cover it. She had been doing so more and more lately. Thankfully, it was not uncommon among her people for men, women, and children to occasionally paint their faces for daily life. No one would know . . . this time.

"Don't you ever say that again," he told her, his face red with fury. "This is your doing—your problem!"

She bit her tongue to keep the fiery retort back, but she let her expression say it all. He might be an angry, hurtful, horrible man, but she would not be cowed. She was Nizhoni; spirited and feisty, as free as the wind, and as wild as the spirit of their people. She would not allow him to crush her. Though she would not continue to bait him with her words, she would let him see how she despised him.

His expression changed and he crouched down in front of her again, his eyes dark as he leaned in close. She clenched her teeth and suppressed a shiver of fear. She would not be afraid. "Maybe it is as you say. Maybe in a few more moons, we will be expecting our own child," he said, his gaze falling to her lips. "We will certainly do our part to make that happen, won't we, wife?"

She narrowed her eyes at him. "For the sake of any children we might have and our people, I hope someday I can find it in my heart to love you."

He laughed. It was a humorless, dangerous sound. "I don't require your love or your heart. I already have all of you that I want."

She felt the pain of his words more clearly than she had felt the sting of his hand. Unfortunately, she had no doubt that he meant what he said. And if it was true, then what kind of life could they possibly hope to build together?

~~~

Nizhoni looked up as the breeze carried the sound of pounding hoofbeats to her ears. She'd just finished stirring the amaranth seeds, making sure they were all patted down into a thin layer and exposed to the dry Colorado air before leaving her wickiup. Drying the seeds thoroughly would preserve them for her people to eat throughout the coming year; leaving moisture in them would spoil the lot. If the amaranth seeds spoiled, they would be left without the nutritious food source they depended on for survival so getting them dry was imperative, even if it was backbreaking work.

Seeing soldiers coming, Nizhoni took a moment to stretch out the kinks that had developed as she'd crouched over the seeds. She didn't know how Shy Fawn and the other women her age did it. Watching the soldiers ride up to the edge of the village and dismount, she started toward them.

With news of their arrival spreading quickly, children hurried to their mothers, and women ushered them swiftly inside their wickiups, out of harm's way. A ruckus arose as several of the braves went to meet them, calling back and forth to each other as they did so. They seemed wary, though curious. Nizhoni wondered if the braves recognized them as the soldiers they had encountered while hunting.

She moved cautiously toward the group, holding back from joining them, but wanting to hear what was being said. The soldiers were trying to talk to the braves, and the braves were trying to talk to the soldiers. Neither group understood the other.

Fire Maker turned, and she instinctively knew he was looking for her. Nizhoni stepped forward from among the curious women who were gathering, and he motioned for her to come. Reaching him, she winced as he roughly grabbed her arm and pulled her through the small crowd. She subtly tried to twist free as his fingers dug into her arm. Her face was already painted; if he didn't lighten his hold, she would have to paint her arm as well. He released her as they reached the front of the group, and with a clear view of the soldiers, she quickly saw it was the same five who had visited before. Fire Maker gestured from Ezra Taylor to her and grunted.

"Hello," Major Taylor said, clearing his throat.

Nizhoni nodded in cautious greeting.

"I've come once more to see if you have any information about the whereabouts of the Comanche. As you likely know, we came upon them last week, but they fled. We picked up their trail again yesterday, and tracked them to about five miles from here, but then lost it. They seem to be good at disappearing. I know you're observant people and I wanted to see if you've come across any signs of their whereabouts or perhaps seen their fires."

Nizhoni turned and carefully relayed the major's words to her husband and the braves surrounding him. The men discussed among themselves for a few moments. She hoped Fire Maker would relay the braves' reports that they had not seen the Comanche. Instead, he turned back to the soldiers, his expression hard as he sized them up.

"What is information on their whereabouts worth to you?"

Major Taylor tipped his head as Nizhoni translated, his eyes narrowing a bit under the bill of his dark blue forage cap. "Those Comanche stole some of your friends' horses when they were out hunting. They are our common enemy. I did not come to hire you. I came to work together for the good of us all."

"I do not work with soldiers!" Fire Maker retorted hotly. He pounded his fist against his chest. "I am Fire Maker, son of Chief

Great Mountain of the mountain people. If you want our help, what do you bring in hopes that we will lend our expert tracking skills to these dogs who have none?" He gestured at the soldiers with an arrogant flip of his hand.

Nizhoni looked at the ground as she translated, unable to meet the soldiers' eyes. Before she'd finished, the men behind the major exclaimed their offense. She glanced up and instinctively took a step back at the angry expressions that filled their faces. Her courage faltered as she listened to the threats a few of them flung toward her husband; dread filled her as she watched them try to convince Major Taylor to deal with Fire Maker's impudence with force.

She knew enough to know what could happen if natives insulted soldiers. She'd heard stories from Alex about how the army dealt with defiance. She'd seen the newspapers during her time with the Applewoods. Oh, if only Chief Great Mountain were still alive! In self-preservation she took another step back and then another, but Fire Maker shoved her back toward the soldiers, keeping her in the middle of the group.

Glancing at her husband, she wondered if she needed to translate the conversation taking place between the soldiers. But behind Fire Maker, the braves were shooting nervous glances at one another. They didn't speak the white man's words, but it was clear they understood their body language perfectly—they comprehended what was being said. She had to assume her husband did also, though he didn't show it. Fire Maker stood perfectly still, his arms crossed, his feet planted, his hard face void of emotion.

The group of soldiers drew her attention again as Major Taylor raised a hand, signaling for silence from his men. They followed his command, though they looked disgruntled and vexed. They had clearly not appreciated Fire Maker's insinuation that they were incompetent.

Worried, Nizhoni braced for whatever would come next. For a split-second Major Taylor's gaze flickered to her and then, just as quickly, it was gone again. But in that moment, though she couldn't explain it, though it was so brief she couldn't even grasp it, the look in his eyes had quieted the alarm coursing through her. Her fear settled a little.

He took a few steps forward, bringing himself directly in front of Fire Maker. He didn't look happy.

"Chief Fire Maker, I've come in good faith in an act of brotherhood, attempting to work together to protect both property and life for all our people. I'm going to ask you once more, have you seen sign of or crossed paths with the Comanche?"

Fire Maker's expression turned mocking, and his answer was quick. "You and me, we are not brothers," her husband scoffed. "You are foolish to imagine yourself great enough to be considered a brother to Fire Maker, chief of Great Mountain's people."

Nizhoni stared at her husband for a long moment, disappointed that he would not just tell the truth, frustrated by the arrogant foolishness that ruled his life, frightened by the possible repercussions. Why could he not see the truth in what Major Taylor was saying? Why would he not accept the soldiers' help and offer his own in return to oppose a common enemy? Why did he withhold his cooperation? Was it truly necessary to demand payment in exchange for his collaboration? Wasn't the safety of the tribe and their possessions profit enough? Was it truly worth the possibility of vexing the army for his own personal gain? For his own personal pride?

What about his people? What of Walks With Power, Stands Tall, and the others who had lost their horses to the raiders, only to have them returned at the hands of the soldiers? What about their village and their people? If the Comanche raided their camp, they had much to lose. Fire Maker had much to lose. The soldiers weren't asking for their help to track down the renegades and oust them from the area, only for their information. Why did he have to be so altogether disagreeable?

"What did he say?" Major Taylor asked stiffly, his unwavering gaze still on Fire Maker. Though the major could not understand the words, he clearly knew he'd been insulted.

Nizhoni turned slowly toward him. She looked at the soldiers that flanked him and drew in a deep, steadying breath, trying to summon her courage to translate the words Fire Maker never should have spoken.

"Actually, I don't even want to hear it," Major Taylor continued after a moment. "I got the gist of it." He turned and motioned for his soldiers to mount up.

Suddenly, she stumbled forward as Fire Maker shoved her from behind. "Tell him! Tell him what I said! Tell him he will never be worthy of calling himself my brother! Tell him if he wants our help, he must pay greatly. Tell him! Do your job and translate, woman!"

"He says you are not worthy to call yourself his brother," Nizhoni said, taking a few steps after Major Taylor, feeling caught between a rock and a hard place. Though she was frightened of the soldiers, she was even more afraid of disobeying her husband. The soldiers would leave, but she would go home with Fire Maker. She was loath to bring his anger against her if he was so set on bringing the wrath of the soldiers against himself. "He says if you want his help, you have to make it worth his while."

Her words elicited another round of furious protests from the soldiers. With red faces, a few of them said things Nizhoni wasn't eager to translate. For a moment, she wondered if one of them would rush her husband. They clearly felt personally insulted but just as obvious was their fierce loyalty to their leader; Fire Maker's slur toward the major had seemed to anger them more than anything else. Before any of them made a move, though, Major Taylor spun on his heel to face Fire Maker again. He clenched and unclenched his jaw, but when he spoke, his words were measured, his tone controlled. "I will not let your pride and greed make me do something I'll regret. My offer to work together stands."

Nizhoni translated nervously, not sure if either of the men glaring so intently at each other were even listening. For a tense moment, they stood staring at one another, both glowering with intimidation. Suddenly, Fire Maker spit on Major Taylor.

"Fire Maker!" she gasped, looking at her husband in dismay before turning back to the major. Ezra Taylor had shown restraint, but she feared this new insult would be too much.

Drawing his explosive anger with her exclamation, Fire Maker shoved Nizhoni powerfully to the ground before turning on his heel and stalking off. After an awkward moment, his braves turned and followed their chief, disappearing into camp. From the ground, Nizhoni watched them go, her heart falling. Why, when he could make peace, did Fire Maker choose to make war?

"Are you alright?" Major Taylor asked grimly, reaching down to help her up. After a brief hesitation, she accepted his hand and let him pull her to her feet.

"Yes, I'm fine," she answered, straightening her buckskin dress, trying to convince herself she was. In truth, her knees and palms were smarting where they had been scraped when she fell, her embarrassment was stinging, and her anger was smoldering.

What gave Fire Maker the right to treat her so? Why did he feel the need to push her around when she was willing to be a good wife to him of her own volition? She would joyfully work alongside him to serve their people, if only he could offer her some sliver of kindness and respect—even the slightest common decency.

Major Taylor stared after where Fire Maker had disappeared. "Why are you even with him?" he questioned, his voice both accusatory and filled with disgust.

Nizhoni's dark eyes darted to the major, surprised by his question. She considered him as she tried to formulate an answer. As she did, her anger began to dissolve into despair. Did he really not know? Was it possible that he still hadn't heard the fate of the Applewood men? And yet, his parents had both passed and he'd been away. Who would have told him?

Choosing her words carefully, knowing she couldn't risk angering the spirits by speaking of the dead, she replied, "Things aren't as they were. Mother Emaline and Raya have returned to the East."

Major Taylor turned from staring after Fire Maker, to look at her. She felt unnerved under the steady gaze of his hazel eyes. Instead of looking angry as he had, his face had filled with sorrow and sympathy, and the emotion in it touched her. She could see he shared her sense of loss.

He glanced up at his men, who were mounted and ready, their horses prancing and snorting nervously, clearly eager to get moving. Turning back to her, he stepped closer, dropping his voice. "Yes, I heard. After I was here last time, I went to town and asked around. I—" He paused to steady his voice. "I'm so sorry, Niz. I'm sorry for your loss, and I'm sorry I wasn't there when it happened. Alex was my best friend. I should have been there. I should have been around to help you and Emaline after . . . I owed him that much."

She shook her head and dropped her eyes, dismissing his apology. Inwardly, she wondered how life would be different if he had been. He didn't owe it to them. He had no obligation. But if there would have been a man around who could have helped them get on their feet—who could have helped sustain them just for a couple of months to give them time to make sense of their grief and decide what to do next with logic rather than emotion, how would things have been different?

Would Mother Emaline and Raya have found a way to stay in Colorado Territory where they could all be together? Would Chenoa have been able to stay with them instead of returning to her father's house? Would she herself have been thinking straight enough to refuse Fire Maker's proposal as she had the first time he'd asked for her hand in marriage? Would her life be happier, better, less stressful, without the constant fear of making him mad?

But Major Taylor hadn't been there, Mother Emaline and Raya had left, Chenoa had gone home, Niz hadn't had the time to grieve in privacy, and she hadn't acted with logic. It didn't matter how things could have been different; things were how they were.

"You don't owe anyone anything," she answered sincerely. "The Applewoods . . . all of them . . . were so proud you were off on another adventure. Don't doubt that."

He cleared his throat gruffly. "I just . . . I wish I'd been there. I helped out with the mill here and there, I knew how things worked. If I'd been there that day, instead of off fighting . . . well, maybe I could have gotten that door open in time."

She looked up into his face, and her heart began to ache, seeing the regret that mirrored her own. He wished Alex was still alive as much as she did. She could see it. Somehow, just knowing that helped. But regret couldn't override logic. She shook her head. "The logs were too heavy. We would have needed a dozen men or a team of horses to move them. And by the time we realized what was happening . . . well, it was too late anyway."

"That's what they said in town. But still . . ." He shifted his weight and drug his hand over his face.

Niz dropped her eyes to the rocky soil, biting her lip, trying to keep the grief at bay. She wouldn't feel it. She couldn't. Not here. Not now. Not with Ezra Taylor standing in front of her. But all her reasoning didn't feel like enough. A wave of loneliness crashed over her. She missed her husband. She missed Mother Emaline, Raya, and Chenoa. She missed her brothers-in-law, the family they had been, and the life they had shared. Suddenly, an idea brought her head up, and hope fluttered to life in her heart.

Mother Emaline and Raya were out of reach in Cincinnati, but Chenoa was still in the area living with her father. Niz's mind worked quickly, and she determined she would find Chenoa's house the next time she visited town. Maybe seeing her would help fill the void. And Chenoa knew how to read. Perhaps she would read her letters to her, and she would not only get to see her dear sister-in-law but also hear news of Raya and Mother Emaline.

"When you asked around in town, did you hear anything about my youngest sister-in-law? Chenoa?" Niz asked hopefully. "She didn't leave with Mother Emaline and Raya last fall."

Major Taylor nodded, his eyes resting on her again. He seemed reluctant to answer. "The storekeeper said as much when I asked if any of the family was still in the area. But he went on to say she left this spring with a man from Idaho Territory."

"She left?" Niz's heart sank. "Why would she go to Idaho Territory?"

Chenoa had been delicate and easily frightened. It was hard to imagine her going off into the unknown. Niz had pegged her for someone who would always stay close to home. And she remembered seeing Idaho Territory on one of Alex's maps. It was far away. Would Chenoa even have been able to survive the journey? Her heart twisted in concern.

He shrugged one broad shoulder. "Something about an aunt."

She couldn't help it; her head fell forward, and her shoulders slumped. The comfort she had hoped to find in seeing Chenoa and finding out what was in the letters had gone out like a small flame on a stormy night. Grief welled up within her. But she couldn't feel it. Not here. Not now. Giving a tiny shake of her head, she drew herself up straighter. As she did, she winced. Fire Maker's shove earlier had tweaked her back; no doubt thanks to having crouched over the amaranth seeds for so long. She moved slightly, trying to ease the tightness. She saw the man in front of her notice.

Major Taylor cleared his throat. "Alex wrote me that he was going to be a father."

Nizhoni felt as though the wind had been knocked out of her. To talk about the Applewoods, Alex, and the tragedy was painful enough, but to have him mention her child . . .

"Did you . . .?" He didn't finish his sentence, letting it trail off instead as he studied her face.

She lifted her chin and shrugged, trying to stop feeling all the emotions his words brought up. "I worked too hard helping to put out the fire. Everyone told me to sit down and rest, but I didn't. I couldn't. And I was punished for my folly."

He took the cap off his head and pushed his hand through his thick, dark brown hair, then put it back on and drug his hand over his face again. She discreetly took the opportunity to run her fingertips under her eyes, making sure none of the tears that were threatening had managed to leak out.

"You're bleeding," he said, reaching out and grabbing her arm.

He released her as quickly as he had grabbed her, but even still, she threw a nervous glance back over her shoulder, suddenly remembering that Fire Maker could be watching. If he was . . .

But Fire Maker wasn't in sight, nor were any of the braves. He was likely drinking with his friends, celebrating his brilliance in offending the army. Relieved, she relaxed.

Bending her arm, she saw that Major Taylor was right. She was bleeding from deep scrapes on her elbow, no doubt caused by her fall. She accepted the handkerchief he held out to her and wiped up the trail of blood that was making its way toward her wrist.

His face hardened. "That brings me back to my original question. Why in the world are you with Fire Maker?"

Surprised, Nizhoni drew back. "I . . . I told you. Things are different now."

"But out of all the men you could have chosen, why him? After how good Alex treated you, how could you be with a man like that?" He sounded disgusted—frustrated—maybe even angry.

Nizhoni drew herself up straighter, both embarrassed and offended. "Fire Maker is my husband."

"A terrible one!" he retorted. Tipping his head back, he stared up at the sky for a moment. Niz stayed quiet, wanting to argue, but knowing he was right. What could she say? Silence seemed the best option. He took a deep breath and leveled his gaze at her again. "Can I help you?"

After a brief pause, she slowly shook her head. What could he do? What could anyone do? She'd made a bad decision and now she had to live with it.

She watched his eyes fall to her cheek. Embarrassment flushed through her as she realized he had noticed the fading bruise. She'd thought she had it covered with paint, but his attention made it clear that she hadn't covered it well enough. Humiliated, she put her hand over the mark.

"Please. I could take you away from here . . . away from him. I could help you figure out a new life. Alex would want you to be safe."

She inhaled sharply. Emotions crashed over her defenses. Her head felt like it was spinning in a swirling mix of grief and humiliation. Tears pricked her eyes, and she viciously blinked them back. Her temper flared in response.

"Fire Maker is my husband!" she repeated, more forcefully this time. She had given her word; she wouldn't go back on it.

Major Taylor's hazel eyes snapped in response. "Niz, he mistreats you! Alex never would have allow—"

"Alex is *dead*, Ezra!" Niz shot back, her heart constricting painfully. As her words registered, she shrank back in fear.

For the first time since the day of the fire, she'd spoken her dead husband's name. How had she let herself do it? Her husband, her son, their family, their livelihood, their means—all gone. She was now married to a harsh and selfish man who hurt her. As if she clearly wasn't already being punished, she had dared to speak the name of the dead, offering the spirits even more ammunition for which to punish her. A painful lump formed in her throat and she worried that tears would follow. She took a shaky step back and then another.

"Niz," Major Taylor started, his voice kinder than it had been. Overcome with fear and grief, she gave a slight shake of her head and turned and ran. Her feet pounded the ground as she sought escape from Ezra Taylor, from Fire Maker, from her marital problems, but mostly from the grief that was rising up, threatening to consume her. She couldn't stay in one place any longer. She couldn't give it the chance to swallow her up. She couldn't allow herself to feel all the things, and so she did the only thing she knew to do—she ran.

Five

"Nizhoni, I heard what you did yesterday when the soldiers came."

Surprised, Nizhoni looked up. Her mother's face looked pensive and anxious. "What do you mean?"

"Fire Maker asked you to translate for him, and in front of the soldiers, you scolded him for how he dealt with them," Shy Fawn said, her words a confusing mix of accusation and concern.

"I didn't!" Nizhoni argued, instantly defensive. She'd already pled her case to Fire Maker the night before. "I only was surprised."

He hadn't been convinced any more than her mother seemed now, and his punishment had been swift and effective. Next time, she would hold her tongue, no matter how surprised she was by his actions toward Major Taylor.

"Walks With Power told your sister all about it, and this morning she told me," Shy Fawn went on, continuing to work the hide they were tanning. One day it would be soft leather they would use to make clothing, or perhaps trade, but today, it was still a work in progress.

The hide had been scraped to remove all the remaining flesh, then soaked in a mixture of water and ash to loosen the hair. After scraping off all the hair, her mother had spent the day before working a mixture of brains, liver, yucca, and grease into the hide to tan it before leaving it to soak. Now, they were working the hide over a log—a strenuous task that not only softened it but also helped to scrape off the remaining tanning mixture. Once they were done, they would smoke it over a smoldering fire. It was a long and difficult process, and Shy Fawn's face was red from exertion and wet with perspiration, as was Niz's.

Pushing back her hair, Niz wiped the sweat from her forehead, unable to believe what she heard her mother saying. Could the woman really be taking Fire Maker's side? Had Walks With Power and Ever Flowering also? She closed her eyes and inhaled deeply, trying not to succumb to the sting of betrayal.

"Mother! Major Taylor came seeking information to fight a common enemy, and Fire Maker refused to help, insulted him, and finally *spit on him*!"

She understood she should have shown her husband honor. She knew she was expected to defend him at any and all times, but how did she honor and defend a man who was so reckless and unwise? "I was shocked by his actions and frightened of how the soldiers would respond."

Shy Fawn looked at her for a long moment and then lifted her slender hand in an act of surrender. "We're concerned for you, Nizhoni, that's all." After glancing around, Shy Fawn dropped her voice to a whisper. "I've seen men like Fire Maker before. Not often, but on a few occasions. You have to be careful with them. You can't antagonize them."

"Mother, he—"

"Your spirit burns bright within you. I know that. That fire is beautiful. It's like the heart of our people. Others see it and are drawn to you. Men like . . . well, some men . . . admire it and are captivated by its beauty. You knew that admiration in your first love. Other men only see the challenge to crush it. Power-hungry, they make it their goal to break a spirit like yours. If they can't . . ." Shy Fawn reached over and grasped Nizhoni's hand, squeezing it, her eyes sad. "I'm afraid for you, daughter. The harder you hold on to that fire, the more determined he's going to be to conquer it."

Nizhoni leaned toward her mother. "Am I not already conquered?" she whispered back fiercely. She was angry because it was true. "I am his wife. I'm trapped. I fear the repercussions before I say anything, always wondering how it might be perceived and bring me harm."

"And yet you say it," her mother pointed out, her words both scolding and full of sorrow.

Nizhoni closed her eyes and let that settle. How could she explain it in a way that anyone could understand? "I can't not, Mother. I try, but I cannot force my voice to stay silent. I can't sit back and watch how badly he behaves and not say something about it . . . or let it show on my face."

"Can't you try harder? Dim that fire, daughter. Just keep your mouth shut. Close your eyes if you have to rather than letting him see how you despise him." Shy Fawn paused and her lip trembled. "Sometimes I fear he means to either break your spirit or destroy you in the process."

Nizhoni looked into her mother's dear face, saw the fear that shadowed her gentle brown eyes, and noticed the lines of worry that had gathered on her forehead.

"Mother," she started, letting the word hang in the silence between them. She grasped for some way to articulate that which she didn't even understand herself.

Tears welled up in the kind eyes Nizhoni loved so dearly. "Ah, I see, daughter." Shy Fawn cupped her hand to Nizhoni's painted cheek. "I understand now. If you put out that fire—if you silence your voice—you're already destroyed, aren't you? It's that fire that keeps you going, isn't it?" She waited for Nizhoni's affirmative nod. When she got it, she continued, her voice little more than a whisper. "Breaking your spirit *would* destroy you—they're not two different outcomes; they're one and the same."

Nizhoni swallowed hard and nodded once again. She, too, felt the powerful force of her husband's desire to break her will. She knew he saw it as a threat to his control. She wasn't sure if it was conscious or unconscious on his part, but it was there and formidable, nonetheless. He meant to crush her under his iron fist; would likely only feel triumphant once he had. As her mother said, if he couldn't, he would likely destroy her in the process. Honestly, Niz wasn't sure Fire Maker preferred one outcome over another. But despite the danger, she could not, would not, be silenced.

"Mother, I feel the steadfastness of the mountain peaks, the strength of the sun, the power of the wind that blows through the passes, the heat of a fire, right here inside me," she explained, tapping on her chest. "It reminds me that we're wild and free. I can't ignore it. I can't give it up. I can't extinguish it or else there will be nothing left within me. Like a river without water or a mountain without rock, that's what I'd be if I let him break me."

"The spirit of our people burns bright within you, Nizhoni," Shy Fawn said sadly, patting her cheek. Nizhoni wasn't sure it was a good thing in her mother's eyes, but she put her hand over Shy Fawn's, and pressed it against her face, drawing comfort from the woman's touch.

"I will treat him respectfully, but I will not be silent. I must speak the truth. I can no more bend under his control than our people can bend under the will of the government. They seek to break us as Fire Maker seeks to break me."

Her mother let out an incredulous laugh. "Look at us, Nizhoni. We live on a reservation! We only live on the land the government tells us we can have—a small fraction of the land our people have roamed since time began."

"Yes, but, Mother, we're still free. We're still hunting our native lands, gathering our traditional foods, tanning hides, and making baskets. We're still living the life of those who have gone before us. We might be battered and bruised, but we're still standing. And as long as we're still standing, then the spirit of our people lives on."

Shy Fawn considered her for several long moments. "Then show your husband honor. He is trying to help our people stand."

Nizhoni blew out a frustrated breath and shook her head. "If only that were true, I would be overjoyed to help and honor him in whatever way I could. But I fear he is only trying to help himself."

"But you are married. What helps him helps you. Can't that be enough?"

"Mother, I care about our people. I care about Walks With Power and Ever Flowering and their new baby. I care about Cloud Walking. I care about you. I care about Soaring Eagle and Stands Tall and all the others. No, it's not enough to help myself. I long to help us all." She paused and looked out at the peaks of the high mountains that surrounded them, lost in thought for a moment.

She filled her lungs with the fresh mountain air and considered the approaching thunderstorm that was rolling in for its daily afternoon rain. She loved the storms that came nearly like clockwork in late summer. The lightning, wild and uncontrolled, struck the trees and mountains. Thunder crashed so loud she felt it inside her chest. Rain fell as if the whole land might be consumed in flash flooding, and then, only thirty minutes later, the storm would roll on through. In its wake, everything would be fresh and clean and bathed in the golden light of the sun once more.

"This new soldier, Major Taylor, I think he wants to help us too," Niz continued thoughtfully, putting words to the feeling that had been growing inside her.

Shy Fawn startled, and she glanced up sharply, her brows furrowing together. "He doesn't want to help us, Nizhoni. He's a soldier. They only want to take our land."

"I know that, Mother, I do, but he's not like the rest. I knew him . . . from before. I've heard him talk about the land and the people."

"He's fooling you, Daughter," Shy Fawn protested stubbornly. "You're young, but I've seen many soldiers come and go. They're all the same. They all only want to take for themselves."

"No," Nizhoni argued boldly. "Not this one. He's different. When the braves' horses were stolen on the hunt, the soldiers returned them. You know they could have kept them, seeing as how they found them. But they didn't. And they didn't even ask for anything in return, not even a fair trade. By returning them, they saved all this meat"—she stopped to gesture at the racks full of drying elk meat that surrounded them—"and all these hides from going to waste. Our people will eat many meals because they were willing to return what they rightfully could have taken."

Shy Fawn bobbed her head in concession. Nizhoni reached out and put her hand on her mother's arm, willing her to understand.

"I've seen how he keeps his men in line. Even when Fire Maker provokes and insults him, he doesn't retaliate. He doesn't attack, and he doesn't let his men either. They want to work together to find the group of raiding Comanches. They're providing the manpower. They ask only for any information we might have."

"Our people have trusted the soldiers before. We welcomed them in peace, and they stole our lands and forced us onto reservations."

"This is the land our ancestors have always called home," Niz reminded. Though their brothers to the east and south had been moved onto the reservation, the land their own band had inhabited for generations was within the boundaries of the reservation.

"Yes, well, we're the lucky ones. But they've stolen much land from our brothers and continue to take more and more all the time. Soon, we'll likely be forced off our land too. And when we are, this new soldier won't help us. You'll see." Shy Fawn's face was troubled.

Niz pursed her lips, trying to understand the glimmer of guilt she saw in her mother's eyes. "You always say each man deserves a chance to prove himself."

"Don't use my words against me, Nizhoni."

"Doesn't this man deserve a chance to prove himself as well?" Niz baited.

"No! No, this man doesn't," Shy Fawn said in exasperation.

"Why not?" Niz challenged, not understanding what her mother had against a man who seemed genuine in his desire to work together.

"Because this man's best friend took you away from your people, your village, your family—away from me!" Shy Fawn whispered fiercely, glancing around even as she did so to make sure no one overheard.

Niz sat back on her heels, surprised. She hadn't realized her mother recognized Ezra Taylor. "You're right. He was a friend of the Applewoods. They were good people, Mother. I think we can trust him."

"He may have been a friend to them, but that doesn't mean he's a friend to you—or to us!" Shy Fawn shot back. Sighing, the woman pressed the back of both hands to her forehead, closed her eyes, and took a deep breath. "He is a soldier, Nizhoni, and they're all the same."

Niz slowly shook her head. "I understand what you're saying, but it's different this time. The Applewoods are gone, Mother, and I'm here. He's the commanding officer at the fort, and I think he wants to help us. I think he's someone we can trust—someone we can work with for the good of our people. And I think as long as he's in charge, we don't have to fear the soldiers."

"Time will tell," Shy Fawn said with a tsk. Turning back to the hide, the woman began to work it over the log again. "You are young and I am old, but I have been right before. I told you not to marry Fire Maker. I cautioned you that there was something dark and dangerous about him. You did not listen."

"I know, but—"

Shy Fawn held up a hand to stop her. "Now I am telling you, do not trust these soldiers. The white men are all the same. They want what we have. They take and take and take. They don't care about us. They care only about themselves."

Nizhoni pressed her lips together as she looked at her mother. She tried to hold her tongue. After all, her mother was right. Shy Fawn had warned her against Fire Maker and she hadn't listened. But she hadn't been in her right mind then. She'd been consumed with grief. Now she was thinking clearly.

"But they returned the horses," she finally said, unable to keep the words back.

"Nizhoni! That's enough," Shy Fawn said sharply. "Support your husband. He's trying to keep our people strong."

Nizhoni bit her lip and looked off to the south. "The rain is approaching. I need to move the meat inside."

As Nizhoni stood to leave, Shy Fawn caught her hand. "Please, Daughter, please understand. Forget all this talk of soldiers. We got off course. I'm simply asking you to be careful. Support Fire Maker for the sake of our people. He is our chief. But most importantly, support him for yourself. I couldn't bear to see you get hurt."

The worry in her mother's voice tugged on her heart, and Nizhoni squeezed the woman's hand. "I'll be careful," she promised.

Six

"Nizhoni!"

Looking up, she saw Fire Maker coming toward her through the village. Concern filled her as she wondered what had happened to cause him to seek her out. Pushing herself to her feet hesitantly, she met him near their empty drying rack. All the meat from the braves' hunt had been dried and she had just finishing storing it away to sustain their people through the winter.

"What is it?" she asked, taking in his intense, but guarded, expression.

"I need you to go to the fort for me."

Nizhoni felt her eyes widen. "The fort? But . . . surely any supplies we need, I could just as easily get in town. I know the storekeeper. I can get a fair price."

"I don't need you to buy anything. I want you to deliver a message for me."

"A message?" she echoed. She'd never been sent to the fort with a message before. It had been five days since the soldiers had visited their camp. Could Fire Maker have reconsidered working together to help find the Comanche?

"I want you to find their leader and tell him I know they've lost some horses, so I am willing to trade him some of mine."

Pleasantly surprised, Nizhoni smiled. "That's thoughtful of you, Fire Maker. Indeed, it must be very difficult for them to continue their work when they've had horses stolen. It would be for us."

Fire Maker didn't look impressed. "Take him the message."

"Don't you want to come along to negotiate the price?" she asked, startling as she realized he meant for her to go alone.

His eyes flashed. "The soldier can come to me. Why should I waste my time going to him? He's the one that needs something. If he wants my horses, he can come here to make the trade."

"Alright," Nizhoni agreed easily. If he was willing to trade with the army, then perhaps he was attempting to make amends with the soldiers. Maybe, after giving it some thought, he regretted how he had behaved and was offering a gesture of goodwill. If he needed Major Taylor to come to him to save his pride, so be it. She would gladly deliver his message.

"Come on," he said, starting toward the large corrals that stood at the west edge of the village. "You can ride to the fort, so they can see the kind of horses I have."

Following along behind him, hope sprang to life in her heart. Perhaps, if Fire Maker had reconsidered, there was still something good and decent about him. If he was willing to work with the army, then maybe he really did care about their people, and if he had it in his heart to care about their people, maybe someday he would begin to care about her. Perhaps all was not lost; maybe there was still hope.

At the corrals, she gazed out over the animals, struck by the number of them. There were more than she remembered. "Your herd is growing," she said with admiration.

Fire Maker only grunted, but at least he'd heard her compliment. In return, he selected the most beautiful horse he had, next to his own personal mount, for her. She walked up and ran her hand under the beautiful buckskin's mane, scratching the stunning animal cordially as Fire Maker put on its braided horsehair bridal and reins. She felt touched that he would send her on his second-best horse and hoped it was because she was his wife and not just because he wanted to show off his stock. Deciding she would give him the benefit of the doubt, she moved up to scratch under the horse's forelock as Fire Maker checked its hooves. The horse spooked a little, tossing its head in the breeze and taking several quick steps back, causing Fire Maker to jump out of the way to avoid being stepped on.

"You can't just walk up and touch his head like that," Fire Maker accused, angry.

"I'm sorry, I didn't realize he would spook," Niz answered, taken aback.

"Well, what do you expect when you just grab him? You can't do that. You have to let him get to know you."

"I didn't grab him," she protested, frustrated by his accusatory tone. So much for giving him the benefit of the doubt.

"Yes, you did. I saw you," he snapped. "Clearly, you have no horse sense at all."

Niz stared at him, unable to believe one man could be so consistently unpleasant. She hadn't grabbed the horse, only reached out to scratch his head.

And though it was typically the men and boys who rode and cared for the horses as they were responsible for hunting and warfare, horsemanship skills were important to them all. Men, women, and children all learned how to ride—and to ride well. Many generations ago, their people had been among the first to acquire horses from the Spanish, and the horse had been an integral part of their culture ever since. They were not only important for transportation, but they were also a measure of wealth and status within the tribe. With how important they were to their people, her father had made certain she knew how to handle herself around horses.

A gust of wind came up and something bright moved, catching her eye. Bending down, she grabbed a piece of red cloth that had gotten stuck in the fence and was flapping in the breeze. She didn't say a word but held it up for Fire Maker to see. The horse spooked again.

"Watch it!" Fire Maker cried. "What are you thinking, holding that up to spook him? If you had half a brain, you would know better."

Nizhoni couldn't help rolling her eyes. No matter what she did, she couldn't win. There was nothing to do but let it go and move on.

"May my mother come along to the fort?" she asked, switching directions. "It seems wise to go in a pair." She wasn't afraid to go to the fort by herself, but it was nearly fifteen miles each way—twice as far as town. It didn't seem prudent to ride off by herself with raiding Comanche, soldiers, and wild animals in the area. Considering the position of the sun, she saw it was already mid-afternoon. It would be dark before she returned. Two together was better than one.

"Are you scared?" Fire Maker taunted as he finished checking the horse's hooves.

"No," she answered honestly.

"You're sure? Aren't you afraid of being alone in the fort with all those soldiers?"

"No," she said again, her tone clipped.

He nearly looked disappointed. For a moment, she almost wondered if he was hoping the errand would frighten her. She pushed her hand through her dark hair and stood a little straighter. She was not frightened, and she would let him see that. It was a matter of honor rather than fear that drove her request. She wanted to be accompanied so that Fire Maker couldn't question where she'd been, what she'd done, who she'd been with, or that she had indeed delivered the message.

But of course, she couldn't say that. "It just seems wise. It's the way of our people to go together. If I'm sent alone, our friends will wonder why."

Fire Maker narrowed his eyes at her. "Fine. Shy Fawn can go." He selected another fine horse. "She can ride this one."

"Thank you," Nizhoni said, breathing a sigh of relief. Though she couldn't put her finger on why, she was beginning to feel a twinge of discomfort with the errand. She hoped he was genuinely seeking to make amends with the army, but knowing him like she did, she couldn't help doubting his intentions. She got the uncanny sense she was being used.

His expression never changed. "Make sure you tell that soldier he can have horses if he wants to make a trade."

Nizhoni nodded. "I will." He turned away. "Fire Maker, it's getting late in the day. We may need to make camp on our way home and finish our ride in the morning," she continued. If they had to make camp, she didn't want her absence arousing his suspicion.

He paused mid-stride. "Fine. I'm sure Cloud Walking will share her dinner tonight."

Nizhoni's chin jerked at the nonchalant way he answered. There was something dangerous and sinister in his tone. She worried about it as she watched him leave the corral and disappear into the village. Inhaling deeply, she started off toward her mother's wickiup.

With her father having passed away two years earlier, it was only her mother and Cloud Walking who shared their dwelling now. When her youngest sister married, the couple would likely move into the wickiup with her mother, but for now, it was just the two of them. If she took her mother along to the fort, Cloud Walking would be left alone.

The sixteen-year-old had caught the eye of a young brave, and they all happily expected him to make an offer of marriage soon. It was a good match. Nizhoni would never forgive herself if she left her sister alone and anything happened to disrupt that. She wished she trusted her husband to protect the young woman in her absence, but she didn't. He knew how deep her love for her sisters went, and sometimes she worried what length he might go to in order to use them against her.

As she approached, her mother looked up. A happy smile spread across Shy Fawn's face. "Hello, Nizhoni. Have you come to visit us? Sit down and help us make beads out of these porcupine quills. I want to start on your sister's cradleboard soon. I've been planning the design, and I think these beads will be perfect to use with the red ones you brought me from town."

"I'm sure it will be beautiful, Mother," Nizhoni started. She had no doubt it would be—her mother was an expert at beaded designs. Shy Fawn had worked hard to pass down the art to each of her daughters, but only Cloud Walking seemed to have inherited their mother's special knack for it. With the two of them working on the cradleboard, Niz knew it would be a work of art.

"Well, sit down and help, and we'll see soon enough."

"Fire Maker has sent me on an errand to the fort."

"The fort?" her mother questioned, looking up quickly. "Why the fort? Don't you usually go to town for supplies?"

Nizhoni nodded. "There's a message he wants me to deliver to Major Taylor. He said you could come along. We'll ride, so it's not a far journey, and it might be nice to have a change of scenery."

Her mother looked at Cloud Walking and then back at Nizhoni. "Alright. Sure. That sounds nice." Shy Fawn sent her a brave smile. "I'm not going to say no to an afternoon with my eldest daughter."

"The horses are strong, and there's no rush to get back, so I thought you could come too, Cloud Walking. We can ride double on the way there, and you can ride with Mother on the way back so the horses each have a rest."

Cloud Walking's eyes lit up. "Really? Do you mean it?"

Nizhoni nodded, smiling at her sister's excitement. She knew the teen had never been off the land of their people. To her, a trip to the fort would be a grand adventure. To Niz, it was the best way to keep her safe.

Shy Fawn looked unsure. "Are you certain that's a good idea, Nizhoni? She's so young. Is it wise to take her to the fort with all those soldiers around?"

"Please, Mother, let her come along," Niz encouraged. She wasn't sure Cloud Walking would be any safer in the village than she would be in the fort if Fire Maker had something up his sleeve, but she didn't say so. It was only a sense, and she didn't want to share suspicions without facts. So instead, she stuck to persuasion. "It would be good for her to see something new."

Her mother still looked doubtful, but finally she nodded in concession. "Alright, if you're sure."

Cloud Walking jumped up. "I can go?" she asked, seeming breathless.

Nizhoni glanced at her mother, who sighed and nodded. Cloud Walking's answering smile was bright.

"Take your sleeping mats," Niz instructed. "Depending on how late it gets, we might have to spend the night along the way."

"I'll pack us something to eat," Shy Fawn offered.

"Thank you. I'll meet you at the river in ten minutes."

Nizhoni left to gather her things before hurrying to grab the horses Fire Maker had ready and get to the river. She wanted to be on their way before he noticed Cloud Walking was going along.

Her mother and sister were waiting when she arrived. After giving them a hand up, she pulled herself onto the back of the buckskin. Splashing through the shallow river, they were soon across it and on their way.

For the first time since Fire Maker approached her about going to the fort, Niz relaxed. There was a storm coming up from the south, as expected, but it surely wouldn't be long in passing. The sun was shining; the temperature was pleasantly hot, her sister was chattering joyfully, and the high mountain peaks were beautifully shadowed and moody under the white clouds scurrying across the blue sky. The feel of the wind stirring her long black hair, the afternoon alone with her mom and sister, and the amiable message from Fire Maker, all made her feel happy. Perhaps, for once, she would get to be part of making peace.

The thunderstorm came up quickly, and they took cover under a grove of evergreens, working together to make a quick brush shelter to keep them dry despite the rain. Once the storm passed, leaving behind the sweet aroma of rain-dampened vegetation, they emerged from their makeshift shelter, pulled themselves up onto the backs of their horses, and started on their way to the fort once more. They reached their destination just after five o'clock. The late summer sun was still bright, and the air was still warm. Nizhoni was glad about that. Riding into the fort in the dark would have been much more intimidating.

As it was, the place was swarming with soldiers, and they all seemed to notice them at once. Heads turned and necks craned as they rode in. Nizhoni felt her skin crawl with apprehension. She felt completely at ease in town, where she knew people and they knew her, but she was not familiar with the fort, nor did she feel comfortable in the presence of so many soldiers. From all she'd heard, she knew her mother was correct. Many of them wanted only to take what did not belong to them.

Though she wasn't necessarily frightened, she didn't feel completely safe, either. Even Alex had chosen not to take her to the fort. He'd frequented it often enough, getting the news, and shooting the breeze with the soldiers, but he had always thought it wise to leave her home.

But that was before Major Taylor was in charge, she reasoned. Surely Alex would have trusted his best friend to keep the peace, and since she had been sent with a message, she would have to trust him as well.

"Where can I find Major Taylor?" she asked the watching soldiers as she brought her horse to a stop. Her mother stopped beside her.

"What do you want with him?" one of the soldiers asked, his expression full of suspicion.

"I've brought him a message," Nizhoni replied calmly.

"Oh yeah? And what kind of message would that be?" another of the soldiers questioned.

"A message from Fire Maker, chief of the mountain people," she answered directly. She would not be secretive or elusive. She believed being forthright and honest was always the better option.

"Why would a chief send a woman?" the first soldier jeered.

"Not just a woman. Three women," another scoffed.

One of the soldiers stepped forward, separating himself from the small crowd of men. "Because she's the only one in her village who can speak English," he answered. "She's Fire Maker's wife."

Nizhoni recognized him as one of the soldiers who had been with Major Taylor at the village, and she watched him, wondering what would come next. Last time she'd seen him, he'd been red faced and angry. He'd looked ready to attack when Fire Maker had spit on his commanding officer. Now, he appeared wary but resigned.

He reached for the bridle of her horse. "Come on, ma'am. I'll take you to the major," he said, leading her mount past the soldiers. Her mother and Cloud Walking followed behind.

"Thank you," she answered, grateful for his assistance. The fort appeared large, and she wouldn't have known where to begin. The other soldiers stared after them for several moments before turning back to their business. Relieved, she redirected her attention to the man leading her horse. He seemed grim. She wasn't sure if he was displeased to see her in the fort, or if he was worried about the message she brought. Either way, she couldn't blame him.

She undoubtedly didn't belong at the fort, and his dealings with her husband had been unpleasant. At least this time she brought a more amiable message than she'd been able to translate in the past, but he had no way of knowing that.

Nizhoni glanced back at her mother and noticed that she seemed pale, though her face was expressionless. Cloud Walking, on the other hand, looked flushed and excited. She was watching the buildings and soldiers they were passing with rapt attention and wide eyes. Both fear and wonder showed on her face in equal measure.

Niz looked around again, realizing how unfamiliar and strange everything must look to her sister. The fort was very different from their village as well as their winter camp—the only towns her sister had ever known. "This man is taking us to the major. I will deliver Fire Maker's message, and we will be on our way," she explained in her native tongue, knowing her mother and sister hadn't understood anything that had been said.

Shy Fawn nodded, remaining expressionless. Cloud Walking looked somewhat disappointed, but mostly relieved. She continued to watch their passing surroundings with wide-eyed wonder.

As they continued deeper into the fort, soldiers stopped to stare. Nizhoni imagined that just as Cloud Walking wasn't accustomed to seeing the sights of the fort, the soldiers weren't accustomed to seeing native women riding through their encampment. They likely looked as foreign to the men as the soldiers looked to them. She considered again the irony of perspective.

In her village, their clothing, hairstyles, and way of life were perfectly normal and the ways of the white man were foreign, uncivilized, and frightening. During her time with the Applewoods, she'd realized that most white folks felt the same about them. Differences often felt dangerous and scary, no matter which side you were viewing them from. But she had learned from Alex that sometimes what people had in common was more important than any differences between them. People were people, and generally speaking, they all just wanted safety, security, and love—a good life for themselves and their families.

The soldier brought her horse to a stop and turned to look up at her. "This is Major Taylor's. You'll likely find him in his office. First door on the right."

Niz looked up at the two-story, sawed board house in front of her. It was the first she'd seen in the fort. A veranda came off the second floor, providing shade for the porch. A large window was situated to the right of the front door, and several others were scattered across the building. She wondered if it was Major Taylor's home or simply a place where the fort's commanding officers worked.

Turning back to the soldier, she wondered if she dared ask him to see her inside. She suddenly felt very hesitant to enter, not knowing who all would be present. Perhaps Major Taylor was in a meeting, busy, or upset she had come? What if he didn't allow natives into his office, or felt that she was overstepping or intruding? He had spoken to her freely in her village, but would things be different here?

But she was not one to hold back nor shy away from difficult things. She reminded herself of that again now and slid off her horse. Fire Maker had sent her with a message, and she meant to deliver it.

Seeing how soldiers nearby were gawking at her mother and sister with open curiosity, she paused beside the soldier who was still holding her horse. "Would you keep an eye on my mother and sister while I deliver my message? Please see that no harm comes to them."

The man looked at her for a long moment, his expression still grim, before giving a slight nod.

"Thank you." She turned to her mother. "This soldier is going to watch out for you while I'm inside. I won't be long." Shy Fawn bobbed her head in agreement, and Nizhoni climbed the stairs.

Taking a deep breath, squaring her shoulders, and lifting her head, she went through the open front door. She found herself in a hallway with doors on both sides. Turning to the first one on the right, she knocked. She heard a muffled command to enter, reached out, and turned the knob, taking a deep, shuddering breath as she did so.

Speaking with Major Taylor in her village was one thing. Coming to his office in an army fort without being summoned was altogether different. She didn't know if she would be welcome. Besides, she'd run away from their last conversation, and that knowledge had rankled inside her ever since. She was embarrassed by how she'd reacted to the memories, frustrated that she had shown weakness, and upset by how she'd given in to her emotions. Usually she did so well keeping them under control, but that day she hadn't.

Keeping her chin raised as she pushed the troubling memory away, she stepped into the room. Major Taylor glanced up briefly, continuing to write on a piece of paper as he did so. Suddenly, he dropped his pen and jumped to his feet, his face revealing his surprise and bewilderment.

"Niz? What are you doing here? Is there trouble?" he asked, coming around from behind his desk to meet her, a look of deep concern replacing his surprise.

She shook her head. "No, there's no trouble. I've come with a message from Fire Maker."

"Is he here too?" Major Taylor questioned, glancing out the door she'd left open.

"No, he's not," she answered, choosing not to share what her husband had said about the army coming to him if they wanted his horses. "He had to stay in the village, but he asked me to deliver his message."

"Alright," Major Taylor said, seeming puzzled. "What's the message?"

"He said he knows you've lost horses to the Comanche, and if you're in need, he has some he can trade you."

Major Taylor tipped his head and considered her. "Really? Fire Maker said that?"

Nizhoni nodded. "He even sent me with two of his horses so you can see what kind of animals you'd be getting."

"Did he?" He still seemed suspicious.

"They're outside. I rode one and my mother and sister the other."

Major Taylor went to look out the window. "We could use a few," he said after a long moment. He turned. "Did you just ride in from your village?"

Niz nodded.

"Did you see any sign of the Comanche?"

She shook her head.

"Did Fire Maker send any braves to escort you?"

"No." He didn't look pleased. "It's not so far, and the weather is good," she continued.

"You shouldn't be out by yourself." His tone was firm, sounding every bit the commanding officer that he was.

She drew herself up taller. "I'm not by myself. My mother and sister have come. We're capable, Major Taylor, not delicate. We're strong, and we know how to take care of ourselves."

Major Taylor considered her for a moment, and she braced for the argument she saw coming. Instead, he gave a slight shake of his head and smiled. "Believe me, I don't doubt that."

Something stirred in her heart. For the briefest moment, he had looked at her like Alex used to—as if she was a wonder, like her bravery was something to be admired. The realization made her heart ache. She'd forgotten what it felt like to be respected.

Turning, he looked out the window again for a long while. "But a homestead was attacked night before last. It's not safe for you ladies to be out unaccompanied."

"Attacked?" she questioned. There had been peace in the valley for years. "The Comanche?"

"We believe so," he answered grimly.

She felt fear prick her heart. She didn't want war any more than the settlers did. The warriors of her people were strong and skilled, but a raiding war party brought death and destruction wherever it went. If the hearts of the Comanche were set on violence, she didn't want them anywhere around. Especially when she had her mother, Cloud Walking, Ever Flowering, and her friends and people to think about. Especially when it would be men such as Walks With Power, Stands Tall, and Lean Elk—men with wives, families, and children—who would be called upon to protect them. She knew they would do so, but at what cost? They couldn't lose them.

Her mind hummed. A worry of similar proportion was the backlash that attacks could bring upon her people. They were at peace with the settlers in the area. Would the Comanche's actions jeopardize that? Would their neighbors see them as separate tribes or view them all the same? Her heart sank, already knowing the answer.

"If I knew anything about the whereabouts of the Comanche, I would tell you," she said sincerely.

Major Taylor nodded. "I believe you. What I want to know is if your husband and his braves would." He paused and Niz stayed quiet.

She couldn't speak for Fire Maker, nor did she think Major Taylor would want her to. He would know as well as she that they were empty words. She couldn't pretend to know her husband or influence him any more than he could.

"Have you heard about the trouble on the reservation?" he continued after a moment.

She shook her head. "We'll hear the news from the other mountain people when we gather for the winter."

"A few months ago, Congress took back a large portion of your people's land in the San Juan region."

"There was talk of it last winter. An agreement had already been signed by many of the chiefs."

"Well, now it's official," Major Taylor told her, his expression grim. "They say your people can still hunt on the land as long as there is peace with the white people." Niz nodded. She'd heard as much in the winter camps. "My concern is that the politicians in Washington won't care which tribe is raiding. If they hear there's trouble near the reservation and that settlers are getting attacked by Indians, there's a good chance they won't wait to hear the details."

Nizhoni's eyebrows shot up as his meaning struck home. "The hunting rights could be taken away?"

He nodded. "Have you not read the agreement?"

She shook her head.

"You should. Your people need to know what it says, Niz. Fire Maker needs to know. So do the other chiefs. I have a copy I found in a newspaper. You should read it and take it back to Fire Maker and read it to him. This winter, you could read it to the others."

He went back to his desk and began rifling through paperwork, clearly looking for the newspaper in question.

"I . . . I'm sure they already know what it says. I'm sure the chiefs have read it."

"But what if they haven't? It's imperative that peace is kept, Niz. That's why I want to work with Fire Maker to find the Comanche. Your people have more to lose than just a few horses. Don't you see? If you read the agreement to your husband, maybe he would see that and be willing to work with me."

"Fire Maker makes his own decisions," she answered slowly.

Finding the piece of paper he sought, he held it out to her. "Niz, I'm trying to help. I don't like what's being done to your people. It's not right. But I can't protect you by myself. We will only succeed if we work together. Please, try to make Fire Maker understand. Read the agreement to him. Make him see how desperate the situation is."

Embarrassment stirred in the pit of Niz's stomach, and she fixed her dark eyes on Major Taylor as she tried to decide what to do next. Should she tell the truth? Simply refuse the agreement and make up an excuse? Or take it, knowing full-well that she couldn't read it? Surely others at their winter camp knew English; many bands of their people would come together there. Perhaps one of them would be able to make out the words, she reasoned. If not, maybe she could find someone to read it to them . . . maybe a trapper or trader who wandered through.

But Ezra Taylor was looking at her so intently, willing her to agree. She believed that he sincerely wanted to help her people, and she appreciated it immensely. Not only was he not against them, as it felt many soldiers—as well as the U.S. government—were, he wanted to help them. He was only one man, and she knew he was no match for a system bent on destroying their way of life, but his desire to help right the systematic wrongs was touching.

And from the perspective he had just shared on the agreement that had been signed, she understood why he was so desperate for Fire Maker to understand and work together to put an end to the raids. If hunting rights were revoked, Nizhoni knew it could only mean war.

Her people had been hunting and gathering on those lands for centuries. They needed their hunting grounds to feed their people. If the soldiers tried to tell them they could no longer hunt there, she knew her people would revolt. Conflict would come. Lives would be lost. And in the end, the army would undoubtedly do what it had done in so much of the country already, and her people would be pushed back, deeper onto the reservation, with less and less of the land they loved, the way of life they knew, and the resources they needed to survive.

"Niz?" He seemed confused by her silence.

Despite the embarrassment that filled her, the sincerity and concern she saw in his hazel eyes drew her to honesty.

"I can't read," she admitted slowly, the words sticking in her throat even as she spoke them. The truth made her feel thick and dull. But her admission did not phase Major Taylor.

"Can anyone in your village read?" he questioned. His expression stayed open, no condemnation or judgment showing in his hazel eyes.

Niz shook her head. She was the only one who could make the white man's words; certainly no one else could read them.

"Then you have to learn."

"I don't want to," she responded honestly. It wasn't that she didn't want to be able to read, only that she didn't want to learn. She didn't want to stumble over letters and words, looking foolish and sounding ridiculous. Besides, who would teach her? Raya had been willing, but she'd wasted the opportunity.

Major Taylor stared at her, looking aghast. "You love your people, I know you do. Alex used to talk about how much you loved them and how you planned to go back together to live among them and help however you could. I see how you look at them now, how protective of them you are . . . how you want to know what's going on."

"Of course, I love my people," she interjected.

"Then you have to learn to read," he told her, making it sound obvious. "You must be able to read what documents say before chiefs sign them. Don't you see? If none of you can read, the government—people—can take advantage of you. They can tell you whatever it is you want to hear, but you could legally be signing something very different that would hold up in a court of law." She raised her chin, not liking the sound of that, knowing he was right. He grabbed a quick breath. "You're a smart girl, Niz. You can speak English as well as anyone. You understand the language. You understand the meanings of the words. If you want to do what you can to protect your people and your way of life from the government, then you have to know how to read—and write—English."

Niz closed her eyes for a moment and inhaled deeply through her nose. His reasoning made sense. Her people did need someone who could read and write English well to make sure they weren't being taken advantage of. For now, they had Major Taylor to deal with, but that may not always be the case. If he was reassigned, they could face a commanding officer who was not fair or just or sympathetic to their plight.

As of yet, their small band had not had run-ins with the federal government; chiefs of different bands of their people had dealt with the treaties and made agreements over land. But that may not always be the case. And if the government came, her people needed someone who could stand up for their rights and fight with the same weapons the politicians used—words.

Still, all the reasoning in the world couldn't keep her stomach from churning. The very idea of learning to read made her feel unwell. It was daunting. She hated feeling dull.

A breeze blew through the open window, setting her long, dark hair to dancing, and she pushed it back behind her shoulder as she opened her eyes and took another deep breath. Major Taylor was still watching her. "Well?" he asked.

"How would I learn?" she asked hesitantly.

His smile was quick and bright. "I have books that will get you started. And my soldiers and I will accompany you back to your village"—he held up his hand to silence her protest—"to trade for the horses with Fire Maker. I'm assuming since he hasn't come with you that he wants us to come to him."

Niz nodded in reply, having all but forgotten the errand she had been sent on in the midst of their conversation since.

"Well, I'll see if I can teach you how to use the books on the way. Then, whenever I visit the village or you're sent here, we'll go over any questions you have and read together to make sure you're getting the sounds and letters right."

Nizhoni cringed. The idea of reading aloud to anyone, especially Major Taylor, to see if she was making errors was repulsive. "What if Fire Maker won't allow me to learn?"

"Surely, once you speak to him about how it would benefit your people, he won't object."

Nizhoni couldn't keep the doubt from showing on her face.

"And even if he does," he continued, "I'm sure you'll figure out a way to continue your studies if you really want to. Like I said before, you're a smart girl. And this isn't a luxury. Literacy—being able to read and write—is a necessity for the good of your people. If you love them as you say you do, and want to help them, this is how you can do it. Educate yourself so you can advocate on their behalf."

"You're right," she consented. She needed to learn to read. If she had to learn in secret, she would. At least then she would be ready to help if the need arose.

"Good," he replied, turning briskly toward a bookcase he had in the corner of the room. He began to run his finger over the spines of the books, glancing over the titles. She watched, realizing she hadn't laid eyes on a book since her days at the Applewoods'.

Suddenly, she remembered the little stack of letters she had stashed between the hides in her wickiup. "Perhaps," she started before thinking better of it. Common sense settling in, she let the word dangle, embarrassed to finish her train of thought.

Major Taylor selected a book before glancing over at her. "Perhaps what?"

"Well, I have a stack of letters that I believe are from Raya and Mother Emaline . . . maybe even Chenoa, I'm not sure . . ." she told him hesitantly.

A look of understanding filled his face. "You can't read them." Cringing, she shook her head in reply. "Would you like me to read them to you when we get back to your village?"

"No," she answered quickly. Fire Maker would never allow such a thing, and she didn't want him to know the letters existed. He wouldn't understand how precious they were to her—he would only see them as a threat. If he knew about them, he would undoubtedly destroy them. Besides, when she opened those letters and heard the words her dear family members had penned her, she wanted to be alone. She didn't know what emotions their letters might bring up, and she didn't know how her heart might respond. Thus, better to be by herself when she read them.

She saw a look of surprise fill Major Taylor's face at her quick response, and she hoped she hadn't offended him by refusing his offer. "I . . . I would rather read them myself, if you'll teach me."

His smile was instant, and he gave a quick nod. "Good idea. Better to read them for yourself than to have them read to you. We'll get you reading, and you can look forward to that along the way. It can be your motivation to keep going." He paused. "But please, once you've read the letters, will you tell me how they are? Emaline was like a second mother to me." His face clouded with regret, and Niz knew he was once again wishing he had been there when the tragedy happened. He cleared his throat. "I'd like to know if she's settled and doing well or still in need. If she is, maybe I could help."

"I will," Niz promised, her admiration of Ezra Taylor growing. If he would take care of his best friend's widowed mother, he really was as good of a man as Alex had made him out to be.

Hearing one of the horses whinny outside, Niz glanced out the window. She could see her mother and sister through it, still atop their horse, the soldier holding the halters of both mounts. "I should get headed back to the village."

"It will be dark before you reach home. Stay here at the fort, and we'll ride out with you first thing in the morning," he said. Like earlier, his tone didn't leave any room for argument. It was clear Major Taylor was used to being in charge, but that didn't silence her.

"I don't know, sir," Niz replied, doubtfully. "Do you think that's wise? My mother and younger sister are with me. When I was with . . . the Applewoods, they never brought me here. They didn't think it was a good idea. To think of spending the night within the fort . . ." She raised her chin. "We brought our sleeping mats. We'll be fine in the forest."

He shook his head. "It's safer for you here. I'll see that no harm comes to you."

Niz looked at him uncertainly, doubt creeping in. Her mother was right. Just because he'd been a friend to the Applewoods didn't mean he was a friend to her and especially not her mother and sister. It wasn't that she doubted him personally—Alex had always made him sound like a man of strong character and principles, and he'd given her no reason to question that. But if the fort wasn't a safe place, as Alex had believed, to what length would Major Taylor go to protect mere acquaintances? Could she trust him? With their honor and their lives? Surely he was a busy man with much to do—did he even have the capacity to watch out for them?

Standing behind his desk covered in papers, wearing his dark blue frock coat with the two rows of gold buttons down the front and oak leaves as rank insignia on his shoulder knots, he looked every bit the soldier that he was. He seemed sincere in wanting to help her people, but they had learned things weren't always what they seemed when it came to the soldiers. One might appear as if they were coming in peace but have a hidden agenda. The thought made her sad. She hoped that wasn't the case with Major Taylor. He'd been her husband's best friend. He was her last tie to Alex, and she wanted to believe he really was as honest and genuine as Alex had been.

She watched his face soften. "Niz, you can trust me," he said, his deep voice steady, his hazel eyes unclouded and sincere. He sent her a sad smile, and he suddenly seemed much less a soldier and much more the man who had sat at her family's table.

She dropped her gaze as she nervously picked at the hem of her buckskin dress. It was worrisome that he had so easily been able to read her thoughts.

"Believe me, I won't let anything happen to you on my watch, or to your mother or sister either. Watching out for you is the least I can do after Alex . . ." he paused, cleared his throat, and turned and walked to the window. Leaning against the wall as he looked out, he started again. "You'll be safe here. There are rooms upstairs. I'll sleep down here. No one will get by me. And your sister might enjoy the excitement of a night in a house. She looks like she's taking it all in," he finished with a chuckle.

Nizhoni followed his gaze and saw that Cloud Walking was indeed looking around intently, her eyes still wide. She smiled. "It's her first time off the lands of our people. Everything is new."

Major Taylor tipped his head, and his lips lifted in amusement. "Wonder what she'll think of the furniture . . . the table and chairs and a bed?"

"She'll likely end up sleeping on the floor, no matter how comfortable the mattress is," Niz mused. "I did my first month with . . . the Applewoods. The mattress was too soft. I felt like it was suffocating me."

"Why don't you ever speak of him? You never say his name." Major Taylor looked curious, not condemning.

Niz took a deep breath and crossed her arms, wrapping them around herself like a barrier against the memories. "I don't want to anger the spirits," she answered honestly, with a slight shrug.

"I wondered if it was something like that." She didn't respond, and he turned back to the window. They were both quiet for a moment. "Does it bother you when I say his name?"

She thought for a moment and then shook her head. It hadn't bothered her when Raya or Mother Emaline spoke about him either. "They're not your spirits. And especially here ... it feels like a different world."

He took that in but didn't turn from the window. "For the record, if you ever need to, you can talk about him with me. Whether or not you say his name." He shifted to face her. "And if it ever feels okay in this world, know that you can speak his name when you're here ..."

Niz turned her dark eyes toward him and met his steady gaze for a long moment. Though she didn't think she would take him up on it, it felt like the kindest offer. In a world where she was afraid to speak about Alex, worried it would offend the spirits and her new husband, there was something comforting about knowing she could talk about him if she wanted to.

"Well, let's go get your mother and sister and settle the horses. You three can eat here with me, and after dinner, I'll find the other book, and we'll start your studies. You can have your first lesson today. How does that sound?" he continued, pushing back from the window.

She took a deep breath and nodded. "I hope you're a good teacher. I might try your patience."

He laughed as he gestured for her to lead the way outside. "I guess we'll see."

Seven

After finally convincing Shy Fawn that the safest option for them was spending the night at the fort under Major Taylor's protection, Nizhoni insisted on making dinner in exchange for the man's hospitality. She wasn't someone who was comfortable with handouts. It was important to her to make good trades—and cooking dinner in exchange for a safe place to sleep felt like one.

As she went about her task, she had Cloud Walking help her, teaching her sister about the white ways of cooking. Niz enjoyed being back in a kitchen, something that had been so familiar during her time with the Applewoods. She mixed biscuits and threw together a stew, while her mother sat at the table and chopped vegetables for her.

Major Taylor had left after getting them settled, and Niz was more than happy to have his kitchen to herself with her sister and mother. The two of them had never visited the Applewoods', but cooking dinner together was like getting to show them a bit of the life she had lived during her three years away from the village.

It wasn't that she wanted to go back, or that she wanted Cloud Walking to follow in her footsteps, but being able to share it with them did help to connect two chapters of her life. Somehow, that felt comforting.

Major Taylor came back in time for dinner, bringing a few officers along with him, and they all sat together at the table to eat. Though the men were quiet as the meal began, soon they began to converse, falling into what seemed like their usual camaraderie.

Major Taylor had explained earlier that they typically ate together and had asked if that would be okay or if it would make Niz and her family members uncomfortable. Happy to have a group to cook for again, she had readily agreed to make dinner for them all.

As they ate, the women sat quietly. Shy Fawn and Cloud Walking couldn't understand what was being said, but Cloud Walking watched the soldiers with open curiosity. Seeming mesmerized by their foreign conversation, the way they used their utensils, and the presence of so many white men in one room, the girl barely remembered to eat her food. Shy Fawn seemed apprehensive at first but appeared to relax when the soldiers paid them no mind. Niz, on the other hand, listened intently to every word that was being spoken.

At first, the men's conversation was stilted and, she guessed, heavily censored. The officers talked about the weather and how rations were holding up. She kept her eyes on her plate, hoping they would forget she was there and soon begin to talk about something of interest. When she finally glanced up, weary of the proper conversation men relegated themselves to in the presence of women, she met Major Taylor's eyes and couldn't help sending him a pleading look. He smiled in reply.

Turning to his friends, he cleared his throat. "I think we're boring our guest. Nizhoni is the wife of a chief and very invested in the goings-on of her people. I have it on good authority that she's a student of the land, loves exploration and geography, and—as she reminded me earlier—is quite capable." Another smile. Nizhoni's heart gave a wild kick. How did he know those things? Alex must have shared in one of his letters how much they enjoyed learning and exploring together. "Please, don't worry about sticking to genteel conversation, gentlemen. Trust me, she can handle it. Just carry on as normal. I heard the post made it through this afternoon. What's the news?"

After a nervous glance her way, the man she believed to be Major Taylor's second-in-command, Captain Blackwell, offered the top headline of the Rocky Mountain News that had arrived with the post earlier that day. The other officers' interest was piqued, and the conversation took off as the captain filled them in on the details of the story.

When Major Taylor glanced her way, Niz sent him a grateful smile. The conversation never slowed again until plates were clean. Thirstily, she drank in every detail as she overheard updates on politics, news from the rest of the country, and the local trouble that was going on.

Niz learned that rumors of statehood were circulating throughout the territory as lawmakers looked to the future. Lieutenant Colonel George Custer had found gold during his expedition to the Black Hills, and a gold rush was beginning. The dry summer in northern Colorado was raising concerns about water rights as the Poudre River had gone dry and settlers were trying to navigate the drought. Niz soaked it all in, tucking the information away, following along by recalling maps of the territory and the country that she had studied with Alex.

Hungry for adventure, Alex had loved studying the geography of the newly emerging nation, and especially the territory in which he lived and explored. It had been that hunger for adventure that had taken him to Niz's village and that longing for the unknown that had united them. As Major Taylor had alluded to earlier, they had loved studying maps and making plans for future exploration together. Now, she listened intently, understanding at last why Alex had found the fort so intriguing. The conversation, the updated news from the rest of the country—it was all so fascinating.

The talk turned to the group of raiding Comanche. She learned they had indeed come from the Great Plains and, being pursued by the army, had sought refuge in the mountains. Evading the soldiers, they had made their way across the continental divide and were once again causing problems, angry over being forced onto a reservation. While Niz could understand their grievances, she hoped they would ride on through. She didn't want them staying around making trouble for her people. She listened to the men puzzle over the fact that while two homesteads had been raided, one attack was violent, while the other had only resulted in stolen livestock. The officers threw around speculations, trying to work out the mystery, the problem, and the solution.

The soldiers were polite but otherwise paid her and her family members no attention. That was a relief to Niz, and she saw it was to her mother as well. Shy Fawn continued to seem more at ease as the meal went on. The officers were outspoken about enjoying the food, and Niz was glad. She enjoyed cooking and found combining flavors a form of art. It was always fun when people appreciated her effort and enjoyed their meals. When they were finished, they thanked her for the food and headed out the door. Cloud Walking helped her do the dishes while her mother sat and worked on the beads she had brought along in a satchel.

Major Taylor had been sitting at the table, reading one of the newspapers that had just arrived, but when Niz glanced back, she noticed the paper was lying forgotten as he watched Shy Fawn work. After a few minutes, he glanced at Niz as she dried dishes, and then back at Shy Fawn. "What are you making?" he asked curiously. With a smile, Niz translated.

Shy Fawn looked up quickly, startled that the soldier was talking to her. She shyly explained that she was making beads out of porcupine quills to decorate the cradleboard she was making for her daughter. Nizhoni translated her mother's words, and Major Taylor's face filled with surprise.

"Do I understand congratulations are in order, then?" he asked, turning his hazel eyes toward Niz. "Fire Maker must be very happy."

Niz felt color spring into her cheeks. "Uh, no, it's my sister Ever Flowering. She will have her baby when the snow is deep."

"Ah, I see. This sister?" he asked, motioning to the young woman beside her.

Niz laughed. "No, not this sister. She's too young. This is Cloud Walking. Ever Flowering is between us in age. She married shortly before I returned home to my village last year."

"Cloud Walking," he repeated, looking at the girl who was washing dishes at the dishpan. "How do you say it in your language?"

Niz told him, and he repeated it. Cloud Walking glanced up and laughed. Niz, Shy Fawn, and even Major Taylor laughed too. Nizhoni pronounced it for him once more, gave him a few tips, and he tried it again, more successfully this time. Cloud Walking nodded and turned back to her dishes. "And your mother, what is her name?"

Nizhoni told him, and he repeated it until he could pronounce it decently well also. Shy Fawn smiled and nodded approvingly, clearly pleased that he was trying.

"Shy Fawn, Cloud Walking," he said in their native tongue. "Now that we've been introduced, we can be friends, and whenever I see you in your village, I will remember the day I had the honor of hosting you in my home." Nizhoni translated the rest for him.

Seeming happy, Shy Fawn and Cloud Walking nodded in reply. Niz smiled at Major Taylor, grateful for the kindness he was showing her mother and sister. He wasn't showering them with attention, which would have made them uncomfortable, but he wasn't ignoring them either. He was showing them dignity and respect. She appreciated that.

"So is the plan still to go back to the village with us tomorrow to trade with Fire Maker?" she asked, turning back to the dishes she had yet to dry.

"Yes. I'll take the four soldiers who accompanied me before and ride out with you. Maybe we'll get lucky and the braves at your village will have some news about the Comanche. It would be nice to apprehend them and trade for horses, all in one trip." His mouth tipped up in a rueful smile. "It's not likely, but one can dream." He picked up his newspaper again.

"The officers who came to dinner weren't soldiers you usually ride with," she observed.

"No, we don't often ride out together. We split up to lead patrols while others stay behind. Someone has to be here to keep the fort in line."

"Are you glad you joined the army?" she asked curiously. He had been so set on going. She wondered if it had proven to be everything he imagined.

He raised an eyebrow at her in question and then laid his paper on the table again, as if agreeing to a conversation. She smiled faintly, glad. Over the past year, she'd had her fill of silent evenings. "There are a lot of good men here," he answered. "Some not good ones, too, but more good than not."

"You didn't answer my question," she pointed out, putting a bowl away in the cupboard and then straightening to dry the next one.

Major Taylor sat quietly for a moment and then shrugged. "I'm not sure I have an answer. In some ways I'm glad. In other ways I'm not."

"You became a major very quickly," she observed. "It was only four years ago that you joined. You must have done very well."

"It was luck."

Niz tipped her chin before shaking her head, sending him a doubtful smile. "I don't buy it. You're a good leader, Major. Your men respect you. That's plain to see."

He shifted in his chair and cleared his throat, seeming uncomfortable. "Well, thank you, but it really was luck. I unintentionally made some very powerful connections."

She sent him a questioning look.

"There was a train hold-up. Some of my soldiers and I happened to be on board . . . and so were some very powerful men. We disarmed the robbers, and they showed their appreciation with a promotion. After that, one thing just kind of led to another."

Niz took that information in with a nod. She wanted to ask him to tell her the story—she remembered he had a knack for telling them—but she got the sense he didn't want to talk about it. "How did you get stationed here?" she asked instead.

"Powerful connections, remember?" He sent her a self-deprecating smile. "New leadership was required, and they knew I came from the area. With my firsthand knowledge of it here they decided I would make a good fit."

"You don't seem very happy about that."

He rubbed the back of his neck. "It's not that. The assignment came with another promotion. I should be grateful. I *am* grateful. It's just . . ."

She smiled, understanding. He really was like Alex. "You would rather be off on a grand adventure."

He smiled back. Settling into his chair, he stretched out his long legs and crossed his ankles, getting comfortable. "Yes. When I enlisted, I wanted to see the West. I wanted to go with Custer on his expedition into the Black Hills, or be sent up to the Canadian border, or down into the desert. That's what I dreamt of—exploring places very few have gone, figuring out how to survive in and bring peace among the unknown. But, thanks to the politicians I met, I haven't left Colorado Territory."

"Maybe someday," she sympathized, feeling the longing in his words. She remembered Alex feeling the same way, his feet always antsy, his desire for something new forever brewing below the surface.

"Yes, maybe someday," he agreed.

"If you could go anywhere, where would it be?" she asked, watching him. She'd missed talking about faraway places and the world of possibilities that laid beyond the mountains.

His eyes lit up. "Oregon—to see what all the fuss is about. I want to see the Pacific . . . explore the coast . . . see a whale spouting off in the distance."

She laughed. "Of course you do." He really was Alex's best friend. "How long—"

"Nizhoni," her mother reprimanded sharply, interrupting. "You are not here to make friends with the soldier. You were only sent to deliver a message."

Nizhoni turned quickly back to the dishes, her cheeks growing warm, embarrassed and feeling guilty over her mother's correction. The woman was right. Fire Maker would be livid to know she was in Ezra Taylor's home, drying his dishes, enjoying a pleasant conversation. But if only her mother could understand how much she had missed casual conversations like this—and how it felt like she was talking to Alex again in some way. How many evenings had they spent just like this? Him reading a paper or book or studying a map while she put their house in order and went about her work, conversing easily as they did so. But Ezra wasn't Alex, and her mother was right.

"What did she say?" Major Taylor asked curiously.

"She just reminded me to mind my duties." With a rueful smile, Niz lifted the bowl she was drying in demonstration and then turned her back to Major Taylor. "Dishes don't dry themselves."

"Hm," he responded thoughtfully. "Well, like I said earlier, I could help you with those."

"No, I've got it," she responded, forcing her voice to sound cheerful, even though she was already missing the casual, happy feel of their conversation. The mood in her wickiup was always so strained. In all things, at all times, she had to tread carefully. It was exhausting.

But her mother was right. She had been sent with a message, not to make friends; so she continued with her task in silence.

When she had finished drying the last dish and put it away in the cupboard, Major Taylor folded his paper. "What do you say we pull out those books and give you your first reading lesson? Then we'll all get some sleep, seeing as how we're heading out at first light."

"Sure, just let me empty the dishwater."

With a slight smirk and a faint shake of his head, he pushed himself to his feet, looking as if the very idea was ridiculous. "I've got it. I'll go ahead and do a night check on the horses while I'm out. Be right back."

Niz watched him go. As soon as the door shut behind him, she spun to Shy Fawn. "Mother, please do not read into this. I promise I'm not trying to make friends with Major Taylor, but when he comes back in, he's going to start teaching me to read."

"Out of the question. You've talked to him enough for one evening."

Niz winced, sending Shy Fawn a pleading look. "Mother, hear me out. When I delivered Fire Maker's message earlier, Major Taylor explained that the agreement we heard about last winter, where the government is taking back our lands but allowing our people to hunt on them, it comes with a condition. We have to live in peace with the settlers, or those hunting rights will be revoked. Maybe the chiefs know that, but I never heard word of it. He's worried the problems I told you of with the Comanche could jeopardize that." Niz paused, having sped through the explanation, hoping to have the matter settled by the time the major came back into the house. She watched as the severity of the news settled over Shy Fawn.

"Our people need those lands to hunt on. Without them, how will they feed their families?" her mother protested.

"Exactly. Major Taylor provided a copy of the agreement and told me to read it to Fire Maker to help him understand how desperately he needs to work with the soldiers to catch the Comanche. It's not for their sake, Mother, it's for ours! And Fire Maker doesn't see that."

"So tell him! He'll understand how important this is. He'll do the right thing." Niz could see that even as her mother spoke the words, more full of hope than certainty, she couldn't keep her doubts at bay.

"He won't listen to me. You know that."

"So read him the agreement."

Nizhoni made a face. "I can't read," she admitted.

"And the soldier is going to teach you?" Shy Fawn asked dryly.

"Trust me, I wish there was another way," Niz answered sincerely. "I wish I already knew how, and this wasn't even an issue."

"Why didn't you have your sister-in-law teach you?"

"I didn't want to look dim-witted."

"And now you will." Shy Fawn sent her a pointed look. "In front of the soldier."

Niz couldn't suppress a shiver of dread and distaste. "It's for our people, Mother. I can do it if it means helping them," she said, trying to reassure herself as well.

The front door opened, and she looked at her mother with pleading eyes. How humiliating would it be to first have to admit that she could not read, only to be convinced that for the sake of her people she needed to, and then have to decline because her mother forbade it? How terrible would it be if her people needed someone to read a treaty down the line, and she had to admit to the entire tribe that she couldn't help them? She would let them all down.

"Surely you see the benefit in Nizhoni learning how to read the white man's words, Mother," Cloud Walking said off-handedly. "If it weren't for her, our people wouldn't even be able to communicate with the soldiers."

Niz sent her sister a look of gratitude as Major Taylor walked into the room and set the dishpan in its place. As he took his seat at the table and pulled the books in front of him, Niz turned slowly back to her mother, her eyes full of questions.

Shy Fawn inhaled deeply. "You're right. You both are. There's value in you learning to read. Our people need someone who can. Go ahead."

Cloud Walking sat down beside their mother to help with the beads, sending Niz a saucy smile as she did so. It was clear the teenager thought she owed her. Niz narrowed her eyes at her, not liking being beholden to anyone—especially not her little sister.

"Ready?" Major Taylor asked obliviously, his voice cheerful.

Suddenly, the reality of what came next hit her. All the things she had felt whenever Raya or Alex tried to persuade her to read came rushing back. Dread over the coming lesson filled her. Slowly, she crossed the kitchen and sat down in the chair beside him, her actions unhurried and hesitant. Seemingly unaware of her reluctance, Major Taylor slid a book in front of her.

"This is the letter A. A-a-apple. You try it."

For just a moment, she stared at him, wondering if he truly was going to make her repeat after him. And in front of her mother and sister, too. Her irritation stirred when she saw that he was. He nodded to her to go ahead, and she pushed her dark hair out of her face and sighed. "A. A-a-apple."

Shy Fawn chuckled, and Niz pinned her with a glare. "What? I see now that this is good for you, Daughter."

"Good," Major Taylor encouraged, drawing Niz's attention back to the book. "B. B-b-bear."

Their lesson continued until they had made it all the way through the alphabet twice. When Major Taylor was satisfied with her progress, he gave her the book they had been using along with another and sent the women upstairs to get some sleep. Shy Fawn had relaxed during the lesson, seeming to enjoy Niz's discomfort so much that she even patted Major Taylor's shoulder as she passed him on her way out of the kitchen.

Niz felt disgruntled and raw from embarrassment as they climbed the stairs to bed. But when she shut and locked the bedroom door behind them and her mother told her she was proud of the effort she was going to for their people, she couldn't stay mad.

Alone in their room, Nizhoni began to show her mother and sister around the space, pointing out and explaining the looking glass, bowl and pitcher, chest, and curtains. Though at first they protested, she finally convinced them to lie down on the bed. Hesitantly, they did so, and when they laid back, their eyes were so round that it made Nizhoni laugh. Shy Fawn and Cloud Walking laughed, too. Finally, Shy Fawn rolled off the side of the mattress onto her knees on the floor. Pushing her hair back she said, "Who could ever sleep on something so soft? That wouldn't be comfortable at all."

"You get used to it," Nizhoni assured her.

"Did you sleep on one of these beds?" Cloud Walking questioned, pushing herself to her feet.

Nizhoni handed her sister her bedroll. "Yes, I did. For three years, and you'd be surprised how comfortable it became. Especially in the mornings. I never wanted to get up."

They laughed together as they rolled out their mats and laid down; the bed remaining empty throughout the night.

The next morning, they set out with the soldiers at first light. Cloud Walking rode double behind Nizhoni, and with Shy Fawn riding beside them, they led the way home. Nizhoni thought of the readers she had stowed away in her satchel and repeated the letters to herself as they rode, picturing them in her mind as she recalled their sounds. She was determined to know them by her next lesson, whenever that might be.

The miles passed quickly and silently, save the hoofbeats of the horses and the morning songs of birds. They came upon a herd of elk grazing in a meadow who only raised their heads and looked at them with their big, gentle eyes before going back to their breakfast. Nizhoni inhaled deeply, feeling as if she breathed in happiness as much as she did air. She loved the mountains, the animals that lived there, and the bright blue sky that stretched out above them like the canopy of the bed they'd slept beside the night before. She loved the wildflowers that bloomed, the trees that offered shelter, warmth, and medicines, the wind that played in their boughs. She was smiling and light-hearted by the time they rode into camp. But that happy feeling didn't last.

From the moment she saw Fire Maker, she knew it was not going to be a pleasant meeting. There was a glint in his eyes, like a cat who was about to pounce on its prey. She cast a nervous glance at Major Taylor. His expression was guarded, and she wondered if he felt the same premonition. She cautiously followed the men back to her wickiup, wondering what Fire Maker was up to. She didn't have to wonder long.

As soon as they were inside, Fire Maker announced the exorbitant amount he wanted for his horses. When Major Taylor declared it highway robbery, Fire Maker only shrugged and declared it was all about supply and demand. It was a fair price, he argued, because of the scarcity of horses in the remote mountain region. The army needed horses, and he had them, he reasoned. The only question, according to Fire Maker, was if the major was man enough to provide his soldiers with what the job required.

As the men argued, it quickly became clear to Niz that it had not been goodwill, remorse, nor a willingness to work together that had led Fire Maker to offer his horses to the army, as she'd hoped. Rather, he had clearly spotted an opportunity to make a large profit. Whether he wanted money that would set him up in the rapidly changing world around them, resources to buy three reasonably priced horses for every one he sold the army and thus increase his herd and social standing among their people, or cash with which he would send her to buy tobacco and firewater, she didn't know.

Major Taylor quickly grew exasperated, trying to keep things civil, and his men grew angry and offended. Fire Maker appeared to enjoy their frustration. Clearly reveling in it, their distress seemed to make him feel powerful. He plainly thought he held all the cards. Niz felt caught between the men as she translated.

When the price had finally been agreed upon, Fire Maker declared the two horses he had sent Nizhoni and Shy Fawn to the fort on, not for sale, nor were any of the others of similar quality. Once again, Major Taylor had to give curt orders to his men to keep them in check as their anger raged. More arguing took place, but the soldiers were forced to settle for the lesser stock of Fire Maker's herd or walk away empty-handed.

Standing between them, Niz could sense how much Major Taylor wanted to make a deal with Fire Maker to demonstrate his willingness to work together, but her husband wasn't making it easy. Finally, Major Taylor left with three horses, but he left frustrated and upset. There was no doubt he had been swindled, but Fire Maker was right—he had the upper hand. The army did need horses, but even more importantly, Major Taylor knew how crucial cooperation between the tribe and the army was.

After the disappointing trade had finally been made, Nizhoni watched Major Taylor and his men ride off toward the fort, their new horses in tow. Sick to her stomach, she felt like she should go after them and apologize for what she had unknowingly led them into. Major Taylor had been kind to her family, concerned about her people, honoring to her late husband, and she had set him up to be tricked and cheated. Turning back to her husband, her frustration barely in check, her dark eyes smoldered.

"Aren't you going to congratulate me on a successful trade?" he taunted.

"Fire Maker, how could you do that?" she demanded, following him back into the wickiup. "How could you ask so much and then offer them your worst horses?"

Fire Maker's handsome face turned angry. "They didn't have to take them."

"They did, and you know it! They need horses! Several of theirs have been stolen."

Fire Maker smirked. "Lucky for me."

"How can you think that? You may have won this battle, but you forget we have to live beside them. They're not going away, no matter how much we would like them to! And now, when there's actually an officer who wants to work together to keep peaceful relations between our people and the army, you do this?"

Her husband glared at her. "Whose side are you on? You're my wife. You should be congratulating me. You should be grateful I'm such a good businessman. You should be singing my praises. Instead, you're whining that I didn't give our enemy my best horses. I knew you weren't the brightest star in the sky, but I at least thought you were loyal."

"I am loyal! I want to sing your praises. I want to congratulate you! Believe me. But how can I when you're putting our people in jeopardy with your foolish tricks and greed?"

He roughly grabbed her jaw, holding her in place, forcing her to look at him. "You act like they're the wounded party, Nizhoni, but *we're* the ones who have been wronged! They take our land, our homes, our wild game, our way of life, and they certainly don't care if we're getting a fair deal. So, tell me—why should I worry about being fair to them? I'll make all I can off the army, and you won't make me feel bad about it."

"I understand you want to make a profit, but that was more than that!" she shot back, her eyes snapping. The grip he had on her face hurt, but she was too upset to care.

"What was it?" he challenged.

"Revenge!"

He laughed a dry, humorless laugh and released her with a shove. "Well, then I'll take my revenge a hundred times over. I made a great deal of money today."

"Is that all you care about?" she questioned, clenching her fists in anger.

"What else is more important?" he mocked.

"So many things!" He raised his brows in question. "Peace, for one! And our people, honor, honesty, love . . .'"

He narrowed his eyes at her. "Do you think I care about any of that?"

Her anger soared, even as she felt sick to her stomach. "I would certainly hope so."

"Then you're sure to be disappointed. In this world we live in now—their world—money rules, Nizhoni, and I will have it." He paused and gave her a deprecating smile. "Who knows, for the right price, I might even trade you."

"How could you say such a thing?" she asked, her voice trembling with emotion. "You'd better not mean that. I'm your wife, Fire Maker!"

"Yes, you are!" he exploded in reply, reaching out and grabbing her arm. He gave her a shake. "Which means I can do with you what I want! Like trade you for the highest price. You are nothing to me, Nizhoni! I could easily replace you. As I should after that stunt you pulled with Cloud Walking. Don't think I didn't notice that you took her with you after I said she would cook me dinner!"

Niz shook with stress and anger as he brought her sister into the fight. Glaring at him, she sized up her opponent, seething as she tried to determine the best path forward. Remembering that this was now about Cloud Walking too rather than simply herself and Fire Maker, she decided to avoid the subject altogether and distract him instead. "Replace me?" she taunted. "Who else would marry you after the way you've treated me? Everyone sees it!"

"Only because you go around whining and complaining, making me out to be a villain, showing off the smallest bruises, telling them I did it to you when it was your own clumsiness."

"I tell no one!" Nizhoni argued, her voice rising.

He glared at her. "I am Fire Maker, chief of our people, the richest man in the village. I would have no trouble getting another bride and one who would even be worth something to me at that . . . a woman who could actually give me a son."

Nizhoni narrowed her eyes, too crushed to even respond to the arrow he had shot her with. She could not win this fight with Fire Maker; he didn't play by any rules, not even truth. He would break her heart in the process of breaking her spirit.

Instead, she tried to take a step back and make sense of the mess that had just been created with the army. "I went to the fort in good faith. I showed the soldiers your horses just as you told me to. I told them you wanted to trade. Because I believed, Fire Maker, that you were doing something good . . . that you wanted to show your cooperation with the army, that you wanted to make peace."

"Yes, you did. And they came, which is why I sent you. They never could have believed a simple woman like you could be clever enough to trick them."

"But I wasn't tricking them," she protested. "I went in good faith. I believed you were trying to do the right thing." She thought maybe, just maybe, if he knew she believed he could be, he would rise to the occasion and become the kind of man he had the potential to be.

Fire Maker laughed. "Then you don't know me very well, wife." He kissed her hard, nothing gentle or loving about his kiss, then shoved her away from him. "Everyone used to say you were clever. This proves how wrong they were." He laughed again as he walked out the door.

She resisted the urge to vomit. He had played her like a puppet. Blind to his schemes, she had marched to the beat of her foolish husband's drum. In the process, she had unknowingly led Major Taylor and the soldiers right into the trap he'd laid for them.

Alone in the wickiup, Nizhoni clenched her hands into fists. She was humiliated that she had played into Fire Maker's plan and furious with him for using her. His careless words had made her blood boil, as did the fact that she believed he meant what he'd said. Nothing spoke louder to him than money. Not her, not the ways of their people, not his conscience, not the spirits. The only thing that drove him was his greed, fueled by selfishness and control.

Overcome with frustration, she wanted to yell or cry or punch something. Yet, nothing she did could change reality. Nothing she could say or do would soften nor hurt Fire Maker. He was aloof and untouchable. He held no love for her. He had only collected her like he collected fine horses—to be paraded about to show off his status and power, to make himself look better, and to make other men jealous.

The worst part was, she had no doubt that what he said earlier was true—she was under no false illusions that he wouldn't trade her if the price was right. With their winters spent among many other bands of their people, even if he had to look beyond the thirty-five wickiups that comprised their village, he surely could and would find another woman to replace her. And he was sure to do so without a second thought. She was dispensable to him.

The truth of it made her stomach churn, and she nearly began to heave. Instead, she stuffed the feelings down, forcing her anger into submission.

Knowing there was nothing she could do about her husband, Nizhoni turned to unpack her satchel instead. Taking out the books from Major Taylor, she carefully hid them under the hides with her letters. She was surer than ever before that Fire Maker would not want her to learn to read, no matter how it might benefit their people. Unless she could figure out some way that reading would benefit him, she knew he would strictly forbid it. In fact, if he knew the books came from Major Taylor, he would likely burn them just for good measure. And so, it was better to keep the books hidden and learn in secret. That way, if a time came when her people needed her, she would be ready.

Eight

S itting in the twilight, a slight smile lifted Nizhoni's lips. She had her knees drawn up to her chest, her buckskin dress smoothed down over them. There was a slight chill in the air, reminding her that the seasons would soon be changing. She was glad she had put on her buckskin leggings when she'd been out gathering seeds earlier. Now, they kept her legs warm, even in the evening chill.

She watched across the fire as Ever Flowering and Walks With Power sat together, talking quietly among themselves. Ever Flowering was speaking to her husband with bright eyes and a happy expression, and he was listening intently, his arm draped around her shoulders. Whatever she said made him laugh, and he pulled her in closer, pressing a quick kiss against the side of her head. Their conversation must have turned to the baby, because they both looked down, and Walks With Power put his hand against her abdomen. She was just starting to show, and Niz thought she was the cutest pregnant woman she'd ever seen. Ever Flowering covered her husband's hand with her own. When she looked back up at him, her face was nearly glowing.

Watching the sweet scene play out, Nizhoni's heart swelled with joy, even as it ached with a piercing sadness. She remembered what that felt like. She remembered what it was like to be in love, to feel hopeful about the future, to share the dream of a baby with someone you couldn't wait to start a family with. She remembered the excitement of carrying a child, the sensation of feeling them move and roll within you, the pride in her husband's eyes whenever he put his hand against her stomach to feel the baby. She smiled again. She was so glad her sister was getting to experience such a wonder.

Turning her eyes out toward the darkness that had gathered around their village, Nizhoni noticed the trees were like lacy black shadows against the darkening twilight. Stars, bright and clear, were beginning to appear overhead, adorning the sky like the most beautiful beadwork. Somewhere nearby, an owl hooted. The silvery music of the river floated to her through the darkness like the melody of life in their summer camp.

Breathing deep, her smile grew. She loved the mountains. She loved the land. She loved sitting outside around a fire, watching it crackle and burn. She loved the earthy smell of the wood smoke mingled with the fresh scent of the pines. She loved how it felt when the wind stirred her hair all around her and the way she relaxed when she breathed deeply of the fresh mountain air.

She wished the peace she experienced in nature would last. If only it went deep enough to soothe her troubled heart at all times, everywhere. Instead, the sweetness of it was fleeting, confined to moments such as this. Breathing it in, she sat quietly, savoring it.

In the stillness, she caught the words of Soaring Eagle's grandfather from where he sat at a nearby fire, children from the village gathered around him. He was telling the stories of their people. The children sat transfixed, hanging on his every word, and Nizhoni listened closer, just as gripped. She loved hearing the elders tell the stories that had been passed down for generations. They were responsible for educating the children in the ways of their people, and the young ones gathered around to listen whenever they started storytelling. Though she'd been hearing the same tales since she was young, she still hung on every word. After several minutes, Niz's eyes grew heavy, the cadence of his soothing old voice relaxing.

"Great-Grandfather, what will happen if The Great Father keeps taking more and more of our land?" a young voice piped up, sounding frightened.

Nizhoni felt her heart prick, and she turned her head to watch as Soaring Eagle's brother, Lean Elk, gathered his daughter onto his lap, holding the little one close.

"We cannot allow it, little one. Our people are connected to this land. If we lose our land, we will lose our way of life," the old man answered.

Nizhoni turned back to the fire, her heart aching. Wise Hawk was right. They couldn't allow it. And yet, how would they stop it? The government took more of the land with each passing decade. The wild game was being killed. The native plants they depended on were being plowed under. Though they were more sheltered from the advancement of the white man than the tribes who lived on the plains and in the East, even from members of their own tribe, they still felt it pressing in against them. What would happen once they no longer had enough resources to meet the needs of their people? What would happen if they no longer had access to the different camps and areas they migrated to throughout the year, following the seasons? Her heart hurt. She wanted to help. She wanted to do something to ease the little girl's fears about the future—the same fear that she knew weighed on Lean Elk and Wise Hawk also—but what could she do? What could any of them do?

Suddenly, she recalled the books she had hidden under the hides she slept on. Her mind felt foggy and thick every time she picked them up, and her opportunities to do so were infrequent between her daily chores and trying to find chances to read in secret. But now, with renewed determination, she rose from the fire, bid her family goodnight, and retreated to her wickiup.

Fire Maker was still with his friends Tall Peak and Black Bear, drinking the firewater and telling stories, so she might have awhile. Retrieving the books, she laid down facing away from the entrance in order to have time to stash them should Fire Maker come home. Struggling to find enough light, she squinted at the page, trying to make out each letter and recall its sound. She repeated them to herself over and over.

She may not enjoy the task, nor the feeling of being dim-witted, but she did desperately want to help her people, and learning to read and write the white man's words was one way she could do so. It may not help them today or tomorrow, but if she stuck with it and learned, perhaps, when the need arose, she would be ready. She had to believe that, because without being able to help her people communicate, Niz didn't know what else she had to offer. And the one thing she liked less than feeling dull was feeling helpless.

~~~

"Nizhoni!" Cloud Walking was panting and out of breath.

Niz looked up, surprised to see the girl, concerned by what it meant. Ever Flowering had suffered with a slight fever during the night. Thinking a tea might help, Nizhoni had walked far down river gathering willow bark she could use to make one. She'd stopped to bathe when she came upon a secluded bend in the river. The late summer morning was warm and the water refreshing. Having finished, she had just started home, feeling relaxed. But Cloud Walking had come at a run, and as Nizhoni's calm shattered, alarm coursed through her.

"What is it? Is Ever Flowering worse?"

Cloud Walking shook her head. "No, she seems better. It's Fire Maker. He sent me to get you."

"Fire Maker?" Niz asked in surprise.

Cloud Walking nodded. "The soldiers are here. Major Taylor is trying to speak to him, but he can't understand. He needs you to translate."

Nizhoni's heart settled. That made sense. Fire Maker needed her to translate. She breathed a sigh of relief, grateful it wasn't anything more serious. Calm settled over her again, and she looped her arm through her sister's as they started toward the village.

"So, how is Strong Pine?" she asked, watching Cloud Walking's face as she did. The girl blushed as Nizhoni had expected she would.

"He's good. He asked me to go on a walk with him this evening."

"And you said yes?"

"Of course. He . . . uh . . . he said he wants to start a family with me."

Nizhoni caught her breath in surprise. She hadn't known an offer had been made. She wondered if her mother knew, or if Strong Pine had made it in private. Though she was personally overjoyed at the declaration, she watched her sister's face curiously. There was a hesitation there that she hadn't expected. "And is that what you want?"

"Yes. I mean, I think so."

"You're not sure?"

Cloud Walking sighed. "He's a strong brave, and I think he'll grow into a good man."

"I agree," Niz said. The young man seemed honest. His father and grandfather were good men. They had taught him to honor family and their people. Though he was still young, he only took what was needed and honored the animals and the land. Nizhoni didn't see any of the selfishness or pride in Strong Pine that she saw in her own husband. She thought he would make a good match for Cloud Walking. Yet her beloved little sister looked conflicted. "So what's stopping you from saying yes?"

"I—I keep thinking about the fort . . . about the houses and the feather beds and the soldiers . . . so many soldiers."

Nizhoni groaned. "Cloud Walking, no! I didn't take you there so that you could want that life."

"But you chose that life!"

"I didn't!"

"You did! I was only twelve when you left, but I remember how excited you were . . . how your eyes shone the day you left the village."

"I didn't choose that life, Cloud Walking. I chose a man . . . I chose my husband. I didn't care about what kind of shelter I would live in or what kind of bed I would sleep in. I didn't marry him to escape our village or because I thought the ways of the white man were better. I married because I had fallen in love, and I wanted to be wherever he was, whatever that looked like." Grief started to well up in her heart, and Niz pushed it back down. This wasn't about her. This was about Cloud Walking, and she had to set the record straight or her mother would never forgive her.

"But you were happy then, in that world. Now, you're miserable," Cloud Walking said guilelessly.

Nizhoni thought quickly and shook her head. "No, I was happy because of a man. And now, at times, I'm miserable because of a man. It had nothing to do with the way of life I was living. Living in this world, with our people, living in harmony with the earth, this is where I'm happiest. I love this life we live. And it's only because I loved my husband so much that I could stand to leave it. It wasn't because that one was better or won me over."

"What if Strong Pine is like Fire Maker?"

"He's not," Nizhoni assured, tucking away the knowledge that her little sister was more aware of how things really were than she had given her credit for.

"How do you know? Perhaps he is fooling us as Fire Maker did. What if, once we marry, he treats me the way Fire Maker treats you?"

Nizhoni lifted her chin. "He didn't fool me."

Cloud Walking sent her a knowing look. "Really? You married him knowing he was like this?"

"I'm married to a chief," Niz said, her pride burning. It was embarrassing to know that everyone, including her little sister, knew what Fire Maker was like. When she had told him as much, she hadn't imagined that meant sixteen-year-old girls too. Cloud Walking was barely more than a child. To feel the sympathy of her mother or Ever Flowering was a different thing than feeling pitied. She had become someone her little sister didn't want to end up like, and that stung. "And he didn't fool me. I knew what he was like. That's why I turned him down the first time he asked for my hand in marriage. I only said yes because I was blinded by my grief.

I wanted . . . comfort . . . to not feel so empty and alone. I knew what he was like, but I was too dazed by my loss to think clearly."

Cloud Walking's face softened. "I'm sorry, Sister."

Nizhoni took a steadying breath and propped up a smile. "Well, believe me when I say Strong Pine is not the same. I could tell with Fire Maker back before the tragedy . . . I would be able to tell with Strong Pine too. And I think he seems like a fine young man. A young man our people can be proud of . . . a young man *you* can be proud of."

Cloud Walking blushed and nodded, but Nizhoni could see the issue wasn't settled in her mind. "What will you tell him?"

"That I need more time to decide."

"What are you hoping more time will tell you?" Nizhoni prompted gently. "Strong Pine is a good man. He would be a good match for you."

"What if I love another man?" Cloud Walking asked slowly as she watched the uneven ground they were walking over.

Nizhoni's eyebrows shot up in surprise. "Do you?"

"I don't know. Maybe." The sixteen-year-old's face looked conflicted.

"Do I know this man?" Niz asked, hoping Cloud Walking would confide in her. She hadn't realized there was anyone else who had caught her sister's eye. She had assumed the girl was as interested in Strong Pine as he was in her.

"Look, there's Fire Maker waiting for you. He doesn't look happy. Let's run, Sister, and keep you out of trouble!" Cloud Walking, forever light on her feet, grabbed Niz's hand and began running, her long braids flying out behind her. Niz ran, too, spurred on by the storm cloud on Fire Maker's face. He clearly hadn't appreciated waiting.

When they got to the edge of camp, they slowed, and Cloud Walking broke off to go back to their mother. Nizhoni continued on alone.

"Where have you been?" Fire Maker demanded.

She showed him the bark. "I was collecting it for Ever Flowering. She woke with a fever during the night."

He caught her arm and pulled her forcefully toward their wickiup. "The soldiers have come. I need you to translate."

Ducking inside, she saw Major Taylor and the others sitting around their fire. Major Taylor nodded to her. "I'm glad you've come. We need your help."

"I'm sorry to keep you waiting. I wasn't in the village. My sister had to find me," she explained, quickly laying aside her satchel full of willow bark. Approaching the fire, she sat down in her usual place between Major Taylor and Fire Maker.

"It's okay. You didn't know we were coming."

"Ask him what he wants," Fire Maker instructed with a grunt. He obviously didn't like being left out of the conversation.

"Fire Maker wants to know why you've come," she said, turning back to Major Taylor.

"Tell him I need more horses."

Nizhoni's eyebrows shot up in surprise. She couldn't believe he had come back for more after the price Fire Maker had demanded last time. He nodded, and she turned and translated his message to Fire Maker.

Her husband looked pleased. "I have a few more I can part with."

"Good. We're doubling our patrols. Another homestead was attacked two nights ago."

"The settlers must be starting to think you cannot protect them," Fire Maker sneered.

"We need more horses to conduct additional patrols," Major Taylor continued after Niz finished translating, as if he hadn't heard. "We will catch those responsible, and when we do, they will be brought to justice for their crimes." His statement sounded like a promise, and Niz looked at Fire Maker nervously as she translated. The undercurrents in the air were tense.

"Well, I hope you know I will have to charge more for these horses, seeing as how I don't have as many in my herd as last time," Fire Maker answered.

"I was guessing you would," Major Taylor agreed grimly. "And I will pay it, only this time I want to see the horses before agreeing to a price. And I was informed after my last purchase that I need you to sign a bill of sale to make the trade official."

"What is this bill of sale?" Fire Maker asked suspiciously, looking caught off-guard.

"It's just paperwork. The government seems to love it. I will buy your horses, but to do so, you must sign the papers, stating the agreed upon price and that the horses belong to me."

"What if you're using this bill of sale to try to trick me?" Fire Maker asked, his eyes narrowed.

Major Taylor's hazel gaze stayed steady. "You're welcome to read it for yourself before you sign it to see that the price and animals are what we agreed upon." Nizhoni caught her breath as she watched Fire Maker shift uncomfortably as she translated. Major Taylor went on. "Assuming you can read, of course. If you can't, surely there's someone in the village who can."

Fire Maker drew in a deep breath through his nose, seeming angry. She knew why. Major Taylor's erroneous assumption had made him feel inferior, and feeling inferior made men like her husband angry.

Fire Maker glanced at her. "Can you read the white men's words?" he questioned, his eyes darkening. Nizhoni shook her head, wondering what Major Taylor was doing. Though she was not at fault, she would likely bear the brunt of her husband's anger. "We will not sign your 'bill of sale,'" Fire Maker said decisively.

Major Taylor held Fire Maker's gaze for a moment, then stood. "That's too bad. We need your horses, and we're willing to pay your price, but we cannot buy them if you won't sign. I got in trouble for not having a signed bill of sale last time. My higher ups informed me I couldn't let it happen again."

Fire Maker stood too. "Hold on." Major Taylor paused just inside the hide that served as their door. "Surely we could come to an agreement with this paper."

Nizhoni could plainly see her husband's displeasure at seeing a chance for profit slip away.

"No. It's the only way I have authorization to make a deal. If you want to sell more horses to the army, Chief Fire Maker, you must find someone among your people who can read and write to sign the necessary paperwork on your behalf." Major Taylor tipped his head. "Or else find someone who can learn."

Ezra Taylor left the wickiup, followed by his soldiers. Fire Maker looked at Nizhoni. "Why can't you read?" he demanded angrily.

"I never learned." Had Major Taylor done this on purpose? Had he anticipated the opposition she would face from Fire Maker and come up with a plan to help her?

"Could you?"

"I'm sure I could, if I had someone to teach me," she answered, thinking of the books hidden under her bedding. She'd studied them half a dozen times in the week since Major Taylor had given them to her. She was ready for another lesson but had been unsure how to go about getting one.

Fire Maker grunted. "Who could teach you?"

"Someone who knows English I suppose."

Fire Maker stood still for a moment, thinking, before following the soldiers out of the wickiup. Niz trailed after him.

"What if I wish for my wife to learn to read?" he demanded, catching up with Major Taylor. "How could she learn? Could you teach her?"

Niz kept her eyes on the ground as she translated.

"I'm a soldier, Fire Maker, not a teacher," Major Taylor said dryly. For just a moment, Niz glanced up at him, surprised by his words. He nodded to her to translate, and embarrassed, she quickly did so, feeling slightly hurt by how indifferent and callous he seemed now after being the one to encourage her to learn. Major

Taylor shrugged. "I suppose we'll just have to find someone else to buy horses from."

"Wait. If Nizhoni can learn, you'll buy your horses from me?"

"Yes. We came planning to buy."

"Do you know anyone she can learn from? Someone who could teach her?"

Major Taylor rubbed the back of his neck. "There is a woman in the fort—one of the soldier's wives—who teaches people to read on occasion. Your wife would have to know at least her letters before the woman would teach her, though. That's one of her requirements."

Fire Maker grimaced.

Major Taylor rubbed the back of his neck again. "I suppose I could spare a little time today to give her a first lesson and see how she does. If she can learn her letters, then I suppose I could talk to the woman at the fort and see if she would be willing to teach her." Major Taylor seemed annoyed by the entire dilemma, and Nizhoni felt her pride smarting as she translated his words.

"What does the woman charge to do this teaching?" Fire Maker questioned.

Major Taylor shrugged. "I don't know, but surely less than you charge for one horse."

Fire Maker crossed his arms, thinking over the situation. Finally, he nodded. "Fine. If my wife's smart enough to learn, she'll learn to read so she can sign this bill of sale you require."

Niz felt her cheeks flush as she translated the humiliating words.

Major Taylor nodded. "Fine. Once she does, we'll be back for more horses."

Fire Maker settled his gaze on Nizhoni. "This soldier will give you your first lesson. Make sure you pay attention and learn what he teaches you so the woman in town will take you on. The sooner you learn to read and write, the sooner I can trade more horses."

"I'll do my best," she promised.

He glared at her. "I don't want your best. I want you to make it happen." He gave her a little shove toward Major Taylor, and then spun and walked away, calling out to a few braves as he did so. Nizhoni watched Fire Maker and the others leap onto the backs of their horses and ride off toward the south.

Major Taylor watched them go before glancing back at Niz. "Why don't you get your books," he told her, his voice kinder than it had been.

As she quickly did so, she mulled over the situation, sorting through both the hope and humiliation it had brought up within her. When she emerged from the wickiup with the readers, Major Taylor and his men were no longer in sight. Confused, she wandered through the village until she spotted them twenty yards beyond the last wickiup. Three of the soldiers were resting against tree trunks and one had stretched out in the grass nearby, his head in his hands, his eyes closed. Their horses grazed nearby. Major Taylor was sitting on a fallen log, his hands clasped loosely between his knees, his eyes on the river.

As she went to join him, Niz recognized that he had settled close to the village but not in it, where it was out in the open and everyone could see them without being close enough to overhear their lesson. Though she wasn't certain it had been intentional, she was grateful. He seemed to be taking care with her honor, not giving room for speculation, guarding against any fits of jealousy Fire Maker might be prone to, and she appreciated it. She sat down a reasonable distance from him, and he looked over and smiled at her—his first smile of the day.

"You found a way to work it to Fire Maker's advantage that I learn to read and write," she observed cautiously. Had that been his intention? She wasn't certain. He'd been hard to read since she entered her wickiup; nothing like the open, unguarded man she'd spoken to in his office.

He shrugged. "The army likes its paperwork."

She liked that he had neither confirmed nor denied his part in it. She returned his smile. "Thank you."

"Have you learned the letters and their sounds?" he asked, easily steering the conversation back to its intent.

"Yes, though I've been struggling with this one," she said, flipping through the pages.

"Ah. Z. It says z-z-zebra."

She made a face. "It looks like a painted horse."

He laughed. "So it does. But no, it doesn't say h-h-horse. It says z-z-z, like zebra."

She nodded in reply, repeating the sound after him.

"Good." He turned back to the first page. "Let's start at the beginning. You tell me the letters and their sounds this time."

They went letter by letter though the book, Major Taylor coaching and correcting her when needed. When he was satisfied, he began teaching her how to put the letters together to make words. She could read several small, easy words by the time he stretched and declared they needed to be starting back to the fort.

"Do you think the woman in town will teach me now?" she asked hopefully. She wanted to learn to read for the sake of her people. She also hoped she wouldn't have to tell Fire Maker she hadn't been able to learn all she needed to.

"Yes, she'll teach you," Major Taylor answered easily.

Nizhoni was glad, and a smile filled her face. "How will I find her?"

"I've arranged for her to come here to your village every other day this week. You can see how you get on. Then next week, if you like her, you can come to the fort every other day. The week after, she'll come back to you again. If you keep that up until you leave for your winter camp, you should have learned quite a deal—enough to read the bill of sale and sign for Fire Maker. Then you'll leave for the winter with him feeling happy that you helped him make a good trade."

Niz considered him for several moments, wanting to thank him for the plan he'd concocted, for making arrangements for her to learn to read, and for caring enough about her people to put time and effort into equipping them with the knowledge they needed to avoid being taken advantage of in the future. She wanted to tell him that his creative solution to her dilemma with Fire Maker reminded her so much of Alex—that this was something her late husband would have done. Literacy was something Alex cared about and valued. It was something he would have insisted upon, should he have foreseen her going back to her people. However, she decided not to say any of it, afraid she would get emotional if she so much as started. Instead, she opted for something safer. "I'm surprised you want any more of his ridiculously expensive horses."

Major Taylor chuckled and looked out toward the river. "It seems buying a few over-priced horses is a small price to pay to get to help. You're worth educating, Niz, and your people are worth protecting."

She looked down at her hands where they lay folded in her lap. She remembered Fire Maker's parting words and the look she'd seen in his eyes. It was only too obvious that he expected her to be too dull to learn. She bit her lip, feeling the shame of his low expectations.

"Hey." Major Taylor reached over and tugged on a strand of her long black hair. "For the record, you're doing really well. Fire Maker doesn't realize what a smart wife he has, and we won't tell him for fear that he'll think up some way to profit off your wits, but you need to know you're picking this up incredibly quick. It's not usually this easy."

She shook her head, encouraged by his compliment, but knowing she didn't wholly deserve it. "It doesn't feel easy."

"Trust me, you're doing good."

She kicked at some loose rocks with her moccasin. "It must still be too time consuming to teach me, though, given your other responsibilities. Thank you for finding someone at the fort who could continue to instruct me." She didn't blame him for needing to find someone else, and she was grateful he had. She wouldn't have known who to ask.

He was quiet, and she risked a quick glance up at him. He was smiling again, and his expression was kind. He bumped her shoulder in a friendly gesture. "It's no chore to teach you, Niz. But I started thinking about how soon you'll be moving down to your winter camps, and with a fort to command and doubling patrols, I knew I couldn't get away enough to guarantee you're reading before you leave. Besides, I doubt Fire Maker would have been agreeable to me teaching you on an ongoing basis, nor would I blame him. There's no way he would appreciate seeing his wife learning from another man . . . especially her late husband's best friend. And I didn't want that coming back on you. Ms. Langston was happy to help, so it seemed like the best path forward."

"Thank you," she said, truly meaning it, "for thinking of all of that."

"You're welcome." He stood to his feet and stretched. "Well, we'd best be heading back. I'll send Ms. Langston out with an escort tomorrow."

"She, um, she is agreeable to coming to my village? She knows I'm . . . not white?" Niz asked, trying to find the words. Not many of the white women she had met would be willing to help a native woman, and they especially wouldn't be agreeable to coming to her village to do so.

"She is. Ms. Langston is the best kind of woman. You'll like her," he promised.

Niz nodded in reply, trusting his judgment. If he thought it would be okay, that was enough for her.

"What will she require to teach me? What will she want in payment or trade?" Whatever it was, she wanted to be able to talk to Fire Maker about it and have it ready when the woman arrived.

Ezra shook his head. "Ms. Langston said literacy is too valuable to put a price on. She's not coming to get paid."

Niz gave him a tight smile. "I appreciate that, I do, but I'd feel better if I could make it worth her while. She's coming all this way . . ."

"Well, next week you'll go to her."

121

"But it's still going to take her time. It's not fair that I would get a new skill and she would get nothing."

Major Taylor's hazel eyes settled on her face, and his mouth tipped up in a smirk.

"What?" she asked defensively.

"Not everything has to be fair, Niz. Sometimes, people just want to help."

"I know that!"

"Do you?"

"I just . . . I want to make good trades. I want to walk away feeling good about what I got but with the other person feeling good too."

"A trait your husband doesn't share."

Niz laughed, caught off-guard by his quick observation. "No, we don't see eye to eye on that, do we?" Or many other things she wanted to add but didn't.

Ezra considered her for another moment and then shrugged. "Maybe getting to help is enough. Maybe in Ms. Langston's mind, that is a good trade. Who are you to judge what she finds valuable?"

Niz narrowed her eyes at him, his words backing her into a corner. Despite what he'd said, it still sat ill with her.

"But you led Fire Maker to believe there would be a charge."

He grinned and shrugged. "I thought I'd leave that door open. Do with it what you will."

She tipped her head and studied him, amused.

"Oh, hey, I almost forgot, but I brought these for Shy Fawn," he said, reaching into the pocket of his frock coat. Her heart warmed—he'd said the name in her native tongue. He hadn't gotten the pronunciation right, but it didn't matter—he'd tried. She took the small paper bag he held out. "In case she wants them for the cradleboard. Or anything she's working on. I don't know. I saw them and thought of her," he finished, seeming less sure of himself than usual.

Curious, Niz opened the bag and looked inside. It was full of tiny, beautifully colored glass beads. A smile filled her face, and she glanced back up at him, her eyes sparkling. "She's going to love these! Thank you!"

"Are you sure you don't want to trade me something for them?" he teased.

Her eyebrows raised in surprise before her eyes narrowed, and her lips pursed.

He cleared his throat and smothered his grin. "I hope she does. Please tell her she does beautiful work."

"I will."

He took a step backwards. "I'll see you next week when you come to the fort for your lessons. Make sure Fire Maker sends you with an escort. Until we find the raiding Comanche, it's not safe for you to be out on your own." He sent her a playful smile as he turned. "And if he objects, remind him that without you, there are no more horse trades. It's in his best interest to protect you."

Her heart warmed as she watched Major Taylor walk away. He had brought a gift to her mother to honor her art. Shy Fawn would be pleased. He had teased her, reminding her not to take herself too seriously. And what was infinitely more, he had found a way to make her indispensable to Fire Maker.

It had been a week since her husband had told her he could easily replace her, but now, that was no longer true. Unless he could find someone else who could speak and read English, his trade with the army depended on her. Major Taylor was giving her more than literacy and a way to help her people; he was giving her dignity.

Nine

Nizhoni felt nervous all morning as she waited for Ms. Langston to arrive. She wondered what the woman would be like and what she would think of her village, of her, and of Major Taylor's task of teaching her to read. As far as Niz knew, it would be the first time ever that a white woman had stepped foot in their village. With Ms. Langston's willingness to help, Niz hoped with all her heart that everything would go well and that the interactions would be pleasant.

With Fire Maker's blessing, Niz spent an hour that morning going over her letters and reading and re-reading the words Major Taylor had taught her. Though it hurt her brain and made her skin crawl, she even went on and tried to sound out some new words on her own. The process was painstakingly slow. But if Major Taylor and Ms. Langston were putting so much effort into giving her the opportunity to learn to read so she could help her people, she would give her all to make it happen.

After studying, she worked on coiling a new basket and stirred the last of the drying amaranth seeds that they had collected two days earlier. They had finished gathering all the amaranth they would take from all the different patches that grew within walking distance of the village. The rest they would leave on the plants. Soon the seeds would fall to the ground and ensure a new crop would grow for them to gather again next summer. That was the way of honor—taking only what was needed and leaving enough to replenish itself.

Sitting down to continue working on her new basket, she smiled as Ever Flowering came and sat beside her. Niz expected her sister to start relaying a story or ask a question; when Ever Flowering didn't, she glanced over at her curiously. Noticing that the young woman looked flushed and tired, she leaned over to lay her hand against Ever Flowering's face.

"Your fever is back," she told her sister.

"Is it?" Ever Flowering replied listlessly. "I don't feel sick, just incredibly tired."

"It's probably just a passing ailment, but better to be safe than sorry. I'll make you some tea. Why don't you lie down and rest?" Nizhoni suggested, jumping to her feet. By the time she'd finished her reading lesson with Major Taylor the day before, her sister's fever had broken. As a result, she hadn't brewed any of the willow bark she'd collected, hoping the fever was gone for good. Now that it was back, she certainly would. "If you're tired, you should sleep. It's hard work growing another human being!" she reminded cheerfully.

Bringing her sleeping mat out for Ever Flowering to lie down on, Niz helped her get comfortable and then set about making her tea. The bark from the willows had many medicinal uses, and she was thankful their camp had large numbers of them growing along the riverbanks.

When the tea had finished brewing, she turned back to Ever Flowering and found the girl asleep. Knowing it would help, Niz roused her sister and helped her sit up to drink. They chatted as Ever Flowering sipped the bitter tea and when she finished, Nizhoni helped her get comfortable in the sunshine again. But even in the warmth of the sun, Ever Flowering shivered. Niz went inside to retrieve a blanket. By the time she settled it over her sister and pulled it up to her chin, Ever Flowering was sleeping again.

"Good. Sleep it off," Nizhoni said, bending down and gently kissing the young woman's forehead.

For as long as she could remember, Ever Flowering had been her dearest friend. Barely a year apart in age, they had grown up together, sharing a camaraderie that ran deep. Nizhoni had been five and Ever Flowering four when Cloud Walking was born. While they loved and adored their baby sister, fussed over her and spoiled her with their affection, their youngest sibling had never made it into the depth of the friendship and bond they shared with one another.

It had been Ever Flowering who had hidden beneath the blanket with her the night the grizzly bear had wandered into camp, looking for his next meal. It was Ever Flowering who had climbed trees with her, shared her berry picnics, and helped her to safety when a flash flood had caught them unaware in a canyon. It was Ever Flowering who had dreamt of the future with her when Alex Applewood first started visiting the village, and Ever Flowering who had held her as she wept after his death. It was Ever Flowering who had tried to talk sense into her following Fire Maker's proposal, and Ever Flowering who always seemed to know what Niz was feeling, even when she didn't know herself. Over the years, Ever Flowering had stuck by her side through thick and thin, tried to get her out of trouble whenever her fiery personality got her into it, and helped calm her down when she was running hot.

Nizhoni smoothed the damp, dark tendrils of hair back from Ever Flowering's face, and pulled the blanket up further before going back to coiling her basket. As she coiled, her mind raced ahead to the baby Ever Flowering would soon welcome, making a list of what all needed to be done before its arrival. Ever Flowering had always been there for her, and now, she would be there for Ever Flowering—and for her baby. Whatever it took. She wasn't going to let anything happen to either of them.

Hearing horses approaching from the east, she looked up. For the last twenty minutes she had all but forgotten about the visit from Ms. Langston. But now, apprehension came crashing over her again as she saw two soldiers and a woman approaching the camp on horseback. Setting aside her basket, she quickly pushed herself to her feet. Smoothing her buckskin dress with the intricate beadwork around the neck, she took a deep breath and went to meet them.

The soldiers, dressed in their dark blue uniforms, were ones who always visited with Major Taylor. The first was the soldier who had taken her to his office when she visited the fort. She was glad Major Taylor had sent him. He seemed level-headed and friendlier than the others. The second had always seemed decently self-controlled as well. They had both helped to restrain their comrades whenever Fire Maker was particularly offensive to the major. Other than a passing glance, though, Nizhoni didn't pay either of them much mind as her attention was immediately captured by the woman they accompanied.

Ms. Langston wore a fine cotton gauze dress of lined rose and cream. The straw hat tipped over her expertly styled golden hair had matching rose ribbons trailing down from the back, and creamy lace fell like a waterfall from her neck. Her skirt was full, with more ribbons and lace, and the back of her dress was bustled. Niz had seen bustles in a Godey's Lady's Book that she had poured over with Raya and Chenoa, exclaiming over the fashions of genteel women, but she had never seen one in real life. She tried not to stare. Ms. Langston's fancy clothes barely compared, though, to the beauty of her creamy complexion, dainty features, and large, crystalline blue eyes. Niz had only seen women so lovely in pictures, and yet, here was one in her very own village.

She instantly felt all too aware of her buckskin dress, her raven-black hair blowing free in the wind, the two feathers she had tied near her scalp, her sun-darkened skin, her womanly figure, and her soft leather moccasins. Her appearance couldn't be more different from that of the fair and willowy woman in front of her. Her awareness pricked her pride, and she lifted her chin and met the woman's eyes, determined not to allow insecurity to plague her.

"Ms. Langston, I presume? I'm Nizhoni. Your student for the next few weeks. Thank you for coming," she said briskly.

Ms. Langston simply looked at her for a moment, wide-eyed, before her eyes drifted from Niz to the village and then back to Niz. Suddenly, she blinked slowly, took a deep breath, and propped up a shaky smile.

"Hello," she answered. "I apologize for staring. I've always wanted to visit a village. I'm just trying to take it all in. It's a very surreal moment, you know, after imagining it for so long."

Nizhoni's eyebrows shot up in surprise, and despite the woman's melodious voice and timid smile, suspicion rose up within her. Who was this woman and why had she agreed to come in all her finery? Why had she always wanted to visit a village? Was she there to gawk at the people she had read about in the newspapers?

"I see you're wary of me, and I don't blame you. I truly don't. You don't know me from Eve, and here I am acting rude and making you feel like a spectacle." The woman reached out and beseechingly took Niz's hand in both of her daintily gloved ones.

"The truth is, my late husband was raised in an Indian village. See, his ma and pa got sick when they were coming west to California in the rush of '49. Their wagon train left them behind, scared the sickness would spread, giving them time to get better. Well, they didn't get better. In fact, they perished, leaving my husband, just a child of three all by his lonesome. Thankfully, a group of Pawnee found him. He was always glad it wasn't the Sioux, but perhaps that was just because the Pawnee and Sioux were enemies. I don't know. Well, the fact is, the Pawnee *did* find him and took him in and raised him. When he was a grown man, at the encouragement of his Pawnee parents, he began scouting for the army. Many of them did, you know, and considering he wasn't truly Pawnee, it made sense that he would form some life for himself back among his own people.

"Anyway, I met him at Fort Sidney in Nebraska in '70. You see, my father was the commanding officer there. Daddy wasn't too happy about me and Robert, but I couldn't help it—I was enamored. Robert was truly one of a kind and just the most wonderful man. Well, after seeing how deeply we loved each other—and much cajoling on my part—Daddy finally gave his consent, and we were married. When Robert got sent out here to Colorado Territory, I came along. Daddy hated to see me come west, of course, but I just had to be with Robert. I couldn't bear to be apart from him. Honestly, I still can't." Ms. Langston paused to blink tears out of her clear blue eyes.

Nizhoni watched, stunned. She'd never heard someone be so forthright with their life story.

"I'm sorry. That was a lot. Too much. I talk when I'm nervous. I overshare," Ms. Langston continued, her pretty face turning down into a sad pout. "But I promise there's a point to all of this. And the point is, Robert always told the most interesting stories of his life with the Pawnee. He was going to take me back to the village one day, so I could meet his Pawnee family, and see for myself what he spoke of so fondly. He . . . well . . . he's been gone for a few months now. We never made it back to his village." Ms. Langston stopped and blinked back tears again.

"I was afraid I would never get to see all that my mind had imagined these past four years. You see, I'm set to return to my father at Fort Sidney in just over a month's time, with the last group out of here before winter sets in. That's why, when Major Taylor asked if I might be willing to come here and instruct you in reading, I jumped at the chance. I always welcome the opportunity to help a fellow woman and make a new friend—there's so few at a fort—but this also is a dream come true for me. I do realize that's so much more than you probably needed to know, but I just wanted you to understand why it means so much to me to be here."

"We're not the Pawnee, Ms. Langston," Nizhoni said slowly.

"No, I know. Of course you aren't. I didn't mean to offend. I realize you are a different tribe with your own unique culture. There are surely many differences, but . . . even still. Maybe I can picture the village he grew up in just one iota more after visiting your village here, and somehow, I suppose I hope that will make me feel a little closer to him . . . or perhaps help me find closure . . .

or at least connect the life I dreamt of to the one I'm living. I don't know. I suppose that sounds silly." Ms. Langston sent her a very nervous and apologetic look, and wrung her hands together. "I do hope you'll forgive me."

Nizhoni's heart twisted, and she took a deep breath. "No, it doesn't sound silly. I—I understand actually."

"Do you?" Ms. Langston asked, her blue eyes round again.

Niz nodded and looked out over the land for a moment before turning back to the woman before her. It *had* been a lot for an opening speech—never before had she heard one like it—but Niz *did* understand, and she liked the woman's frankness. Ms. Langston had spilled it all instead of leaving her to wonder.

"I do," Niz answered. "I also married a wonderful man from a different world. A tragedy happened, and I returned home to my village a year ago after three years of marriage. I recently visited his world again and it . . . it helped. So yes, I do understand." Nizhoni gave the woman a sympathetic smile. Though they were strangers, they now had something in common.

"I can't promise to match your frankness. We're private people, Ms. Langston," she continued. "We don't like to share about ourselves as we don't want that knowledge getting into the wrong hands and being used by our enemies. I can't promise to answer all your questions, but you are welcome here."

"I understand. Thank you for welcoming me," Ms. Langston replied with a wobbly smile.

"Thank you for agreeing to teach me to read. It's very kind of you and I appreciate it very much."

"Shall we begin your lesson?"

Nizhoni nodded and motioned to the fallen tree she had sat on with Major Taylor. The soldiers, coming back from watering the horses, stood nearby where they could keep watch over Ms. Langston. After a fleeting look of despair, the finely clad woman sat down carefully on the fallen log. Watching, Nizhoni cringed. "I'm sorry, I wish I had a chair to offer you. Next time, I'll bring a blanket to spread."

Ms. Langston laughed. It was a lovely sound. "No, it's my fault. I don't know what I was thinking wearing my best dress. It's quite likely already been ruined by the ride. I suppose I just wanted to make a good impression, and it felt like a rather momentous occasion to me."

"Just a plain, everyday dress may be better suited to that ride," Nizhoni agreed. "Though this one is beautiful."

"Yes, I suppose you're right. I shall remember for next time. So Major Taylor said you know your letters and are working on short words."

Niz nodded and opened her books. Together, they went over the letters and then reviewed the words she'd learned with Major Taylor. When they had finished, they moved on to new words.

To Nizhoni's relief, Ms. Langston was a patient and encouraging teacher. She didn't make Nizhoni feel like a child with exuberant praise, nor did she make her feel dull for not knowing things. Niz appreciated her teaching style and found herself liking the woman more and more, despite her initial misgivings. When Ms. Langston and the soldiers left an hour and a half later with promises to return again in two days' time, Nizhoni breathed a sigh of relief, thankful for how their visit had gone. Despite her dislike of learning something new in the presence of another, she wasn't dreading her next lesson, and that was certainly something.

She determined that on Ms. Langston's next visit, she would give her a tour of the village and introduce her to her mother, sisters, and friends. Ms. Langston was going out of her way to help her. She wanted to make sure the kind woman got something out of the bargain as well. Niz wanted it to be a good trade for them both.

Wandering back to the village, she stopped to visit with the women and children who had gathered at the edge of camp to get a glimpse of the white woman. They remarked on her hair that was the color of the sun and inquired about her odd shape. Niz tried to explain that a bustle was part of white women's fashion (though she herself did not understand why) and invited them to meet her guest when she gave Ms. Langston a tour of the village following her next lesson. When she made it back to her own fire, she found Ever Flowering was still sleeping. Niz sat down with her books again and went over what Ms. Langston had taught her. Once she felt good about her progress, she put her books away carefully, intending to return them to the major in pristine condition.

With her studies done, she went back to coiling her basket. When Ever Flowering awakened a while later, the fever had left her, and she said she felt much better. She stayed to hear about Ms. Langston and the reading lesson, help Niz tighten her coil, and dream about the baby.

That night, Fire Maker asked how long it would be before she could read the bill of sale. Though disgruntled when he heard Major Taylor had predicted it would take nearly until they left for their winter camp for her to learn, Fire Maker only told her to try harder and hurry up with it before letting the topic go. He had finished his dinner by then and left to join his braves for the evening. Knowing he would be gone from the wickiup until late, she wandered over to her mother's fire, taking the basket she was working on with her.

An hour later, when their mother stepped out to check on Ever Flowering, Niz turned to Cloud Walking, her curiosity too much to contain. "Ever since our talk yesterday, I've been trying to guess who else you might have taken a liking to. Please, won't you tell me who it is? I won't tell anyone!"

She didn't like being left in the dark. If she didn't know what was going on, how could she help, guide, and protect those she loved?

Cloud Walking blushed and shook her head.

"Come on, Cloud Walking. Please?" Nizhoni begged. She'd been going over the other young men in the tribe over and over again and could think of no one else who seemed better suited for her sister than Strong Pine.

"I'm not ready to share yet. I don't know, maybe I never will be. It's possible nothing will come of it," Cloud Walking said, her last words bringing a cloud over her young face.

"It's clear you hope something will."

Cloud Walking shrugged in reply but said nothing more. Disappointed, Niz resigned herself to the fact that she was not going to find out who Cloud Walking was interested in. The girl had always been disappointingly good at keeping information close when she determined to do so. "Well, how was your walk with Strong Pine last night?"

"It was good," Cloud Walking answered, never looking up from the metate and mano she was using to grind seeds for their mother. Before she'd left the wickiup, Shy Fawn had announced she needed flour to use for the morning meal.

Nizhoni sifted her fingers through the tiny beads her mother was making out of porcupine quills and collecting in a basket. They were so small, yet she knew they would turn into a beautiful work of art in her mother's capable hands. "That's it? Just good? There's nothing else to report?"

Cloud Walking shrugged. "He's a nice young man."

"And?" Nizhoni pressed.

"And . . . he kissed me last night," her sister told her with a shy smile.

Nizhoni's eyes widened. "Did he?"

Cloud Walking nodded with a laugh. "Don't look so surprised. It isn't the first time."

"It isn't?" It was hard for Niz to accept her baby sister was old enough to be kissed.

"Nizhoni!" Cloud Walking cried, still laughing. She threw a cushion at Niz, hitting her in the chest. "I'm not a child. He's trying to convince me to become his wife and start a family together, remember?"

"But Cloud Walking . . . walks alone in the dark . . . kissing . . . you should be careful. You may not understand it yet, but too much time alone isn't wise. Perhaps you should take me with you next time Strong Pine asks you to go on a walk with him."

Cloud Walking's laughter died, and her expression turned indignant. "I understand!" she protested. "I understand exactly what you're talking about, Nizhoni. I'm not a child! I know how things work."

"Cloud Walking," Niz started, trying to soothe the offended teen. "That came out wrong. I know you're not a child. You're growing up. Sometimes, it's just hard to remember that. I'll always think of you as my kid sister." She held up her hands in concession. "But I know that you're not. You're a young woman now, with a beau and an offer of marriage and . . . and even your first—" Cloud Walking shook her head. "Second—" Another shake. "Third?" Nizhoni tried to keep the dismay out of her voice. Deciding she'd rather not wait for an answer, she plunged ahead.

"Anyway, you've been kissed. I just want to remind you to be careful. There's an order to these things. You keep saying Strong Pine is trying to convince you to start a family, and by that I assume you're speaking of marriage. But knowing you're not a child anymore, I want to remind you that you know—and he knows—that the ways of our people say he needs to present you with a gift and there must be a ceremony before you actually start a family."

Cloud Walking sent her a sassy look. "You know that's not the only way. Our people also consider the marriage official if we—" Cloud Walking stopped short as Shy Fawn ducked through the entrance.

Nizhoni sent the teen a look only an older sister could send but held her tongue with their mother back in the room. Clearly her little sister was not as innocent as she'd thought if she knew about the other way their people considered a marriage official.

When their mother stepped out to grab the start of the cradleboard she had left outside, Nizhoni wasted no time. "Don't you dare, Cloud Walking! Get the gift, have the ceremony—for mother's sake. You're her last daughter to marry!"

Cloud Walking rolled her eyes. "I know that," she answered dryly. "I was only pointing out that it's not the only way. Besides, I'm not even sure I want to be Strong Pine's wife, so don't worry. I'm not going to agree to anything—one way or the other—until I'm certain of what I want."

"Well, make sure that you don't," Niz conceded grimly, feeling far from relieved. She remembered what young men could be like when they fancied themselves in love. Strong Pine cared deeply for Cloud Walking. Niz could see it every time he looked at her sister. But he needed to keep his kisses to himself. There was a proper order to things and she was not above reminding him of it if need be.

Shy Fawn came back in with the base of the cradleboard that she was fashioning out of ponderosa pine, and the conversation ended. Cloud Walking sulked, and Nizhoni glowered.

Frustrated by her own naivety, Niz realized the situation was much more serious than she'd first assumed. What she had imagined being innocent and adorable young love that would eventually result in a marriage proposal sometime in the next several months, had already progressed into a legitimate relationship complete with physical affection and plans for the future—and all without her knowing! As Cloud Walking's big sister, she wasn't sure how she felt about that. What was even more disturbing was knowing that Cloud Walking's crush, whom she couldn't figure out, though she was certain it couldn't be anyone as well matched, was robust enough to keep the young woman from Strong Pine, even when the brave was seriously pursuing her.

"My, it's quiet in here," Shy Fawn observed, her attention still on the cradleboard. "What were you girls talking about while I was checking on your sister?"

"Nothing," Cloud Walking answered quickly.

"Yes, nothing," Nizhoni agreed grumpily.

"It seems like a serious nothing," Shy Fawn teased gently.

Unable to hold back a smile, Nizhoni turned her attention to her mother. "How was Ever Flowering?"

Lines of worry appeared on her mother's forehead. "Coughing."

"Is the fever back?" Niz questioned.

Shy Fawn shook her head. "No, just a cough tonight."

She considered her mother's face. "Do you think it's serious?"

Her mother hesitated and Nizhoni's heart skipped a beat. "It's too early to jump to conclusions. We'll make sure she rests, eats well, and sleeps well, and give her the medicines from the earth. There's no reason to doubt she'll be feeling better very soon," Shy Fawn finished, propping up an encouraging smile.

Niz hoped her mother was right, but she couldn't shake the worry that filled her. Shy Fawn began telling stories from childhood, and Nizhoni and Cloud Walking listened intently, never tiring of them no matter how many times they'd heard them before. But tonight, even her mother's stories weren't enough to make Nizhoni forget all that troubled her.

When Shy Fawn and Cloud Walking were ready to sleep, she walked home feeling grim. More than ever, she realized she needed to keep close tabs on her youngest sister's love life as well as Ever Flowering's health. She was desperate to keep those she loved happy, healthy, and safe, and she would do whatever it took to make that happen.

Ten

The next morning, Fire Maker and most of the men set off on a hunt. With the potential of winter weather just over a month away, they were eager to fill their meat stores so that when they left for their winter camp, they would have plenty of food to get their people through. Nizhoni was thankful they were good providers, and even more thankful that there was still wild game to hunt to keep their bellies full. Though they heard stories that game was growing scarce on the far side of the mountains and out onto the plains, they hadn't seen it. The herds of elk in their high mountains were still abundant, the mule deer still frequented the riverbanks in strong numbers, and there were still plenty of bighorn sheep to find if one knew where to look.

She contemplated the animals, the westward expansion, and what it meant for her people as she moved quietly through the woods. Stopping near the river, she set a little snare for rabbits who came to drink. She had already set several, hoping to catch enough to make a big pot of stew for her loved ones while the men were away hunting. Every meal she could gather fresh from the land was a meal they didn't have to take from their stores for the winter.

Niz collected acorns from the thickets of Gambel Oaks as she went, adding them to her satchel. Today she was only taking the occasional ripe one, but soon they would all ripen, and she would come back with the other women to gather them in earnest. That's when they would have to be most vigilant to watch out for bears, who also liked the nutrient-rich nuts. Still, she stayed alert and watchful as she worked.

When her snares were set and her satchel was full, she headed back to camp. Her heart settled as she walked, her worries from the night before not seeming quite so ominous in the light of day. Ever Flowering had woken up feeling better, except for a slight, nagging cough that persisted, and Cloud Walking had seemed much improved in humor. Nizhoni surmised the teenager had likely just been tired from the day and a little on edge, eager to prove her independence. With Fire Maker away, the next few days spread out before her, gloriously peaceful and uncomplicated.

For a few days she wouldn't have to worry about his temper, suspicion, or selfishness. She wouldn't have to feel guilty about not being with child or fearful that he would come home having had too much to drink. She wouldn't have to worry that the soldiers would come and Fire Maker would bait them into a confrontation, stress about having his meals ready exactly when he wanted them, or constantly be anxious about saying the wrong thing. Weary of the tension in their home, she was thankful for the break.

The day passed happily as she went about her work and studies. That night, she made dinner for her mother, sisters, and her friend Soaring Eagle and her small son. They ate the flat bread, dried elk meat, and fresh huckleberries together around her fire. Laughter and conversation filled the evening as they sat outside her wickiup late into the night, enjoying one another as they all worked on their individual tasks.

Nizhoni continued to weave her basket, Shy Fawn worked on the cradleboard for Ever Flowering, Soaring Eagle nursed her son to sleep, and Cloud Walking hemmed a pair of buckskin leggings she was making to wear when the snow began to fall. At their urging, Ever Flowering just rested on her sleeping mat.

When the group finally began to disperse for the night, with both Fire Maker and Walks With Power away, Nizhoni encouraged Ever Flowering to sleep over. She was glad she had when Ever Flowering woke up shivering and drenched with sweat in the middle of the night.

"I thought the fever had gone," Ever Flowering whispered, her teeth chattering.

"It will. It's just a little relapse," Niz soothed as she settled another blanket over her sister and stoked the fire.

She brewed Ever Flowering more tea and helped her sit up to drink it. Once the tea was gone, Niz dipped a cloth in water and washed her sister's face before draping it over Ever Flowering's forehead. When the fever persisted, she wrapped wet cloths around her wrists and shins as well.

In the morning, though Niz struggled to keep her eyes open, the fever had vanished again. That made the restless night worthwhile. In fact, she was so much improved that when Nizhoni tried to convince her sister to stay in bed and rest, Ever Flowering protested. She was only a little tired, she said, but otherwise felt fine.

Knowing Ms. Langston and the soldiers would be there before the sun rose too high in the sky, Nizhoni hurried to check her snares. Finding she'd had success, she processed the harvest, and prepped the dinner she would cook later. Finishing her preparations, she hurried through her wickiup, tidying up. After her lesson, she planned to give Ms. Langston a tour, and if the woman had been dreaming about what a native village might look like for four years, she wanted to make sure her home looked nice. Ducking back out into the sunshine, she realized it was later than she'd thought. She walked quickly to the edge of camp with her books and a blanket, hoping the little group hadn't already arrived and been left waiting.

But the place where they had met was empty and the mountain meadow still. Spreading her blanket over the fallen log, she dropped down with a relieved sigh. She'd made it in time. Waiting for Ms. Langston, she tipped her face up to the sky and breathed deeply, pausing to soak in all the summertime beauty for the first time that day.

The heat of the August sun stirred the sweet scent of late summer, releasing the smell of sagebrush and baking grasses into the air. The wind was gentle, softly rustling the aspen leaves overhead. Their silver-green shimmer caught the light, flickering pretty patterns over the ground beneath. The low hum of insects and the occasional call of a hawk circling above the treetops combined like a symphony with the faint sound of women talking and children laughing in the nearby camp.

Relaxing, Nizhoni closed her eyes for a moment, and yawned, her restless night catching up to her. Her thoughts began to drift. Hearing Ms. Langston's story forty-eight hours ago had been difficult. It had brought it all back—her loss, her longing, her shattered hopes. Yet, it had helped too. Though she was sorry for Ms. Langston's pain, it was oddly comforting to know the young widow understood how she felt and vice versa.

Opening her eyes again, she saw three horses on the horizon. The sight of them brought the familiar ache back up again. But though grief lingered heavy in her chest, today—in the hush of the mountains, beneath the expanse of the heavens—something deep and great stirred. It was almost like the wind rustling the leaves, but deep inside her. The ache did not leave, but it softened. A tragedy that still held so much heartache, suddenly got drenched with deep peace. She took several moments to soak in the moment, unaccustomed to peace so deep that it seemed to go beyond the natural beauty surrounding her, beyond her loss, beyond her grief, beyond her worry about her sisters, Fire Maker, or her people. In that moment, peace held her.

Uncertain of what was happening, her eyes did a wide sweep of the land—painted with wildflowers clinging stubbornly to the end of their bloom, and distant peaks dusted with snow. The world felt both eternal and fleeting. Again, something stirred within her. Something solid and sure, timeless and all-knowing. She grasped after it, not comprehending what it was but feeling a holy presence, nonetheless.

A horse whinnied as it crossed the river. She turned toward it, distracted from the stirring, the peace, and the whisper of something she couldn't quite make out.

The soldiers dismounted and helped Ms. Langston down. The golden-haired woman had come in a sensible blue calico today, with a matching—though rather plain—hat, but somehow managed to look just as stunning. The blue of her dress brought out the vibrant blue of her eyes, and for a moment, Nizhoni found herself staring. Once she recovered, she noticed the youngest of the two soldiers, one she hadn't seen before, seemed to be having the same problem.

"Nizhoni! How good to see you again. It's a lovely day, isn't it? I am just so pleased I get to spend it out riding in the wonder of God's green earth rather than staying stuck away inside my house, doing the baking as I should be. Do you smell that smell? Tell me, what is it?" Ms. Langston bubbled, coming forward.

Niz had forgotten just how forthright and talkative Ms. Langston was. Recovering from a brief stunned silence, she breathed in the scent of the warm summer air. "It's sagebrush, Ms. Langston."

The golden-haired woman looked taken aback. "Please, don't call me Ms. Langston. That makes me feel so old and . . . widowed. It's Marigold . . . between us ladies," she tacked on, looking pointedly at the young soldier who had still not managed to drag his eyes from her. The other soldier, the one who had helped Niz find the major at the fort, elbowed the younger one, sending him a warning look.

"We'll be over here if you need us, Ms. Langston," the slightly older soldier said, dragging the younger one—who looked to be barely old enough to shave—a short distance away to stand guard.

"Thank you, Sergeant Green," Marigold answered. She turned and moved to join Nizhoni at the fallen log. Her cheeks grew pink. "Thank you for bringing a blanket this time. You didn't need to. I wore an everyday dress today. I feel so silly about last time. I don't know why I wore my Sunday best. I'm sure you think me frivolous."

Nizhoni shook her head, slowly coming out of the daze that Marigold Langston always seemed to bring on. She was so talkative, so pretty, so lively, so honest, so . . . much. It was a little overwhelming, but Nizhoni liked her. She'd spent her entire life being a little extra herself, and she appreciated Marigold's enthusiasm. She smiled. "No, don't feel silly. I remember how it felt to wear beautiful dresses. Sometimes, you just need to wear one to remind yourself you're strong enough to face the day."

Marigold's blue eyes grew wide and then filled with mirth. "That's exactly it! I could not have said it better myself." She paused. "You know, now that you say that, I think maybe I wore that dress because it was Robert's favorite. I didn't have the conscious thought, but I wonder if I didn't wear it just to give myself courage . . . the confidence and courage that he used to give me. Hm!" She shrugged her thin shoulders, seeming amused. "That's so interesting, isn't it? All the thoughts we think that we never know we do, and the conversations we have with ourselves without words. What a wonder!" she exclaimed again with a little laugh.

"Was your dress spoiled?" Niz asked, worried. It must have saddened Marigold if she'd ruined her husband's favorite dress.

The blonde waved the thought away. "Oh no! If there's one thing I'm good at, it's laundry. It came clean, and I got the smell of horses out of it too. Thank goodness!" She opened the first book. "Alright, where did we leave off?"

The words were getting harder, and Nizhoni grew frustrated with the lesson and with herself. She wanted to *know* how to read, but she didn't want to *learn* how to read. It was hard and made her head feel thick. Marigold was kind and encouraging, but Niz still found herself gritting her teeth, just focusing on making it through. Her head ached by the time they were finished. Marigold gave her instructions to practice the words frequently in her absence.

"I know it's hard," Marigold said as she stood, "but if you keep at it, it *will* get easier. And it'll be worth it in the end."

Niz nodded, but she didn't feel convinced. With her head pounding like it was, she felt like sending the books back to Major Taylor via Marigold and never looking at them again.

Marigold reached out and put her hand on Niz's shoulder with a kind smile. "Once you learn to read, it's not something you forget. It's one task that will stay done, and those are rare, so that's something. You won't have to learn it ever again."

"Thank goodness for that," Nizhoni muttered.

She should have learned from Raya. Though that would have been difficult, too, at least it would have been done and over with.

"I suppose I'd better be going—like I mentioned earlier, it's baking day."

Sergeant Green choked nearby, drawing their attention. "Sorry," he said, holding his hand up to signify he was good.

"Anyway, I'll be back again day after tomorrow," Marigold promised.

Nizhoni forced herself to stand, too, and continue as planned, headache or no headache. "My husband and the other braves are gone hunting, so the camp is quiet. If you would like to see our village, today would be a good day."

Marigold's face lit up. "Truly?" Niz nodded. "Oh, I would love that! I've been hoping, but I didn't want to be rude and ask. But genuinely, I wouldn't have minded if your husband and the braves were here. I wouldn't have been frightened. Unless they wouldn't have been agreeable to having a stranger in their village. I do understand that, I promise I do."

Honestly, Nizhoni wasn't sure what Fire Maker and the braves would make of Ms. Langston. Fire Maker had agreed to have a woman out to teach Niz to read. But she didn't know how he would react to the pretty young widow, and she had no faith in his manners, his inner compass, or his wisdom. That was why she'd elected to continue her reading lessons outside of camp where Major Taylor had started them. She'd known Fire Maker's pride would keep him from seeking them out, and she thought the distance best. Niz certainly didn't want him doing or saying anything that would offend Marigold or bring the wrath of the army down upon them all. It just seemed like a better idea to show Marigold the village when he wasn't around, and the hunting trip had presented the perfect opportunity to do so.

"It's not that," she assured. "Come on. Let me introduce you to some people, and I'll show you my wickiup."

"Your what?" Marigold asked, her blue eyes widening.

"My wickiup . . . my home."

"Oh! I thought your people lived in tipis?"

"No, that's mostly out on the Great Plains where the buffalo are plentiful," Niz explained. "Here in the mountains, we have brush shelters your people would call wickiups. We use what we have. Kind of like how back East people live in sawed board or brick houses but here in the West most settlers live in log cabins."

"Around Ft. Sidney many of the homesteaders live in sod houses. I suppose we all use what resources we have available."

Niz nodded. "Exactly. I saw a picture of a sod house in a newspaper once. It had grass on the roof."

Marigold smiled brightly. "Yes, they do! And inside they smell musty like the earth, though many people whitewash the walls to make them feel brighter and cleaner."

Niz shook her head faintly, trying to imagine what it would be like to live in a house with white walls. Other than the hides they hung up for insulation, she'd never known walls that weren't natural wood. "Come on," she finally said, motioning for Marigold to follow. "I'll take you to my wickiup and then show you around the village."

The women relayed their plan to Sergeant Green before heading into camp. The soldiers stayed behind, visibly relaxing once Niz shared that Fire Maker and the braves were out hunting. Her people watched as they passed, staring unashamedly at the white woman. Ducking under the hide that hung at her doorway, Nizhoni led the way into her wickiup. Marigold followed, wide-eyed as she stepped into the dim interior.

Knowing how fascinated she had been when she went into the Applewoods' cabin for the first time and seen how they lived, she gave Marigold a thorough tour. She pointed out the hides that were stacked several deep to give them a soft place to lay, and the wool blankets and hides that she rolled up for her sleeping mat. Niz showed her the differences between the conical shaped, open weave baskets they used for gathering and the tighter coiled baskets they used for food storage. She set her new pitched basket in Marigold's hands.

"This one is coiled the tightest and covered with sap. Look what's inside."

Marigold peered into the basket and sniffed it. Her brows drew together as she looked up at Niz. "Is it water?"

Niz smiled brightly. "Yes! Very good! We use these pitched baskets to store and carry water."

"Why not use pottery? I read many natives do."

Niz nodded with understanding. "Our people are nomadic. We follow the food and the seasons. We're constantly moving throughout the year. This is our summer camp, but soon, we will go to our winter camp at lower elevations. This camp is small, only thirty-five wickiups, but at the winter camp we will join with other bands of our people to swap news, share stories, and rest, so it is large. Moving so much, we need items that are strong. These baskets don't break as easily as pottery—they're hearty. We don't have to worry about them breaking and spilling all our water when we're far from the river."

Niz turned and spread her arms toward the structure. "Our homes are simple for the same reason. We only have what is functional and practical. These brush shelters are easy to build and dismantle. The conical shape helps them stand up to the wind, rain, and snow. It's stable even when the ground is uneven, and they're easy to construct using what we have available—aspen and pine. We build our fires in the middle like so, and leave openings overhead for the smoke to go out. Some bands of our people wrap their shelters in canvas, kind of a mix between tipis and wickiups."

Niz opened baskets and showed her the dried berries, meat, nuts, and seeds within. "These are a metate and mano. Sit down in front of it on your knees."

Marigold did, and Niz sprinkled some seeds over the flat metate. Demonstrating how to hold it, she put the round mano in Marigold's hand and taught her how to use it. She showed her the pieces of rawhide they used for plates, their turtle shell bowls, hollowed gourd dipper, her metal knife with the shaped antler handle guard, and its ornate blue and white beaded sheath. Marigold took it all in with wide-eyed wonder. Finally, Niz showed her the doll her mother had made her from traded muslin when she was a child, adorned with seed beads and horsehair.

Marigold ran her fingers over it softly. "It's beautiful. The beadwork is so intricate."

Niz smiled. "My mother worked hard on it."

"She must love you very much to put so much effort into decorating your doll."

Niz smiled again and nodded. Even when Shy Fawn scolded and fussed at her, she knew it was born of her deep love. "She does."

She returned the doll to the satchel under her hides for safe keeping and pointed out the differences between the elk, deer, and sheep hides she slept on. Encouraging Marigold to run her fingers through the coarse furs, she said, "In the winter, we hang hides around the inside of our shelters to insulate us from the cold. With hides on the walls and the fire burning, we stay quite warm."

"That's what Robert said," Marigold agreed, her eyes misty. "He wore buckskin and had a big buffalo robe. He said he was warmer in that than he ever was in a wool coat."

Nizhoni nodded. "I'm sure that's true. I wore dresses and coats like you when I was married, and hides are warmer."

"What's it like coming back after being away?" Marigold asked curiously, still running her fingers through the fur of the elk hide.

"I missed my family and my people, so it's good to be home, with them," Nizhoni answered carefully. She wouldn't open the lid on anything unpleasant; she wouldn't talk about how much she missed Alex or share about her troubles with Fire Maker. All that mattered was being back home with her people.

"Do you miss your husband?" Marigold asked, her voice very solemn, her blue eyes very large and very sad.

"He won't be away long," Niz said, looking down. She wouldn't express just how thankful she was to have him gone. "They'll hunt only a few days, a week at the longest."

"No, your first husband. Alex. Major Taylor told me about him. He told me how he was his best friend, about the fun they had, and . . . and about your husband now."

Nizhoni caught her breath, upset for a moment that the major had shared her story with Ms. Langston. She wondered what all he had told her, and if Marigold had agreed to come out of pity. She could hardly bear the thought of it.

"Are you and the major close?" she asked instead, lifting her chin a little, choosing not to respond.

"Somewhat, I suppose. He was a friend of Robert's, but I didn't know him well. Over the past few months, I've gotten to know him a little more. He's been kind enough to check on me to make sure I have everything I need and to help me arrange transportation back to Fort Sidney. He's been helpful as I've dealt with Robert's death and decide what to do next. He seems like a wonderful man."

"Yes," Nizhoni answered simply. "He does."

There was an awkward silence before Marigold threw out her hand imploringly. "I'm sorry if I shouldn't have brought up your husband."

For a moment, Niz's hardness held before she felt it crumbling. She let out a deep sigh. "It's not that. I can't speak of the departed. I don't want to anger the spirits. And . . . it hurts to think of . . . how things were. I'd rather think of other things."

"The spirits?" Marigold questioned, seeming confused. Suddenly, her face filled with deep compassion. "Oh, I see. I'm sorry. That must be very difficult not to be able to reminisce or share your pain or talk about him. I don't know how you do it. Everything I think comes right out of my mouth; sometimes it even comes out my mouth before I think it, which is most inconvenient at times. Robert used to say I couldn't have a thought without saying it."

"You're not at all worried? About speaking of the dead?"

"No," Marigold answered, her blue eyes clear and unguarded. "I serve a different, God, Nizhoni. The God I serve is to be greatly revered and respected, and I do, but I'm not afraid. I know He loves me, and His actions are based in that love, not rage. I don't want to grieve His heart, and I live my life accordingly, but I don't live in fear of accidentally angering Him. A number of years ago, I encountered the perfect love of God, and once I did, I realized there was nothing to fear because everything He does is loving."

"Nothing to fear?" Nizhoni echoed, recoiling at Marigold's words. "Is death loving? Is you being a widow loving?" Her voice rose with each question. "If your God allows such painful things to happen, how can you believe that? If that's what His love feels like, how can you believe that love is nothing to fear?"

It was the question she'd been asking since the day of the fire—the mystery that made her blood boil and her chest feel heavy. She'd heard it all before.

She was certain the God Marigold spoke of was the same one the Applewoods served—it was always about love with them too: love, faith, and trust. And for the last year she'd been with them, she'd been listening closer and closer. Though she pretended she wasn't, she'd been taking it all in, even as she continued to follow the traditions of her people. Her heart had begun to ask, what if it were true? What if love so deep really existed? What if she really didn't have to live in fear of the spirits, always worried she would disrupt them? What if Jesus Christ really did offer freedom, forgiveness, and hope? What if He really did love and care about His followers?

But then she'd seen the mill engulfed in flames, the black plume rising up to the clouds. She'd felt the heavy smoke in her lungs, the heat of the blaze on her face; staggered under the grief of knowing her beloved husband was inside. Nizhoni had lived through the excruciating pain of watching her infant son take his last breath. Running out of her little cabin, the four walls suddenly too small to hold her grief, the lifeless baby clutched against her chest, she had been greeted with the blackened ashes of the mill, her husband, and his brothers. Her heart had felt like it was exploding, the pain too much to bear. And she had known in that moment that no matter what part of her heart had wanted to believe in the Applewoods' God of love, she could never serve a God whose love felt like that.

She turned tormented eyes toward Marigold and encountered blue pools of peace and compassion staring back at her. Marigold reached out and put her hand on Niz's shoulder. "You may wonder how God could allow such suffering and think it's a reflection of His character, but suffering is part of the world we live in. No matter which God we serve, suffering comes."

Niz inhaled deeply through her nose and looked away, studying the pattern of the wool blanket stretched over her sleeping mat. "I suppose that's true," she finally admitted. After all, her father had passed away in a hunting accident just as Alex had perished in a fire.

Marigold's blue eyes lit up. "But what's most remarkable about Jesus Christ is that He wasn't willing to watch our suffering from the distance and comfort of heaven. He was so moved by the plight of man, that He came to earth at His own peril. He engaged our broken story, shared in our suffering, died an excruciating death and rose again to rewrite the end of the story. He came to give us hope!"

"Hope?" Niz echoed in disbelief. She barely remembered what hope felt like.

"Yes, hope," Marigold answered gently. "Hope that one day suffering will come to an end. Hope that death does not have the final word. Hope that after death comes eternal life—life with Him where there is no more sickness, no more sadness, no more brokenness or imperfection. We suffer now, yes. But He proved that He cares about us, Nizhoni, so much so that He would enter into our suffering so that He could relate to us in it. He didn't stay far off where it was safe. He made a way to draw near so that He could be right here with us through the pain, so we never have to suffer alone."

Niz wanted to cry out that she was suffering alone, but she didn't. She would not open the door on her grief. Not here. Not now.

Marigold's face softened, as if she could read Niz's thoughts. "Nizhoni, Jesus Christ died, proving He was human. He rose from the grave, proving He is God. And the cross proves that He loves us. Though they nailed His hands and feet to the wood, it was His love that kept Him there. He could have called down angels to rescue Him, but He didn't, because while He could have escaped the pain and suffering, it was the cross that gave Him us."

Niz raised her chin. She didn't want to feel. She didn't want to be reminded of the nights she'd spent sitting in Mother Emaline's cabin, listening to Raya read the Scriptures. She didn't want to remember what it had felt like when hope had fluttered in her heart like a fragile seedling emerging from rocky soil. She didn't want to remember what it was like when that hope had been snuffed out by the pain of all she had lost. *She didn't want to feel.* "How can you say all this when your husband is dead?" she asked harshly.

Marigold's blue eyes held hers for a long moment. The woman inhaled deeply before giving a slight shrug of her dainty shoulders. "I am dreadfully sad Robert is gone from this life. I am heartbroken to be a widow, but I don't blame God. I thank Him because He's here with me, helping me get through it. He didn't cause my heartbreak, Nizhoni, rather, He is my only hope to find a way through it. The only thing in the whole wide world that truly offers a lasting way out of suffering is Jesus. Do I fear speaking of Robert since that terrible day? Not at all, because Robert is not dead. Robert is alive. His place of residence changed, but because of Jesus, He lives. And because of that, I will talk about him with total peace and with so much love in my heart, just as I would have when he lived in our home."

Nizhoni stared at her for a long moment, something stirring deep within her again as it had earlier. Peace. She barely knew what that felt like apart from the mountain vistas, the song of the wind in the trees, the fresh morning air, and the evening sunsets. In those moments, nestled in the stillness and beauty of nature, she felt it. But what would it be like to feel it within? What would it be like to be at peace all day every day?

She swallowed hard. Peace in her mind and heart felt distant and unheard of. She felt fear of loss, fear of hardship and pain, fear of the future—for herself, for the ones she loved, for her people. She felt this incredible need to be strong enough to hold everything together for everyone, and the weight of it was crushing.

It drove her—it was the reason she got up in the mornings, the purpose that kept her going when she felt too sad to face another day, the thing that kept her from succumbing to Fire Maker. Long ago she had realized she wasn't on the earth for herself, rather she wanted to use her life to make other people's lives better. She still believed it wholeheartedly. But feeling solely responsible for keeping things good and her loved ones happy, taking the weight of that on her own shoulders, was a heavy burden to bear. Stress, anxiety, and fear kept her mind on overdrive as she sought to keep things from falling apart.

She wondered if the peace she saw in Marigold's blue eyes truly came from her God. Marigold had also experienced great loss and sadness. But there was no hardness, no bitterness in her blue eyes, nor did she seem to be suppressing it, keeping it buried under, afraid of the magnitude of it, as Niz was. Marigold spoke easily and freely of her grief, of her husband, of their love. She was living through the pain, dealing with it as it came, brave enough to face it rather than keeping it stuffed down.

For a moment, Nizhoni was jealous. For a moment, she wished she could do the same. But then reality returned. She couldn't. She couldn't deal with her loss as Marigold was. The truth was, she wasn't free to speak of her grief, of her loss, of her husband or her son. Nor did she want to face it. People were depending on her. What if she broke down? What if she wasn't okay? She couldn't take the chance of dissolving into a mess of grief. She had to stay strong. She had to press on. She had to hold it all together.

Suddenly, Niz felt very tired. Tired, and uncomfortable with the truth she'd looked in the eyes for one brief moment. But like she always did, she moved all the thoughts, all the feelings to the background of her consciousness, pressing them down to do what needed doing. It was time to get back to business.

Turning, she lifted the hide over the door. "Come on, I'll introduce you to my mother and sisters," she said, keeping her tone cheerful.

Marigold wasn't to blame—she had no idea what her words had stirred up. She'd only been answering Niz's question. It was the internal war that Niz raged against—the grief that she refused, the pressure that she carried, and the question—oh, the question she couldn't quite crush—*what if it were true*?

Marigold followed, and Niz led her to Shy Fawn's wickiup. Cloud Walking was sitting outside, sewing her new leggings. A basket full of roots and wild onions sat beside her.

"This is my sister, Cloud Walking," Nizhoni said, gesturing to the girl. "Cloud Walking, this is the woman who is teaching me to read, Marigold Langston."

Cloud Walking watched Marigold with wide brown eyes that nearly looked frightened. But when Marigold smiled brightly, Cloud Walking smiled back.

"How do I say hello in your language?" Marigold asked. Niz told her, and Marigold turned back to Cloud Walking and greeted her in their native tongue. Cloud Walking smiled again.

"How do I say it in English?" Cloud Walking asked Niz. Again, Niz demonstrated, and Cloud Walking said, "Hello."

Marigold smiled brightly. Squatting down on her heels, staying a respectful distance away, she studied the garment Cloud Walking was sewing. "It's very nice work. What is that she's using to sew with?" she asked.

Nizhoni sat down beside Cloud Walking as she translated. Cloud Walking patted the ground beside her and Marigold moved to sit next to her. Cloud Walking handed Marigold the garment and needle, and Marigold inspected it curiously.

"It's sinew," Niz answered. "We collect it from animals. It's gathered from the . . . hmmm, let me think how to say it . . . tendons of deer and elk. We twist it into thread, and it's very good and strong to use for sewing. The needle is one she made from an elk bone. The bone is splintered, and the splinters are trimmed into the rough size and shape of a needle, then ground and polished smooth. She sewed all her clothing this same way—the dress she wears and these leggings that will keep her warm once the snow begins to fall. Even her moccasins she sewed."

Marigold's eyes moved to Cloud Walking's shoes, and a bright smile filled her face. "They're beautiful! The beadwork she did is simply extraordinary!"

"She likes your moccasins," Niz told her sister, and Cloud Walking laughed, though she seemed pleased by the compliment. "Cloud Walking is very good at beadwork, just like our mother. They have a gift for it."

"Yes, I can certainly see that they do. It is beautiful."

Niz relayed Marigold's words, and then asked, "Where is Mother?"

"She went to the river with Ever Flowering. They should be back before long. But look, I gathered these for you to use in the stew later," Cloud Walking said, gesturing to her basket.

"What did she say?" Marigold asked curiously.

"With most of the men gone, I'm making dinner for my family later. She gathered these for the stew."

"What are they?"

"Those are wild onions, and those are kind of similar to what you call potatoes. They are native to the land. We do not plant or cultivate them, but we harvest them."

"May I try a tiny bit of one?" Marigold inquired.

"No! You wouldn't want to now. They're very bitter and would make you sick. Cloud Walking will boil them in clay to make them less bitter before washing them and adding them to my stew," Nizhoni said before turning and relaying the conversation to Cloud Walking. Leaning over, Cloud Walking took several of the potatoes and put them in Marigold's hand so she could have a closer look.

"Boil in clay?" Marigold asked, her eyes widening as she rolled the little tubers over in her hand. "How did she learn to do that?"

"Our mother taught her, just as her mother taught her, and so on. Our people know the plants of the earth, the trees, and the animals. We know what plants heal and what plants harm. We know what insects to eat, and which ones can make you sick." Nizhoni laughed as she watched the color drain out of Marigold's face. "I know eating insects sounds very odd to you, but our people consider them a valuable food source in years of scarcity. We harvest our food from the earth, moving with the seasons, gathering and hunting what's available. In early summer, sometimes we gather grasshoppers and crickets, chop them up, and mix them with berries to make little fruit cakes that can be eaten on the go. Other times, we add them to stews or grind them up like flour. They're not my favorite, but they make do when our meat stores run low."

"Well, you certainly have lots of knowledge. If I was ever to get lost in the woods, I most assuredly would hope it was with you," Marigold declared.

"We're still learning. If you get lost, get lost with our mother," Cloud Walking said with a laugh when Niz finished translating.

"She's right," Niz agreed.

Marigold smiled warmly, rolled the small potatoes over in her hand once more, and then handed them back to Cloud Walking with a nod of thanks. "Will you put crickets in your stew?"

"No, I snared three rabbits this morning. I already dressed them and have them waiting for the stew," Niz said proudly, gesturing to where her rabbits lay, covered with a cloth. Discerning the direction of the conversation, Cloud Walking lifted the cloth to show off their dinner. Marigold lost a little more color in her face.

"My, that is quite . . . resourceful of you," Marigold stammered, seemingly trying to be brave, though she only succeeded in looking a little ill.

Niz laughed. "Did your husband not hunt?"

Marigold grimaced. "All the time. But he didn't bring it in the house until it no longer resembled an animal. Nowadays, I prefer the bins of salt pork at the store." She paused. "Though it's not an easy life by any means, us army wives aren't like settlers. There are always plenty of men around to do the dirty work. There's so few of us in forts that I daresay we're a little spoiled by frontier standards."

Niz gave her an understanding smile. "I know dressing a rabbit probably seems a little distasteful, but it's not so different from butchering a chicken, and I did that while living with the Applewoods. It seems like that often falls under even civilized women's tasks."

"West of the Mississippi, that's probably true. I've butchered plenty of chickens in my time," Marigold conceded. "Not that I enjoy the task, but when they stop laying, I must say it is a treat to have fried chicken."

"Yes, it certainly is. Fried chicken was one of my favorite meals at the Applewoods!" Niz said, her eyes sparkling. "Here, things are different. We're hunters and gatherers, not farmers, so we harvest what the earth has to give us. We steward the earth's resources carefully, not taking more than we need, not depleting it. We store up food in the summer and fall to get us through the deep snows and cold temperatures until the earth gives its bounty again. So if I can gather meals for my loved ones instead of dipping into our winter stores, I will gladly do so."

"That makes sense," Marigold said firmly. "Who all will you cook for tonight? Major Taylor said you're a wonderful cook."

Niz warmed at the compliment. "Did he? That was kind of him. Tonight, I will cook for my mother and my sisters, Cloud Walking and Ever Flowering, and my friend, Soaring Eagle . . . and anyone else who wonders over to our fire when it's time to eat! Ever Flowering is with child and hasn't been feeling well. Soaring Eagle has a young son. Since I do not, and am able-bodied and enjoy it, it makes sense that I would cook for our group."

"Well, I wish I could stay and join you for dinner, but I'm not sure my escorts would be eager to be gone from the fort after dark. Nor do I want to presume on Major Taylor's good nature. He loaned me his men to escort me, and I should return them at a decent hour. Which reminds me, I'd best be heading back. Oh!" Marigold exclaimed with a jump.

Cloud Walking and Niz began laughing and couldn't stop. Behind Marigold, Lean Elk's small daughter had crept up to touch the woman's golden hair. Now she stood transfixed, petting Marigold's bright tresses.

Turning, a bright smile filled Marigold's face. "Hello!" she said warmly.

Leaping Water jumped back, her brown eyes wide and sparkling, a shy smile on her face.

"It's alright, you don't have to be scared," Marigold said, holding her hand out to the girl.

Leaping Water stared at her, holding back, and then looked at Nizhoni. Niz smiled and nodded to the girl. When she did, Leaping Water took Marigold's hand and went to sit beside her.

"They say your hair shines like the sun," Niz told Marigold, her eyes dancing.

"They?" Marigold asked.

Niz motioned to their left, and Marigold turned to see several children hiding behind the closest wickiup, peering around its corner. She laughed and waved to them.

"You can come out and say hello," Nizhoni called, and the children came forward, shy and giggling. They sat down beside Leaping Water.

Smiling, Marigold reached up and pulled the hairpins from her hair, letting it tumble down long and loose over her back. The children exclaimed in wonder and immediately stood up and began petting it as Leaping Water had. Leaping Water began to plait and braid the golden strands, talking as she did so. Instantly, all the children were plaiting and braiding Marigold's hair.

"What did she say?" Marigold asked, her head moving this way and that as children clamored to get more hair to braid.

"She said she's never braided the sunshine before," Niz told her with a laugh. Turning to the kids, she shooed them away. "Leave the sunshine alone before it all gets pulled out," she instructed warmly. The kids scampered off and Marigold laughed, watching them go.

"It's so beautiful how children are just children no matter where they live. They're not concerned with all the things we are. They're just children." A happy smile on her face, Marigold stood. "This has been so delightful, Nizhoni. Thank you for showing me around your village and introducing me to your sister."

Niz nodded and pushed herself to her feet. Marigold waved at Cloud Walking and then turned toward where the soldiers were waiting. Leaping Water shyly fell into step beside her and slipped her hand into Marigold's. Marigold smiled warmly at the little girl and swung her hand as they walked.

"If the men are still gone hunting when you come the day after tomorrow, I'll make dinner for you and the soldiers. And your little friend there too. We can all sit down and share a meal together," Niz offered.

"That sounds splendid!" Marigold answered, looking pleased. "I'll look forward to it."

Seeing Shy Fawn and Ever Flowering coming up from the river, Nizhoni waved them over. She introduced them to Marigold and translated back and forth for a few minutes before continuing on. She noticed Marigold was studying the village intently as they passed through it, as if she were trying to memorize every detail. When they made it back to the horses, Marigold sighed and impulsively turned and threw her arms around Nizhoni.

"Thank you for showing me around today! Thank you for giving me a tour of your village and for explaining so many things about how you live. I know Robert didn't grow up among your people, but still, you've shown me so many things he spoke of. It's like a missing puzzle piece in my heart has finally been found. Thank you."

"You're welcome," Niz replied, awkwardly patting Marigold's back. "I'm glad it's helped. I know getting used to life without him—the way it is now—is difficult. I'm happy I could help you find one of the missing pieces."

Niz knew from experience that Marigold's picture was still far from being full. Losing a loved one was like a puzzle being all broken up and scrambled, with some puzzle pieces disappearing altogether and the rest so badly stirred that it took a long time to make sense of it all again. She knew showing Marigold her village wouldn't make everything better, but she did hope it would help.

After promising to be back in two days' time, Marigold and the soldiers set off for the fort, and Nizhoni sighed, both a little relieved and a little sad. Despite the unpleasantness of learning to read, she liked Marigold. She was beginning to feel like a friend.

After giving Leaping Water a hug and sending her back to the village to her mother, Niz sat down in the baking grass, under the warmth of the summer sun. Gritting her teeth, she went over her lesson again, sounding out each word, practicing them over and over, determined to master them when so many were making sacrifices to give her the opportunity to learn.

Eleven

Nizhoni heard the horses before she saw them. Standing up quickly, she peered through the gathering darkness to scan the horizon, looking to see if it was the hunting party returning. As the sight registered, her heart sank. The small group of men riding toward the village were not their men coming home. They weren't even the soldiers coming to see Fire Maker. Though she had not seen them with her own eyes before, Nizhoni instinctively knew the painted men riding toward their summer camp were the raiding band of Comanche.

Turning, she glanced back over her beloved village, feeling as if time froze. She knew what raids between tribes were like. Horses would be stolen, men and women would be killed, children would be killed or taken. Her heart began to break. There wasn't one man, woman, or child in the camp that she was willing to lose—she knew and loved them all. Each had a place—loved ones—if they were lost . . . Yet there were no warriors left in camp beside the elders. Fire Maker and all the braves were gone. Only men too old to hunt, women, and children remained in the village.

But although she was not a man, she knew how to shoot a gun, and she was not going to let the Comanche plunder without a fight. She was the wife of the chief. She would fight to protect her people.

Springing into action, she began yelling at the others, alerting them to the danger. Ducking into her wickiup, she grabbed a rifle and ammunition and ran back out. The camp, which had just begun settling down to its nighttime routine, was suddenly chaotic with activity, people running this way and that.

"Hide the children! Grab any weapon you can use!" she yelled as she ran toward the approaching riders. Around her, women were screaming, children crying out in terror as they got pushed into shelters.

Seeing they had been discovered and no longer held the element of surprise, the raiders gave bloodcurdling war cries. Nizhoni's hands began to shake. Though her people did not live on the Great Plains, she'd heard tales about the Comanche. She knew they often attacked by the light of the late summer moon, just as they were now. They had a reputation for being fierce, strategic, and violent. She had selfishly hoped that their aggression would be reserved for the settlers and army they blamed for taking their lands, but it seemed it wasn't to be.

Nizhoni wished there was time for her people to disappear into the tall grasses along the riverbanks or fade into the forests. But already, the warriors were nearly upon them. In only thirty more seconds, they would be in camp. Raising her rifle, she took aim and fired. One of the warriors grabbed his arm. She took aim and fired again. The man on the far edge of the pack fell off his horse. He rolled across the ground and then jumped up, starting toward her on foot. Feeling someone beside her, she looked over in time to see Wise Hawk raise his rifle in his old, weathered hands. This time, the running warrior fell to the ground and did not get up.

The warriors shot back. Nizhoni and Wise Hawk ducked behind the wickiup they were sheltering behind. Even so, Nizhoni felt something like a searing knife graze her arm. She looked down grimly as bright blood instantly soaked through her torn buckskin. She'd been grazed by a bullet. Giving a shout of anger, knowing it was only the beginning of the bloodshed for her village if they didn't fend off the attackers, she raised her rifle and pulled the trigger. Beside her, Wise Hawk did the same. Again, a warrior fell to the ground. She wasn't sure by whose bullet he had fallen, but either way, there had been a dozen warriors, and now there were only ten. And one of those ten was wounded.

"You should hide, Nizhoni," Wise Hawk said, his weathered face full of sadness, his words and actions slow, despite the speed of those approaching. "You are too beautiful to be out here. They will find you and capture you."

"I will not leave our people!" she told him fiercely. "I will help you defend them."

Wise Hawk looked at her for a long moment. "At what cost to yourself? You've suffered much this year. Can you endure more?"

Nizhoni shut her mind to the fear his question brought up. People she loved were in danger—people she would give anything and everything to protect. She was not going to protect herself and leave them at the mercy of the raiding tribe. She couldn't. There was no one else to defend them. She would protect, not be protected.

She reloaded and fired again. Thirty feet to her left, a shot rang out, and she looked to see another elder wielding his rifle. Nearly at the same time, an arrow sped out toward the raiders, and Nizhoni saw Cloud Walking beyond the elder with a quiver of arrows on her back and a bow in her hands. She wanted to cry out to her sister and order her to disappear among the river reeds, but she knew they needed help, and Cloud Walking was a good shot.

Everything felt like it was happening quicker than lightning could strike. The Comanche were returning fire and drawing ever closer. Two more women came to join the defense, their children undoubtedly stowed away by now. But Nizhoni knew it wouldn't be enough. Could four women and two old men hope to be any match for ten warriors, schooled in the ways of war?

Suddenly, the Comanche were upon the camp. Nizhoni had to turn in toward the village to take aim now. Their war cries were adding to the chaos. Adrenaline pumped through her veins. She took aim more carefully and pulled the trigger of her rifle again, knowing that a stray bullet could have a heavy cost now that the Comanche were among them. Her shot hit one of the warriors in the arm, and he let out a guttural scream, then spun his horse around. His eyes were blazing as he looked across the distance at her.

"Nizhoni, run!" Wise Hawk whispered urgently. "Disappear and he will assume I fired the shot!"

"No! Please go, Wise Hawk! Let me answer for my actions," she argued hurriedly. The elder was so valuable to the tribe, and she loved him dearly—she couldn't leave him to face her consequences. Still, fear tapped a fast, irregular rhythm in her heart. Everything within her was screaming at her to run, to hide, to escape the coming pain.

His face full of rage, the Comanche warrior dug his heels into his horse, starting back toward them at a gallop.

"I'm afraid it's too late for either of us, my girl," the old man said grimly. With trembling hands, Nizhoni pressed her back against the wickiup, reloading her rifle as quickly as she could. She knew instinctively that she wasn't going to get it loaded in time.

Suddenly, like the sound of deliverance, a bugle call rang out through the moonlit night. Above the chaos of the raid, they all heard it. The warrior stopped his horse short, looking up toward the east. The Comanche yelled out to one another, and just as suddenly as he had turned toward them, the warrior spun his horse and sped off in the opposite direction. They raced through camp like streaks of lightning, the hoofbeats of their horses making the ground shake.

The Comanche were going for the horses; one of the warriors was opening the gate to the corral. She knew she should be terrified of what Fire Maker would do if his precious horses were lost on her watch, but all she could feel was relief. The Comanche were leaving the camp. The raid was ending. Niz could barely believe her eyes. Again, the sound of the bugle call came.

With pounding hoofbeats and shouts filled with foreign words she didn't understand, the Comanche suddenly were gone, melding into the night, several of the horses from the corral running along with them. Niz sank to the ground, her body trembling, overcome with relief. She would soon check on the others, but she needed a minute to get her bearings first. Silently, Wise Hawk leaned heavily against the wickiup, placing his hand on the top of her head for comfort. Only seconds later, the soldiers were upon the camp, their horses stretched out long, their flanks foamy with sweat.

"Niz!" Major Taylor shouted.

Pushing herself to her feet, she quickly moved out from behind the wickiup she'd been sheltering behind. Waving to get Ezra's attention, she watched relief flood his face.

"Which way?"

She pointed in the direction the Comanche had disappeared in, and he rode out without stopping, his men thundering along behind him.

With the Comanche and the soldiers gone and the attack over, an eerie stillness fell over the village. Niz let out a deep, deep sigh, and sank back against the wickiup again, her legs suddenly feeling too weak to hold her. From somewhere nearby, the sound of a woman crying broke through her consciousness. Rallying, she straightened, looking for the source of the sobs.

It didn't take long to find it. Noon Day Sun, the elder between her and Cloud Walking, had been struck down. He lay with his rifle still in his hands. His daughter had found him and was down on her knees by his side, weeping over her father. Niz took the scene in, her heart wrenching with grief. She had often sat at Noon Day Sun's knee to learn the oral history of their people. For as long as she could remember, Noon Day Sun had been a pillar in their community, offering wisdom and guidance, teaching the young ones, and providing stability and strength.

Moving toward the fallen man, Niz put her hand on his daughter's shoulder and squeezed. "After I check on the others, I'll be back to mourn him with you," she promised.

Seeing Noon Day Sun's family—daughters, granddaughters, and nieces—coming out of hiding and moving toward him, Niz left his daughter to her loved ones. Refusing to give into her tears, she began making her way through the village, taking in the damage, seeing who needed help. Snow Flower had been run over by one of the Comanche's horses, and her leg was badly broken. Nizhoni helped carry her into her daughter's wickiup and held her hand while the bone was set. Once the worst was over, she left her to the capable care of her daughter and the medicine man.

Back outside, she saw Wise Hawk on his knees on the ground, cutting his hair with his knife. Nizhoni knew what that meant, and her heart dropped. Someone he loved had died. Around him, Soaring Eagle and her sister-in-law were weeping and wailing. Niz could barely find the strength to approach them. She wanted to run from the grief and horror she knew she would find. But she was the wife of Fire Maker, chief of their people; in his absence her people looked to her for leadership. More importantly, she was their friend. So she walked toward them when she wanted to run away.

On the ground before Wise Hawk was Lean Elk's little daughter. The sweet little one had been asking her great-grandfather questions around the fire only a short time back and swinging Marigold's hand just hours earlier. Niz had hugged her that very afternoon before sending her home to her mother. Now, the child lay broken and lifeless. Moaning in grief, Nizhoni went down on her knees beside Soaring Eagle. The pain felt like too much. It didn't seem possible. It had only been earlier that day that the little girl had been giggling and braiding the sunshine.

"My baby, my sweet baby," Leaping Water's mother wailed.

"What happened?" Nizhoni asked Soaring Eagle sorrowfully. Grief was rising inside her, and she put a hand to her throat, pressing back against the ache that made it difficult to draw a breath.

Tears dripped off Soaring Eagle's face as she shook her head. Carried in a sling of fabric wrapped around his mother's neck and shoulder, her little boy peeked out at Niz, looking frightened. "I ran down to the river with Two Hawks to hide in the grass. I didn't see what happened."

"I had put her to bed. I checked on her, but she was asleep. I ran out to see what was happening. She must have woken and followed me," the grieving mother wailed. "I saw her come out the door, but I was too far away to reach her. I screamed at her to go back inside, but the warriors were already riding through camp. She got caught under the horses' hooves." The woman dissolved into sobs, Soaring Eagle and Wise Hawk along with her. Niz wept with them.

When she finally rose again to continue making her way through camp, Niz discovered that had been the worst of it. There were a couple others who had received minor injuries in the chaos, and one wickiup that had been damaged. Several horses seemed to be missing, though she wasn't familiar enough with the herd to know how many, which ones, or whose. Knowing some were, dread sat like a rock in the pit of her stomach. If any of them were Fire Maker's . . .

But the biggest surprise came when, an hour or so later, an unknown child was discovered sitting at the edge of camp. With her people looking to her for leadership, Niz was immediately summoned. She sat down in front of the small child, who was barely more than a baby, studying him.

"Hello. What's your name?" she asked gently. The child was so young that she doubted he could talk yet, but still, she watched for a look of recognition when she spoke. There was none. He simply looked at her blankly. Puzzled, she turned to the woman who had found him. "He doesn't understand our language. He can't be from among our people."

"But where did he come from?" White Bird asked.

"I don't know," Niz answered, peering at the little one through the dark. She couldn't make sense of it. The Comanche raided, two people were killed, a few others wounded, horses were missing, and now there was a child who hadn't been there before. It made no sense. Had the child been with the Comanche? Had he been riding with one of the warriors and fallen off the horse? She pursed her lips, trying to think of what to do next. Her headache from earlier had only grown in intensity with the stress and her eyes burned from the tears she had shed. The adrenaline of the attack had faded, and she was dreadfully tired. She wanted to curl up on her mat and sleep. Yet she was the wife of the chief. In Fire Maker's absence, it was up to her to decide what happened to the little one.

"Who found him?" Niz questioned.

"Myself and Singing Sky."

"Have either of you laid hold of him yet?" Niz knew, according to the ways of their people, whoever touched the child first claimed him. It would be up to that person what happened to him in the days ahead. If he was discovered to be Comanche—now a blatant enemy given the raid—the one who claimed him could ransom him, trade him, or adopt him.

"No, we wanted to get you first," White Bird said nervously. "My wickiup is damaged. With that and my children, my hands are full. So are Singing Sky's. We don't wish to be burdened with a captive."

Niz nodded. Taking a deep breath, she held out her arms to the child, and he slowly, hesitantly, leaned into them. He rubbed his little face against the shoulder of her soft leather dress, and her heart skipped a beat.

"I will decide what to do with him tomorrow," she told White Bird. She reached out and put her hand on the woman's shoulder. "What we all need now is sleep. I know your shelter was damaged. You and your children can sleep in mine tonight."

The woman nodded. "Thank you, Nizhoni."

Niz squeezed White Bird's shoulder. "Tonight, there has been loss and great grief, but we must not forget it could have been so much worse. I know you will hold your young ones close tonight. Go ahead and get them settled. I'm going to take this little one to my mother's fire where I can get a better look at him and then I will join you."

Lifting the boy in her arms, Nizhoni carried him to Shy Fawn's wickiup. Her mother was sitting by the fire, and Nizhoni could instantly see the exhaustion and worry etched across her face. But when Niz stepped into the light and the woman's eyes fell on the boy, surprise lifted her expression. "Who is this?" she asked.

Nizhoni sat down by her mother with the boy on her lap. "We don't know. White Bird and Singing Sky found him sitting at the edge of the village."

Shy Fawn's brows furrowed together. "Comanche?"

"I don't know. That's my only guess. I can't imagine where else he would have come from. It all happened so fast, but I didn't see a little one with any of the warriors. Nor can I guess why they would have brought a child along when they were raiding."

Shy Fawn left and brought back some dried berries and a dipperful of water. "He doesn't look old enough to be off his mother's milk, but let's see if he'll take something. He's likely hungry."

Shy Fawn held the dipper to the little boy's lips, and he looked up at her and then at Nizhoni with his big, dark eyes. Nizhoni nodded and gave him a smile of encouragement, and he drank. Some of the water ran down his little chin, and she gently wiped it away. When Shy Fawn held out the berries, he smiled, revealing little white teeth. He reached out and grabbed them with his chubby fist before cramming them into his mouth.

"He looks to have lived around a dozen moons, don't you think?" Nizhoni observed, smoothing his inky black hair. The child must be somewhere around a year old. He was walking but clearly hadn't been for long.

"Yes, likely around there," Shy Fawn agreed contemplatively. She reached out and took hold of his foot, studying the little moccasins he wore. "The sole is buffalo hide, and I don't recognize the patterns of this beadwork. These fringes on the back, too, are not our way. He is not of the mountain people."

"No, I don't think he is," Nizhoni agreed.

"What will you do with him?"

Finished with his berries, the little one looked at Shy Fawn and opened and closed his little fist. Nizhoni chuckled. "It looks like he's still hungry."

As her mother went to get more berries, Nizhoni studied the little boy she held on her lap. His eyes were big and brown, his nose and brows delicate, his mouth and cheeks full, his skin lighter than her own. His little tuft of black hair was still baby soft. There was a good chance he was Comanche and had somehow ended up in their camp by mistake. But although he likely belonged to the enemy, in that moment, all she saw was a baby who needed her help. Startling, she reflected that her own son could have looked similarly. In that one realization, she knew what she would do.

"I'm going to keep him," she declared when Shy Fawn reappeared.

Her mother nodded knowingly. "I thought you would." She held out more berries to the child, and he grabbed them up, filling both fists this time.

With the berries out of her hands, Shy Fawn sat down and leaned back against her wickiup, closing her eyes for a long moment. "I'm tired," she admitted.

"It's been quite a night," Nizhoni sympathized, looking with concern upon her mother's weary face.

"When I saw you run by with your rifle, I was afraid, Nizhoni. But more than that, I was very proud. You led our people well tonight."

"I wish I could have done more. Our people are grieving," Niz said, pressing her fist against the ache in her chest.

Shy Fawn reached over and laid her hand against Nizhoni's cheek. "You did all you could."

"I'm only thankful the army was somehow right behind them and sounded their bugle when they did."

Shy Fawn nodded. "If it hadn't been for them, the loss tonight would have been much graver."

"How is Cloud Walking?" Nizhoni asked.

"Sleeping."

"Good. When I saw her, I wanted to send her straight home to hide, but I was so proud, too, Mother, that she ran toward danger instead of away from it to protect the women and children of our tribe. She's a good girl."

Shy Fawn nodded. "I felt the same. But she's not a girl anymore, Nizhoni. It's hard to accept that she's no longer a child, but she's not. She's a woman, and her bravery tonight proved that."

"Yes, it did," Niz agreed, realizing that her sister's actions had spoken that truth louder to her than any marriage proposal Cloud Walking had received. She could see now that her sister was indeed old enough to be kissed, old enough to start a family, old enough to be considered a woman and not just a little girl. She mulled that over, even as she moved the conversation on. "How's Ever Flowering?"

"Also sleeping. The excitement was too much for her. I'd hoped hiding her in the tall grasses along the river would protect her and the baby she carries, but it wasn't enough. The fever is back. I put her to bed as soon as the danger was over."

"That's good, Mother. I'm glad you saw to her." Nizhoni reached over and squeezed her mother's hand. Shy Fawn was always so wise and courageous. She knew what needed to be done and did it. Nizhoni was thankful that the woman had allowed her and Cloud Walking to rally a defense while she saw to Ever Flowering. In her sister's expecting state—and especially with her recent sickness—Ever Flowering's care had to be priority.

"I still need to see to you," Shy Fawn said, pushing herself to her feet again.

"I'm fine," Niz protested, but still, her mother came to squat beside her. She had to set her teeth as her mother pried and prodded at the bullet wound.

"Thankfully, it went all the way through. It took out a chunk of your flesh, but it only grazed you," Shy Fawn said, inspecting the path of the bullet. "Another quarter inch and it would have put a hole clean through your arm."

"Even then, I would have been glad it was my arm and not my chest," Nizhoni said, breathing deeper as her mother finished her perusal.

Shy Fawn went into her wickiup and came back moments later. Soon, she had mixed a poultice out of natural medicinal items she produced from a little satchel. Spreading the poultice on a bark strip, she tied it over the bullet wound.

"That should do for tonight. We'll check it again in the morning. For now, you look dead on your feet. So does that little one."

Nizhoni looked down and saw that the child's eyelids were indeed growing heavy.

"Take the boy and go get some sleep. The sun will rise before you are ready."

Niz nodded, knowing her mother was right. Standing, she settled the little one on her hip, embraced her mother, and made the short walk back to her own wickiup. Tiptoeing over White Bird and her sleeping children, Niz laid down on her mat with the baby. When she tucked him in against her where he would be warm, he nuzzled his face against her chest, fussing a little. Her heart began to ache again, knowing what he wanted. She wished she had milk with which to nurse him. As her mother had guessed, he had clearly not been weaned. She reached down and traced the line of his little face with her fingertips. He turned his big brown eyes up to her.

"I wish I had a child of my own, so I had something to give you," she whispered to him, knowing he couldn't understand her but saying it anyway. Grief and longing rose up in her heart. Her own son would have only been a few months younger. Had the child lived, she could have shared her milk between them. She looked at the little face staring up at her and imagined, just for a moment, that it was her child. Hers and Alex's. She knew it wasn't, but it helped her aching heart to dream. Besides, she had claimed him. He belonged to her now. Finally, she had a son. She cuddled him closer.

He blinked long and slow, then began fussing again. Knowing he'd already had a snack and was likely seeking comfort more than nourishment, she began to pat the little one's back in rhythm, humming to him softly, hoping the only comfort she could offer him would be enough. She watched his eyelids go shut and then open, shut and then open, shut and then open, slower and slower until at last they didn't open at all. She cautiously stopped patting. When he didn't wake, she closed her weary eyes. Sleep soon overtook her too.

Twelve

Nizhoni's sleep was fitful, her dreams haunted with the nightmare of the evening they had just lived through. Over and over, she heard the heart stopping sound of war cries. Time after time, she saw the angry face of the wounded Comanche as he sped toward her and Wise Hawk and felt the panic of knowing he would reach them before she could reload. The heartbreak was agonizing as she watched people she loved weeping for their loved ones on repeat. Again and again, she heard the pounding hoofbeats of horses bearing down on their camp, the very sound of them stirring terror, chaos, and suffering.

Suddenly, Nizhoni woke with a start. In the stillness of her wickiup, the sound of hoofbeats still filled her ears. Dread hit her like a rock as she realized it wasn't a dream at all. She jumped up even as fear gripped her.

Through the darkness, she could see White Bird's eyes were open wide, her face revealing her fear. The children were still sleeping. Only the little mystery boy was beginning to rouse. Niz quickly covered him back up, shielding him from the cool night air, and pointed to White Bird and then the child. White Bird nodded in understanding, and Niz grabbed her rifle and ran from the wickiup.

The sky was dark, the stars bright. She figured it must be several hours until dawn still. The village was quiet as she raced toward the sound of the horses. No one seemed to be moving. If anyone else had heard the approaching riders, they must be hiding.

With all her heart, for the second time that night, she wished the men were in camp. Though she had been thankful for his absence when he left, now she wished Fire Maker hadn't gone. Surely, despite his selfish nature, he would fight to protect their people. She wished Walks With Power, Lean Elk, Stands Tall, Strong Pine, Black Bear, and all the others were there, rushing toward the intruders instead of her. If only she could be rousing the women and moving the children toward the tall grasses along the river, working silently alongside her mother and sisters instead of running toward danger, alone with a rifle. Filled with anxious panic, she tried to be silent as she ran, wanting to see who was coming before they saw her.

As she sprinted through the village, she debated on whether she should call out to alert the others or continue on without a sound until she was certain of the facts. If they were in danger, would it be better to let the enemy think they had the upper hand while they quietly disappeared into the night? Or would it be best to cry out and let the approaching riders know they had been discovered and no longer held the element of surprise? Her mind grappled with the options, the strategies, and the possible repercussions. She wished the braves were there to make the decision. They would know how to best handle things. At the very least, she wished she could wake Wise Hawk and seek his counsel. But there was no time. As it was, there was only one wickiup left between her and a clear line of sight. In another moment, she would know exactly who was riding toward their village.

Fear rose up within her until it seemed to consume her. Her traitorous stomach churned, nearly causing her to be sick. If the Comanche had returned . . .

But when she rounded the wickiup, she saw it wasn't the Comanche at all. Major Taylor had just stepped out of his saddle, flanked by two dozen mounted soldiers. Seeing him, her knees went weak, and for just a moment, she stumbled. He reached out and grabbed her arm, steadying her.

"Niz!" He said her name as if a thousand pounds had suddenly been lifted off his shoulders. Relief was written all over his face.

As her terrible fear dissolved at the sight of him, she was suddenly overtaken by the indescribable, wholly improper desire to throw herself against his chest and weep. She was safe. Her sisters were safe. Her people were safe. She was no longer solely responsible for defending them in a midnight raid. Now there were armed soldiers under the leadership of a commander who had not come to attack, but to help. She was certain of it.

Thankfully, she got herself under control in the nick of time. Instead of shamefully flinging herself into the arms of Ezra Taylor, she propped up a wobbly smile, blinked back threatening tears, and found her balance again, standing firm on her own two legs, even if they were shaky.

She barely had time to register her success, though, before Major Taylor pulled her into a bear-crushing hug, letting out a great sigh as he did so. After inhaling deeply, he released her, stepping back. "It sure is good to see you in one piece," he told her. "When we came through earlier, you were covered in blood."

"Oh," she responded numbly, her thoughts and emotions spinning out of control. Her heartbeat had yet to return to normal, the panic she had felt still making its way slowly out of her system. Gratefulness was flooding in behind it, and she still felt dangerously close to breaking down in sobs of relief. She felt as if she'd never been so glad to see anyone in her entire life, and Major Taylor's quick embrace had been comforting and reassuring—a physical demonstration that she was indeed safe.

"Are you alright? What happened?" he pressed.

She closed her eyes for just a moment and gave a slight shake of her head, trying to clear the haze and rein in her chaotic thoughts. "I'm fine. It was just my arm. A bullet grazed it."

"You were shot?" he asked, his expression full of alarm as he grabbed her arm and inspected the white bark bandage.

"Barely. My mother tended to it. It's not serious."

"Thank goodness for that." He exhaled hard, released her, and stepped back. "We've been tracking the Comanche for the past two days but had lost their trail. When we headed toward your village only to realize they were also . . . all we could do was pray that we would make it in time. We knew the hunting party was out of camp and that you women and children were here alone. I'm guessing the Comanche knew that as well. They often raid this time of year, and usually at night. Out on the plains, they call that the Comanche moon," Major Taylor explained, pointing up at the full moon. "We knew they would raid somewhere, but we didn't expect it to be here. I guess the temptation of all those horses must have been too great to pass up when they realized the men were gone."

Niz's mind spun with questions. The Comanche had a moon named after their raiding? How had everyone known the braves were gone? Why were Ezra and the soldiers on their way to the village to begin with? Why hadn't Fire Maker foreseen what a temptation the herd of horses would be to the raiders and taken precautions? Why had he left them in danger instead of working with the army to keep them safe? Where were the Comanche now? Would they return to finish what they'd started?

Despite the questions pounding through her head, Niz stayed quiet. Major Taylor's hazel eyes were unguarded, his expression open. She could tell he wasn't holding back, and she waited for the story she saw was coming.

"Once we picked up their tracks and realized where they were headed, we rode here as fast as we could. We knew the Comanche had the jump on us. When we got to the ridge and saw them swooping down on your camp . . . Niz, the only thing I could think of was to sound the bugle. We were too far away for anything else. We couldn't get to you in time." He seemed pale, even in the moonlight.

"It worked."

"Thank God." He paused. "Was anyone else wounded?"

Her heart constricted painfully. "Yes. One of our elders and a little girl were both killed. A few more were injured, one wickiup was damaged, and several horses were stolen."

Ezra closed his eyes and exhaled as if he'd been struck.

"Hey," she said, reaching out and putting her hand on his arm. Her adrenaline was fading, her thoughts calming, her senses returning. With their return, the regret and guilt in his expression registered. She waited until he looked at her again. "This could have been so much worse. We will deeply grieve those who were killed, but we could have all met that same fate tonight, Major Taylor. We would have fought bravely and done our best to hide the vulnerable and survive, but the old men likely would have been killed, the children would have been taken and sold—given the Comanche camps are so far away—and the women would have been—"

"Stop," he told her, lifting his hand. "I don't need you to tell me. I've seen it." He cracked his knuckles, staring past her for a moment. "Seven homesteads have already been raided. At nearly half of them it's . . . it's been the same."

"Then you should know how grateful we are that it wasn't worse—that you and your soldiers showed up when you did, blew your bugle when you did," she told him, her voice gentle.

She understood men like him. Alex had been the same way. If complete success wasn't achieved, they counted it as a failure. If even one person had been injured, Ezra Taylor would feel like he'd failed them. He wouldn't stop to count success by each person who had been spared . . . but she would.

"You saved a lot of people from suffering greatly tonight. This—raids from other tribes—this happens in our world. We know it's a possibility. We've seen it before. I have bad dreams about it. But you stepped into that reality tonight, and . . . you saved us. As odd as it feels to say, I'm really glad the army is around," she finished, smiling up at him. "Thank you for what you did—all of you," she said, turning to the others.

Her sisters, her mother, her unborn niece or nephew, her friends, her loved ones—they were all alive still because of Ezra Taylor and his soldiers. When he'd realized the Comanche were headed toward their village, he could have looked the other way, letting the tribes fight it out between themselves. He could have counted it a relief to have them out of his hair; many officers would have. He could have left them to their fate, deciding it was none of his concern. He could have taken Fire Maker's stance and refused to lend his aid, knowing there was nothing in it for him and his men. But he hadn't. He'd come to their rescue. "You did a good thing tonight. We are grateful."

He closed his eyes again and let out a deep breath. She could see he was still struggling to accept the defeat of not having saved them all.

"Did you catch the Comanche?" she asked.

He shook his head. "No. We lost their trail in the dark. We'll set out again at first light."

"Don't worry. You'll catch them," she told him, truly believing it.

His doubtful expression showed he clearly didn't share her optimism.

Reaching out, she squeezed his arm gently. "You will."

He pulled his hand over his face. "You're right. We will. We have to. It's just been a long day."

Niz nodded compassionately, understanding, fighting the urge to give the discouraged man in front of her a hug. He'd gone above and beyond for them and yet he was ending the night feeling the sting of failure. But he didn't need a hug—what he probably needed was sleep. She took a step back, determined to let him be on his way no matter how much she wanted the comfort of having him and the soldiers stay.

"Is it alright if we make camp nearby?" he asked, easing back a step too. "Not here, of course, but close enough that we can keep an eye on your village in case they circle back around? With the men out hunting, I'd feel better if we did."

More relief flooded her. When she went back to bed, she could sleep well. Ezra and the soldiers would be nearby if there was trouble. "Yes, absolutely."

He nodded. Turning, he pointed. "We'll make camp there, then." It was where she met with Ms. Langston. Far enough away to be separated from the village but close enough to be within earshot.

"Alright."

He let out another deep sigh. "Alright," he echoed. He started to turn as his men set off for their temporary camp.

"Wait!" she said suddenly. He turned to face her again. "You said you were on your way here when you found out the Comanche were also. Why were you coming? You said you knew the men were hunting. Was there something you needed to tell us?"

He put his hand to his head, seemingly in despair. "Niz, I'm so glad you reminded me! In the commotion of tonight, I'd completely forgotten. There was a boy. I was bringing him to you. Did you find him? One of my soldiers dropped him off just outside of camp, not knowing if the Comanche would run or turn and fight. He had meant to keep him out of danger if things went bad. Did he wander in? If not, we'll start a search for him. I only hope he didn't go toward the river . . ."

"No, we found him!" she assured, rebounding from the shock of what he'd said. The soldiers had brought the boy? "He's safe. I had him with me."

"I thought you would." Ezra's voice was warm.

"But . . . where did he come from?" she asked, trying to make sense of it. "He's not of my tribe. We figured the Comanche had somehow left him behind."

Ezra clenched his jaw and readjusted the cap he wore before answering. "The last homestead that was raided was a trapper and his wife. Not sure what tribe she was from, but she was a native. They had both been killed, and their animals taken. We found the boy hidden in a trunk when we got there. I'm guessing he'd been asleep when his mother hid him inside it, but he was awake and crying by the time we arrived."

Niz inhaled sharply in shock and horror. She stared out into the darkness beyond Ezra, her thoughts spiraling. The boy was an orphan. Her heart twisted as she pictured his precious little face and processed the fact that his parents had been murdered. Suppose the army hadn't found him! The poor boy would have starved to death. And yet, didn't her own people hide their children when attacked? Wasn't it the natural inclination? Because sometimes it worked, as it had for the little boy, who was currently sound asleep on her sleeping mat. Surely that mother had only thought to save his life out of love for her son, and she had succeeded in doing so, but Niz's mind was frozen in the horror of what would have happened if no one had found him. She shuddered.

"Don't," Ezra told her. "Don't picture it. Stay in this moment. Focus on how it ended, not on how it could have."

Refocusing on him, she nodded, knowing he was right. Taking a long, deep breath to steady herself, her head began to clear a little as the initial shock wore off.

"So . . . you were on your way here to . . . bring him to us?" Niz asked, trying to absorb the information Ezra had shared and what all it meant. The little boy wasn't Comanche after all. He was a child of mixed race. No wonder his skin was light.

Niz's head was spinning. Her heart was full of compassion for the parents who had been attacked, aching sadness for the little one, questions about his mother and her tribe of origin, thankfulness the soldiers had found him before he starved, and confusion about why Ezra had thought to bring the child to them instead of back to the fort. Still, she was thankful he had. If he hadn't, the Comanche would have been able to plunder at leisure. Very likely, many of her people would have met the same fate as the boy's parents.

"No. I was bringing him to *you*."

"To *me*?" she asked, her eyebrows lifting in surprise.

Ezra considered her for a long moment. Finally, he drew in a deep breath and shrugged. "You might hate me for this, but it's been a long night, so I'm going to say it anyway. I know he can't take the place of your baby, Niz, but I figure you're a mother without a child and he's a child without a mother. He needs you, and I think you need him."

"You want me to adopt him and raise him as my own son?" she questioned, surprised by his boldness.

Ezra's face broke into a smile brighter than the full moon. "I might be wrong, but if I know you like I think I do, Niz, I'm guessing you've already decided to do just that."

Her conversation with her mother came instantly to mind, but she tossed her hair and narrowed her eyes at him for good measure. "Just because you're right doesn't mean you know me."

His smile broadened into a grin. "Fair enough." Reaching out, he squeezed her shoulder. "Goodnight, Niz. I'm glad you're safe."

"Goodnight," she echoed, watching him swing into his saddle and set off toward the place where he and his men would camp until the sun rose.

With a deep sigh of relief, she turned back toward the village. Her people were grieving tonight, as was she, but they were alive to grieve, and for that, she was thankful. As she wound her way back to her wickiup, the glorious feeling of being safe washed over her. Ezra had told her to stay in the present, and it was a good place to be. The little boy had been found. The soldiers had come. The Comanche had fled. They hadn't come back as she had feared. Ezra and the army were camped nearby.

Suddenly, she felt very sleepy. Seeing White Bird waiting just inside the door of her wickiup, a war club in her hand, Niz told her in a whisper what had happened and that they were safe. The woman's relief was evident, and tears began rolling silently down her cheeks. Understanding, Niz gave her a reassuring hug before stepping over the children and settling on her mat again.

With a yawn, she snuggled down under the blankets next to the boy. She looked over at his little face, so peaceful in slumber, and leaned down and kissed his sweet cheek. The poor little dear was an orphan, in need of love and care. Her heart filled with warmth. Ezra had brought him to her.

"My son," she whispered, a smile lifting her lips.

~~~

Major Taylor and the soldiers rode out at first light. Nizhoni felt for them as she listened to them leave, her own eyes still heavy and gritty after the short night. They had gotten even less sleep than she had, and already they were off again. They must be exhausted. Rolling over, being careful of her injured arm, she went back to sleep until the child beside her stirred.

Again, he wanted to nurse. Niz's heart hurt for him even more than it had the night before, now knowing he was longing for his dead mother. Never again would he be satisfied by his mother's milk, hear her voice, or be comforted by her familiar arms. And for what? For a few stolen horses and a dozen men's anger to be avenged? She knew across the village, Leaping Water's mother must be feeling the same way. Her daughter was gone, her beautiful little life cut short. And for what purpose? The senseless violence was maddening, sickening, and devastating. Grief rose up within her, and Niz's stomach churned at the injustice of it all. As the little one rubbed his face against the fabric of her dress, searching for milk, she nearly began to weep for him.

Niz tried soothing him as she had the night before, but this time, he wouldn't be soothed. He began to fuss, and she knew he must be hungry rather than just seeking comfort. Lifting him in her arms, she got up quickly, grabbed some breakfast for the two of them, and left the wickiup, doing her best to let White Bird and her children sleep.

Outside, she sat the boy on the ground. Taking his little dimpled hand, she led him away from camp where they wouldn't disturb anyone. The night had been frightening and sad. She wanted people to be able to sleep as long as they could before waking up to face the grief the day would carry. The bodies of their loved ones would have to be prepared and buried according to the traditions of their people and mourning practices commenced. The day ahead promised to be difficult and full of sorrow, and her heart grew troubled just thinking about it.

Rubbing her hand over her face, Niz thought back to Ezra Taylor's words the night before. *'Stay in the present,'* he had said. It had been good advice then, and it was good advice now. Determined to follow it, she refocused on the little boy whose hand she was holding.

Obviously as enamored with the sunbathed morning and his surroundings as she normally was, he toddled along beside her, closing his eyes and smiling up at the sun, then grabbing at the grasses as they walked by. He jabbered happily as they walked, his tone expressive and delighted, his words unrecognizable. She wasn't sure if he was speaking his mother's native tongue or his own baby language. Either way, he seemed quite content to be in the fresh air and sunshine.

Happy with their distance from camp, Nizhoni sat down on a grassy patch of ground. When she held her arms out to him, the child toddled into them with a big, toothy smile, and she laughed in delight, kissing his cheeks before settling him on her lap. Though she couldn't nurse him as his mother had, she hoped cuddling him close would give him the comfort he longed for. In the safety of her lap, he took the small pieces of dried meat she tore off for him and ate them greedily. When they had eaten all the meat she had brought, she offered him seeds and then more of the dried berries he had enjoyed the night before. When his hunger was satisfied, the little one stood and began to toddle around, exploring the world around him. Nizhoni watched quietly, enjoying the chance to study him in the light of day.

Dark hair and dark eyes, lighter skin, chubby, kissable cheeks—he was everything she had imagined her own child looking like. His smile was bright and quick to appear, and a dimple peeked out from his right cheek every time it did. He really was a darling child, and her heart swelled with joy as she watched him toddle about, squatting to examine the little treasure of a pinecone, the beauty of a wildflower, the wonder of a stick. He picked up a small rock and carried it with him in his clenched hand. Finding another, he gave a little chuckle of delight as he hit the two rocks together. He did so over and over until, in his uncoordinated actions, he mistakenly hit his thumb instead. Tears gathered in his big brown eyes, and he let out a wail as he came toddling back to Niz at an unbalanced run. She held out her arms, and he fell into them, rubbing his face against her shoulder and then showing her his injured thumb. She kissed it, and he smiled. Soon, he was up exploring again.

Watching him, her breath caught as she realized what happened to his family could have happened to her and Alex if the mill hadn't burnt. Seven homesteads in the area had been raided. Could the Applewoods' have been one of them? It was something they'd never worried about as there had been peace in the area for years. It was only the arrival of the Comanche that was throwing off the balance.

Guilt filled her as she remembered hoping the Comanche's aggression would be reserved for the soldiers and settlers they thought had wronged them. Those settlers had been her neighbors, people just like the Applewoods. Had things been different, it could have been them. And the soldiers... the prospect of a raid at the fort frightened her too. Major Taylor, Marigold, even Sergeant Green—they were all good people whom she had come to care about. She didn't want anything to happen to them either.

Shaking her head, she looked back at the boy and hoped again that Major Taylor and the soldiers would apprehend the Comanche. They needed to be caught. Things needed to go back to normal, where people didn't have to be afraid to lay down their heads at night, where mothers didn't have to hide their babies in chests to save their lives, and where darling children weren't trampled while running to their mothers.

Sighing, Niz glanced at the village. Seeing activity, she stood and scooped the boy up, wincing as her injured arm protested. Once the pain began to ease, she started toward camp. The boy seemed quite content to be carried, and she rejoiced in the weight of him in her arms—arms that had been empty for far too long.

"Since I don't know what your parents called you, you'll need a name," she told him as she walked. He sucked on his finger and looked at her. "I think Walks at Night would be fitting, seeing as how you walked into camp after dark. What do you think? Do you like that?"

The small boy simply stared at her, and she tickled his tummy, eliciting his endearing smile. "Maybe the next time we see the major, we'll ask him to take us back to where you lived with your parents. Maybe some of your things are there . . . your clothes or a blanket or a toy . . . anything that would bring you comfort while you get used to life here. What do you say to that?" Another tickle, this time drawing a throaty chuckle. The happy sound made Niz laugh, too, and she kissed his little cheek again, unable to help herself.

With the village awake, they proceeded with the traditional mourning practices for their loved ones. Once the bodies had been taken to a high place and laid out on scaffolds that took them closer to the sky, everyone made their way back to camp.

Weary and full of sorrow, Shy Fawn changed Nizhoni's bandage slowly, using the task to allow them both a chance to regroup. She ground and applied a poultice, packed moss over it, and then tied a strip of bark over the moss. Once the wound had been bandaged, Niz and Shy Fawn visited those who had been injured, helping however they could. When Walks at Night began to rub his eyes, Shy Fawn took him back to her wickiup to nap while she checked on Ever Flowering. Niz and Cloud Walking worked alongside White Bird to repair her wickiup while he slept. As the sun began to sink toward the western horizon, Nizhoni gathered everyone in the village together, and they discussed what should be done if the Comanche returned.

With the government trying to force the Indians onto reservations, tribes hadn't been raiding each other like they once had. Much of their energy and focus now was on survival rather than expansion. As a result, their people had grown lax in their preparation for such an event. With the Comanche in the area, Nizhoni knew that was a luxury they could no longer afford. They needed to have a plan in case they were attacked again, especially with the braves out of camp. Nizhoni looked to Wise Hawk, Blue Flower, and the other remaining elders to lead the conversation, asking them to teach them what their people had done in the past to survive. A plan was put in place, and everyone—including the children—were made aware of their part in it.

Older children were designated to gather the younger ones based on the part of the village they lived in. Several women were put in charge of getting the group of children to safety. Wise Hawk, with his old heart heavy within his chest, gathered the young ones around him and taught them how to hide in the forest, to run as silently as the wind, and breathe as undetectably as the animals. He taught them how to survive until the hunting party returned in the case of an ambush that left the village annihilated. He told them that no matter what the days ahead held, to continue to follow the ways of their people, to stick together, and to remember who they were.

While Wise Hawk taught the children and the mothers who had been chosen to tend them, Nizhoni and another of the elders instructed the rest of the women in a defensive strategy. As darkness fell again, although apprehension built within her chest, Niz knew that if another attack was launched, they were now equipped with a plan to defend themselves. How successful it would be, she wasn't sure, as they were likely still no match for those trained in the art of war. They far outnumbered the Comanche, however, and that was something. At least with a plan, she felt they had a chance.

When she finally laid down on her sleeping mat that night, Niz jumped at every little noise, barely able to sleep at all during the long midnight hours. But when the sun rose again, the village stood quiet and calm. Walks at Night woke hungry, and for the second morning in a row, she led her new son out into the glorious sunshine to enjoy their first meal of the day together.

Tired from three nights in a row of little sleep, Nizhoni laid down on her side in the mountain grasses, her head propped up on her hand as she watched him wander and explore. Seeing the curiosity on his little face and listening to his exclamations of delight with each new treasure he discovered, something deep pulled at her heart.

To watch a child's response to the world was refreshing, calming, and somehow stirring. She wanted to experience the day with the same simple innocence. The heart within her chest began to ache. She wished for just a moment that she could be as unconcerned and trusting as Walks at Night, knowing she had someone who loved her looking out for her. Distant phrases that had been spoken by Marigold, Mother Emaline, Raya, and Alex played through her mind. Words about a Father who loved them, who watched over them, who made a way for them—and the longing within her grew. If only it were true.

Walks at Night tripped on a rock and fell, letting out a wobbling wail before starting to cry in earnest. Nizhoni jumped to her feet and went to him, lifting him up and brushing off his little skinned knees. His scrapes were starting to bleed, so she took him to the river to wash them, singing to him as she did. Still whimpering, he clutched her dress in his fists and rubbed his teary face against her. Finally, he rested his head against her shoulder and began to suck his thumb, quieting as he did. When his scrapes had been washed and he had settled, she set him back down, and he toddled off again. This time, she pulled out her books and began to study, glancing up frequently to keep a watchful eye on him.

In the commotion of the raid, she had forgotten all about learning to read. She hadn't so much as opened her books since it happened. But the Comanche were not their only enemy. With the government closing in around them, learning to read felt as necessary as making a plan in case of another attack. Though it was an invasion of a different kind, with very different weapons, she had no doubt that war with the government—in one shape or another—was imminent. And currently, they were as unprepared for it as they had been for the Comanche. She wasn't sure whether or not Marigold would come, given the danger, but if she did, Marigold—the one person who could help them get ready—would be arriving within the next few hours and Niz hadn't done her part. She hurried to study.

Near midday, Niz saw Ms. Langston and her escorts approaching. Pushing herself up from the log she'd been waiting on, she stretched. Despite all that had happened, she'd still successfully managed to learn the new words she'd been assigned, and she was glad about that. She also felt incredibly grateful that Marigold had still come—and was still willing to teach her.

Before the horses had even come to a stop, Marigold was waving, her smile big. Niz's heart felt heavy and sad after the events of the past forty-eight hours, but she couldn't help waving back.

"What happened to your arm?" Marigold asked as the soldiers helped her down from her horse. Niz noticed Sergeant Green wasn't with her, only the young one who had accompanied her the last time and a new one.

"Oh, I was shot during the raid, but it's fine. My mother has been seeing to it," Niz answered absentmindedly as she brushed the question away. Though it was painful, it seemed so trivial compared to what others had endured that she didn't want to speak of it.

The new soldier cocked his head to the side, alarm showing on his face. "The raid?"

"You were shot?" Marigold questioned at the same time.

Niz studied them both, confused. "Major Taylor didn't tell you?"

"Tell us what?" the soldier demanded.

"He's been out on patrol. I haven't seen him since before we were here last," Marigold explained.

Niz's brows drew together in concern, even though she tried to tell herself not to worry. Major Taylor was a trained soldier riding with other trained soldiers. They were likely still pursuing the Comanche, and that's why they hadn't returned yet.

"Tell us what?" the soldier repeated.

Niz quickly relayed the events of the raid. The soldiers' alarm appeared to grow, and they wanted to know all the details about how many Comanche there had been, which way they had gone, and what weapons they had been carrying. She told them everything she remembered. Marigold only had one question: was everyone alright?

The young woman's deep blue eyes filled with tears when Niz told her that the little girl who had braided her hair and held her hand the last time she'd visited had died before the day's end. Seeing Marigold share their sorrow solidified the friendship she'd felt growing between them, and Niz had to push her own grief back, closing the door to it, in order to avoid shedding her own tears. The soldiers were antsy as Niz told Marigold about Walks at Night, who was playing on a blanket she had spread, clearly nervous as they continually scanned the horizon.

"We should head back to the fort," the new one said, interrupting.

"Head back? Why, we haven't even started our lesson yet!" Marigold protested.

"It's not safe for you to be out here, Ms. Langston," he cautioned.

"Well, I'm already here. Let us at least do our reading. Then we'll head back right away," she promised. She turned sadly to Niz. "Though I was so looking forward to joining you for lunch."

"Another time," Niz told her, knowing the soldier was right. If the Comanche were to come across the small group between the village and the fort, the two escorts likely wouldn't be enough. They needed to return Marigold to the safety of the fort. She also hadn't remembered to prepare a meal, nor was it a good time to host one.

The soldiers reluctantly agreed, and Marigold and Niz sat down to begin their studies. Though Marigold didn't seem overly concerned about the Comanche, the soldiers plainly were. They were on high alert as they waited for them to finish and encouraged Ms. Langston more than once to hurry. Niz couldn't blame them. They were likely eager to return their charge to safety and share the news with Ezra's second-in-command.

While Marigold promised to make the lesson as quick as possible, she was clearly smitten with Walks at Night. She bounced him on her knee and played with him while listening to Niz sound out words. Before she left, she insisted that the two of them stay with her the following week, seeing as how Niz was to visit the fort for her lessons. She reasoned that given the present threat of raids, it seemed much safer to stay at the fort and minimize the risk associated with travel; especially now that there was a child to consider. Besides, she persuaded, then Niz could have a lesson every day and she would be reading just that much sooner because of it.

Niz couldn't argue that Marigold's reasoning made sense and agreed to stay if Fire Maker allowed. Satisfied with her answer, Marigold and the soldiers left. Niz stood with Walks at Night, watching them ride away, hoping wholeheartedly that they would make it back to the fort safely—and that when she arrived in a few days' time, that she would learn that Major Taylor and his men had arrived safely back as well.

Thirteen

"You cannot trade him!" Nizhoni argued, alarmed, astonished, and outraged all at the same time.

The hunting party had arrived back in camp just an hour earlier. The news of the raid had quickly spread, and the braves had joined Lean Elk, as well as Noon Day Sun's sons and grandsons, as they mourned their loved ones. The women had solemnly begun processing the hunt, leaving the men to grapple with the events that had taken place while they were away. Still, the women were outside skinning, cleaning, and slicing, just as Niz should be. Instead, she was standing in the middle of her wickiup, feeling as if the wind had been knocked out of her.

Fire Maker had approached her outside, grabbed her arm, and wordlessly pulled her away from her work and into their wickiup. He had not bothered to greet her, kiss her hello, or ask any questions about the Comanche's raid. He hadn't even inquired about her injury. Instead, he said he'd heard about the child she'd taken in and bluntly stated his intentions for him.

"It's done all the time, Nizhoni. Captives are traded to increase the wealth of the tribe." There was no remorse, no softness, no concern in his tone, only arrogance and disdain.

"But—"

"You know it's true. It's what the Comanche would have done with any one of you that they captured." He stopped and let out an unpleasant laugh. "Well, maybe not with you. They likely would have found another use for you. But anyone else, and you can't deny it."

Niz wanted to slap him for saying such a horrible thing. Her hand burned to do so. How could he speak such sickening words? How could he act as if he wasn't the least concerned that their village had been attacked or worried even the tiniest bit about her safety? She knew he was cruel, but she hadn't believed he was completely heartless. She had assumed that somewhere deep down he held some sort of affection for her, even if it was very small. But if he could laugh about what could have happened should the Comanche have captured her, she knew she had been mistaken. Her stomach churned, and anger exploded through her. Still, she kept her hand at her side, refusing to give in to the temper that wanted to rule her. Just because he was badly behaved did not mean she had to be. Instead, she would fight with logic.

"Walks at Night is not Comanche," she told him, trying to stay calm. "We didn't conquer his people. He's not a captive. He was brought to us for care and protection!"

"By whom?" Fire Maker demanded, his voice taunting. "The soldiers?"

She suspected he already knew the answer. That would explain why he was so against the child before even laying eyes on him. It would make sense that jealousy was fueling his behavior. She'd been very careful not to tell anyone that Ezra had brought Walks at Night to her, not wanting the news to make it back to Fire Maker. But with the child's arrival being such a mystery, she'd had to divulge that the soldiers had brought him to the village. It seemed even that had been a mistake. She raised her chin. "Yes."

"Why would they think I would want another mouth to feed? Why would they assume I would take in another man's child? Hm? Why would they think we would want him, Nizhoni? Why?"

"I do want him!" she cried.

"Well, I don't!" he yelled back. "The child will be traded to a neighboring tribe. End of story."

Niz pressed a hand to her stomach, panic and anger growing within her. The child had been brought to her to love, care for, and protect. His parents were dead. He had been planted in her heart.

They had both lost much—she a son, he a father and mother. But they had each other. She had claimed him as her own. She drew herself up to her full height. "The child will not be traded."

Fire Maker's eyes flashed fire. "How dare you challenge me? He will. I've made my decision."

"You're wrong!" she cried. "I claimed him! *I* took hold of him! This is not your decision, Fire Maker! You may be chief of this village, but according to the ways of our people, the child belongs to me, not to you, and I *am* keeping him!"

Fire Maker clenched his fists, but Nizhoni didn't flinch. She would not be cowed, and she would not be conquered. Not in this. She would not lose this battle.

"I can make you change your mind," he threatened.

"You cannot," she disagreed, keeping her gaze steady. She wasn't scared of him. Nothing he could do to her would hurt more than losing Walks at Night. In the dull spark of his eyes, she saw that he knew she spoke the truth. He turned and considered the child, who lay on her mat napping.

"He's as ugly as they come. I doubt he would even bring enough to make it worth my time to barter a trade," Fire Maker said, sounding disgusted.

His observation cut her heart, but she tried not to show it. If he needed to spew cruel words to ease his smarting pride, so be it. Walks at Night would stay.

Taking a deep, calming breath, she laid her hand on her husband's arm. Surely, *surely*, somewhere deep within, he must have a heart. "We have both wanted a child. Maybe this is the spirits' answer to our prayers. They have given us a son."

"You can pretend he's your son if you wish, but we both know he's not. And he will certainly never be mine," Fire Maker scoffed, hitting her hand away. With that, he stormed out of the wickiup.

Nizhoni watched him go and then turned and looked at the child sleeping so peacefully. He was worn out from a morning of playing outside in the sunshine. He had been with her for four days now, and she loved him more with each passing day. Somehow, in such a short time, he had become part of her heart.

Fire Maker was wrong. Walks at Night *was* her son. And every cruel thing he'd said had cut her because of it. Squatting down on her heels beside her sleeping mat, she dropped her head into her hands. After several deep breaths, she raised it again. Quiet and still, she watched the boy sleep. Fire Maker could rant and rave and say what he liked; she would never let him trade her son.

Straightening again, she sighed and pushed the weight of her long hair over her shoulder. So much for hoping Walks at Night would be something good between her and Fire Maker.

Some part of her had begun to hope that maybe, just maybe, even though he wasn't their biological son, the darling boy would find his way into Fire Maker's heart. They had both wanted a child; perhaps having one in their home would be something they could unite over. She'd spent the last few days telling herself that their marriage—Fire Maker—couldn't be as bad as she believed. Somewhere deep down, there had to be something good in her husband. Maybe a child would bring that out in him. Maybe a child would bring them together.

She'd almost convinced herself that Fire Maker would return from the hunt, hear their tale, feel real concern for her, and realize he did care about her after all. Maybe the raid would cause something protective and good to rise up within him, and he would become the husband she knew he could be. The men in their tribe were strong and fiercely protective. They valued their wives and their children. They were men of honor and loyalty. She had almost convinced herself that deep down her husband had to be like them. But their conversation had proved again that he clearly wasn't.

The disappointment she felt was acute. It rose up within her, threatening to overwhelm her. Tears stung her eyes. But she couldn't give in to them. Not now. If she started crying, she didn't know if she could ever stop. Her life with Fire Maker stretched out bleak and miserable before her. Some part of her had to hope that this wasn't all there was, that things could change, but that hope was becoming harder and harder to cling to.

Walks at Night turned over in his sleep. Giving herself a little shake, Niz started into motion again. Her life didn't just include Fire Maker anymore. It also included Walks at Night, and for that, she would be thankful. All the love, all the happiness, all the devotion she wanted from Fire Maker and wanted to give in return, she would lavish on Walks at Night. Though he was an orphan, she was determined he would never want for love and belonging. Not while she lived. His parents may have died, but he had a mother.

With a new resolve, she stepped out of the wickiup and began helping once again to process the harvest.

~~~

The next morning, knowing she couldn't put off talking to Fire Maker about going to the fort for her reading lessons any longer, Nizhoni mustered up her courage and set off to look for her husband. She found him out among the horses and was glad—it seemed to be one of the places he was happiest.

"Five of my horses are missing," he told her as she approached, his face stormy.

Her heart fell. "I knew several stampeded with the Comanche. I wasn't sure how many or who they belonged to," she answered carefully.

He shook his head in apparent disgust. "You would think I could have trusted you to look after my animals while I was away. Instead, you lost five of our horses and ended up with some other man's child."

She stared at him in disbelief. Is that really all he was worried about? Didn't he even care enough about the lives that were lost to throw that back in her face too? "I did my best to protect our village during the attack!"

"Well, your best wasn't good enough, was it?" he mocked.

Niz took a deep, calming breath and reminded herself that when she'd set out to find him, she'd done so expecting some kind of confrontation. It was rare to talk to her husband and not have conflict. She'd planned to stay calm and reasonable, no matter what. "Fire Maker, I'm sorry about your horses, but I was more concerned about our people that night. You lost a few horses, but Lean Elk lost a daughter! Noon Day Sun's children lost their father. We all could have been killed. Truly, five horses is a small price to pay, isn't it?" she asked, hoping to help him see reason.

"That's your opinion," he shot back. "Those horses were incredibly valuable!"

"Fire Maker!"

"Don't take that tone with me! Lean Elk has other children."

Niz bit her tongue to hold back the angry replies but couldn't keep from clenching her fists at her sides, unable to believe what she was hearing. He made it sound as if he would rather have lost people than horses. It was unfathomable to her.

Fire Maker noticed and narrowed his eyes at her. "I was planning to sell those horses to the army assuming you're ever smart enough to read. Your incompetence cost me a great deal of money!"

With something between a huff and a growl, he turned back to his work. "I'll get my horses back. Watch and see. No one steals from Fire Maker and gets away with it!"

Unable to help herself, she rolled her eyes. He certainly had a knack for making everything about him. But, she reminded herself, this wasn't about him; it wasn't about either of them. One wrong step from Fire Maker could come back to hurt their entire village. Anxiety crowded out her frustration. "Please, however you're planning to get them back, just think of our people. If you make the Comanche angry and they return, we could lose more than horses."

"You are telling *me* to think of our people? You forget I'm the chief! These are *my* people, Nizhoni. Not yours. Don't pretend you know better than I do."

She cleared her throat. The conversation was not headed in any kind of positive direction. She'd searched him out for a reason, hoping to find him in good humor. Instead, she'd only succeeded in making it worse. "You're right," she conceded. "You're the chief."

He ignored her.

"This is the week I'm to go to the fort for my reading lessons. Ms. Langston is expecting me today."

"Can't you read yet?" he grumbled. "If you weren't so slow, I could have sold those horses before they were stolen."

"No, but I'm getting much closer. Ms. Langston is a very good teacher, and she's pleased with my progress," Niz said, plowing ahead.

He didn't respond.

"She mentioned when she was here last that perhaps I should stay with her at the fort this week, rather than going back and forth."

"Why would you stay at the fort? She went back and forth. You can too."

"Well, with the Comanche raiding . . ."

"Stop being so dramatic. You'll be fine," he told her, sounding annoyed.

Niz closed her eyes and counted to ten. "Alright. I'll go back and forth. Will you please escort me? Or send someone to do so? It doesn't seem like a good idea for a woman and child to travel by themselves so many miles, given the events of the past week," she reasoned, her voice strained as she struggled to stay pleasant.

She wished he had offered to escort her on his own accord or, at the very least, arranged an escort for her. If only he wanted to protect her. His lack of concern served as a reminder of the lack of worth he placed on her, and it stung. She wanted to be cared about. She wanted to be valued and loved.

"You're taking the kid?" he asked, sounding surprised.

"He's my son. Who else would look after him?"

There was a brief silence as he continued to brush his horse. "No one can spare the time to escort you back and forth to the fort all week because you're too scared to make the trip by yourself," he told her, making the very idea seem ridiculous.

She watched him, frustrated. "Well, could I stay, then? Ms. Langston said I could stay with her."

"You'd like that, wouldn't you? A whole week back in the white man's world!"

She shook her head. "That's not what this is about. I love our village and our people!"

He laughed at her.

"Fire Maker, I'm learning to read for you!" she cried, growing upset. "All so that you can trade horses to the army."

"Who would make my dinner and tend my fire if you're off at the fort all week? Have you even stopped to consider that? You have duties here, Nizhoni. You can't shirk them just because you're scared."

"I'm not scared," she started.

"Yes, you are," he argued.

She felt the pressure inside her building again as her temper flared. It wasn't fear that drove her request. It was wisdom! And it wasn't fair that he was always trying to tell her about herself. Only she had the right to do that. Still, she knew he wasn't in a place to recognize the injustice, no matter what she said. Responding in anger would only result in anger. So instead, she tried to tamp down the fire that was growing inside her and respond reasonably. "I'm sure one of the braves would welcome you at his fire."

He shook his head. "You can go back and forth."

She sighed. She wasn't afraid. But it *was* a long distance to travel by herself three times in a week. Normally it was a risk she would take, but with the Comanche in the area, it didn't seem wise.

Major Taylor had suggested reminding Fire Maker that his trade depended on her, but Niz had hoped she wouldn't have to go to such lengths. She had wanted to believe her husband would be willing to offer her protection of his own free will. Again, her hopes had come up empty. "And what if something happens to me?"

"I'll find another wife," he answered easily.

Her chin jerked as she absorbed his cruel words. "And who will read your bill of sale then? Will she be able to sign your name? Will your next wife speak English? Who will translate for you when the army comes? Or do you plan to learn? I could teach you if you'd like," she offered, knowing he'd never take her up on it. To accept her help would be to admit he needed it, and he would undoubtedly see that as acknowledging a weakness.

He was quiet for a long spell. Finally, he said, "Fine. Go. Spend the week. But you'd better come back knowing how to read. Don't bother coming back until you do."

Nizhoni clenched her teeth. She didn't know if she could learn everything she needed to know in a week. "If you mean that, I might be gone longer than planned. I honestly don't know if I can learn that quickly."

"I mean it. We'll be just fine without you," he said, his smile sardonic. He made her feel dispensable and unimportant. His words and his mocking tone cut. Still, she could see he thought he had her cornered. He was twisting the knife. He was punishing her for wanting to stay at the fort, counting on her loyalty to their people to keep her from agreeing to an indefinite absence.

And it was working. Her heart hurting, Nizhoni thought of her mother, Cloud Walking, and Ever Flowering. She hated to be gone for an indefinite amount of time with Ever Flowering sick and Cloud Walking making decisions about her future. Soaring Eagle and her family were grieving. Snow Flower was still recovering. To the best of her knowledge, the Comanche were still raiding—what if they returned while she was away?

But she did need to learn how to read before they left for their winter camp. The Comanche had to be stopped. She had to be able to read the government's agreement to Fire Maker so he would see how important it was to keep the peace—even if that meant working with the army. Otherwise, hunting rights could be revoked by the time they returned next summer, and what would happen to their people then? Glancing up at the aspens, seeing how the green leaves were less vibrant than they had been, she knew she didn't have much time left. She had to give herself the best chance of learning.

What was more, she had a child to think about now. Staying at the fort would be safer for Walks at Night than making the trip back and forth. He had already been orphaned once. She didn't want him to know any more suffering at his tender age.

"Alright. I'll stay at the fort until I can read." She paused and looked out over Fire Maker's herd of horses. "Which horse would you like me to ride?"

"I don't know how long you'll be gone. Without knowing that, I can't spare a horse. Maybe I'll need it before you get back."

"You have so many, and you can only ride one at a time," she said carefully, fighting hard to keep her temper under control.

She saw him glance at Walks at Night, who was riding on her back in the rudimentary cradleboard she had quickly constructed for him. "I can't spare any. You'll have to walk. And it works out since you'll be staying so long—there's really no rush. You can take your time."

"It's nearly fifteen miles."

He glanced up at the position of the sun. "Well, if you leave now, you'll probably make it before the afternoon rains start. If not," he shrugged, "it might feel refreshing after such a long walk."

She closed her eyes and took a deep, calming breath before she said anything she might regret. When she opened them, Fire Maker was watching her. It was almost as if he was taunting her to say something, but she refused to give him the satisfaction. If he wanted her to walk, so be it.

"That's true. And I do love going on walks." She watched as her cheerful answer gave him a moment of uncertainty. She turned. "I'll be back when I can read."

Returning to their wickiup, she quickly packed some provisions and her books in a bag that she tied to the side of the cradleboard along with her sleeping mat, told her mother and sisters goodbye, and set off. Fifteen miles through the mountains on foot, carrying supplies and a little boy, was going to take a while. She might as well get started.

Six hours later, she arrived at the edge of the fort. She had indeed been caught in the afternoon rains about two miles back. The storm had come at an inopportune time when there had been no cover near enough to reach. The trees that had once been there had long since been cut down to provide lumber for the fort, leaving her and Walks at Night without shelter as thunder shook the mountains, lightning flashed, and rain pelted them as it fell from the heavens in sheets. Contrary to what Fire Maker had said, there had been nothing refreshing about it. Thus, she arrived tired, soaked clean through, with a pounding headache and a screaming child who was not enjoying being wet any more than he had enjoyed the thunderstorm.

Nizhoni lifted her chin as she felt soldiers staring as she walked the road that lay along the southern side of the central parade ground. She passed the store, armory, and infirmary. As she did, the soldiers whispered between themselves, some of them pointing. No one tried to stop her, so she kept walking. She'd hoped she would see someone she recognized and could ask directions to Marigold Langston's house, but so far, all the faces were new—and there weren't many of them. The fort seemed emptier than it had before. Deciding she would go to Major Taylor's office first, as she already knew where that was, she continued toward it, hoping with all her might that he had returned from chasing the Comanche.

With twenty feet to go before she reached his front porch, she watched in relief as he came out the door, another soldier right behind him. He seemed to be in a hurry, but as his hazel eyes landed on her, he smiled, sent the soldier behind him on ahead, and changed course to meet her. As he drew closer, his smile faded.

"Here I was going to say it was a fine day for a visit, but it looks like you got trapped out in the less fine part of the day," he said, clearly trying to sound lighthearted but succeeding only in seeming concerned.

She shrugged her drooping shoulders. "The storm hit when we were a couple of miles out," she explained, raising her voice to be heard over her crying son.

"Ah, no trees to shelter under," he said with an understanding nod. "Wait—a couple of miles? The rain passed an hour ago."

"I wasn't moving quite as quickly as I was when I first set out. I also stopped and tried to calm him down, but . . ." she shrugged again. "He wasn't in the mood to be comforted."

Exhausted, she considered that maybe she just wasn't any good at being a mother. Nothing she'd tried had worked. Despite the added threat Walks at Night's crying brought, she hadn't known how to comfort him. She caught her lip between her teeth, discouraged.

Major Taylor's eyes narrowed. "Are you saying you walked here? Carrying him?"

"It's not that far," she told him, feeling a little defensive for a reason she didn't fully understand. She was a capable woman. She didn't want him to think she was weak or incapable.

"It's fifteen miles!" he argued. "Why didn't Fire Maker send you on horseback?"

She raised her chin a little. "He couldn't spare a horse."

Major Taylor's jaw clenched and unclenched, and his hazel eyes gazed past her for a moment, as if needing time to collect himself.

"It's okay, really. I'm capable of walking, Major Taylor. Like you said, it's a fine day. The walk gave us time to enjoy it."

He sent her an exasperated look and then stepped forward and lifted Walks at Night, still in his cradleboard, off her back. "I suppose Fire Maker didn't send an escort for you either, did he? And will you please call me Ezra already? It's not like we just met."

"Thank you," she told him as the weight was lifted off her shoulders, taking a moment to roll her neck, avoiding both questions. "I thought a cradleboard would allow me to continue to get things done, but he's just about too big for one."

"Yes, he is," Ezra agreed, seeming grim as he turned the cradleboard so Walks at Night could see them. "And I'm sure he felt a little heavier with every mile."

His attention shifted back to her. "You're avoiding my question. Are you seriously going to tell me Fire Maker didn't send you with an escort? Even after what happened last week?"

Stepping forward, Nizhoni began to unlace Walks at Night from the cradleboard Ezra was holding. "Everyone was busy."

He shook his head in disgust, his lips pressed together. "I'm sure they were."

Choosing not to respond, Niz smiled and talked quietly to her son as she undid the laces that held him securely in place, hoping he would finally stop crying. With her attention on him and feeling himself being freed from the board, the little one did stop. He looked at her out of big brown eyes fringed with dark lashes, still wet with tears. He sucked his thumb and watched her, then kicked his legs with obvious glee as she finished with the leather ties and pulled him free of his pouch.

"Here, I'll take him. You're surely worn out," Ezra said gruffly, taking Walks at Night from her arms. "I'm assuming you're here to see Ms. Langston? Unless you've come with another message from Fire Maker . . ."

"No, I'm here to see Ms. Langston. I was coming to ask for directions to her house."

"Good. I'll show you the way, then, and we'll get you two inside where you can dry off."

Nizhoni fell into step beside Ezra as he led the way past the stables and barracks along the eastern edge of the center grounds. "I can take him since you've got the cradleboard," she offered, realizing belatedly that he was carrying everything. "He's heavier than he seems, and he is my son."

The sun finally broke out from behind the dark cloud—Ezra Taylor smiled. For just a moment, she let herself enjoy the warmth of it. "Yes, and I'm the one that dumped him on your doorstep. Don't worry. I've got him."

Feeling more cheerful now that her load had been lightened and Walks at Night had stopped crying, Niz flashed him a brilliant smile in return. "I'm really glad you did. I can't tell you how much I've enjoyed having him."

"Good. I'm glad to hear it." Ezra looked down at the boy in his arms. "He is a cute little guy, isn't he?"

"He is," Niz agreed, reaching over to ruffle Walks at Night's wet hair, hoping to help it dry.

When the boy squirmed and leaned toward the ground, Ezra set him down and took his hand. Niz noticed that he slowed his pace as Walks at Night toddled along beside him. She wasn't sad about it. After the long walk, the leisurely pace and pleasant conversation were nice.

"I'm sure Ms. Langston has some hot tea that will warm you both up, and when I saw her earlier, she said she was making a treat for you two. I don't know what it is, but I'd be cautious. Ms. Langston isn't known for her baking skills."

Niz laughed. "Good to know."

"Actually, if you have time, maybe you could give her a cooking lesson after she gives you a reading lesson. I'll make sure you have a ride and an escort back to your village whenever you're done."

"I'd love to," Niz said, pleased by the idea. She would feel better if she could give Marigold something in exchange for the reading lessons she'd been receiving. "And I'll have time. Ms. Langston invited me to stay the week with her rather than going back and forth. That way, I'll be able to read with her every day."

"Did she?" Major Taylor looked pleasantly surprised. "And Fire Maker agreed?"

"More or less. He told me not to come home until I could read."

"Well, I know it will be hard for you to be away from your village, but we'll enjoy having you—both of you—around while you're here. And," he gave her a rueful smile, "I'll be sure to have my billfold nearby whenever you're ready to return home. I'm guessing I'll have some horses to buy."

"You . . . you actually need the horses you're planning to buy from him, don't you?" she asked, worried that he could possibly be doing it just for her—so she could learn to read.

"We need horses. We've had several stolen."

"Good. Because I wouldn't want . . . I mean . . . it would be ridiculous for you to . . ." she stammered, not knowing how to finish the sentence without being rude.

He smiled again, and her heart warmed. His smile was so sincere, so unguarded, so simple. It wasn't mocking, condescending, or forced. He was kind, happy, and amused, and he wasn't trying to hide it. "Trust me, Niz, we need horses."

They walked in silence for a few steps. "So," she said, dragging the word out. "Do you often get to sample Ms. Langston's baked goods?"

He chuckled. "No, not often. But it's something you don't quickly forget once you do. Here we are. This is her house."

Nizhoni turned just as Marigold flung open the front door of her log home. Somehow it felt surprising that it wasn't ornate or beautiful. It didn't actually fit the occupant at all. But it did fit the fort. It looked the same as every other house they had passed on their way down the road that followed the center ground's northern edge. Maybe that's what felt the most surprising of all.

Marigold, beautiful and smiling, rushed across the small front porch and down onto the street to meet them. Embracing Niz, she exclaimed in astonishment as she did so, already too much in forward motion to stop. "Why! You're soaked through!" she said, laughing as she drew back.

"We got caught in the rain," Niz explained.

"It's a lovely day, but you must be freezing. If we were out on the plains, you would be sweltering, even though it is the first week of September. That rain would have felt refreshing. But not at this elevation! Come on inside! I have a fire going. And I've been baking!" Marigold declared happily, looping her arm through Niz's, pulling her forward. Ezra followed with Walks at Night and the cradleboard.

At the front door of the cabin, the acrid smell of smoke hit them, hanging so thick in the air that Niz's eyes began to water. Marigold continued happily on as if she hadn't noticed. "It's getting so late I was worried you wouldn't be coming, but here you are. I'm so glad! But before we speak of anything else, I have to know—can you stay over for the week? I do hope so! It would be so wonderful to have someone in the house again. I've been making so many plans!"

Niz blinked rapidly, trying to clear her eyes, even as she caught Ezra's look that plainly said, 'I told you so.' She quickly looked away, fighting the urge to laugh. "Yes, we'll stay here at the fort with you if you're sure you don't mind," she answered.

"Wonderful!" Marigold exclaimed, her bright eyes and smile conveying her delight. "And I don't mind at all! I was so hoping you would, I was thinking we could—"

"Ms. Langston, let's give Niz and . . . I forgot to ask, what are you calling this little guy?"

"Walks at Night."

"It's fitting," Ezra said approvingly. "Well, let's give Niz and Walks at Night a chance to change into something dry so they can warm up. In the meantime, why don't we open the windows? The air is so fresh after the rain earlier. Then you can proceed with making your plans for the week," Ezra suggested, sending their hostess an amused smile.

Niz watched the look exchanged between Ezra and Marigold and wondered for a moment if the major was sweet on Ms. Langston. Ninety percent of her hoped he was. He was a good man, and Marigold was a good woman. They shared a common thread of compassion, and both treated others with dignity and honor. Marigold had proven she was not opposed to the unknown when she married Robert and followed him West, so she was likely to support Ezra's adventurous spirit. They would be a good fit. Yet, as Niz lifted Walks at Night and headed to the back bedroom Marigold directed her to, some part of her felt sad.

It wasn't that she was interested in Major Taylor; she was already married, and happily or not, she was a woman of honor. She wouldn't give space or a place to anything else. But Ezra was her last tie to Alex, and a part of her felt sad thinking about losing that.

"That's so selfish of me," she whispered to Walks at Night as she nestled her face against her son for a moment, seeking comfort in having a little one to hold and love. Alex was gone, and Ezra had never been anything but kind. He deserved to have a good life, full of love and laughter. Marigold would certainly provide both.

She sat Walks at Night on the floor and quickly changed him into dry clothes. As she did, a memory of Alex came to mind. It had been a little over a year into their marriage, and he had just received a letter from Ezra. Ezra had written him about life in the army, detailing the things he had seen and done. Alex had been restless all evening after reading the letter, and Niz knew he was feeling left behind and pulled to adventure. After they'd gone to bed, she'd stared up at the ceiling through the darkness, feeling slighted that after a year of marriage, he was longing to be somewhere else.

"Hey Niz, do you ever think about going off into the unknown, seeing something you've never seen, doing something you've never done?" Alex had asked into the silence.

"You clearly do."

"Yeah, I do. All the time. But I can't."

"Because you have a wife?" she had asked bitterly. "And I hold you back?"

His laughter had filled their small cabin. "Is that why you've been so stormy all night? You think I feel like you're the reason I can't go exploring?"

"Aren't I? You were footloose and fancy free before you got married. Now, you're chained to this homestead."

He'd reached across the distance separating them and pinched her lightly in the ribs, making her jump. "You goose." She'd batted his hand away. "I was chained to this homestead the day my pa died. Mother needs me. So do Luke and Will. But one day . . . Will's almost a man now. Once he is, we'll stick around a bit to make sure he and Luke are getting by alright, and then we'll head out into the wild unknown . . ."

"You promised we would live with my people once you got the mill situated!"

He'd laughed again. He was always laughing when she was feeling prickly. For some maddening reason, he'd always thought it so amusing when she got worked up. "So we will. But give me a year to explore first. Maybe two . . . or three."

"Alex!"

"Okay, no more than two, I promise. We'll ride off together into the unknown . . . see things you've never dreamt of . . . sleep under the stars without a fire to dim their light."

"That sounds cold," she'd pointed out.

"I'll keep you warm," he'd answered, his voice full of promise. Rolling over, he'd propped himself up on his elbow and looked down into her face. "We'll explore, just you and me, see what there is to see, take in the wonder of it all . . . together."

"What makes you think I'll come with you?" she'd challenged.

He'd leaned down and kissed her; the kind of kiss that always made her heart pound wildly and her breath quicken. "Because we were made to be together. Life wouldn't be worth living without you."

"Well, I'd be fine without you," she'd quipped, even though they'd both known it wasn't true.

"Oh, yeah?" he'd asked with a laugh. "We'll see about that!" He'd kissed her again, just the way she liked it, until she'd wrapped her arms around him and kept him close even when he attempted to draw back. "You still think you'd be fine without me?" he'd teased.

She'd made a face.

"Seriously, you'd go with me, wouldn't you, Niz?" he'd asked, looking down at her, smoothing her hair back from her face. "It wouldn't be any fun without you."

"Of course I'd go with you," she'd answered, her voice husky. The truth was, she couldn't have imagined a day without Alex. He was like the sun and the moon, the tall mountains and high valleys to her—vital to her very existence. Wherever he went, she would go too.

He'd bent down and kissed the tip of her nose. "That's what I've been thinking about this evening. I wish Ezra had this—what we have. He's out having adventures, but he sounds flat . . . empty, maybe. Like they just don't matter as much as they once did. Perhaps that's part of growing up—of becoming a man instead of a boy. You still want to have fun, but you want someone to have it with. Without that, the excitement's just gone out of it. This . . .you . . . love—it makes it all meaningful. Without it . . . it's just not. Life loses its luster. It's not all you expected it to be. Ezra's letter tonight, it made me feel . . . sad for him. I hope he finds a love that makes all his adventures meaningful someday."

Niz had watched Alex's face through the darkness, in wonder over this man who seemed to her a philosopher hidden beneath the ruggedly handsome mountain man exterior. She'd run her hands up into his hair and pressed her full lips against his. In that moment, there had been no room in her thoughts for any man but him.

Blinking heavily, Niz came back to the present, the memory passing with a deep ache. She wished she could go back and relive that conversation. She would tell him that she'd been wrong—she wasn't fine—and that he'd been right. Life was no fun without him. She wished she could feel the tenderness in his kiss again and the joy of his embrace. She wished the future still felt bright and rosy and life full of meaning. But those things were just a distant memory now.

Walks at Night, who had been playing with the fringe on her dress, tired of his play, and leaned toward her, burying his face against her neck. She kissed his soft cheek and reminded herself that although she had lost the love of her life, her life was not void of love. And in the love that remained, her life found meaning. Her sisters, her mother, her friends, her people, and now Walks at Night, still filled her heart with purpose. And though some part of her still felt sad, she rejoiced that Alex's wish for Ezra might be coming to pass. Maybe Ezra was finding a love that would render all his adventures in life meaningful too.

Nizhoni stood and pulled out of her satchel a calico dress she had kept from her time as an Applewood. She was glad she'd remembered to pack it before leaving her village. Dust flew as she shook it out. Like her doll, it had been relegated to hiding between the hides for the past year. Thankfully, she had kept it wrapped in brown paper, and it still smelled more like the lavender sachet she'd packed it with than leather. Changing into it, she ran her hands over the cotton fabric. It seemed like a lifetime since she'd worn it.

Though she was proud of her people and proud of who she was, she would spend the week living among the more than one hundred soldiers stationed at the fort. As she would be staying with Marigold, who lived on the opposite side of the central parade grounds as Major Taylor, the man could not be expected to be around every moment of every day. He had a job to do. And while he'd kept his soldiers in line thus far, she knew the whole camp likely didn't share his perspective on the Indians. It would be better—safer—for herself, Walks at Night, and Marigold if she blended in as much as possible while she was there.

At first, she'd been conflicted about changing her appearance to fit in, but she'd had plenty of time to think about it during her walk. She'd concluded that changing out of her buckskin was not being untrue to herself, as her past as an Applewood was also part of who she was. For the week, she would step into that part of her identity and embrace it, knowing her past, though complicated, was all a part of her. Her time in her village as well as her time as Nizhoni Applewood combined to make her the woman she had become.

Opening the bedroom door, she found Ezra and Marigold involved in a serious conversation. They stopped talking when she entered, and both looked at her in surprise. She shrugged and tucked her hair self-consciously behind her ear. "I . . . I figured it would be best to blend in while at the fort."

Marigold rose quickly. "You, my dear, do not blend in, and it has nothing to do with the clothes you wear," she said, coming toward her. "You are too beautiful to blend in anywhere. You couldn't be missed even if you were in rags." Marigold reached for Walks at Night, her smile for the little boy big and bright. "Isn't that right, darling?" she cooed to the toddler. "You have an awfully pretty mama!" He laughed and kicked his legs, clearly delighted by the attention. Niz turned away, embarrassed by the compliment. She veered towards the open window and stood looking out of it. A cool breeze was coming in, chasing away the heaviness of the burnt aroma. A group of soldiers was practicing a drill on the parade grounds.

"Niz, you don't have to do that," Ezra told her, standing up and moving to the other side of the window, facing her. "Don't worry about being here at the fort. You're safe. Everyone knows you're here in peace, as Ms. Langston and I's guest."

She simply nodded.

"If you have any trouble at all, you come get me at once, do you hear? Don't hesitate. Either one of you." Both women nodded, though Nizhoni wondered about the intensity of his tone.

"With the Comanche making such trouble in the area, everyone is a little jumpy," Marigold explained, her expression sympathetic as she settled on a chair with Walks at Night on her lap. He promptly scooted off, and toddled around the room, inspecting everything.

Niz looked at Ezra expectantly, wanting an update. She knew it wasn't a conversation a man—especially a soldier—typically would have with a woman, but he'd been candid with her before. She wanted to know what was going on.

He hesitated for only a moment. "We captured three of them—they're locked up in the guardhouse—and two others fell in the skirmish." He looked grim, and she realized he was saddened by the bloodshed, regardless of the necessity. "Their friends aren't happy. Two more homesteads have been hit since the raid on your village."

She winced. Two homesteads in five days.

"At one, the horses were stolen in the night, but the family was left unharmed. At the other, the animals were taken and the man, a bachelor, was killed."

"Why do they continue to use violence at one and not the other?" Niz questioned.

Ezra shrugged. "We can't figure it out. About half the raids are violent and half aren't. They're so merciless at the half that it makes no sense why they wouldn't use any violence at all at the others." He looked uncomfortable and unwell with the words he was speaking.

"Do some fight back while others let them raid uncontested?" she questioned.

He shook his head. "The bachelor was murdered in his bed. I doubt he even knew they were there."

Niz shook her head, saddened by the senseless violence. Ezra kept talking, but for a brief moment, her mind flashed back to the moment she'd first seen the Comanche coming. The dread. The fear. The panic. Again, she heard them release their terrifying war cries, and she shivered.

"Hey." Ezra reached out and put his hand on her shoulder. "You okay?"

She refocused on his face and propped up what she hoped was a convincing smile. "Yes. I guess I must still be chilled from getting caught in the rain."

For just a moment, something unreadable flickered through Ezra's hazel eyes. She watched it, trying to figure out what it was. Was it frustration? Pain? A desire to make it better? Did he know she'd just had a flashback? Did he have them too?

"Come stand by the stove and get warm," Marigold suggested, looking up from her play with Walks at Night. "Obviously you're still chilled. Your hair is still damp."

"She's right," Ezra told her, turning her by the shoulders, and gently directing her back to the stove. Niz couldn't argue that the heat felt nice and held her hands out to warm over the cast iron.

Ezra crossed his arms over his chest. "Anyway, as I was saying, I have patrols out all over the area, leaving only enough soldiers here to defend the fort. The settlers are scared. Living so near the reservation has felt safe with your people at peace, but now, the Comanche are using the vastness of your lands as a place to disappear and launch their attacks from . . ." Ezra sighed. "People are frightened, Niz. Please be sure to stay inside the fort, and whenever you're ready to return home, I'll make certain you have escorts."

The gravity of what he wasn't saying set in. "Settlers, people in town, they don't know the difference between my people and the Comanche, do they?" Niz questioned. "They don't see us as separate tribes." She paused, watching his face. "They blame us, don't they?"

"They know your people are peaceful. Things will get back to normal. We just need to stop these raids so that everyone stops making assumptions and starts asking the right questions before taking action," Ezra answered, sounding strained.

Niz considered him for a long moment, realizing how difficult it must be to have the responsibility of keeping peace when hardly anyone was willing to cooperate. And yet, despite the pressure, he remained strong, kind, and compassionate. "You're doing a good job, Major Taylor. I know it isn't what you wanted, but I'm glad your powerful friends sent you here."

He pulled his hand over his face, and she could see he didn't feel like he was doing well.

"The Comanche would have come whether you were here or not," she continued, meaning every word. "If you weren't in charge, who would be? And would they have shown the restraint and wisdom that you have?"

"You should withhold your praise until we see how all this plays out," he answered gruffly.

"Do you think the government will revoke our hunting rights?" Niz asked. It was a question that had been weighing on her mind ever since their last conversation at the fort. As the problem with the Comanche continued to grow, so had her anxiety. Knowing that the settlers were now blaming her people, expanded it even more.

Ezra met her eyes for a long moment. "I don't know," he answered honestly. "We need to stop the raids."

"That's enough of all this talk about raids," Marigold declared, standing. "I've been baking!" When the blonde whisked past them to the cupboard by the table, Ezra sent Niz a pointed look. "I burnt the cookies beyond repair, so those aren't an option," she continued, drawing a grin from Ezra, "but the bread turned out marvelously, and I have a jar of raspberry preserves!"

"It sounds wonderful, Ms. Langston, but I'd best be on my way. I have paperwork I have to finish before the end of the day," he said apologetically, the grin gone when their hostess turned back around from her cupboard. Ms. Langston's face fell. "But I'm sure Niz is hungry after her walk, and Walks at Night, also," he offered.

Marigold looked at Niz, and Niz nodded helplessly, not wanting to hurt her new friend's feelings. Marigold's face brightened. "Wonderful. Let me just spread these preserves and make a pot of tea, and I'll bring it over!"

"I'm headed out. Thank you for your hospitality, Ms. Langston." Ezra settled his dark blue forage cap on his head.

Unwillingly, a part of Niz felt sad that he was leaving. She still had so many questions and so many thoughts about the Comanche. Being able to talk to Ezra about it was a relief. He actually included her in the conversation and seemingly thought her worth the discussion. And the kindness in his handsome face made her feel safe.

Marigold sent a farewell over her shoulder as she went about putting on the kettle. Starting for the door, Ezra paused in front of Niz. "I'm glad you're staying for the week. Please don't worry. You're safe here." He smiled as he reached down and tousled Walks at Night's hair. "And for the record, I like the buckskin."

Niz looked up, surprised by his last comment, but he was already out the door. She watched through the window as he walked away. Fire Maker had made her feel unimportant and dispensable. Settlers she used to call neighbors were turning against her and her people. She was in a place where it felt safer to blend in rather than be herself, where it didn't feel like she was valuable, likeable, or equal. And Ezra had just left her feeling like he preferred her just the way she was. His comment was a reminder that being herself was enough and maybe even preferable to trying to blend in. She inhaled deeply, taking a moment to process that.

"Alright, go ahead and bring that hungry little guy to the table," Marigold said, sounding happy. When she turned with her tray full of delicate teacups, a little tin cup for Walks at Night, and a plate full of bread with preserves, Nizhoni could clearly see how pleased her friend was to have company, and she understood it. She could only imagine how lonely the cabin must feel since Robert died. Marigold had no sisters or mother close by, no friends that she had known her entire life as Niz did. It was only her in the middle of a fort, all by herself.

Niz scooped Walks at Night up and sat down at the table, holding him on her lap. Marigold served the tea, and Nizhoni tasted it to make sure it wasn't too hot before helping Walks at Night drink his. As Niz sipped her own, she began to feel warm from the inside out for the first time since the rain had begun. Marigold served her a slice of bread, and she cautiously took a bite, heeding Ezra's warning. To her surprise, the bread was fluffy and delicious. When she looked up at Marigold, the woman's face made her laugh out loud.

"The major warned you about my baking, didn't he?" she said, her pretty features turned down in a pout. Niz stayed quiet, not wanting to incriminate a man who had been nothing but kind to her.

"Oh, don't bother. I know he did. They all know I'm a terrible cook. Robert was dear to eat what I fixed him, but he was no liar. He didn't pretend I was any good in the kitchen, but he always said he didn't mind." Marigold's face brightened a little. "He didn't marry me for my culinary skills—I was upfront and honest with him about it before the wedding. He knew what he was getting into. When we first arrived here, everyone expected he must eat so well with a wife to bake for him. There aren't many of us out here on the frontier, you know."

Niz nodded. She knew that to be true.

"Well, at first his friends asked to come for dinner—they planned to get some good home cooking—but no one came more than once. Within the first week, people stopped asking. Now I have a . . . a reputation," she finished with a miserable harumph. "But it's not really my fault, you know. My father is an army man. My mother and I followed him from camp to camp during the first year of The War Between the States. I helped her bake bread for the soldiers, so that's why I can make that, but I hadn't the chance to learn much else. She spent most of her time tending the wounded, and I stayed busy helping her."

Niz helped Walks at Night with another drink of his tea while watching Marigold twirl a strand of her golden hair around her finger absently. "What happened?" Niz asked gently, even though she could guess—she recognized that look of suffering.

"Living conditions were poor. Mother got sick and died very suddenly. I was only eight when she passed. After that, Father kept a cook. He wanted to send me away to boarding school back East, but I was all he had left. He couldn't bear the thought of it, and I didn't want to go. So, he let me stay and brought in a governess. I minded my studies and helped in the medical tent whenever the opportunity arose. That's what I'm most fascinated by; I love helping a sick man heal. But I never learned much more about cooking. The bread is lovely, though, isn't it?" she finished hopefully.

"It really is," Niz agreed truthfully. Walks at Night reached for another bite, and she tore a piece off and put it on the table for him. "First of all, I think your mother would be very proud of the woman you've become, even if you have a reputation."

Marigold looked pleased.

"Secondly, it just so happens that among my people, we like to make trades. And, as you know, I know my way around a kitchen. What would you say to me trading you lessons? I'll teach you to bake and cook, and you can teach me to read."

"Oh, you don't have to do that," Marigold answered sheepishly. "I'm terrible at it, but I suppose we all have things we're bad at."

"Well, you don't have to be bad at this. I'm sure the men are exhausted and hungry after all these extra patrols searching for the Comanche. You can bake cookies for them to boost their morale, and when you leave the fort and head home to your father, you can go with your head held high and a new reputation in tow."

Marigold's answering smile was bright. "I would like that."

"Good! Let's start with raspberry preserves," Niz said, showing Marigold her bread. She had carefully nibbled away around the edges, where there was very little of the ruby red jam.

"Oh!" Marigold said, with a dismal laugh. "I know it's terrible!"

"It's not terrible, it's just . . . tart," Niz argued. "Did you forget to add the sugar?"

"Sugar?" Marigold asked, her blue eyes wide. "But berries are naturally sweet."

Niz couldn't hold back a grin. "Yes, it sounds like preserves are the perfect place to start. But first, let me put Walks at Night down for a quick nap."

Once she had washed the boy up, swaddled him, and strapped him into his cradleboard to sleep, she laid him in the back bedroom and sang softly to him until he fell asleep. When she returned to the main room, Marigold suggested they start with reading. Marigold stood behind her and braided her black hair into a beautiful style as Niz read aloud, going slow as she stumbled over words. Marigold was extra patient, thoroughly seeming to enjoy the chance to do someone's hair, and the afternoon wore on pleasantly.

After reading, Niz and Marigold worked together to make a small batch of preserves and while it was cooling, they cooked their dinner. Niz taught about techniques and flavors as they went along and the meal turned out well. Once the kitchen had been put back in order, they played with Walks at Night and spent the evening working on projects. Niz began sewing Walks at Night a new outfit out of buckskin she had brought along, and Marigold mended uniforms she had taken in.

When the hour grew late and Walks at Night began to rub his eyes, Nizhoni rolled out her sleeping mat on the floor of the main room. Marigold retired to her bedroom, and Nizhoni laid down with her son, singing and patting him until he fell asleep. Lying quietly in the darkness, she took in the details of the home.

The outside of the house certainly did not reflect its occupant, but inside, it fit Marigold. The curtains hanging at the windows were vibrant; the quilt draped over the rocker was cheerful and bright; the checkered tablecloth was red and cheery. Even the oil lamp was made of green glass. The chairs had colorful cushions with beautiful stitching, and the tea towels were embroidered with pretty florals. Everything was beautiful and happy, just like Marigold. Niz smiled, feeling happy too. If she had to learn to read and be away from her village, she was happy to be there, in the vibrant and cheerful home of a friend.

Niz was nearly asleep when a noise on the front porch startled her. Her thoughts returned to the conversation earlier, and she lay awake in the darkness, listening. She heard the unmistakable sound of footsteps, and her heart began to race, wondering why someone would be on Marigold's porch so late, after the house had clearly gone to bed. Rising silently, being careful not to disturb her son, she tiptoed to the window on the opposite side of the door from where she'd heard the noise. Standing off to the side, she carefully moved the colorful curtains just enough to have a view of the front porch.

At first, she didn't see anyone. She waited patiently, determined to know who was out there. If she didn't, sleep would be elusive. The Comanche raid was too fresh, the tension between the settlers and the natives too high for her to feel unconcerned.

Something stirred in the shadows near the porch floor, and she squinted through the darkness, trying to make out what she was seeing. There was a dark form near the ground, but she couldn't decipher more than that. She stood watching for several minutes, trying to make sense of why a man would be on the floor of Marigold's porch late at night. Was it a soldier deep in his cups and simply trying to find somewhere to sleep it off? Or someone with ill intent, who was waiting to make sure everyone was asleep before making their next move? Were there soldiers who were angry about her being in camp? Or someone who knew a beautiful widow lived in the house alone?

It was likely nothing. There was a very good chance there was a harmless explanation. But even though she hadn't rested well for almost a week, ever since Ever Flowering's midnight fever and then the raid, Niz knew she wouldn't be able to sleep for wondering. She glanced at Walks at Night, so peaceful in slumber, and thought of Marigold, who had opened her home to them even in such a precarious time. She couldn't let anything happen to either of them.

Tiptoeing back across the room, she opened her satchel and pulled out the revolver that had belonged to Alex. Though she'd brought it for the walk, she felt better having it in her hands, knowing she wasn't defenseless. Moving silently back to the door, she cracked it open. She could see a man's boots off to the side where she had heard the noise. Her heart hammering, she counted to ten, took a deep breath, and then opened the door wider and slipped out, both hands gripping her revolver. If there was trouble, she could head it off and protect her son and Marigold. If there wasn't, at least she would know and be able to sleep.

As she stepped out onto the porch, a board creaked. She froze, but it was too late; the dark form on the porch moved. Through the shadows, she saw two eyes looking at her.

"Don't move," she said, her voice low and dangerous. Whatever was going on, she was going to take care of it—and without waking her little one.

There was a shocked silence. "Niz?"

She rocked back a step, surprised by the familiar voice.

Fourteen

"Niz, lower your weapon. It's just me."

The man sat up, moving into the moonlight. Relief flooded her as the familiarity of his face registered. She lowered her revolver and squatted down on her heels to his level, her heart still racing. "Major Taylor! What are you doing here?" she whispered accusingly.

"I could ask you the same thing."

"I'm staying here," she retorted, irritated that she had been frightened for no reason. "What are you doing lying on the porch?" Now that she was outside and closer, she could see that he was sitting on his bedroll. "Were you planning to sleep here?" she asked incredulously.

"As a matter of fact, I was," he answered, seeming annoyed.

"Why?" she demanded. The man had a large house and a comfortable bed not far away. It made no sense. Unless there was something he wasn't telling her . . .

"What I would like to know is why, if you thought there was danger out here, as you clearly did," he said, pointing at her revolver, "did you open the door and come out?"

"I needed to know who was out here," she said simply.

"No, you didn't," he answered bluntly. "You should have stayed inside where you were safe."

Niz lifted her chin, his chastisement adding fuel to her irritation. "Excuse me? Do you know who is inside that door? My son and a woman who has been nothing but a friend to me! How could you think I would stay hidden inside instead of coming out to secure their safety?"

"And what of your own safety?" Ezra challenged, his tone matching hers. "Hm? What if I had been a dangerous man, Niz?"

"I can take care of myself!"

He suddenly reached out and batted her hand, knocking the revolver free, causing it to fall to the ground with a loud thud. She gasped. "How dare you?" she cried, too livid to remember to whisper. "What if that had gone off when it fell? My baby is inside!"

"You had no business coming out that door!" he hissed, barely keeping his voice quiet. "I easily disarmed you in one move!"

"I wasn't ready!" she objected. "For your information, I had a much better hold before I realized it was you."

"Niz, don't you understand? Anyone who wishes you harm wouldn't hesitate to use force to disarm you. And I didn't even have to!" Frustration was written all over his face.

"I told you! I wasn't ready!" she argued, her eyes fiery in the darkness. "What would you have had me do, Ezra? Stay inside and simply wait to be attacked? I'm not the kind of woman who worries and waits. I take action!"

"You should have laid down with Walks at Night and gone to sleep! I told you not to worry! I told you that you were safe! You should have known I would protect you."

"Should I have guessed you would be sleeping on the front porch?" she shot back, offended by his scolding. She clenched her hands into fists, her frustration rising. "Go home and sleep in your own bed while you have the chance. You don't have to protect me, Ezra. I can take care of myself!"

"You might think that, but it's not true when you keep doing reckless things like leading a defense against the Comanche, walking fifteen miles through the wilderness alone, and sneaking out late at night trying to thwart danger!"

Niz's eyebrows shot up. "Excuse me?"

Unfazed, he shrugged his broad shoulders. "Which part do you need me to clarify? Did you not do all those things within the past week?"

She glared at him. "Do you not understand?" she accused, her voice rising. "I don't go looking for danger! I don't choose it! I only do what I have to do. Things aren't like they were. My husband and my father are dead! I don't have anyone to protect me anymore!"

"You have me!" He threw his hands out in demonstration. "And I am trying my best!"

"Ezra!" she cried. "You're not Alex!" She was too mad to even care she'd spoken his name. "You have no obligation—" He shot up, and she stopped as she scrambled to her feet too. She could feel his frustration from the top of her head to the bottom of her toes. It was radiating from him, matching and mingling with her own.

"Do you think I don't know that?" he asked, his voice incredulous, taking a step toward her as he spoke, his angry gaze intense in the darkness. "Sometimes I wish with all my heart I was because then I could—" He stopped short.

"Could what?" she questioned, raising her chin, daring him to finish. What had he been about to say? Order her around? Tell her what to do?

He clenched and unclenched his jaw. "Alex is gone, Niz. And I am doing my best to be a good friend to him even now."

Her heartbeat quickened. Some part of her felt sad. She'd known he was helping her because he felt an obligation to Alex. She'd known that. But this felt different. This felt like pity, and it whipped up the flames of her anger.

"That's what this is?" she asked, her voice suddenly low and trembling, his last statement making her angrier than anything else he'd said, even though she didn't completely understand why. "Befriending my tribe, speaking to my mother and sister, protecting us from the Comanche, helping me learn how to read, buying horses from Fire Maker . . . it's all out of pity, isn't it?"

"For heaven's sake, Niz. You're tired. I'm tired. Let's not do this—" he groaned, but she continued as if he hadn't spoken.

"It's out of some duty you feel you have to my dead husband, isn't it? Does doing so ease your guilt that you weren't there the day he died? Or that you weren't there the last years he was alive because you were too busy off having an adventure?"

"No, that is not what this is," Ezra argued, his voice strained.

"Save your breath, Major Taylor. I don't want to hear it! I don't want your pity! I'm going inside, and in the morning, whether I can read or not, I'm heading home, and I don't want your horse and I don't want your escort, and I don't want anything from you ever again!" she cried, beginning to shake from emotion.

To be pitied was worse than being in danger. To be no more than a duty was far more terrible than being on her own. Some part of her had thought he was her friend, that he actually cared, but no, once again, it wasn't about her or who she was as a person. *It was about a man wanting to prove something and using her to do it.*

She whirled, reaching for the door. But before she touched the latch, Ezra caught her wrist and swung her back around.

"Niz, stop! You want to know what this is about?"

She glared at him.

"This is what it's about!" Cupping his hand to the back of her neck he covered her lips with his own. For one heart-stopping moment, he kissed her thoroughly and passionately. His strong arms wrapped around her, pulling her to him and holding on like he planned never to let go.

For a moment, she stood frozen in shock. As the shock subsided, another moment passed as she found herself being drawn into the intensity and emotion of his kiss. She could feel his hunger and longing, and his tenderness was like a taste of honey after a year of drinking vinegar. Then, her wits returning, she pushed him back with a gasp. "Ezra! I'm married!"

"I know you're married," he shot back. Suddenly, she watched his anger dissolve into despair. "You've always been married."

"What's that supposed to mean?" she questioned, stunned.

He watched her for a long moment, silent, and then shrugged. "I never meant to love you, Niz, but I fell in love with you just like Alex did. You're strong and spirited and vibrant and so full of life and beauty, and it just happened before I even realized it was." He swallowed hard. "But Alex was my best friend . . . more like a brother really, and I could never do anything to hurt him. So I stayed until after the wedding and then left to join the army." His lips lifted in a sad smile. "You were so mad the day I left because you thought Alex would rather be leaving with me to have another adventure. What you didn't know was that I would have given anything to be in his shoes, staying home with you."

"Ezra . . ." Feeling lightheaded, she sank back heavily against the door. What he was saying was a shock. She'd never had even the slightest inclination as to his feelings. It was hard to comprehend that so many assumptions she'd made about why he'd left had been so wrong.

"When I was assigned to come back here, I would have happily gone anywhere else, and it had nothing to do with adventure. I missed Alex and you and the Applewoods, of course, but over the last four years, I'd figured out how to move on. I was scared that I would come back and find myself right back in the same predicament—face to face with the fact that I was in love with a woman I could never have. When I got back, I decided I would stay away for a while, just until I could get my head on straight. I planned to ride over and see everyone once I mustered up the courage. This trouble with the Comanche came up, and I ended up riding out to your village before that happened. I never thought you would be there.

"I wanted to help your people, Niz. I still do. What's being done isn't right. I know I can only do so much—there's a lot of red tape, and people in high places that call the shots, but as far it depends on me, I wanted to be an ally—someone who did all they could to help. I was excited about this post for that one reason alone, but when we rode out to the village to meet with Fire Maker and you walked in . . . I couldn't believe what I was seeing. I honestly thought my eyes were playing tricks on me. I'd always pictured you living happily with the Applewoods; I never expected you to be at the village. And then to find out you were married . . . again." He clenched and unclenched his jaw. "Only this time, it's not even to someone I love like a brother—it's not even to someone who at least loves you and treats you well. In fact, he's terrible to you, and it took every ounce of restraint I had not to knock him out when he pushed you to the ground."

He stared at the porch floor for several long moments and then finally sighed. "So now you know. I don't want to help you or protect you out of duty or guilt or pity. Trust me. That's not enough to make me sleep on a hard porch floor one of the few nights I've actually been home in the past two weeks rather than out on patrol." He shrugged one broad shoulder. "It's love, Niz. I want to help you however I can and protect you and equip you and care for you because I feel like my heart would be ripped out of my chest if something happened to you. I'd rather die a thousand deaths than see you hurt or scared or troubled. Niz, I . . . I love you."

"Ezra," she started again, her eyes wide, her thoughts feeling thick, her heart hammering. She felt dangerously near tears at the terrible hopelessness and sorrow of it all. She was married to a man who didn't love her, who held no fondness for her, who didn't care for or protect her, all while a good and wonderful and incredibly handsome man stood before her professing his true and enduring love, and she couldn't offer him anything in return—not even hope.

His smile in the light of the moon was sardonic. "I know. You're married. To another man." He drew a deep breath. "And you're a woman of honor, and I hope I'm a man of honor too. So I want you to know that I will never speak of this again, nor will I do anything to make you feel uncomfortable. I never meant to in the first place. I just couldn't let you believe you were nothing to me but a duty. On the contrary, it was duty that kept me away." He drug his hand over his face. "Think of me as a friend who truly cares, and that's all. It's enough. Let me protect you. Let me fuss over you all I can from a distance. Give me that. And I'll give you uncomplicated, pure friendship in return."

Niz stood staring at him, not knowing what to say. She rarely found herself speechless, and it was an uncomfortable feeling. The love, pain, and admiration in his hazel eyes was making it hard to think; her own emotions were even less helpful. Dropping her gaze to the porch floor, she tried to figure out a path forward. Finally, she nodded. "Alright, friend. Come, tell me why you're sleeping on the porch. And I want the whole truth this time. You can't tell me anything less," she said, crossing the floor to sit on the top step, her legs suddenly feeling very weak.

She didn't know what to make of his kiss, his declaration, or his explanation. She felt shocked by what he'd said and appalled that she'd had no idea. She was sad for the years he had missed out on with the Applewoods because of her, guilt-ridden that she had been kissed by Alex's best friend, ashamed that it had happened while she was married to another man, and mortified that some part of her had delighted in his kiss. And in the midst of all the emotions, she couldn't deny how comforting it felt to be loved again after the loneliest year of her life.

Even being the confident woman that she was, being unloved by someone who should have loved her had taken its toll. Somewhere deep in her heart, she had begun to own her husband's indifference and feel unlovable. She felt thirsty for affection, for warmth, for love. Some part of her wanted to return Ezra's kiss and get swept away in passion and tenderness and longing. But that's not who she was, nor was it who he was. Instead, she was going to push all the emotions down deep and pretend they had never had the conversation they'd just had.

She was married to Fire Maker. And whether or not he deserved her loyalty or loved her well, she was a woman of honor, integrity, and faithfulness. No matter how aggravating her husband was or how wonderful Ezra Taylor was, she knew who Nizhoni Applewood was. She would not change nor compromise that. She was greater than her lack, stronger than her desire, deeper than the moment.

Ezra dropped onto the stair beside her with a sigh. "Niz, the truth is, there's a lot of people not feeling too friendly toward the Indians right now. It's not your tribe that's causing the problems, and I know that, but not everyone understands that you're different tribes—different people. They think in blanket terms, and right now, those thoughts aren't too good. My men have been cleaning up the aftermath of some pretty brutal attacks these past few weeks, and they're angry. I've said what I can say, and I sure hope no one would do anything dumb, but I'm not going to take any chances. Not with you. You came here at my request. You're staying in the fort I have command over. I *will* keep you safe while you're here. Even if I have to sleep on the porch to make sure I can do that."

She nodded as she took that information in. Things must be bad if he felt such a drastic measure was necessary. "Did something happen this evening? You didn't seem as worried this afternoon . . ."

"There were some men who saw you walk in that aren't happy you're here," he answered simply. "They think maybe it's a trick."

"A trick?"

"Yeah. They think you're a spy, sent to gather information about how many soldiers are stationed here or how many horses we have." He bent forward over his knees and settled his elbows on them. "Or that maybe your people are planning an attack and you'll cause a diversion while they sneak in or maybe you'll attack from the inside while they attack from the outside."

"If only they knew how bad I was with a gun," she answered dryly.

He bumped her shoulder with his. "Your aim's not bad. It's your grip. I can help you with that."

"I'd appreciate it." She sat, thinking for a moment. "What were they planning to do with me?"

"We don't need to go into it."

"I asked for the whole truth, remember?"

He cracked his knuckles and looked out into the darkness for several long moments. "They figured they could take you captive and trade you back for a ceasefire. They know you're the wife of a chief."

"It's not Fire Maker causing the trouble," she reasoned. "He has no sway over the Comanche. Our village was attacked too."

"I know. I tried to tell them. But all they see is Indian. They don't know the Comanche from the Lakota from your people. All they know is that you're the wife of the chief, so they assume you could become a bargaining tool."

"Even if it were Fire Maker causing the trouble, I wouldn't be a tempting enough trade," she admitted honestly.

His only answer was a sound of disgust. They were both quiet for several minutes. "I think it would be best if you stay inside while you're at the fort," he finally said, breaking the silence.

She bit her lip. The outdoors felt like a part of her. She recoiled at the very idea of being shut up inside. And Fire Maker had told her to stay until she could read. She didn't know how long that would take, but the thought of staying indoors—with a toddler—for however long it did, was suffocating.

"Please," he entreated.

"I will if you think it's necessary."

"I do."

"Do you think I should go home? Would it be better? Safer? For Walks at Night and myself . . . Marigold . . . you?"

"If you're here, at least you're within my reach."

Despair settled over Niz as she realized he was right. With Ezra there to protect them, she and her son were safer in the midst of a fort full of people who wanted to take her captive than they were in their own wickiup with their own people because her own husband didn't care about their safety. In fact, Fire Maker was likely the greatest danger. But there were others to think of—Marigold and Ezra's safety mattered too. If only the soldiers could understand how far their suspicions were from the truth . . .

Suddenly she laughed—it was either that or cry.

"What's funny? I don't see anything remotely amusing about this conversation," Ezra commented dryly.

"I was just thinking how ridiculous it is that they assume I'm here spying and making plans to attack, when in actuality I'm here looking ridiculously dimwitted as I sound out the smallest words. That, and teaching Marigold how to season her skillet, so she doesn't burn everything." She paused. "And how ridiculous it was that I assumed someone was on the porch wanting to do us harm when in actuality you were out here to protect us."

He chuckled too. "It is easy to assume the worst, isn't it?"

"I wish we didn't. I wish we could see one another for what's on the inside, not what's on the outside. I think we'd see we are much more like some people and much less like others, and that where our similarities truly lie would surprise us. If only we could see a person's heart instead of their face." There was a brief silence. "Don't you?" she asked cautiously. She would have thought Ezra would understand.

"I rather like your face."

Startled, she laughed as she glanced over at him. Realizing he was watching her, she quickly redirected her attention up to the stars instead, color rising in her cheeks. Drawing her knees up to her chest, she smoothed her skirts and wrapped her arms around them. "Is me being here putting Marigold in danger?" she asked, getting back to the point.

"Robert was a really likeable guy, and a friend to everyone. He's only been gone a few months. No man would dare to lay a finger on his widow for fear of what the others would do to him if he did. Besides, Ms. Langston is admired by nearly every man here; most would marry her on the spot if she'd take them. Believe me—she's in no danger. Haven't you seen how they stare at her? They adore her."

A slight smile touched her lips. "Yes, I've seen." It was hard to miss. "I actually—" she stopped abruptly, leaving her sentence dangling awkwardly.

"What?" he asked curiously. She shook her head, reluctant to finish the thought. "I thought we were speaking the whole truth," he prompted.

Niz shrugged one shoulder and took a deep breath. "Earlier, when I went to change, I thought maybe you were sweet on Ms. Langston." She turned to look at him, trying to gauge his reaction. "Honestly, I kind of hoped you were. She's a wonderful woman, Ezra, full of joy, beautiful . . . and available."

He sat quietly for a moment, staring off into the distance. She wondered if her reasoning was striking home. Maybe hearing it from her own lips might make him think logically about the situation. The reality was that no matter how much he thought he loved her, there was no future for them, and they both knew it. Marigold could assure his happiness now and for years to come. It just made sense. She wondered if it did to him too. Part of her sincerely hoped so. But some selfish, horrible part of her would be sad if it did.

Finally, he looked back at her. His hazel eyes were intense. "I've told myself the same thing a dozen times."

"You said yourself that she's the best kind of woman," she reminded softly. "I'm certain she could make you happy."

He searched her face. "Only if she had hair as black as a moonless night, eyes as fathomless as the peaks of a hundred mountain ranges, skin as silky as young aspen leaves." His attention dropped to her mouth. "And the most compelling dimple in her lip that makes a man unable to think about anything else but kissing it."

He glanced back up to meet her eyes again. Mesmerized by his words, Niz felt incapable of looking away. "I could love her if she had a spirit as free and untamable as the wind, the essence of the wildflowers that bloom in mid-summer, and the strength of the tall pines that continue to grow and flourish, despite freezing temperatures and spells of drought," he continued. "Only then could she make me happy. But then she wouldn't be her anymore—she'd be you."

His words wrapped around her heart like a warm fur on a cold winter day. In them, she felt beautiful, desirable, and exciting. She thirstily drank in the tender adoration in his eyes, feeling no more capable of looking away than could a man dying of thirst walk away from a clear mountain stream. Finally, she succeeded in doing so. Fixing her gaze on the house across the road so it wouldn't turn back toward him, she forced her tone to be lighthearted as she asked, "What are you? A poet?"

He chuckled and shook his head. "Not a poet. Just a man who was told I must speak the whole truth." His smile faded. "Your parents named you correctly, Nizhoni. You are Beautiful. Beautiful in every way. That's what I call you in my thoughts. I never call you Niz. I always call you Beautiful."

She sat up a little taller; she *felt* a little more beautiful. Still, she bumped his shoulder. "I thought you made me a promise."

"I forgot to tell you that promise goes into effect tomorrow," he answered lightly.

"Oh, does it?" she asked, unable to hold back another laugh. He'd said it so casually and cheerfully.

"Mm-hmm," he answered. She could hear the smile in his voice.

Telling herself not to do it, she glanced over at him again, and her eyes met his. His gaze was full of so much love and admiration, and despite all her efforts to push down the emotions and the feelings, they were rising back up, threatening to consume her, drawing her to him. Despite her resolve and her determination of who she was—and wasn't—she was being swept away by the emotion in his hazel eyes, his rugged good looks, and the longing that was emanating from him.

For just a moment, she was tempted to lean in for a kiss. She was hungry for comfort and affection, and he appeared only too willing to give it. Still, she stayed where she was, unmoving, knowing she never could. She was married. And regardless of Fire Maker's actions, that meant something to her. A promise was a promise.

Ezra reached out and brushed his knuckles softly down the side of her face. "Go to bed, Beautiful, before I kiss you again and have to apologize for it later." His voice was strained and sad.

She didn't want to leave. And in that one fact alone, she pushed herself quickly to her feet and hurried to the front door, as much for his sake as hers. He was a good man. She didn't want to hurt him, and she didn't want to be hurt. She wasn't free to love him. His love and her integrity were both too valuable to tarnish, and thus, together was no longer the place to be.

"Goodnight, Ezra," she whispered softly, pausing at the door. Opening it carefully, she slipped silently inside and crossed the room to lie down beside her son.

She heard Ezra settle down on the porch again, and she closed her eyes and forced her mind to be still. Tears ran down the sides of her face and dampened her dark hair, refusing to bend to her will as her mind had. She could refuse to give place to the chaotic emotions and thoughts, but this time, she couldn't control her tears. Exhausted, she fell asleep with one thought standing out among the rest—regardless of the troubles that were swirling and the big emotions and shocking declarations, with Ezra outside, she felt safe.

Fifteen

Feeling safe, Niz slept well for the first time all week. By the time she woke in the morning, Ezra and his bedroll were gone. He sent a note instructing them to stay inside. When Marigold read it aloud, Niz's heart warmed, thankful he had thought to send one so she wouldn't be forced to tell Marigold of their late-night conversation. It felt too raw to share. Still, after the note had been read, she stood looking out the window at the September sunshine, thinking everything over, and her heart grew heavy.

"I'm so sorry if our being here has put you in danger or become an inconvenience. We will certainly return home if you feel it would be better," Niz said, turning from the window toward her friend. Fire Maker and Ezra could both be dealt with; Marigold deserved to have a say. It was her home, after all.

"Don't be silly!" the golden-haired woman responded, continuing to play with Walks at Night, kissing both of his palms and then blowing on them, tickling his little hands. The boy erupted into hearty giggles that made Marigold laugh too.

"Marigold, I'm serious. We'll be returning to our village once I learn to read, but this is your home. You'll be staying here among these soldiers, who likely don't think you should be housing us."

Marigold turned. "Do you think I care? If I cared, would I have married Robert? Would I have visited your village?" Marigold scooped Walks at Night up off the floor and came to stand before her. Reaching out, Marigold laid her hand on Niz's arm. "Meeting you and getting to host you in my home for this week—or however long it takes you to read . . . don't think it hasn't crossed my mind to sabotage our lessons!" Marigold told her with a twinkle in her eye. "It is the bright spot in a few really hard months. I will not let the opinions of a few ignorant soldiers steal the joy of having you both here. You have become my dear friend, Niz, in the middle of a dreadfully lonely season. And you and this little bundle of cuteness"—Walks at Night chuckled expectantly, just seeing Marigold look his way—"are just exactly what I've needed. I've felt so terribly blue, and I was dreading going back to Fort Sidney, knowing more of the same lay ahead. You two have given me hope. Even if I don't know what the future will bring, you've cheered me up and proved to me that smiles and laughter can still fill my days."

Niz smiled faintly. "You're sure?" she asked just once more, feeling she must. She didn't want Marigold's reputation to be tarnished.

Marigold sent her a look. "I'm sure. Stay as long as you like! And certainly until you teach me to make biscuits as light and fluffy as the ones you made this morning."

Niz laughed. "I can do that."

"Good. What if we go ahead and make those cookies for the soldiers today as planned? Perhaps doing so would ease their minds, and they would see you mean them no harm. Maybe it would give them a better opinion of the Indians and be an olive branch of peace."

"Or maybe they would think I was trying to poison them and throw the cookies away."

Marigold laughed at Niz's gloomy prediction. "Then I'll eat one in front of them to prove they're safe. For now, why don't you get out your books, and you can practice while I watch this little darling? Once we put him down for his nap this afternoon, we'll go over your lesson together."

Agreeing, Niz spent the morning practicing reading on her own. After lunch, she taught Marigold how to lay a pot of baked beans for supper before putting Walks at Night down for his nap. They spent his naptime studying together, and when he woke, they mixed a triple batch of cookies, methodically running them through the oven until they'd all been baked. The still-warm cookies covered the kitchen table, and Marigold stood staring at them with shining eyes.

"Not one is burnt!" she declared happily.

"Well, there was that one pan . . ." Niz reminded her honestly.

"Those cookies are in the garbage, so they don't count," Marigold explained quickly. "Not one of *these* beauties are burnt. And I measured and mixed all the ingredients myself!"

"Yes, you did," Niz agreed. Though she'd kept a very watchful eye on the measuring process, and had reminded Marigold to add sugar, which she seemed to be particularly good at forgetting, the happy woman had indeed measured and mixed the dough all on her own.

"Now, let's do your hair, and you can change into your calico, and we'll get these cookies delivered," Marigold continued, pushing away from the table.

Niz looked at her doubtfully. "Ezra told us to stay inside."

Marigold tipped her head. "Niz, we both know you're never going to make it inside all week without going stir crazy. You're not a woman who stays tucked away. Change your dress to show them we're really not so different, and we're going to go give those soldiers a reason to change their minds." Niz hesitated. "If anyone has anything to say about it—including the major—I'll not hold back from giving them a thorough tongue-lashing. I know these men, and I'll see that they behave themselves. And if there's trouble we can't handle, which I highly doubt there will be, Major Taylor is close by."

Persuaded, Niz changed out of her fringed and beaded buckskin into her brown dress patterned with a scattering of small peach and gold floral sprays. As Marigold styled her black hair just the same as her own golden tresses, Niz's excitement grew. She hadn't even been inside for twenty-four hours yet, and already she was missing the fresh air and sunshine. Finding a way to free herself from house arrest while she learned to read sounded wonderful.

And Marigold's rationale made sense—if she had been told to stay inside because Ezra was worried she wasn't safe with the soldiers, then the logical solution was to make friends out of her enemies. Baked goods in a remote fort on the western frontier seemed like a reasonable place to start.

When they were ready to go, Marigold took Walks at Night's hand, leaving Niz to carry the cookies, and they set off in the sweet calm of late afternoon. Despite wary looks, pointed fingers, and a few rude comments, which were met with thorough scoldings from Marigold, everyone accepted the cookies. Marigold did indeed eat one of the treats in front of their most skeptical connoisseurs, and eventually all the soldiers risked a first bite. Once they did, their eyes lit up. Their next question was always the same: "You made these, Ms. Langston?"

"I most certainly did!" she answered proudly. "With my friend Nizhoni's help, of course! She's here teaching me to bake this week in exchange for me teaching her to read. Just wait until you try the biscuits we'll be making!"

Most of the men visibly relaxed as they finished their cookie and accepted another, clearly happy to be passing a few moments in small talk with Marigold. Niz chimed in to the conversation when she had something to add, and her presence was tolerated. She told the soldiers that they would bring fresh cookies around the next day, adding that it was to their good fortune that Ms. Langston needed the practice. Most of the men cheerfully agreed. A few stayed skeptical and bad-humored, but Niz never felt the need to go for Ezra. With any attacks staying verbal, Marigold's charm proved to be a formidable opponent for even the most grizzled soldier.

They visited Major Taylor's house last, anticipating that he would shut down their cookie distribution as soon as they did. Niz felt nervous as they knocked on his door, worried about what he would say, but her anxiety was wasted. He wasn't home. As nervous as she had been, a twinge of sadness ran through her when she realized they wouldn't get to see him after all. Things always seemed better when Ezra was around.

They left his cookies on the porch and headed back to Marigold's. Niz walked her eager student through baking cornbread to go along with their beans, and they were just putting their dinner on the table when a hard knock came at the door.

"I'm guessing that's Major Taylor," Marigold said, her cheerful tone undampened. "Why don't you let him in while I set him a place and pour the tea?"

"I can set him a place and pour the tea while you invite him in. It's your house," Niz pointed out, trying to sound as cheerful as Marigold. She wasn't eager to face him. Last night, she had agreed to stay inside. While she looked forward to the prospect of having him join them for dinner, she dreaded the initial confrontation.

Marigold sent her a charming smile. "I'm guessing he's here to speak with you. You're the one who left the house when you weren't supposed to."

"Because you encouraged me to!" Niz exclaimed with a gasp.

Marigold laughed, her blue eyes merry. "True enough. Go answer the door, darling. You're not one who runs from a fight, and I'll be here for backup if you need me."

Nizhoni turned slowly toward the front door, grumbling to herself. It was Marigold who had hatched the plan and persuaded her to go against Ezra's orders. But her friend was right—she wasn't easily cowed. Giving herself a little shake, she stood straighter and took a deep breath. They had done nothing wrong.

She swung open the door to see that it was indeed Ezra standing on the front porch. His face was grim, and he wordlessly held up a cookie, his brows lifting in question. She raised her chin, and he just shook his head.

"I thought we talked about this, and you were going to stay inside."

"Well, I did plan on it, but we baked a lot of cookies that we needed to share."

Suddenly, his hazel eyes turned amused, and he tried to smother a smile as he shook his head again. Reaching out, he tugged lightly on a strand of dark hair that had fallen out of her elaborate hairstyle. "I should have known I couldn't contain the wind."

Her eyes brightened as she smiled in reply. She'd been expecting a scolding, had prepared for a fight. Instead, his comment was casual and lighthearted.

"Major Taylor, come join us for dinner!" Marigold invited from the stove.

"I gladly will. I was hoping I had correctly timed my visit to result in a dinner invitation."

Niz watched over her shoulder as a happy smile filled Marigold's face and knew instinctively that Ezra's comment had been intentional. He was purposefully building Marigold's confidence and refuting her reputation, just as he constantly was for Niz. Her heart warmed at the realization.

When she turned back toward him, he tipped his head questioningly. "So . . . may I come in and join you for dinner? Or should I stay out here?"

Laughing even as a blush started to form on her cheeks, she stepped back out of the doorway, allowing him to enter.

"You know, I was not happy with the two of you on my way over here," he said, addressing both women as he walked in and shut the door behind himself.

"You seem in good spirits now. What changed your mind, Major?" Marigold asked cheerfully as she placed the steaming teapot on the table.

"I ate one of these cookies. They'd put any man in a better mood." Marigold and Niz laughed, and so did Walks at Night, simply because the women did. Ezra grinned at the chuckling boy and picked him up. Niz could see he intended to give the boy the cookie he held.

"Not before dinner!" she told him quickly. "He's had too many already."

Ezra looked at her and then Walks at Night and made a face. "Sorry, little guy."

Clearly disappointed, Walks at Night began to fuss and reach for the cookie. Niz moved forward to take him, but Ezra stepped around her and sat down at the head of the table with Walks at Night on his lap. "Don't worry. I've got him tonight. You go ahead and eat. I'm sure you don't have too many uninterrupted meals anymore."

"Are you sure?" Niz questioned doubtfully. "You have to make sure his food is cut small."

He gave her a pointed look. "Seriously? It's beans. How do you get smaller and easier to chew than beans? Besides, who do you think fed and cared for this little guy when we first found him? I assure you, I can handle this."

Niz hadn't considered that, and conceding, she sat down at her place across from Marigold.

"So, all kidding aside, did you ladies encounter any trouble today when you were out making your deliveries?" Ezra asked casually, breaking Walks at Night's cornbread up into small pieces before beginning to eat his own dinner.

"No, nothing notable," Marigold answered. "The soldiers seemed to like the cookies. We told them we'd be back with more tomorrow, and everyone seemed to be looking forward to it."

"Good. I'm glad to hear it. And I don't blame them. They really were good cookies."

"Thank you," Marigold said, clearly pleased with the compliment.

"They tasted really familiar. I think I've had some like them before."

"It was Mother Emaline's recipe," Niz offered. "My former mother-in-law," she explained to Marigold.

Ezra's smile was instant. "That's it! I knew I recognized them. She used to keep that blue crock on the cupboard full of them."

Niz nodded, the memory bittersweet.

"Alex and I used to take a handful every time we went in the house," Ezra remembered aloud. "And she never once scolded us for it."

"She loved seeing people enjoy them," Niz agreed.

"Speaking of Emaline, have you read your letters?"

Niz shook her head, thinking of the envelopes she had slipped into her satchel for safekeeping. She'd been too nervous to leave them behind. "I can't read well enough yet. Hopefully soon."

"Maybe by the end of the week," Marigold suggested. "You're improving a lot every day."

"Maybe so," Niz agreed half-heartedly. She wanted to read them, but at the same time, part of her didn't. She wasn't sure she was prepared to face the emotions they would stir up. She reasoned she still had more to learn before she could make out the small, hand-scripted words. Surely by the time she could, she would feel ready.

The three of them shared a pleasant conversation through dinner, and Ezra upheld his promise perfectly. It was almost as if their conversation the night before had never even happened. In fact, if it hadn't been for his one casual comment about the wind, Niz would have wondered if she had dreamt it. As she watched Ezra talk and laugh with Marigold, telling them about his day and asking about theirs, she began to question if maybe she had. Perhaps the comment earlier had been a coincidence. There certainly was no sign the conversation had taken place—he seemed completely normal.

After they were done eating, Ezra sat on the floor with Walks at Night and played while Marigold and Niz did the dishes. When Walks at Night screeched, Niz turned and watched as Ezra chased the little boy on hands and knees, drawing happy shrieks and peals of laughter from her son. When she turned back to the pan she was washing, she realized Marigold had been watching too.

"He's good with him," Marigold observed with a smile.

Niz nodded. "Yes, he is."

"They must have really bonded when the major was bringing him to you," Marigold said, turning back to her drying.

"I'm sure saving a child's life connects you to him," Niz agreed thoughtfully. She hadn't given much thought to where Walks at Night's home was or how long he'd been with Ezra before they arrived. It hadn't occurred to her that they had formed a bond during their time together, but it made sense. She could only imagine what it must have been like to come upon the raided homestead, find the parents, hear the crying, search for the child, only to open the trunk and find him. She shivered. She was only grateful Ezra had found him in time.

"I bet Fire Maker is missing him this week. Once you get used to having a little one around, it must be hard to have them gone."

Niz held her tongue, not saying the first—or second—thing that came to mind. "Fire Maker had barely gotten home from the hunt when we left. I don't know that he's had time to grow accustomed to having Walks at Night around yet," she answered carefully. She wouldn't tell her friend that her husband had wanted to trade the child.

Marigold watched her for a moment before offering her a smile. "Well, I'm sure when you get back, he'll soon be smitten. Walks at Night is such a darling, I can't imagine anyone not falling head over heels in love with him once they spend a little time with him."

"I can't either," Niz agreed, though her heart felt heavier than it had since she arrived. In the cheerfulness of Marigold's house, she'd nearly forgotten about her problems at home. Now, she worried her lip as she grew anxious about what the days ahead would hold. Would Fire Maker one day warm to Walks at Night as Marigold predicted? Would he become a loving father? Or at least treat the boy kindly? Surely he wouldn't treat him as he treated her . . . Not even Fire Maker could continue to withhold his care, protection, and love from a child, especially one as sweet as Walks at Night . . . could he? Pressing her lips together, Niz began to worry what would happen if they someday had their own child.

Even if Fire Maker learned to accept him, if a baby was added to the mix, would he treat his own son better than he treated Walks at Night?

The small boy shrieked again, much closer this time, and she looked back just as he toddled into the back of her legs, clinging to her skirts and giggling as Ezra came across the floor after him. Ezra's frock coat had been discarded and his dark hair tousled in places from their wild play, but Niz couldn't help noticing he'd never looked more handsome. Stopping, he glanced up at her and smiled before reaching out and catching Walks at Night up in his arms. Wrenching her skirts from the little boy's fists, he pushed himself to his feet.

"Come on, buddy. Let's let your mama and Ms. Langston finish up." He carried him back to the other side of the room and sat down on the ground with the toddler on his lap. He picked up the two wooden spoons Marigold had given the boy to play with, hitting them against each other as only a man would. Walks at Night's eyes lit up, and he reached for them.

Niz dropped her eyes back to her dishes. Would Fire Maker ever crawl around on the floor, chasing after Walks at Night, just to make the boy laugh? Her heart sank, already knowing the answer.

She dunked the last pot through the rinse water and handed it to Marigold to dry. Emptying the dishpan and putting it away, she breathed a sigh of relief as she finished the last chore of the evening. Crossing the room, she settled down in an empty chair, seeing that Marigold had just sat down as well. As soon as she did, Walks at Night toddled over and rubbed his face in her skirts. Lifting her son, Niz snuggled him close. Her heart felt full as he rested his head on her shoulder and began to suck his thumb. A wave of gratitude overwhelmed her—she'd spent so long yearning for a moment just like this.

"Looks like someone's getting sleepy," Marigold said affectionately.

Ezra stood and stretched. "Can't say that I blame him. I have some paperwork I still need to finish up tonight, so I'd best be headed home." He snagged his coat off a nearby chair.

"I'm glad you joined us for dinner, Major Taylor," Marigold said, getting up and crossing the room to where she'd left a tin full of cookies on the cupboard. Retracing her steps, she offered it to him. "We saved these for you. And there will be fresh ones tomorrow."

Ezra peeked inside the tin and grinned. "Thanks! I was hoping there were more of these." He paused, his face turning serious. "Listen, I'll be headed out on patrol again tomorrow, but I've arranged for Sergeant Green to stay. I've asked him to watch out for you ladies, so he'll be sticking close. Don't hesitate to reach out to him if you need anything at all."

"That was thoughtful of you, Major, thank you," Marigold said with a dazzling smile as she settled back down in her favorite rocker with her mending.

"You're welcome. Captain Blackwell will be in command in my absence. He knows you're here, Niz, and he knows why. He'll keep a watchful eye on things."

"How long will you be out on patrol?" Niz asked, trying to sound casual. Though she trusted the arrangements he'd made, the fort would seem empty without him.

"I should be back by the end of the week. You'll still be here, won't you?"

"Well, I'm supposed to stay until I can read, and I don't know that I'm too close to achieving that, so I would think so. Unless Ms. Langston plans to kick us out."

"You know that's not likely," Marigold piped in happily.

"Good. Niz, when you're ready, I want to arrange an escort for you back to your village. Deliver your cookies if you must, but please don't leave until I can do so."

Niz nodded in understanding.

"Well, thank you both for a nice evening and a wonderful dinner. I'll check in when I return." He paused beside Niz to reach down and tousle Walks at Night's hair. "Goodbye, little guy. See you soon."

"Be safe," Niz told him. Ezra held her gaze for a split-second longer than necessary, then turned toward the door. Leaving, he shut the door behind himself. A couple of hours later, lying beside her sleeping son, Niz heard footsteps on the front porch. This time, she only smiled and rolled over, tucking Walks at Night in close. Whatever tomorrow brought, tonight they both had someone looking out for them.

Sixteen

The next few days passed quickly and pleasantly. Mornings were full of cooking and cleaning, then studying while Marigold watched Walks at Night. After lunch, Niz put her son down for a nap while Marigold ran any errands. Once he was asleep, Marigold listened to her read aloud, taught her new words, and instructed her in spelling and penmanship. When Walks at Night woke, they baked cookies or biscuits and walked around the fort, distributing them to whatever hungry soldiers were around. Sergeant Green always seemed to be nearby, and Marigold piled a handkerchief high with cookies for him each day in thanks. Once the baked goods had been distributed, they returned home for Niz to teach Marigold a new dish to make for dinner, before ending the night with more reading and sewing.

Niz enjoyed the full, happy days at Marigold's. She enjoyed the companionship, the peace that seemed to permeate Marigold's home, and the happiness that filled the four walls. Marigold was cheerful and talkative and Niz found herself liking the woman more and more each day. Marigold adored Walks at Night, was a patient teacher, an eager student, and friendly and generous to everyone they came in contact with. Though Niz missed her mother and sisters, her people, and the village, Niz's lighthearted days with Marigold were a welcome respite from the silent tension that filled Niz's own wickiup.

Friday evening, they were out delivering cookies when, unexpectedly, there was a flurry of activity. Soldiers started shouting, and suddenly everyone was running. From fifty feet away, Sergeant Green turned and yelled, "Go home! Ms. Langston, Niz, go home!"

Hearing the urgency in his voice, Niz caught Walks at Night up in her arms. She barely had time to turn before she felt Sergeant Green's hand on her shoulder, propelling her toward Marigold's house. Looking over, she saw he was pushing Marigold too.

"I know it's not ladylike to do so, but run!" he commanded, seconds before the first gunshot rang out.

They didn't have to be told twice. Catching up their skirts, they ran for Marigold's house. Men were shouting and gunfire filled the air. Frightened, Walks at Night began to wail. Above the commotion, Niz heard the unmistakable sound of war cries. Reaching the house first, Marigold ran up the steps and pulled open the front door. "Come on, Niz! Hurry!"

Holding the screaming boy against her chest as she crossed the last few feet, Niz rushed inside, thankful to have reached the relative safety of the house. Marigold shut and barred the front door, then led the way through the house to her bedroom. "We'll be safer here in the back," she explained hurriedly, kneeling down behind the bed against an interior wall. "There's less of a chance of stray bullets finding us."

"Take him. I need to get my revolver," Niz said, pushing the crying boy into Marigold's eager arms. She ran back to the front room and grabbed the gun, holding it tightly, remembering what Ezra had said about her grip. If only he were at the fort instead of out on patrol!

For a moment, Niz paused to look out from behind the curtains. She caught a glimpse of the Comanche warriors riding on horseback through the fort, and her heart sank. No doubt they had come for their captured friends.

In that moment, she knew that all she'd been doing throughout the week—distributing cookies, talking to the soldiers, reassuring them that she came in peace, educating them that not all tribes were the same—was now for naught. They would surely think she had some part in the attack, just as they had feared. All the progress she'd made was dissolving before her very eyes.

Letting out a long sigh, she turned and hurried back to the bedroom, knowing the best thing she could do was to protect her son and Marigold should the need arise. Dropping to her knees beside her friend, they worked together to quiet Walks at Night.

Once he had stopped crying, Marigold turned to Niz, her beautiful blue eyes wide. "What's going on out there?"

"The Comanche have come," Niz answered dully. "Likely for their friends. There aren't enough of them to stage a full-blown attack. We'll be safe in here . . . unless they start the fort on fire."

"Niz . . . the soldiers . . . they'll blame you."

"I know." She took a deep breath. "I'll head home at first light."

"But Major Taylor said—"

"He's not here," Niz answered, wishing he were. "And he didn't know the Comanche would come."

Suddenly the gunshots stopped. An eerie silence fell over the fort. The women looked at each other and waited, wondering if the fighting would start again. When it didn't, Marigold stood slowly. "Is it over?"

"I would think so," Niz said somberly. "The Comanche were badly outnumbered. They weren't going to engage in conflict any longer than necessary. They surely disappeared just as quickly as they came."

Marigold nodded and started for the door. "I'd best go see to the wounded."

"I'll come with you." Niz grabbed her cradleboard and began to lace Walks at Night into it. Tears gathered in his big brown eyes again, and he began to fuss.

"No, Niz, that's not a good idea. Stay here."

Niz shook her head as she handed Walks at Night one of the cookies that still lay cooling on the kitchen table. Then she hoisted the cradleboard onto her back, settling the burden strap around her shoulders.

"I can help. I know they'll blame me, Marigold, but if I stay hidden away, won't that confirm that I have a reason to hide? Let me help you tend the wounded. Let me prove to them that I'm not their enemy." Marigold still looked doubtful. Niz raised her chin, refusing to let her friend's doubt stir her worry. "With so many soldiers out on patrol and the doctor away, they'll likely need all the help they can get. You've been doing this since you were a child—taking care of the wounded after a battle, and so have I. We can work together."

"It might be dangerous," Marigold warned.

Niz shrugged. "Much of my life is. I can't stay here when people need help. It's not in me."

Marigold hesitated one more moment, then nodded and opened the door. Together, they headed toward the infirmary. The doctor was away tending to a community closer to Denver that was suffering from an influenza outbreak, but the infirmary still seemed to be the reasonable place to take the wounded. Turning onto the street it sat on, they saw soldiers carrying in their injured comrades as expected. Marigold picked up her pace, her face filling with compassion. Niz followed, hurrying to keep up.

As they approached the door, two soldiers were just coming out. One of them glanced over and his face distorted in anger. Seeing there was going to be trouble, Niz braced for it.

"What are *you* doing here? Haven't your people already done enough damage today?" he shouted, adrenaline still clearly pumping through his veins.

"They're not my people," Niz argued.

"You come here and pass out cookies, and the whole time you've probably been sending them secret messages at night giving them intel about this fort."

"She hasn't!" Marigold interrupted indignantly.

"Now they've attacked, and three good men have been killed, and many more injured!" he bellowed, continuing as if Marigold hadn't spoken. "This is *your* fault! *You're* to blame for these men's deaths, and I aim to see you arrested and locked away with the rest of your kind, even if I have to do it myself."

Niz closed her eyes for a moment, absorbing the numbers he'd shared. She understood his anger and frustration. She'd felt the same way after the Comanche raided her village. Faced with loss and destruction, one wanted someone to blame.

"My people too were attacked by these raiders," she said, raising her voice so that everyone nearby could hear her. "Just last week. We also lost loved ones. One of our grandfathers and a sweet little girl. She was only six years old. We grieved for them just as you grieve for your friends. These who came are not my people, and I promise I don't want them here anymore than you do. Not at your fort, not at my village, not in this area. We all want peace and safety for our loved ones."

"Likely story. That's what all spies who'd been caught would say!" the man shot back.

"She's no spy! She's here teaching me how to bake, and I'm teaching her how to read. Nizhoni is my friend! And now she's going to help me treat the wounded!" Marigold said, stomping her foot as she looped her arm through Niz's.

"Over my dead body!" another soldier thundered, moving to block the door to the clinic. "She's not touching our men. She'd likely slit their throats and finish the job."

"Smith, if you know what's good for you, you'll never raise your voice to Ms. Langston again!" Niz turned and saw Sergeant Green coming toward them, carrying the shoulders of a wounded soldier while another man carried his feet. The sergeant was glaring at the man who had spoken harshly to Marigold. Blood was trickling down his face from a cut along his hairline.

"She's no friend of yours, Ms. Langston. She's lying to you and she's lying to us!" the first soldier said, his tone more cajoling as he addressed Marigold.

"She's not lying," Sergeant Green barked, clearly annoyed. "I was there when Nizhoni's village got attacked. My whole patrol was. It was her village that was hit just days before we brought the captives in." He stopped with the wounded man as the soldier he'd called Smith still blocked the door. "Move!" Sergeant Green yelled. The soldier did. Sergeant Green disappeared inside.

"I understand that you're angry, I do," Niz told them. "But I also know there are wounded men inside who need help, and—"

"Not from you," Smith argued. The first soldier grunted his agreement, watching her with narrowed eyes.

She went on, uncowed. "Ms. Langston has been helping the wounded after battle since she was a child. She can help your wounded men, and I can help her."

"They wouldn't want you touching them!"

"Aren't you listening? She's here to help!" Marigold cried.

"Likely story!"

People were hurting. Niz could see the need all around her. She couldn't—wouldn't—sit by and do nothing! "When we were attacked, the army rode in and chased the Comanche out of my village. By doing so, they kept our death toll down to two. Let me help Ms. Langston keep your death toll at three," Niz pleaded.

"She's helping, and that's final," Sergeant Green said, coming back outside. "There are suffering men in need of medical care lying right inside that door. If these two women are brave enough to stomach helping them, we're not going to turn them away. Now get about your business. There are more to carry in." His orders were met with glares. The soldiers didn't budge. "Move out!" he thundered, obviously losing his cool. "Or else I'll go find the captain so he can tell you the same thing. And he'll wonder why you had to be told at all when there are men lying injured in the streets, as will the major when he gets back. I'm sure he'll have a thing or two to say about this!"

Grumbling, the soldiers stepped away from the building and headed down the street. Sergeant Green watched them go, then turned back to face Marigold and Niz. "Carry on, ladies."

Inhaling deeply, Niz nodded, and Marigold determinedly drew her inside the infirmary. The building was small. Four men were on cots, three more laid out on the ground. Five had suffered gunshot wounds, one had been stepped on by a horse, and the last had been struck with a lance.

"So many!" Marigold lamented, her voice full of sorrow.

"The Comanche are formidable warriors. We can be glad there weren't more of them."

"Yes, I suppose that's something to be thankful for," Marigold agreed, beginning to assess the wounded and treat the most serious. Niz handed her instruments, administered chloroform, and took care of the others in between. The soldiers continued to carry in the wounded until the total count in the small clinic sat at twelve.

Marigold and Niz worked late into the night without stopping. Walks at Night fell asleep in his cradleboard. Weary, Niz lifted the burden strap off her shoulders and carefully set the board down, propping it up in the corner of the storeroom, hoping the quiet darkness would keep her son asleep while she worked.

Despite their best efforts, the man who had been stepped on by a horse died just after midnight.

"I knew he had internal bleeding, but I didn't know what to do about it. I'm not a surgeon, Niz," Marigold said, tears in her lovely blue eyes as she drew a sheet up over the man's face.

"You did everything you could," Niz comforted. She'd watched her friend work tirelessly to help the injured man who'd been on the brink of death ever since being brought in.

"But I wish I could have done more," Marigold answered dejectedly. She glanced around the small room, lit by candles, and Niz knew she was wondering how many more patients they would lose before the sun rose. There were two more in very serious condition.

Marigold looked back at the covered form in front of them. "His father was killed in The War Between the States. He was just a boy when his mother received the news." Marigold wiped at tears that were rolling down her cheeks. "I can only imagine how his poor mother is going to feel when she gets this news. Private Reid here was her only son."

"You should go home, Ms. Langston. You too, Niz. Get some sleep. We'll see to the rest," Sergeant Green urged from a chair in the corner. He and a few others were waiting to be stitched up, having suffered minor injuries during the skirmish.

Marigold took a deep breath and shook her head. "Not until everyone has been treated. Come on, Niz, let's remove the bullet from Private Mulligan."

Niz followed, and they worked on through the night. When their candles were nearly burnt out, Marigold sent Sergeant Green back to her house for all she had, along with her green glass lamp. He brought the candles from his barracks as well, and the women worked on by the light of a dozen small flames. During the early morning hours, Captain Blackwell stopped in briefly to check on the injured. Niz recognized him as the man who had shared the headline from the Rocky Mountain News on her first visit to the fort. He smiled and thanked her kindly before turning to discuss the condition of the patients with Marigold as she stitched up Private Mills. He left as soon as he'd heard her report.

They ran out of bandages around three in the morning, so Niz ripped new ones from a bolt of muslin she found in the storeroom. Marigold removed bullets, sutured, and administered morphine to those in pain. Niz bandaged, assisted, and tended, fetching cups of water when the soldiers were thirsty, cushions and blankets when they were uncomfortable, cookies they had baked for those who were hungry. Once they had seen to the badly injured, they moved on to those with minor injuries.

Dawn was just breaking when they finished stitching up the last wounded man. Niz moved to the window and shut the curtains as he left, keeping the room dark for those who were recovering. The chairs that had been brought in for those waiting to be seen finally sat empty. Exhausted, Niz dropped into one of them. Marigold sat down beside her.

"I'm weary down to my bones," the blonde said, putting her head in her hands.

"You did good tonight, Marigold. We only lost one patient. That number would have been much higher if it weren't for you. I think your mother would be very proud."

Marigold flashed her a tired smile. "Thank you. I felt close to her tonight. Most of my memories of her include helping the wounded. She's been gone such a long time, but tonight . . . I felt like her daughter." She paused, emotion showing on her face. "And thank you for your help. I know I tried to persuade you to stay home, but I'm grateful you came anyway."

"Me too," Niz agreed. All she wanted to do was curl up and sleep, but she was glad to have been able to help. Staying at home when people were hurting and in need felt unimaginable. If it was within her power to help someone, she couldn't sit by and do nothing—even if her son would be waking up soon, ready for the day ahead. Surely she could make it to naptime.

The men were quiet. With everyone treated and the room dark and still, Niz struggled to keep her eyes open.

"Let's nap while we can," Marigold suggested, sounding sleepy. "These aren't the most comfortable chairs, but they'll do." She rested her blonde head against Niz's shoulder and was asleep within seconds.

Niz was almost asleep, too, when the door opened, spilling a rectangle of golden morning sunlight across the clinic floor. The injured man lying in its path moaned and shifted in his sleep, turning away.

Blinking heavily and then squinting against the brightness, Niz tried to make out who had entered. She hoped it was the soldier Sergeant Green had promised to send to look after the wounded so she and Marigold could go home and sleep.

"Hey, Niz."

The rich, warm voice made her heart jump. She held her finger to her lips, motioning to her sleeping friend. Ezra shut the door, blocking out the bright light, and sat down in the chair beside her.

"When did you get back?" she asked, keeping her voice low.

"We rode in half an hour ago. I got a report of what happened, and Sergeant Green told me you ladies were over here." He looked out over the men on both the floor and the cots. "How are they?"

"We lost one during the night. Private Reid. Everyone else seems stable now." Ezra's head dropped, and she knew he was feeling the weight of the news. Reaching over, she laid her hand on his forearm, hoping to lend comfort. She'd felt the same way when she'd learned of the casualties in her own camp. "Marigold was wonderful with them," she continued, giving him something positive to hold on to. "You're lucky she was here."

Ezra hesitated and then reached out and picked up her hand. Lifting it to his lips, he kissed the back of it. "The way I hear it, we're lucky you were too. Thank you for helping my men. Sergeant Green told me about the trouble you had last night. He said that even some of the wounded were rude. And yet you stayed up all night to help them. Thank you."

He released her hand, and Niz clasped it tightly with her other, his words warming her heart. Many of the others had seen her as the enemy, but Ezra knew her. Feeling safe and known, she was tempted to lay her weary head on his shoulder and succumb to the exhaustion that made it difficult to keep her eyes open. Fighting the temptation, she attempted to rouse herself. "I haven't heard an update. Were the Comanche successful in freeing the captives?"

Ezra rubbed the back of his neck. "No, and that's something. We still have all those we had caught in custody." He sighed. "But this has to stop. Too many people are getting hurt, Niz. I've got to find the rest of them, but they just keep disappearing onto the reservation. It's like they vanish into thin air."

"You'll find them," she said firmly. "I know you will." She sent him a faint smile and shrugged her free shoulder. "They've got the best man on the job."

He smiled back, but then it faded. "I've got a favor to ask you."

"What is it?" she asked, suddenly worried. She had no more sway over Fire Maker than he did. If he wanted her to ask her husband to help them find the raiders, she would be of no help to him.

"Will you help me speak to the captives?"

Her heart fell. Something else she couldn't help him with. "I don't speak their language."

"Do you speak the signs of the plains tribes?" he questioned.

"Not well." He gave her a questioning look. "I've picked up a few things at our winter camps, but only a few. Some of our people used to live on the plains. Now, since being moved onto the reservation, they winter with us. I've learned a few signs from them, but I can't imagine it would be enough to be of any help to you." She paused. "Don't any of your soldiers speak it? Don't you?" she asked, remembering belatedly that Alex did.

He shook his head. "I could never get the hang of it; I'm not good at languages like Alex was. He communicated for the both of us when needed. I've got a soldier who can speak it, but he's out on patrol, and I need information now. If we could learn anything about the whereabouts of the others, or where they're headed . . ."

"They're not going to give up their brothers," she warned, already knowing it to be true.

"That may be, but I've got to try." He paused. "Will you help me?"

Niz looked at Ezra for a long moment, doubts filling her mind, but longing filling her heart. He'd done so much for them—for her. He'd returned the braves' horses, been patient with Fire Maker, arranged for her to learn to read, filled her empty arms with a child, slept on hard floors to keep her safe . . . She nodded. She had to try. His smile was as warm and bright as the sunshine that had flooded in the door with him.

"Thank you. A soldier is coming to care for the wounded while you ladies get some sleep. He should be here any minute. Once he comes, send Marigold home and meet me at my office."

Niz agreed, then watched as he stood and quietly left. When the promised soldier arrived, she awakened Marigold. While her friend gave instructions to the soldier, Niz slipped into the storeroom. Draping a blanket over the hoop that protected Walks at Night's head, she cautiously lifted the cradleboard to her back, careful not to wake her son. He would be rousing soon, but she wasn't ready for him to just yet. She walked with Marigold until their paths split, and then she and Walks at Night walked on alone.

She noticed how warily the soldiers watched her as she passed, and it saddened and frustrated her. Her eyes burned and her steps dragged from staying up all night, helping their comrades, and still they looked on her with suspicion. Knowing they saw her as their enemy was crushing. The weight of their distrust piled on her already drooping shoulders.

At Ezra's door, she knocked, and then entered, knowing he was likely in his office and was expecting her. The smell of coffee hit her as she stepped inside, and she inhaled deeply, just the scent of it reviving her. Sipping a steaming cup of it in the mornings had been one of her favorite parts of the day while with the Applewoods.

She stepped through Ezra's open office door, but the room was empty. A sketch pinned to the wall caught her attention, and she quietly walked closer, studying it as she drew near. She ran her fingertips softly over the paper; the men sketched on it were undeniably familiar. Alex sat outside a wickiup wearing a buffalo robe and smoking a pipe. He was sitting near the fire, and Great Mountain sat beside him, her father next to him. Her village was in the background. She closed her eyes and pictured the scene in living color, just as it had been the day she stood behind Ezra and watched him sketch it. It had been Alex's eighth visit to her village and Ezra's third and last . . . until he returned with the army. She'd nearly forgotten about it.

"I found that the other day when going through some of my papers," Ezra said from the doorway, making her jump. "I don't know that Alex ever sat for a photograph." Niz shook her head. "I know it's not the same . . . But it's something. I thought I would put it up . . . just to remember. It's a reminder to me of why I'm here and what all this is for."

"It's so lifelike. I feel like he could step off the page . . . like they all could." She wished all three of them would. Great Mountain had been a wonderful chief who had led their people with courage and wisdom. If he were alive, she knew he would be working with the army to protect their people and their hunting rights. Her father had been the strongest, bravest man she'd ever known; he would have shared the burden she carried. Alex . . . She couldn't even go there. She wiped a tear of exhaustion off her cheek and inhaled deeply, determined not to let one tear turn into more. "You're a wonderful artist, Ezra. If you ever decide the army isn't for you, I'm sure you could make a living with your sketches," she said, turning to face him.

He laughed. "You're kind, but I doubt that. It's just a hobby." He held out one of the two cups he carried. "I seem to remember you preferred it to tea."

Surprised, she accepted the cup, her eyes lighting up. She breathed in the rich, toasty aroma before taking her first sip, reveling in the taste of the steaming brew. Ezra chuckled. "I didn't know you loved it that much, or I would have made some for you before now."

"I haven't had a cup since I returned to the village. Sometimes—at the Applewoods—it was the only way I could convince myself to get out of bed on a cold morning," she admitted. "Often, I was looking forward to it before I even went to sleep at night." He laughed as she took another drink. "And you even remembered the sugar."

"Come on into the kitchen. I made breakfast, and then we can head over to the guardhouse and see if we can get anything out of the captives."

"You didn't have to make a meal for me," she protested.

He grinned. "I've been out on patrol for the past three days, and I'm famished. I thought you might need something too. Green said you ladies worked straight through dinner." He helped her lift the cradleboard off her back and set it carefully on the ground.

Walks at Night woke, and he bent to unlace him. "At the very least, I knew this little guy would be hungry."

While he saw to her son, Niz glanced around the kitchen. She smiled as she noticed the place he had clearly set for her. A second plate sat beside the first, holding a biscuit and salt pork that had been cut into small pieces. Her heart warmed at his thoughtfulness, and she set her cup of coffee at her place before turning to accept Walks at Night. Taking the little one, she changed him before sitting down at the table. When she took her seat, her coffee had been refilled.

Ezra folded his hands and led them in saying grace, thanking God for the wounded men whose lives had been spared and asking for wisdom to know how to help bring peace. Niz followed his lead, bowing her head until the prayer was over. She'd nearly forgotten that each meal had begun the same way at the Applewoods. Marigold paused and sat quietly before each meal, and Ezra had prayed when she and her family had joined him and his officers for dinner, but hearing him pray aloud, asking for wisdom and talking to his God about what had happened the night before, stirred a longing inside of Niz.

What would it be like to trust an Almighty God with the small, day-to-day details of your life? Ezra was the commanding officer at the fort—all the soldiers followed his orders. And yet, he was asking for God's help as simply and expectantly as a child might ask for their father's. Niz sat mulling over Ezra's humility, which seemed to go hand in hand with his strong leadership skills. It was clear to see that his men held the utmost respect for him. Still, he was not afraid to admit he didn't know everything and needed help. It was refreshing.

"I'll warn you, the biscuits are a day old and weren't anywhere near as good as yours even fresh," he said cheerfully, interrupting her thoughts.

"I'm just grateful for food," Niz answered, realizing she was hungrier than she'd thought. With a little honey, the biscuits weren't bad. A comfortable silence fell over the table as they all filled their empty bellies. When she was done, she settled back in her chair, watching Walks at Night eat his salt pork. Suddenly, a new question filled her mind. "Hey, Ezra?"

"Hm?" he asked, finishing the last of his biscuit.

"Did you happen to get any of Walks at Night's things from his house? Blankets or toys? I thought having something familiar might be comforting for him."

Ezra's face fell. "No. I wish I had. I didn't even think of it at the time. There was a lot going on, and all of a sudden, I had this kid to keep alive until we got to you."

She shook her head, regretting having said anything at the sadness in his expression. "It's fine. Really. He's adjusting. I was just curious." She paused. "How long was he with you?"

"His family lived several hours north of here. We found him late in the afternoon. We think the Comanche attacked sometime during the night, so he was pretty upset and hungry by the time we arrived. We buried his parents and started your way the next morning."

Niz absorbed the broad strokes of information he was giving her and was grateful Ezra hadn't gone into more detail. With the little boy on her knee firmly planted in her heart, she wasn't sure she could have handled any more. She brushed the dark hair out of her son's eyes as he reached out to grab another piece of biscuit. "When you found Walks at Night, what made you think to bring him to me? How did you know how much I needed him?"

Ezra leaned back in his chair and considered her for a long moment, as if weighing how much to say.

"The whole truth, please."

A quick grin filled his face. "I remember." Still, he hesitated. Finally, he shrugged. "It was his name."

"His name?" Niz questioned, stunned.

"When we found him in the trunk, there was a family Bible in there too. I figured they'd recorded his birth in it like most people do, so I looked to see what we should call the poor kid."

"You know his given name?" she asked incredulously. "Why are you just now—"

"Niz, his parents named him Alex," he interrupted, his eyes on her face.

She stared at him. Shock rumbled through her as her thoughts began to spin. Her son's given name was Alex? That's why Ezra had thought to bring him to her? And he hadn't shared that? "W-why didn't you tell me?"

Ezra's expression was serious as he considered her. "We both know he can't be Alex in your village—in your home. Not if he's going to be Fire Maker's son."

Niz dropped her eyes, and Ezra cleared his throat. She wondered if he knew what she wasn't saying—chances were good that Walks at Night would never be Fire Maker's son, regardless of his name.

"He needed a new name, and I wanted you to be free to pick one, so I didn't tell you. But I also knew as soon as I saw his name written in that Bible that he belonged with you." He paused and cleared his throat again. "Alex had written that if your baby was a boy, you planned to name him Alexander Applewood II." Niz nodded, her eyes on her empty plate. "Seeing his name . . . it felt like a sign from God."

Niz took that in quietly, processing all he had said. Grief rose steadily within her as thoughts of her infant son, Alex, and the dreams they had dreamt filled her mind. Ezra's words had stirred deep emotion, and she started to feel panicky within. Desperate for a distraction, she quickly stood and went round the table, handing him Walks at Night. "You made breakfast, I'll clean it up."

"Leave it. I'll get to it later," he told her, scooting his chair back and standing, the boy in his arms.

"It won't take me long to do the dishes," she argued, not feeling right about leaving them. What was more, she urgently needed something to do to stay busy so she could distract herself from the feelings that were crashing over her, making her head swim.

"I'm serious. Leave them. I'm a bachelor—I do dishes all the time. Right now, let's see what we can learn from the captives and then get you some sleep." He bent down and laced Walks at Night into his cradleboard again before helping her lift it onto her back and starting toward the door. When she hesitated, he turned back. "Come on, Niz. The dishes will wait."

Finally, she followed, too tired to put up any more of a fight. After all, their next errand would also serve as a distraction. On their way to the guardhouse, she started growing nervous. She wasn't a timid person, but she felt apprehensive as she followed him inside. Would she be able to understand anything the Comanche warriors said? And if she could, would she want to? They had considered her an enemy at her own camp, but here, she would be seen as a traitor—something far worse.

The captives were being held in a jail cell. Two soldiers were stationed outside the building. Inside, a soldier stood on either side of the front door. Ezra, suddenly all army major, spoke to the soldiers as they entered, and they moved back to stand against the wall.

A few of the Comanche stood, appearing fierce and angry, when they saw him. Yet, she could tell the exact moment they noticed her. Their eyes began to burn like fire. The warriors in front stepped aside as one in the back moved forward. Niz's heart plummeted and fear clutched at her throat as she recognized the man she had wounded during the raid on her village. A soiled bandage was still tied around his arm. When his eyes met hers, they were full of rage and hatred as they had been that night.

For a moment, she was back beside the wickiup, Wise Hawk beside her, seeing the fury in the warrior's face as he started back toward her atop his horse. She felt the same panic she'd felt that night as she watched recognition flash in his eyes. Though he said nothing, he looked as if he meant to reach through the bars and throttle her with his bare hands. She instinctively took a step back.

But this time, Ezra was standing beside her. The warrior was unarmed and behind iron bars. He couldn't hurt her, and she reminded herself of that as she concentrated on taking deep breaths, pressing down the panic, focusing on refusing to let him see her fear. She raised her chin and looked right back at him.

"Ask them why they come here, over the mountains, and make trouble," Ezra requested firmly, watching the warriors warily.

Niz inhaled deeply, trying to hold herself together despite her exhaustion, apprehension, and fear. "Ez . . . Major, I don't know all the signs," she protested, glancing at the soldiers standing against the wall. They likely didn't know the history between the Applewood family and their major; she didn't want to seem disrespectful of their commanding officer.

"Just try," he encouraged.

Doing her best, she tried to recall what she had learned at their winter camp and perform the signs correctly. The Comanche just stared at her, their eyes burning. When it was clear they weren't going to answer, Ezra said, "Ask them where they're going."

Again she tried, and again the Comanche stood like statues. "Ask them where they camp. And what they want."

Niz's questions were met with stony silence. Ezra clenched and unclenched his jaw.

"I don't know if I'm making the signs wrong or if they're just refusing to respond," she admitted, frustrated.

He took a deep breath in and blew it out. "I guess we're done here. You tried. Let's go."

Ezra put his hand on Niz's shoulder, encouraging her toward the door. As he did, the man from the raid let out a horrific war cry and violently shook the iron bars, creating a sudden ruckus. Startled by the loud noises, Walks at Night began to wail. In the chaos, Ezra jumped in front of Niz protectively as the guards rushed toward the cell and those outside ran in. They all stood ready but unsure, seemingly confused and unnerved by the fearsome cry. Only Niz understood it. She stepped out from behind Ezra in wonder.

"You speak the language of my people," she said incredulously. The warrior's words had been broken, but she understood him.

"What did you say?" Ezra demanded, sounding every bit the commanding officer that he was. The man who had fixed her breakfast was nowhere in sight. In his place was an army major who sounded more than equal to his office.

Niz didn't respond. She was warily watching the warrior, and the warrior was watching her, his rage like a palpable force in the room. Neither of them looked away.

"Niz? Let's go. This was a bad idea. I shouldn't have brought you here," Ezra said through gritted teeth. He put his strong hands on both of her shoulders, determined to turn her toward the door.

The warrior cried out again in fury. "The white man takes whatever he wants!" he shouted. "He steals our lands and our women and our children. He slaughters our buffalo and robs us of our horses. We will not rest until we have stolen from the white man everything he has stolen from our people!"

Twisting away from Ezra, Niz stepped closer to the jail cell, her temper flaring. If the warrior wanted to talk, then so be it. She had plenty to say. "We did none of those things to you, and yet you attacked my people! You killed one of our elders and a sweet little girl," she accused.

"You understand him?" Ezra questioned, clearly surprised.

"Oh, but I wouldn't have killed you." The warrior's face turned mocking, and there was a dangerous glint in his eyes. "I knew it as soon as I turned and saw you. The beauty with the smoking gun. You would have been my captive."

She glared at him, suppressing the shiver that tried to run through her, hiding the fear that made her stomach churn. "You're not here on a noble journey to reclaim what has been stolen from you," she retorted hotly, stepping closer to the cell in challenge, refusing to acknowledge his threat with a response. "You're here in blind rage and violence. You're not here for your people—you're here for yourselves! You're nothing more than common thieves!"

The warrior's face changed, an intense rage filling it once more. "Your husband supplies the army with horses," he said, spitting at her.

"Hey! That's enough!" Ezra boomed, pulling Niz back and stepping in front of her again, shielding her from the warriors.

"Has your husband sent you to the army as he does his horses?" the warrior mocked.

"What's he saying?" Ezra questioned fiercely through gritted teeth, never looking away from those in the jail cell. Niz narrowed her eyes. She wouldn't repeat it. "Niz?"

"Has he?" the warrior pressed. "Wonder what I would have to trade him to have him send you to our camp instead?" His degrading comment drew crude laughter from his companions.

With her temper burning and her cheeks flushed, Niz stepped out from behind Ezra. "Stop!" she demanded. "My husband has not sent me! Not in the way you mean. I've come to learn to read the white man's words to protect my people against having their land stolen like yours was. My husband would not send me here like that or to you!" she said forcefully, hoping it was true. Her last conversation with Fire Maker came to mind, but she pushed the troubling memory away. Now was not the time to doubt.

The man laughed at her. "You and I both know Fire Maker can't say no to a good trade."

Her stomach dropped. Sickening understanding filled her. He knew her husband. With apprehension and suspicion running wild, she felt unwell. The man's expression was taunting, just daring her to disagree.

"Niz," Ezra said, his tone demanding her attention. He waited until she looked at him. His hazel eyes were full of questions, and she looked away, not wanting to face them. "Ask him why they came across the mountains," he continued firmly.

She looked back at the warrior, lifting her chin, and drawing herself up to her full height. "Why did you come across the mountains?" she demanded.

The warrior's silence was mocking.

"Ask him where they camp."

"Where do you camp?" she questioned, her voice rising, her temper barely in check.

More silence.

"Ask him how many of them there are. Ask him what they want."

Niz hesitated, trying to get control of her tongue before she opened her mouth. She wanted to scream at the taunting warrior and tell him exactly what she thought of him and his murdering, thieving comrades, who had come onto their reservation and stirred up trouble for her people. She wanted to tell him what he could do with his crude suggestions and mocking ways. She wanted to remind him that he was imprisoned and had already been defeated. Instead, she smoothed the front of her brown dress, took a deep, deep breath and opened her mouth, determined to ask only what Ezra had requested. "How many warriors are with you?"

The warrior tipped his head, an unpleasant grin filling his face. "Tell me, do you do everything he tells you?" he jeered. "*Everything*? Because you forgot to ask what we want."

He knew what Ezra had said.

Niz spun on her heel and stomped out of the guardhouse, the Comanche's laughter following her.

"I'll see you again! And next time, the soldier won't be there to save you," the warrior called out in promise.

Feeling sick and consumed with anger, she slammed the door shut behind herself. Had she stayed, she certainly would have done or said something she'd regret. Startled by the loud noise of the slamming door, Walks at Night began to cry harder. Despite his wails, she heard the door pulled open and quick footsteps behind her.

"Hey!" Ezra called, jogging to catch up with her. She kept walking. He reached out and grabbed her arm gently, trying to stop her. She pulled away. "Niz, wait. Please wait." When she didn't stop, he matched his stride to hers. "Where are you going?"

"Marigold's," she answered through gritted teeth.

"Give me ten more minutes. Please. You can understand them. Niz, I need you to translate."

"No, you don't," she answered grimly.

"What do you mean?" he questioned, seeming confused.

"He speaks English."

Clearly shocked, he stayed where he was while she continued walking. Suddenly, he jogged again to catch up with her. "How do you know that?"

Finally, she stopped and faced him. "Because he understood everything you were telling me to say in there!" she cried.

Surprise filled his face. "He did? How do you know?"

"Trust me, I know," she said bleakly. A wave of nausea rolled over her as the warrior's words came back to mind. Her temper flared again in response. "You're in charge here! Why don't you try those murderers for their crimes and do away with them?"

He shook his head, surprise still showing on his face. "Niz, there's a proper way to do things. Believe me, they'll stand trial for their crimes. But their sentencing will be handed down by those with the authority to do so."

"You're telling me anyone would bat an eye if five thieving, murdering Comanche went missing?" she demanded. She knew the lack of value that was placed on the lives of the natives. And these were criminals! The government would surely be glad to be rid of them.

Ezra looked at her for a long moment and slowly shook his head again. "I will not take revenge, Niz. Justice will be served, but it will be justice that demands payment for their deeds, not me—not vengeance."

She stared at him, frustrated, wanting to argue. Tears gathered in her eyes, and she quickly looked away, not wanting him to see. She wanted him to eliminate the threat, to take care of the problem—it was within his power to do so. But she couldn't help admiring him all the more for refusing. He wasn't willing to play God. He wasn't willing to render a life worthless, even if it belonged to a murdering, thieving native. Something about that knowledge made her feel safe. He was a man worthy of respect. She dashed the backs of her hands across her eyes, angry at herself for showing emotion, angry at the Comanche for being so terrible, angry at Ezra for being so honorable.

Walks at Night let out another wail, and Ezra reached back and patted the boy. "Hey now, it's okay," he said soothingly. "How could you understand him?" he asked, refocusing the conversation, addressing Niz once more.

She sighed as she started walking again, feeling more eager by the second to reach Marigold's. "It was broken, but he was speaking the language of my people."

"How did he know it?"

"I don't know, but I'm guessing he's picked it up from captives they've taken. The Comanche are a fierce tribe. Some of their lands used to border some of my people's."

Ezra considered her for a long moment. "What was he saying to you?"

She raised her chin. "He said that the white man takes their land and their women and their children, their buffalo and their horses. They're here to take back what has been taken from them," she answered carefully.

"These settlers, they're not the ones who took all that from them," Ezra pointed out.

She sighed and stopped to face him, willing him to understand. "When the white men look at us, they see us all the same. They don't see different tribes, different people, different languages, personalities, ways of life. They see the American Indian."

"I don't," he replied firmly.

"Well, those warriors are the same way," she continued as if he hadn't spoken. "They look and simply see white men—the men who stole everything they held dear. The men who tell them they can't hunt where their ancestors have hunted for generations, who shoot the buffalo they depend on for their very survival, who till up the land that is a part of them." Tears collected in her eyes again, and she quickly tried to blink them away, even as she pressed her clenched fist against the pain in her chest. It was the story of her people too. She felt the sorrow of it deep inside.

"Hey," Ezra said gently, reaching out and putting his hand on her shoulder to comfort her as he had Walks at Night.

Still raw from the things the Comanche warrior had said, she shrugged his hand off and stepped away. He clenched his jaw and crossed his muscular arms over his chest, clearly getting her message.

"Niz . . . what else did he say?" he asked, sounding grim.

She turned her face away. She would not repeat the rest.

"I need to know." He waited. "Why did he spit on you?"

"He said they attacked my village because Fire Maker supplied the army with horses."

Ezra took that information in with a grunt. "I wondered if that led to the attack. What else was said?"

"That was all," she lied, raising her chin.

He was quiet for a moment. "I don't believe you."

"That was all!" she repeated.

"Are you really going to lie to me?" His words were dripping with hurt. "I thought we told each other the whole truth."

She kept her face turned away, her eyes on the mountain peaks beyond the fort, her teeth clenched together. She wasn't willing to share that she'd known the Comanche warrior, that she'd been the one to shoot him, his plans for her if he'd captured her, the fact that he knew her husband, or his intention to trade for her if he had the opportunity. Those details and her fears surrounding them were not something she would share with the man standing in front of her.

"Niz . . . you're shaking," Ezra observed, concern overshadowing the hurt in his voice.

She looked toward Marigold's, longing for escape. "I'm tired," she muttered.

He blew out a deep breath. "Listen. This is my fault. I'm sorry I asked you to translate this morning. I should have waited. You've been up all night; you need to get some sleep." He reached out and gently lifted Walks at Night's cradleboard. "Leave him with me and go get some rest."

"No, I'll take him," she protested, holding onto the burden strap. She did need to sleep, but he was her child. There were only a few more hours to make it through until naptime. She could do it.

"I insist."

"He's my son," she snapped.

"That doesn't mean you can't get some sleep," Ezra answered, sounding frustrated.

"I'll take care of him! Then I'll know he's safe. And you have more important things to do than chase a little boy around, Major!"

The title she had used for him hung heavy in the air between them. She crossed her arms over her chest, using the pressure of them to try to pull herself together. She felt like she was coming apart at the seams. The instinct to flee was strong. Everything within her wanted to run—away from Ezra, away from the Comanche, away from the enormity of emotions that were overtaking her like a mountain wildfire. She could feel the heat of them breathing down her neck, the danger of not being able to outrun them in time filling her with panic.

"Niz, look at me." She didn't. "Please," Ezra requested, his voice firm. She kept her eyes on the mountains. "Niz!" Finally, she did as he asked. His hazel eyes were pools of concern so deep and tender that her heart began to ache. "Listen, I don't know what was said in there, but out here, it's just me."

Her shoulders slumped, and suddenly, she felt completely spent. Her legs trembled, and she worried they wouldn't hold her much longer.

He reached out and put one hand on her shoulder, using the other to tip her face up so he could look her in the eyes. "Look past my uniform and the color of my skin, Niz. I'm just Ezra, your friend. I was there at your village. I shook your father's hand and listened to his stories around the fire. I was at your wedding when your eyes were shining as bright as the sun. I sat at your mother-in-law's table, teased your brothers-in-law, listened to

Raya read the Scriptures after dinner. I helped Alex build the cabin you lived in and move in that ridiculously heavy furniture he made for you. I've sat in your wickiup. I've watched your mother make beads. I could find my way to your village blindfolded. I brought you your son. Niz. It's just me."

Her knees buckled; the weight of everything she carried was suddenly too heavy to stand under. Ezra caught her as she stumbled and wrapped her tightly in his arms, letting her rest against his solid chest as he held her up. His embrace was supportive, not passionate, friendly rather than intimate, so she relaxed there in the quiet shadow of his solid strength while she tried to convince her weary body and ragged emotions to pull themselves together. "Ezra," she started, knowing she owed him some sort of explanation.

He shook his head and quieted her. "Let me take Walks at Night while you get some rest. I won't let him out of my sight, and I'll bring him back to you when he wakes up from his nap. Niz," he waited until she glanced up at him. "You can trust me."

She searched his handsome face and hazel eyes and nodded, feeling very near tears. He was right. Out here, he wasn't Major Taylor—commander of the fort or the army in their area. He was Ezra. He had done all the things he'd listed off. He wasn't his uniform or his skin color; she could see his heart.

This time, she allowed him to lift the cradleboard off her back. As he turned Walks at Night toward her, she leaned forward and kissed the child's little face. His big brown eyes were locked on her, and he was sucking his thumb. "I'll see you soon," she promised her son.

"I'll take good care of him," Ezra said kindly. "Get some sleep, Beautiful."

Afraid she would dissolve into tears, she nodded and turned, starting to walk away from them. Suddenly she spun back. "Thank you, Ezra, for being my friend."

His answering smile was so tender that her tears began to fall, and unable to stop them, she turned and ran, not stopping until she was behind Marigold's front door, alone in the little front room. She wiped her cheeks as she rolled out her sleeping mat and dropped down. She would not think about Ezra or the Comanche or Fire Maker. She would not think about the wounded soldiers or the frightening attack from the evening before. She would not think about her mother or her sisters, returning home, or what the Comanche warrior had made all too clear. She would not think about the fact that her son's real name was Alex, or that the grief felt big enough to swallow her whole. She would not think about any of it. She would do what she had done so many times before and push it all aside, leaving her thoughts empty so sleep could come.

Only this time, as exhaustion caught up with her and sleep swept in, she felt like she was drowning, in over her head, no longer able to keep her face above water. She was no longer capable of holding it all together, and she knew it.

Seventeen

Niz woke to knocking. Her head felt thick, and she had to blink several times to clear her sight. Still groggy, she saw Marigold put down her mending and push herself out of the chair she'd been sitting in. Marigold motioned for Niz to stay where she was and hurried to the door. Her eyelids feeling heavy, Niz closed them. Hearing the front door shut, she opened them again to find Marigold holding Walks at Night.

"Try to sleep. I'm going to take him out for a walk."

Niz nodded and promptly fell back asleep. She woke again when the front door opened sometime later. Marigold came in with Walks at Night toddling along beside her. The shadows in the house were growing long, and Niz knew instinctively that it was evening. Throwing off her blanket, she pushed herself to her feet. "I've slept so long. I'm sorry."

Marigold shook her head with a charming smile. "Don't be sorry at all. I absolutely adored my evening walk with this handsome little guy. He's the best male company at the fort!"

Walks at Night toddled over to Niz and buried his face in her skirt. She settled him in her arms and kissed his sweet cheeks. "Did Major Taylor get along okay with him today?"

"He said he was an angel. They played chase and watched ladybugs, and he said Walks at Night ate a good lunch and napped for three solid hours." The report brought a smile to Niz's face. "I need to head over and make sure the bandages have been changed correctly for the wounded men. Would you want to stay here and make us some dinner? I'm starving, and I'm sure you are as well. I won't be long."

Niz nodded. "I'll do that."

Marigold left with a smile, and Niz took a moment to bury her face against Walks at Night, holding him close and breathing deeply as he snuggled in against her. Waking up, all her worries from earlier had come back, pressing her down with the weight of them. But here, cuddling her sweet child, she found respite and delight in the simple pleasure of loving and being loved. For that moment, nothing else mattered.

Too soon, though, Walks at Night didn't want to be snuggled anymore. He wanted to explore and play.

"Fine, you win," she said with a sad laugh as she sat him down and watched him toddle off toward his wooden spoons. She set about fixing dinner, keeping an eye on him as she did so.

As she worked, she found herself jumping at every little noise. Every door that shut nearby, every creak of the floor, even voices of men passing outside, set her on edge. With each one, she braced, fear springing to life, anxiety overtaking her. What if the Comanche had escaped? What if their friends snuck in to free them? If they were successful, would they leave without her, or would the warrior make good on his threat? Fear churned her stomach. She wholeheartedly hoped she would never see him again.

Dinner was nearly ready when the front door opened. She spun to face it, alarm coursing through her, her eyes finding Walks at Night and making an escape plan in an instant. Relief crashed over her as Marigold's face registered. The blonde entered in a flurry of laughter and talking, Ezra only a few steps behind.

"I hope you made enough for one more," Marigold said happily from the doorway where she was hanging up the light shawl she had worn. Niz looked to the windows and realized it was nearly dark. The days were getting shorter. Autumn was upon them and winter was coming. Even more reason to do what she'd made up her mind to do as she cooked.

"I did." Niz answered, turning her attention back to those in the room. "I figured you might join us and set a place for you," she told Ezra, sending him a smile as her heartbeat returned to normal. "Thank you for watching Walks at Night today so I could sleep."

"We had fun."

"Most bachelors don't know what to do with a child—they're just helplessly lost, as if a baby were a creature from another universe," Marigold said, watching Walks at Night run toward Ezra as she tied on an apron. "But not Major Taylor. You're a natural, sir."

Ezra grinned as he squatted down on his heels to greet the boy, reaching out to tousle his hair. "This little guy makes it easy. He's a good kid."

Niz watched the scene unfold, not missing how Marigold looked at the major with admiration. She couldn't blame her friend for noticing what a good father Ezra would make—it was hard not to. Niz's heart began to ache a little, and she turned to finish slicing the bread. She set a plate of it on the table alongside the venison steaks she had prepared to go with a hash of fried potatoes, squash, and corn. As she went after a jar of Marigold's raspberry preserves (this time made with sugar), she decided that if an opportunity came to encourage Marigold toward Ezra later, she would take it.

They were both dear people. They deserved each other and all the happiness in the world. Surely if Marigold were to set her cap after Ezra, he would not be able to withstand her charming smiles and cheerful golden beauty. He would come around. And Niz was certain he would be incredibly happy once he did. Marigold would make him a wonderful wife. The thought of both of them being happy made her heart happy, too, even though she suddenly found herself blinking back tears.

The dinner conversation was informative and pleasant. They discussed the condition of the wounded, and Niz learned all who had made it through the night were still alive. Ezra shared that he'd gone back to talk to the captives and that they had continued their stony silence. He would be heading out on patrol again in the morning. This time, his patrol would head north; Captain Blackwell would once more be in charge in his absence. They were determined to catch the remaining Comanche and put an end to their violent raiding. Too many people had already died. It needed to end.

As Ezra finished his dinner, he leaned back in his chair, looking seriously across the table at Niz. She helped Walks at Night scoop up the last of his hash and braced for what she knew was coming.

"Niz, I know there were things said this morning when you were talking to the Comanche that you didn't tell me about." She didn't look up. "Will you tell me about them now?"

"No," she answered simply, keeping her eyes on her son. In true Ezra fashion, he'd given thought to setting her up to feel safe enough to share. He'd allowed her to get some sleep, something to eat, and had asked with Marigold present, surely thinking she would feel more comfortable sharing with her friend there for support. Still, she'd given it a lot of thought as she cooked their dinner, and she didn't plan to share any more of the conversation than she already had. Unfortunately, she hadn't learned anything from the Comanche that would help Ezra apprehend them. Everything she suspected she'd learned had to do with only one person—her husband.

"Niz," Marigold started, reaching over and squeezing her arm kindly. "If it's something the major needs to know . . ."

Niz shook her head.

"It's just that we know you want peace as much as we do. Your people have been hurt by the Comanche too," Marigold said carefully.

Niz looked up, stunned. "You think I'm protecting them?" Marigold glanced at Ezra uncertainly, and he cleared his throat and leaned forward in his chair. "I'm not! I want them caught as much as you do!" Niz cried passionately, meaning it with every ounce of her being.

Ezra considered her for a long moment. "We've known each other for a long time, and I trust you, so I'm just going to ask this once. Is there anything that was said today that I need to know about? Anything that would help us find the rest of the Comanche?"

"No," she said confidently, holding his gaze.

"Are you in danger?"

She dropped her eyes as she tore off a piece of bread for Walks at Night. "They're in custody. What could they do to me? Or any of us?"

Ezra clenched and unclenched his jaw as he studied her. "You didn't answer my question. Are you in danger?"

"No," she said, raising her chin, though she couldn't bring herself to look at him.

Ezra hit the table, startling them all. "Gosh darnit, Niz, don't lie to me!"

He slammed his chair back and left the table, stalking over to stare out the window. Walks at Night watched him with wide eyes, obviously alarmed by the loud noise.

"Niz, we just want to help," Marigold said, squeezing her arm again, her blue eyes sincere. "We care about you!"

"I don't need help," Niz cried, pushing herself to her feet, holding her son tightly in her arms. "And I'm not lying."

Ezra spun toward them. "Something happened in there today that greatly upset you. I know it did, because I know *you*. And I know you're not a woman who is easily shaken. If there's trouble . . . if you're in danger, let me help you!"

Niz pressed her fingertips to her forehead, closing her eyes for a moment. He wanted information, but she already knew he wouldn't want to hear what she had to tell him, especially when there was nothing he could do about it. How could she give him what he wanted without hurting this man, who was nothing but wonderful and kind? "The man who was talking to me, the fierce one with the bandage on his arm?"

"Yes," Ezra agreed eagerly with a nod. He appeared relieved that she was finally talking, but she knew his relief would be short-lived.

Walks at Night leaned toward the ground, and she set him down, watching him toddle off toward his wooden spoons. She took a deep breath. "I'm the one who shot him. It was during the raid on my village. He was riding through our camp, and I wounded him. He knew I was the one who did it. I was trying to reload but I wasn't going to make it in time. He had just started back toward me when the bugle sounded. I thought he was going to kill me, but," she dropped her eyes, unable to look at Ezra while she finished, "he corrected me today, saying he intended to take me as his captive instead. If you hadn't come when you did . . . death would have been a kindness."

Glancing up nervously, she watched the color drain out of Ezra's face. She licked her lips, trying to moisten them, trying not to feel her dinner rising up as the memory of that night, the memory of the warrior's eyes earlier, churned her stomach.

"Niz," Marigold breathed.

"Keep them in your guardhouse, Ezra, and I'm in no danger. If they're busted out, they're a threat to us all," she finished shakily. There was no need to go into the rest.

Ezra stood unmoving across the room, his expression a mix of anger, worry, and frustration. She knew it wasn't directed at her, but she clearly felt the power of it even across the distance separating them. For a man like Ezra, who was a protector down to his core, she knew everything inside of him likely wanted to lash out at the man who had threatened her and fight for her honor. But the man had been caught; he himself was the one who had put her in his path once again. She knew that knowledge was likely equally as frustrating.

"Is there anything else?" he asked, crossing his arms over his chest, appearing to brace himself.

"Not that I'm willing to share and not that you need to know," Niz answered, tossing her dark hair. She'd said all that she would.

She wasn't going to share that the man had known Fire Maker or that he had threatened to strike a trade with him for her. It would be pointless; there was nothing Ezra could do about it. She was married to Fire Maker, and sooner or later, she would have to return to him. She scooped up Walks at Night and sat with him on the ground, leaning back against a chair.

"Niz," Ezra started, frustration ruling his tone. She sat up straighter but kept her eyes on her son. "Tell me the rest."

Determined to keep her information as private as Cloud Walking could, she shook her head. He pushed his hand through his brown hair and spun toward the window. After a moment, he turned back to face her. "Fine. Then I'll send Captain Blackwell out to lead the patrol tomorrow. I'd feel better staying here at the fort—with you."

"No!" she answered quickly, her mind humming. "I know how important it is to you to lead your men. Other commanding officers would stay back at the fort to lead from safety, but not you. You value being out on the front lines where you can see and hear and make decisions firsthand, and your men admire you all the more for it. I've heard them talking this week, and they respect you."

"That's true," Marigold added. "They do."

"Niz, that doesn't matter, I can—"

"Ezra! It does matter!" she protested, her frustration growing. This—his willingness to change his plans to be with her, to protect her—this is what it felt like to be taken care of. Valued. Loved. But this wasn't her reality anymore. Her heart twisted painfully. This wasn't real life. It wasn't his place. He couldn't protect her, and she couldn't let him. In the wake of disappointment, her defenses rose, her pain masking itself in anger. "Don't change your plans for me, Major. I'm not your concern!"

"Niz—"

"You can't help me, Ezra!" she cried.

"Alright." Marigold pushed back from the table and crossed the room. Laying her hand gently on Ezra's shoulder, she turned him toward the door. "Go on home, Major. She's right. If you want to help Niz—help everyone—catch the raiders and keep those who have been caught in custody. There's nothing more to be said here tonight. She's safe, and we all know you'll be back to sleep on the porch soon anyway." She smiled knowingly. "Yes, that's right. Sergeant Green told me you slept on my porch to keep us safe. Thank you."

Ezra shifted his attention from Marigold to Niz, frustration filling his expression. Marigold shook her head and pushed him gently toward the door again. "It's not the time."

Finally, he dipped his head. "You're right. Thank you for letting me join you ladies for dinner. And thank you for the meal, Niz. As usual, it was wonderful."

"You're welcome," Niz said from the floor, keeping her attention on her son.

Ezra left and Marigold barred the door and shut the curtains before coming to sit on the floor with Niz and Walks at Night. Leaning back against a chair, Marigold positioned herself to face her. "He cares about you a great deal."

"Ezra was my husband's best friend," Niz said simply. "They grew up together . . . adventured together . . . they were basically like brothers. I don't know if you've been in his office recently, but he has a sketch of him hanging there. Mother Emaline—my mother-in-law whose cookie recipe we used—said they were nearly inseparable in their teens."

"What happened?" Marigold asked, propping her head up on her fist and her elbow on the seat of the chair.

"We got married, and Ezra went off to join the army. Last summer there was a fire at our family sawmill. My husband and his brothers were trapped inside. None of them made it out. My mother-in-law and one of my sisters-in-law went back east to Cincinnati. My other sister-in-law went home to her family's house on the other side of town. I returned to my village. Ezra didn't know about any of it until he got stationed here at the fort. I think now he feels like he owes it to his best friend to make sure

I'm okay. I think it's his way of making it up to him that he wasn't there that day."

"Sometimes I think it's more than that," Marigold said softly.

Niz shook her head, swallowing hard against the painful tightening in her throat. It was time to speak the words she'd determined earlier that she would speak. "It's not. You know Ezra. He's a man of principle. Deep down, he's just trying to do right by my husband." She paused, reaching out to lay her hand on Marigold's arm imploringly. "He is a really good man, though. I know it hasn't been long since Robert, but Marigold, if you can find it in your heart to love again . . . there isn't going to be anyone better than Ezra Taylor."

"I've had the same thought," Marigold said, her blue eyes filling with tears. "I know you're right, and sometimes I think it could work, but . . . I loved Robert with my whole heart."

Niz squeezed her arm gently. "I understand. I do. But wouldn't Robert want you to be happy? To find love again? To be with someone kind and good and honest? Wouldn't he want you to be protected and provided for?"

Her words were like a knife to her own heart. Wouldn't that be what Alex wanted for her also? He would have hated to see her with Fire Maker as much as Ezra did.

"My father will protect and provide for me," Marigold reasoned, wiping tears from her creamy cheeks.

"That's good, Marigold. I'm glad for you," Niz said sincerely. "My father died during the years I was married. He wasn't there to return to after the fire."

"I'm sorry. That must have been very difficult."

Niz nodded, and the silence stretched. "You're fortunate that your father can provide for your needs and safety, but what about your happiness? What about this?" Niz asked, motioning to Walks at Night. "You adore him. I know you dream of children of your own."

"I do," Marigold admitted, tousling Walks at Night's hair. "Even more so since this handsome boy came to stay."

"Well, who better to have as the father of your children than Ezra? You said it yourself—he's a natural."

A slight smile touched Marigold's lips, then she grew serious again. "Why are you saying all this? Why now? You haven't tried to persuade me toward Major Taylor before."

"I just want to see you both happy. He's a wonderful man. I want him to have love in his life. My husband wanted that for him." Niz paused, swallowed hard, and pushed herself to her feet. "You watched Walks at Night while I slept. Stay here and rest while I clean up dinner."

Niz busied herself doing the dishes and wiping down the table while Marigold sat on the floor and played with Walks at Night. When she was done, she came back with a cup of tea for each of them and settled down on the floor again.

Marigold sipped her steaming brew and considered Niz over the top of it. "What was really said today when you were talking with the Comanche?"

Niz dropped her eyes.

"You can tell me. I won't share it. Not even with Major Taylor. You have my word."

Niz took a deep breath. "They were being crude . . . suggesting Fire Maker traded me out to the soldiers just like he traded his horses."

Marigold looked horrified, and a part of Niz felt vindicated. It really was as awful as it had felt. "They wondered how much it would take to have him send me to their camp too."

"Niz." Marigold set down her tea, reached over and took her hand, holding it between both of hers. "What a terrible thing for them to say. They don't know you at all. If they did, they would know you're a loyal and virtuous woman, just as we do." Marigold squeezed her hand warmly. "Don't let them get to you. Like you said, they're in custody. And it's a good thing your husband didn't hear them talking like that!"

Tears burned Niz's eyes. "The worst part is, Marigold, I think Fire Maker would consider it if the price were right . . . and that is absolutely terrifying to me."

"Surely not!" Marigold said with a gasp. Niz simply shrugged. "You must be mistaken. No man would allow such a thing to happen to the woman he loves . . . not for any price."

"Fire Maker doesn't love me."

"Don't say that. Of course he does. Maybe he just doesn't know how to tell you," Marigold said soothingly. "Some men just don't know how to express their feelings."

Niz shook her head. "No, you don't understand. I'm not speaking out of hurt or emotion. He really doesn't, Marigold. I'm only a trophy to him—something to win and possess. His only draw to me is to conquer and control me. I saw it when I was a teenager and he asked me to marry him. But then . . . after the fire . . . I don't know. I guess I was desperate to feel better . . . to be able to move on. I couldn't . . . let myself feel. I just wanted to pretend everything was okay . . . that I was okay. And I thought getting married again might help me do that."

"Perhaps you'll learn to love each other," Marigold offered, clearly doing her best to cling to optimism. "Maybe it's just going to take time."

Niz looked at the floor. "Perhaps."

Walks at Night came and sat down on her lap, rubbing his face against her dress. His eyes were growing heavy.

"He's sleepy."

Niz nodded. She took a deep, shaky breath. "Fire Maker wanted to trade him."

"What?" Marigold gasped. "Trade him?"

Niz shrugged miserably. "The tribes have traded captives for generations . . . sometimes to other tribes, sometimes to the Spanish."

"But . . . how could he? In this day and age? This precious boy?"

"I think he knows how much I love him."

"But isn't that a good thing?" Marigold asked, tears in her crystalline blue eyes.

Niz shrugged. "Not to Fire Maker. He feels threatened by anything he thinks I care about. So, he tries to use my affection as a weapon against me." She inhaled deeply and then blew it back out. "I try to tell myself I'm not, but I'm frightened of what he might do to Walks at Night . . . to my sisters . . . to my mother . . . to me. He's not a good man."

"I wish I could help you," Marigold said sadly, squeezing her hand. "Is there anything I can do? Anything at all?"

"No. There's nothing anyone can do. Not even Ezra," Niz said truthfully. Walks at Night rested his head against her chest, and she let go of Marigold's hand to wrap her arms around him, holding him tight. "I'll figure out a way to protect him . . . to protect all of them. Don't worry. We'll be okay."

"You're a clever girl, Niz, smart and quick. I've seen that firsthand. If anyone can figure this out, it's you," Marigold encouraged. When she spoke again, her voice was gentle. "Tell me about your sisters."

Niz did, and the conversation took a pleasant turn as she shared about Ever Flowering's pregnancy and Cloud Walking's mystery crush. She told Marigold about life with her people, and the tasks that were still coming up before they headed off to their winter camp. Niz told her about her mother, and her friends, and all the wonderful things about life in her village. They stayed up late, talking long into the night. Marigold was resting her head against a pillow propped up on the chair she sat beside, and Niz had laid down on her sleeping mat with Walks at Night, who was soundly sleeping. They laughed together over silly things and poured their hearts out to one another. Marigold shared her fears about traveling back to Fort Sidney, what she was looking forward to about being east of the Rockies again, and reminisced about Robert. Her tears fell freely, and she sopped them up with her handkerchief.

"You don't speak of Alex much," she finally said after being quiet so long Niz had wondered if she was asleep. "I know you said you can't say his name, but . . . do you think about him?"

"I try not to," Niz answered sleepily. It was too late at night to be anything but honest.

"Why? Does it hurt too much?" Marigold questioned compassionately.

"I'm scared it will. So I don't . . . At least I try not to. I try not to think about him or . . . the fire . . . or the baby I delivered months too early." Marigold's face filled with sadness and empathy. "I try not to think about how different things are with Fire Maker than they were with him . . . or how frightened I am . . . or how Fire Maker hurts me. It's too much, Marigold. I'm scared of how deeply I would feel it . . . of the depth of my emotion . . . and so I just keep pressing it down, ignoring it, hoping it will go away, but it never does. And I'm scared because I don't know if there's room to press anything more down. I think I'm full to the top. I'm suffocating in it. I feel like I can't breathe. I keep trying to outrun it, thinking if I just stay busy enough, if I just don't stop, if I don't let myself feel, but . . . I don't know if I can outrun it anymore. It's catching up to me." Niz stopped and gave a self-deprecating laugh. "I'm sure that sounds so ridiculous. I don't know . . . maybe I'm going crazy."

"It doesn't sound ridiculous to me," Marigold said, her voice full of sympathy.

Niz lay staring up at the log ceiling. "I can't even put my finger on it, Marigold. I don't know if it's grief or fear or just the weight of responsibility for my family and my people or if Fire Maker is succeeding in breaking my spirit . . . I just know it's too much. It's all running together. I don't even know what to call it exactly, but I know I feel like I can't breathe . . . like I'm drowning."

"You can't keep pressing it all down, Niz. That's not healthy for you. It's too much for you to carry."

"I don't know what else to do," Niz admitted hopelessly.

"You need to hand it over to someone who can carry that heavy load," Marigold said gently, reaching out and smoothing Niz's hair back off her face.

"Who could I trust with thoughts and memories and emotions I don't even trust myself with?" Niz questioned hopelessly. "Who could I trust with fears about an unknown future? With the pain of today? With the grief of the past? Who could I trust to hold everything together?"

Not even Ezra Taylor could do that.

"Jesus," Marigold answered, her voice suddenly warm and confident. "He said: Come unto me, all ye that labour and are heavy laden, and I will give you rest. Take my yoke upon you, and learn of me; for I am meek and lowly in heart: and ye shall find rest unto your souls. For my yoke is easy, and my burden is light."

Niz mulled over the words Marigold shared. She certainly did feel heavy-laden, and she felt desperate for true, safe, uncomplicated rest. What would it be like to have someone to turn to that invited those carrying heavy things to draw near? What would it be like to trade Him her load that felt too heavy to bear and take His light, easy yoke instead? But how could that even happen? What could be done? She'd gotten herself into a mess. She couldn't expect anyone else—not even God—to get her back out of it.

"I could show you where it says that in the Bible tomorrow if you'd like," Marigold offered. "You could read it for yourself. You're doing wonderfully. You've made so much progress this week."

Niz nodded, even as tears collected in her eyes. This time, in the dim light of the lone lamp Marigold had lit, she didn't even try to blink them back.

"You're leaving, aren't you?" Marigold questioned softly. "That's why you were so insistent Ezra leave on patrol. That's why you've shared everything you have . . . that's why you've stayed up late talking . . . been so open and honest."

"Yes," Niz whispered.

"When?" Marigold asked, her voice filled with sadness.

"Before it gets light."

"But why?"

Niz closed her eyes. Why was she leaving? How could she even articulate it? Especially to Marigold? She'd been gone nearly a week, and she could read decently well now. But it was more than that. "I need to go home. I miss my mother and my sisters. I need to check on them and make sure they're okay. I need to see that Ever Flowering is better . . . she's been sick . . . and that Cloud Walking is using wisdom. And regardless of the kind of man he is, I'm married. My place is with my husband." She didn't add that she needed to be far away from Ezra Taylor, who made her remember what life with love could be like. There was no point.

"Are you coming back?" Marigold asked, beginning to cry.

"No," Nizhoni said softly.

"Please don't say this is our last conversation. You've become such a dear friend," Marigold pleaded, her tears continuing to fall.

"I can't come back. And it's not safe for you to be traveling to my village right now, even with an escort—we both know it. You belong here, and I belong there, but I just want to thank you, Marigold, because you've been such a good friend to me, and I didn't even know how much I needed you, but I did. So thank you . . . for everything."

"Meeting you has been the best thing that has happened to me in a long time," Marigold said, sniffling. "Thank you for reminding me that life is full of unexpected blessings. I will forever consider you my friend. And I will write you when I get back to Fort Sidney so you'll have a letter waiting for you when you return from your winter camp. Please, you must write me back as soon as you do. I'll be thinking of you all winter."

Niz reached out and held Marigold's hand. "Don't go back to Fort Sidney, Marigold. Stay here. With Ezra. Even if you two aren't in love yet, you'd be so good together. Love will grow. Please. I want you both to be happy."

Marigold wiped her eyes with one hand and squeezed Niz's with the other. "I'm not worried about that. How can anyone not love Ezra Taylor? But . . . I just don't know that I'm ready."

"Marigold," Niz started.

"I promise I'll pray about it, okay?"

Niz nodded. She couldn't ask for more. "Thank you."

They were both quiet for a long moment. "I'd better let you get some sleep if you're leaving early," Marigold finally said, squeezing Niz's hand. "I never had a sister, but if I had, I imagine I would have loved her just as I love you."

"I love you too," Niz said, meaning it completely. Marigold had been like a song of joy in her last few weeks, a river of peace, a shelter from the storm. She had reminded her of all things good and wonderful. "Marigold?"

"Hm?" Marigold asked, standing.

"Don't tell Ezra I'm gone."

Marigold was quiet for a moment. "I won't."

"Thank you."

"How are you going to sneak past him? He's sleeping on the porch," Marigold reminded. They'd heard him come a few hours earlier.

"Will you hand Walks at Night out the window to me?" Niz asked.

Marigold nodded hesitantly, as if she wasn't sure she should agree.

Niz looked at the clock. If she left now, she could get several hours from the fort before Ezra woke up. He would leave on patrol heading north, assuming she was still inside, and wouldn't find out she had left until he returned.

"Thank you." Niz stood up and began packing her belongings.

"Wait, you mean you're leaving now?"

"Yes, I'd best get on my way. I'll walk until I find shelter, and then I'll sleep until morning."

"Why not wait? Ezra is leaving in the morning. He won't be here to stop you."

"Surely he'll be leaving Sergeant Green to watch the both of us."

Marigold conceded with a nod. "That's true enough. But you're not a prisoner, Niz. You're free to leave. Major Taylor just wants you to be safe. He wants you to have an escort and a horse when you do. Would it be so bad to let him arrange that for you?"

"Marigold . . . this isn't my life. My husband doesn't care to give me a mount and an escort. And no matter how well-intentioned, Ezra can't protect me. My place isn't here within his reach. It's with my people. I need to live the life I agreed to . . . even if that means no horse or escorts. The sooner I remember that, the better."

Niz straightened from lacing the sleeping Walks at Night into his cradleboard. She tied her sleeping mat and satchel to the side of it. Marigold went into the kitchen while she packed and came back with a handkerchief tied around biscuits and cookies. "Here's something to eat on your walk . . . we both know Walks at Night wakes up hungry."

Niz smiled. "Thank you. And I'll actually enjoy eating these! You're a quick learner."

Marigold laughed and followed her into the back bedroom. Niz gave her a long hug, opened the window, and climbed out of it, dropping the last few feet to the ground. Marigold carefully finagled the cradleboard through the window before lowering it to Niz. Catching hold of it, Niz settled the burden strap around her shoulders, then looked up and sent one last smile up at her golden-haired friend. With a little wave, she started off silently through the night, refusing to jump at every little noise. She was not weak, and she would not live her life in fear. Comanche or no Comanche, she would remain strong and fearless, wild and free.

But before it disappeared, she looked back over her shoulder at the little log cabin, thinking about the kind man who slept on its porch. Once she was in her village, she could effectively shut him out. She could limit the time she spent with him and the conversations they might have. That was the only path forward, and so it's the one she would take, even if her heart hurt just thinking about it.

Ezra had committed to offering her only friendship, and she didn't doubt he would keep his promise, but he wanted more for her than she could have. He wanted her to be taken care of, to be cherished, safe, protected, and loved. Fire Maker wouldn't, and Ezra couldn't. Being her friend was sure to only frustrate, anger, and sadden him. He would feel like a failure if anything happened to her, if he saw the bruises she tried so hard to hide, or was there when Fire Maker mistreated her. She didn't want that for him; she didn't want him to have to carry that load. He would feel like he was failing her and Alex, and yet his hands would be tied. There was literally nothing he could do.

On top of being worried about him—his heart—she was worried for her people. What would Ezra do if he saw Fire Maker hurt her again? What if a fight started and his soldiers and the braves got involved? A brawl could end detrimentally for them all. Her heart couldn't handle that kind of loss.

No, she had to leave. She had to get out of this place where their friendship could grow, away from his principles and his self-appointed duty to protect her, away from what life could be like and back to what life was. She missed her sisters. She missed her mother. She missed Soaring Eagle and all her friends. She needed to check on Lean Elk and Wise Hawk and their family, as well as those grieving Noon Day Sun. The buffaloberries and acorns would be ready to gather soon, and not long after that, they would head to their winter camp. She needed to go home.

"Goodbye, Ezra," she whispered into the night. Turning, she stayed in the shadows, avoiding the soldiers on duty, silently slipping out of the fort and into the darkness beyond. She needed to make it to the cover of the forest before the sun rose.

Eighteen

Niz woke slowly, the familiar interior of her wickiup registering as she opened her eyes. Beside her, Walks at Night was stirring. She had made it back to her village around noon, only to find Fire Maker and the braves gone again. There were only a few weeks left before they headed down to a lower elevation to spend the winter, and they were making their final push to secure food for the cold months ahead.

She couldn't deny that she'd been thankful to find him gone. During her long hours walking home from the fort, she'd attempted to prepare for the conversation they would surely have. Seeing her, he would undoubtedly assume she would be able to read the bill of sale, and he would get to make his lucrative trade. He would want to know where the soldiers were, why they weren't there to buy his horses, and when they were coming. However, he wasn't the only one who would have questions. She had several for him as well. But with him off hunting, that was trouble for another day.

What occupied her thoughts as she lay staring up at the ceiling was her dismay that Ever Flowering was no better. In fact, she was worse. When her sister had greeted her with a hug the day before, Niz had immediately noticed how she could feel Ever Flowering's bones pressing against her. What had been a soft cough here and there in the weeks before she left, had become dry and hollow. It echoed in her chest. In August, Ever Flowering had laughed off the weariness in her steps as they gathered amaranth or processed the men's hunts, blaming pregnancy, and her cough on too much smoke from the fire. Now, it was evident to Niz that it was more than that.

Shy Fawn had reported the fevers had come and gone like shifting winds, hot and fierce one day, leaving Ever Flowering shivering and soaked, only to vanish the next morning as if they had never come. Even in the sunshine of midday, Ever Flowering had been damp and pale, and although she told Niz she was fine, Niz could see her eyes had lost their brightness. In the evening, she'd caught Ever Flowering pressing her hand to her chest when she thought no one was looking, and there was a sorrow in her gentle eyes. It was as if a quiet battle was waging inside her sister's body while she carried life within it. Niz, her mother, and Cloud Walking were powerless to stop it.

Deciding she would go check on her, Niz threw back her blankets and stood. She changed Walks at Night and got them both some breakfast before starting toward Ever Flowering's wickiup. As they walked, Walks at Night's hand in hers, he pointed at the animals in the corrals at the edge of camp.

"Horses," she told him. "Aren't they pretty? Someday you'll ride one. You'll race across the mountain meadows, your arms spread wide and the wind in your hair. That's the best way to ride."

He babbled, sounding gleefully happy, trying to mimic her words as he continued to point. One of the horses snorted and shook its mane, and Walks at Night exclaimed in wonder. Niz laughed, thankful for the happy, carefree moment with her son in the midst of her concern. Suddenly, she tilted her head, studying the horses more closely. There seemed to be several more in the corrals than there were last time the men were out on a hunt. Among them was a beautiful red roan paint that she was certain she would have remembered; its markings were stunning.

"Good morning!" Cloud Walking said cheerfully, falling into step beside her.

"Good morning," Niz answered, pushing the troubling thoughts out of her mind. "How did you sleep?"

"Very well. And good morning to you, fine sir. How are you this morning?" Cloud Walking asked, squatting down to the toddler's level. Continuing his baby babble, he pointed at the horses. "Ah, yes, I see. You're a budding young horseman. Maybe someday you'll be the best rider in the camp," Cloud Walking said, pinching his cheek affectionately before standing back up.

"Cloud Walking," Niz started. "Have you ever seen that paint over there before?"

"Which one? There are lots of paints," Cloud Walking teased.

"The red roan with the white blaze on its forehead and the copper-colored mane and tail. There," Niz explained, pointing.

Cloud Walking looked, then shrugged. "No, I don't remember seeing it. But then again, I'm not out in the corrals much."

Niz tipped her head. That was true enough. She wasn't in the corrals much either. Perhaps she'd just missed it. "Well, it's a beautiful horse."

Cloud Walking nodded. "It is." There was a slight pause. "So, how was your time at the fort? You didn't say much about it yesterday."

"It was good," Niz told her. "Marigold was a gracious host. We did lots of reading, and I taught her to bake."

"Did you see Major Taylor?"

"Yes, though he was out on patrol for most of my stay," she answered, trying to sound casual. She wouldn't share the details of her late-night conversation with Ezra with anyone—not even her sister. Niz had decided to forget the entire incident altogether. There was no room for it among the facts of reality. She was married. She had encouraged her dear friend to make space in her heart for him. Thus, Ezra, his declaration of love, and the kiss had to be wiped off the record of her heart.

"Hm," Cloud Walking responded.

"There was trouble with the Comanche . . . they continue to raid. They even came to the fort, trying to release some of their warriors who were captured."

Cloud Walking's eyes widened. "Really? While you were there? Did they succeed?"

"No, thankfully. The soldiers held them off, though many were injured." Niz paused, pushing away fears that arose with the memories. "Sergeant Green—"

"Sergeant Green?" Cloud Walking interrupted, clearly alarmed, her feet seeming to freeze in place.

"Yes, the soldier who took us to Major Taylor when we visited the fort."

"Yes, I know who he is! He was hurt?"

"No," Niz said slowly. Cloud Walking seemed quite worried.

"Oh, good. It's just, you mentioned him," her sister said, recovering.

"I was going to say that he saw the Comanche coming and sent Marigold and me to safety. We came out once it was all over and tended to the wounded."

"Oh, I see. Well, that was honorable of him. I'm glad none of you were injured." Cloud Walking reached down and took Walks at Night's free hand, swinging it in hers. "Was the major hurt?"

"No, he was out on patrol when it happened."

"Too bad." Cloud Walking's eyes grew wide, and she laughed at herself. "Not too bad he wasn't hurt, too bad he wasn't at the fort. I bet Major Taylor would have stopped them if he'd been there," she finished a bit dreamily.

Niz sent her sister a sideways glance. "Perhaps."

"What? He seems like a good leader, that's all," Cloud Walking said with a shrug.

Niz couldn't argue with that. Ezra did seem to be an excellent leader. She was more convinced of that than ever, having just spent a week watching his men interact with him and then talk about him when he was out on patrol. She'd overheard nothing but good things and deep respect for their commanding officer. But Ezra was the last person she wanted to think about now that she was back home. She'd left the fort to put him out of her mind. He likely was angry with her anyway—or would be once he found out she had snuck away in the middle of the night.

"Has there been any more trouble with the Comanche here at camp?" she asked, changing the direction of the conversation.

"No, not since the raid."

"That's a relief." During her walk home, she'd begun to worry about what she would be returning to. What if the Comanche warriors had circled back to finish what they'd started?

"Sergeant Green was one of the soldiers who chased them out of here."

"Was he?" Niz knew he'd been there, but she hadn't realized Cloud Walking did.

Her sister nodded. "I saw him. After the Comanche rode off. He returned one of my arrows that had missed its mark," Cloud Walking finished sheepishly.

Niz stopped walking. "Did he?"

Cloud Walking laughed. "Was he? Did he? So many questions, Niz. Don't you have any information to share?"

Niz tipped her face up to the sun, taking a moment to let all the pieces fall into place. She glanced back at her sister. "When Marigold and I were passing out cookies to the soldiers, one of them mentioned you were quite good with a bow and arrow and asked if you'd been injured in the raid. But I can't seem to remember who it was." She hadn't thought anything of it when Sergeant Green had asked her—only that it was kind of him to remember her sister—but now she waited to see how Cloud Walking would respond.

"Oh, it was probably him. Sergeant Green. I don't know any of the others."

"But you know him?"

Cloud Walking blushed. "No," she said, drawing out the word. "Not really."

"What's that mean?" Niz asked, forcing a smile, even though warning bells were going off inside her head. Certainly, her sister's crush wasn't on one of the soldiers . . . her mother would never forgive her if it was.

"Well, I mean, he did help us through the fort, and we talked a little while you were inside delivering your message to the major. I taught him a few of our words, and he taught me a few of theirs . . . words like horse, soldier, fort . . . did I pronounce those correctly?" Cloud Walking looked doubtful.

"Yes, you did," Niz answered honestly, her heart racing. Shy Fawn had told her it was a bad idea to take Cloud Walking to the fort, but she'd insisted. She'd thought it would be safer for her sister there, where she could keep an eye on her, rather than leaving her in the village with Fire Maker. If she'd made the wrong call . . .

"And, well, it's silly . . . it was nothing really. I don't even know why I remember it, but . . ."

"Go on," Niz prompted, trying to hide her distress.

"When you were reading with the major that day he came to try to buy horses, well, the soldiers were resting nearby while you read, and I had been upriver washing—"

Niz paled. "Yourself or the laundry?" she interrupted, holding her breath as she waited for her sister's answer.

Cloud Walking made a face. "The laundry."

Niz let out the breath she'd been holding and held up her free hand in a sign of peace. "I'm sorry. Continue."

"Anyway, I was down doing the washing, and Sergeant Green didn't know I was there. He came down to the river to fill his canteen. He asked—well, he tried to ask—if he could stay and watch how I washed the clothes, and I said yes, and he did and . . . I don't know."

"You had a moment," Niz finished knowingly.

"I'm not sure about a moment, but I would recognize him in a crowd now, and I think he would recognize me," Cloud Walking said shyly.

"He's the reason you're not sure about Strong Pine anymore," Niz stated, feeling panicky inside. If their mother found out . . .

"No, that's ridiculous," Cloud Walking said, brushing the thought away.

Niz watched her. "Is it the major, then?" she asked carefully, feeling as if she were struggling to breathe.

Encouraging Marigold to like Ezra was something altogether different from encouraging Cloud Walking to do so. Ezra and Marigold could fall in love at the fort, where Niz wouldn't see it. They could go off and live their happily ever after, adventuring and enjoying each other to their hearts' content, and she could imagine them happy but never have to see it lived out in front of her. She wanted Ezra—both of them—to be happy. But as terrible as it was, she didn't know if she was selfless enough to want to watch his happiness while she continued to live out her lonely life with Fire Maker. Even still, Cloud Walking was a closer fit to his description of what he wanted in a wife. If her sister liked him . . . could she be so selfish that she wouldn't encourage their happiness?

Cloud Walking laughed. "Niz . . . seriously? He's got to be nearly ten years my senior."

"Marriages like that happen," Niz said with a slight frown.

"Well, not for me they won't," Cloud Walking said flippantly.

Though Niz was selfishly thankful Cloud Walking didn't seem interested in Ezra, she didn't love that her sister was talking about him as if he were old. She'd always assumed he was Alex's age, which would make him somewhere around twenty-five. She herself was only four years younger. Did her sister think her old too?

"Well, if it's not Major Taylor and it's not Sergeant Green, who is keeping you from saying yes to Strong Pine?" Niz asked, truly puzzled. She'd been sure for a moment there that it was Sergeant Green.

"Who says I haven't?" Cloud Walking teased, her eyes laughing.

"Have you?" Niz exclaimed. Had Cloud Walking accepted him while she was away? She'd only been gone from the village a week!

"Oh look, there's mother!" Cloud Walking said, reaching down and snagging Walks at Night before taking off at a light run toward Shy Fawn.

Niz followed, taking a deep breath and exhaling all the frustration, worry, and confusion their conversation had brought. "Teenagers," she said under her breath.

~~~

Ezra paced the floor. Niz was gone. Gone from his fort, gone from his reach. Gone. He remembered the Comanche warrior's expression when he had spoken to her, and his gut twisted. He hadn't understood the words, but he'd understood the look in his eyes. With the Comanche in the area, Niz wasn't safe. Not with her wretched, no-account husband. Not when she was hours away, tucked inside her village where he couldn't even protect her. Not with her wild beauty and untamable charm.

He clenched his jaw, the frustration making him want to fight somebody. While he loved that about her, he also lamented it. From Fire Maker to the Comanche, her rare beauty endangered her over and over again. It kept her from him, as men had always been lined up to possess it.

For just a moment, he considered stealing her away in the dead of night and making a run for the Pacific. He could snatch her away from the Comanche, away from Fire Maker, away from all those who sought to hurt her. On the West Coast, far from Colorado Territory, he could protect her. He would chase the shadows out of her eyes and bask in the beauty of the woman he loved and the Oregon coast all at the same time. What could be better?

He drug his hand over his face, the temptation altogether too great. He imagined he could convince her to run away with him if he tried hard enough, and if not, well, he was stronger than she was. Even if it meant throwing her onto his horse, he would do what he had to do to get her to safety. On the way he would hope and pray that once he had, she would relent and let him love her with all the love he'd carried in his heart for her over the past four long years. Either way, at least she would be safe.

But he'd had this conversation with himself before. And the truth came back to stop him just as it had so many other times. He loved Niz. It wasn't just attraction, chemistry, or connection. It wasn't shallow and fleeting. In the depths of who he was, he loved her. And she was married. Still. Always. So, for better or worse, loving her had to look a whole lot more like the true definition of the word. His love for her was better characterized by long suffering and sacrifice. It couldn't be envious or proud. It couldn't be easily provoked, badly behaved, or about him and what he wanted. His love for Niz had to bear all things, believe all things, hope all things, and endure all things, or was it really love at all?

As much as he wanted to steal her away from the pain and the danger that was her life, as much as he wanted to believe he would be enough, he knew her. He knew how much she loved her people and the land. They were part of her. It was where she belonged. He couldn't take her away from that and believe she would still be whole. Leaving like that, leaving all she held dear—she would be broken, a part of her missing. The cost to her would be too great.

And he knew it would hurt him as well. Because as much as he loved her, she didn't belong to him, and he couldn't dishonor her husband, her, or Almighty God and not hurt himself along the way. It wasn't who he was. Achieved like that, any happiness they found would undoubtedly prove to be empty.

No, he could love her in the purest—and only in the purest—sense of the word, but he couldn't have her. Not before, not now.

Over the past weeks, he'd been dreaming that somehow, someway, at least he could protect her. If he just found the Comanche, if he made it to her village in time to stop the raid, if he kept her at the fort where he could watch out for her, he could keep her safe. He'd told himself that would be enough. But she'd left. Without his escort, without telling him, she'd left. She'd stepped out of his protection, beyond his reach, and she'd done it on purpose.

When he'd returned from patrol, found her gone, and gotten the truth out of Ms. Langston, he'd been angry. Really angry. But after a long walk and a lot of prayer, he'd come to understand that he wasn't angry with her—he was angry with himself. Though realizing it was like a punch in the gut, she'd been right to leave. Protecting her had never been his job. He was trying to fill a role that had never been his to fill.

The truth was that Nizhoni wasn't his to protect. As long as she was married to Fire Maker, he had to trust God to do that.

With a deep sigh, Ezra finally admitted to himself that he wasn't even seeing the map pinned to the wall where he'd been attempting to plan their next patrol. Turning away, he slumped down into his office chair, propped his elbows on his desk and dropped his head into his hands. He was in command of the fort. He could offer her his protection just as he did every other resident of the territory. He could equip her to be prepared for and successful in life. And that was all.

He had provided aid to her village when he knew danger was at hand. He was doing his best to protect her people's hunting rights. He had offered her protection while she was at the fort. He had made sure she could read. He had helped her improve her grip on her firearm. He'd done all he could do.

Thinking back to the twenty minutes he'd spent doing the latter made him chuckle. She'd been so irritated and testy, clearly frustrated by what she saw as her own incompetence.

"You want a firm hold to be able to keep your revolver steady," he had started, already amused by the look of utter disdain on her face.

He'd had to drag her away from her books, knowing she would never willingly come to him for help, having discovered that when trying to convince her to learn to read. In preparation, he'd made sure Marigold could watch Walks at Night, so Niz would have no excuses, before coaxing her into trying with the promise of fresh air and sunshine. It had been effective bait on her second morning in the fort, after they had agreed the previous night she would stay inside. That was before she had decided to deliver cookies with Marigold against his direct orders. The memory made him shake his head. As did recalling the way she'd rolled her eyes at him.

"I did assume that was the point. Are we good now? Can I get back to my books? After all, I am here to learn to read."

He'd watched her, trying to hide his enjoyment, knowing it would only irritate her. The fact was, she'd been nervous to be alone with him after their conversation on the porch the night before. She had no reason to be—he intended to keep his promise. But it was that same conversation that had convinced him that she needed instruction. It was terrifying to him that she had come out onto the porch to confront whatever danger was there and then had been so easily disarmed. He couldn't stop thinking about what could have happened if it had indeed been someone who meant her harm.

"Hold on," he'd encouraged. "Start by getting as much of your hand on the grip as possible." He'd watched her wrap her dainty hand around the revolver, and mused that a hand so small and slender could be so strong and capable. "That's it. Put the web of your hand up high on the backstrap. That will give you better leverage against the recoil."

"I hate the recoil," she'd muttered.

"Try absorbing it through your body rather than attempting to overpower it. It helps."

"Alright. Am I done?"

He hadn't been able to hold back a grin. "Really? Are you that anxious to get back to your studies? Those readers must be fascinating."

She'd tossed her head, sending her long black hair dancing in the breeze. She hated being taught anything, especially by him. He'd known that, and he'd been okay with it. She'd kept herself safe with her defenses. He hadn't wanted to take that away from her. Not when she needed it for daily survival. But he'd also wanted her to be able to protect herself.

"Bring your other hand up and wrap it around your first for stabilization. Good. Now find your balance, lean slightly forward, and bring your right foot just behind your left, opening up your stance. Keep your front sight aligned with your target and pull the trigger smoothly to prevent jerking the gun."

"Got it. Thanks," she'd answered and quickly lowered the revolver.

He'd given her a pointed look.

"What?" she'd asked defensively

"Seriously?"

She'd raised her eyebrows in challenge.

"Give it a try," he'd told her.

She'd looked at him hesitantly, and he had seen all the thoughts and emotions she'd wanted to keep to herself playing out in her beautiful brown eyes. Insecurity, worry, awareness, fear. He'd been a student of her for a long time. He knew her far better than she thought he did. He'd had lots of time to watch her while she'd been unaware. While she'd fallen in love with Alex, been focused on the Applewoods, dealt with Fire Maker, and mingled with her mother, sisters, and people, he'd only ever had eyes for her. He'd seen the true Nizhoni, unencumbered by pretense or the walls she erected, and he loved her for it.

He'd given her a reassuring nod, and she'd reluctantly moved into position and lifted the revolver again, doing as he'd instructed.

"Aim for the can on that stump," he'd encouraged, "and pull the trigger."

She did, and there was a loud ping as the can flew backwards off the log.

"Good. See how that felt?" She'd nodded. "Try again."

This time, when she lifted the revolver, he'd watched until she was ready to fire and reached out and bumped her as she pulled the trigger.

"Ezra!" she had cried.

"See how much steadier you were? You didn't even drop it this time."

"Someone could have been hurt!" she'd accused indignantly.

"We're in a shooting range, and I bumped you in a direction where there's nothing you can harm. It's fine." She'd glared at him. "You're missing the point. Your grip is steadier."

She'd let out a sigh, and turned away, lifting her revolver again. He'd watched, remembering the day Alex had bought the gun, picking it for its custom elk antler grip. Sorrow pricked his heart. He missed his friend.

Getting into position, Niz had tested the weight of the firearm in her hand, cocked the hammer, pulled the trigger, and absorbed the recoil. He bumped her off balance again as she fired, and this time it didn't faze her.

"You're right. It is better," she'd admitted reluctantly. She eased back a step, turning to him with a smile as she lowered her weapon. "Thank you."

He'd watched her, studying her face, wondering if she realized how incredibly fascinating she was. He loved how she could go from sassy and spirited to friendly and amiable in the span of half a second. Like the Colorado weather, she was constantly changing, keeping things interesting, but if given the time, she almost always came around in the end. It was almost hard to comprehend that one woman could be so interesting, exciting, and beautiful, all at the same time. He'd stuffed his hands in his pockets to keep from reaching out to brush her dark hair out of her eyes and smiled. "You're welcome."

She had chatted on their way back to Marigold's as if they'd been out on a pleasant stroll, and he had dropped her off at the door with a promise to see her later. He'd wished he were free to kiss her as he had the night before, but he wouldn't do that again. The kiss, as wonderful as it was, had been a mistake. It was wrong. It wasn't consistent with who he was, and he wouldn't allow himself to put her in such a compromising position ever again. He'd already apologized to the LORD for it and determined he wouldn't make the same mistake again. It was enough that he had equipped her with a little more knowledge that would keep her safer and her life a little better.

Coming back to the present, he reminded himself of that again. It had to be enough.

If it wasn't, for his sake and hers, he had to figure out how to give her up completely. He shook his head. Maybe Niz was right. Maybe it was time to move on.

~~~

"So, you've returned from the fort."

Niz looked up, surprised to see Fire Maker. Glancing past him toward camp, she saw the braves unloading their horses. Their wives and children swarmed around them in the late afternoon sun, greeting them. "Yes. It looks like you had a successful hunt."

"We did."

"Congratulations," she said, wringing out a dress. She'd gone down to the river to bathe herself and Walks at Night and had stayed to wash their soiled clothing and blankets too. It was a warm day, and she knew there likely weren't many of those left. She might as well do the wash while it was still pleasant to do so. Clean and fresh, Walks at Night was sitting on a grassy patch, playing with sticks and rocks, and she was just finishing up.

"Since you're back, I'm assuming you can read?"

"Yes, well enough," she answered simply.

"Good. When will the soldiers be here to buy my horses?"

"I don't know."

"What do you mean you don't know?"

"Well, I didn't arrange a time before I left," she said carefully.

"Why not? I thought the whole reason you went was so you could sign the papers they needed to buy my horses." Fire Maker didn't sound happy.

"It was, but I left early."

"So, you went for nothing? Your trip was a failure?" he accused. "I should have figured." He spun to leave.

"Fire Maker, listen and I'll explain!" He stopped walking but kept his back to her. She took a deep breath. "The last night I was there, the Comanche rode into the fort trying to free their captured warriors. They weren't successful, but the next morning Major Taylor asked me to translate for him."

"You only translate for me," Fire Maker ground out.

"I knew you were counting on the army buying horses from you. They'd been so kind to arrange for me to learn to read. With your trade coming up, I thought I could translate just that once to keep them happy."

He scoffed loudly at her explanation. "I hope you didn't try to keep them too happy."

She narrowed her eyes at the back of his head, not appreciating his insinuation. "I read and I baked with Ms. Langston in trade for my lessons. I helped care for the wounded after the Comanche's attack, and I translated one time for the major. That's all."

"Well, I hope they at least paid you for your services," he answered, his tone mocking, leaving her to interpret his statement however she pleased.

She closed her eyes and took a deep breath, refusing to take his bait. "Let me finish," she requested, and he waved her on. "I went in and talked to their leader. He spoke enough of our language that I could understand him." She paused, not wanting to anger her husband but knowing he needed to hear the truth. "Fire Maker, they attacked our village because you supplied the army with horses!"

He didn't even flinch. "I know."

"What?" she asked incredulously.

"It doesn't take a genius to figure that out."

"But . . . if you know . . . why do you want to sell the army more horses? Aren't you worried the Comanche will come back?"

"No."

"But why? We already lost loved ones; several others were wounded. Why antagonize them? Why not wait until they're caught and then trade your horses to the army if you must?" She couldn't keep the accusation out of her voice. All the suspicions her talk with the Comanche had brought up—the ones she'd spent every day since trying to convince herself couldn't be true—were hammering through her head like the beat of Fire Maker's drum when he played it in the wickiup at night.

"Don't question me, woman."

"Why would you endanger your people?" she demanded, undeterred. "The Comanche have shown they have no qualms about striking when you're not here, taking your horses, hurting our most vulnerable. Why would you invite their wrath?"

He spun around, his face like a dangerous storm. "I said don't question me!"

She took a step back. Though the river wasn't deep, she was thankful she had come to the other side of it to do her wash. Fire Maker could cross it easily enough, but somehow the natural barrier gave her boldness. She raised her chin. "There seem to be new horses in the corrals."

He lifted an eyebrow in challenge. "What's that supposed to mean?"

"I'm just saying I noticed."

"I told you I would get my horses back."

"How did you get them back?" she questioned, barely keeping her anger under control.

"It's none of your concern," he ground out, glaring at her.

"You met with them, didn't you?"

"I said it's none of your concern!" he repeated, his voice rising.

"You're working with them, aren't you, Fire Maker? That's why there's no animal tied to your horse, nor to Black Bear's nor Tall Peak's. The three of you weren't hunting. You were raiding. You're stealing horses and blaming it on the Comanche!"

She watched rage fill Fire Maker's face. "Shut your mouth, woman!" he yelled, taking purposeful strides toward the river.

"I don't want to hurt you with this knowledge. I just want you to stop," she continued, taking a step back and then another.

"I told you to shut your mouth!"

"Fire Maker, if this trouble with the Indians continues, the government could take away the hunting rights they promised our people!" Niz hurried to say, continuing to back away from the river as Fire Maker continued toward it. She'd been waiting to share the news until she could read him the agreement, but she couldn't wait any longer. With what she'd discovered he'd been doing, he needed to know.

"What are you talking about?"

"Remember the agreement with the government we heard about at our winter camp last year? The one the chiefs had signed? Well, there's a provision in the agreement that allows the government to revoke the hunting rights if the Indians make trouble with the settlers."

"How do you know this?" he challenged.

"The agreement was printed in the newspaper. I have a copy of it back at camp that I can read to you."

"What does this matter to me? It's not my hunting rights that will be revoked."

"Fire Maker! They're our people! And if they can't hunt on their hunting grounds, there won't be enough resources for them to survive. People will die! Our way of life will be lost!"

"Why are you bothering me with this?" he asked angrily.

"Fire Maker, the government doesn't care which tribe is doing the raiding. If attacks are being launched from our reservation—by you or the Comanche—our people will bear the consequences. Don't you see—these raids must stop! The Comanche must be stopped! You have to stop!"

He stood at the edge of the riverbank, his hands clenched into fists, his face red. "Or what?" he challenged. "If I don't stop, you'll tell your friend?" He looked at her with accusation filling his expression. "Don't think I don't recognize him, Nizhoni. I know who he is! I know he came here before with that dog you called your husband. Is he the real reason you went to the fort? Did you go to see him?"

His cruel words about Alex felt like a punch to the gut. She inhaled sharply and shook her head. "No! I went to learn to read so I could help you—and our people. That's the truth, Fire Maker." She took a deep, calming breath. "But Major Taylor and his soldiers are smart. They will catch those responsible for the raids, and they'll be brought to justice. So please, stop raiding. Help the army find the Comanche," she pleaded. She watched in dismay as rage and jealousy filled her husband's face.

"Oh, they're smart, are they?" he asked, his voice low and dangerous. She raised her chin but didn't answer, seeing he meant to twist whatever she might say. His face grew angrier. "Is that what you want—for them to arrest me? Now that *he's* back, is your plan to work with him to incriminate me?"

"What? No!" she cried, feeling blindsided and unwell. "Where is this coming from? Fire Maker, you're my husband. I want good for you and for our people. I'm not going to tell anyone. I know you're raiding for horses but not harming the settlers. I know you're not murdering like the Comanche. You're only in it for the profit. I know that. That's why half the attacks aren't violent . . . because it's not the same people carrying them out."

"How do you know that? Maybe you have it backwards!"

"Because I know you, and despite your flaws, you're not a murderer," she said, her voice trembling. She only hoped she was right.

"You know nothing!" he shouted, crouching down and sending an angry spray of water up at her.

Surprised and sputtering, she jumped back. As she wiped her eyes, she watched Fire Maker stalking away toward camp. Letting out a ragged breath, she held her head in her hands for a moment, giving herself a moment to collect herself. Then, pushing her hair back, she crouched down to finish wringing out the dress she still held. As she did, her mind spun.

He hadn't denied it.

Truth be told, they'd only been speculations. She had no proof that he'd been raiding or that he'd met with the Comanche. But the questions that had started at the guardhouse had only been growing since as the pieces fell into place in her mind.

Perhaps the Comanche warrior had heard her husband's name from someone, but how had he known that Fire Maker couldn't turn down a good trade? It was certainly true of her husband but not typical of the chiefs of their people. Fire Maker was not like the others. Their men were strong, loyal, and honorable. They weren't all consumed with and driven by greed. So how could the warrior have known that if he didn't know Fire Maker personally? And how did Fire Maker's herd continue to grow, despite the fact that he had sold horses to the army and lost some in the raid? Fire Maker and his two closest friends were good hunters; how had they been skunked the last two times they'd gone out on a hunt? And why else did they often disappear from camp at night?

She had no proof, and yet it all seemed to add up. Fire Maker had to be working in some capacity with the Comanche, and she thought he had to be responsible for the non-violent raids. She didn't know the specifics, but she had to assume he was using the arrival of the Comanche to increase his herd, and thus his social standing. And now, with all sorts of fears and speculations rolling around her thoughts, Fire Maker hadn't denied it.

Niz had hoped she was wrong. All the way back on the long walk from the fort, she'd hoped she was wrong. In the five days she'd been home, she'd hoped she was wrong. Even as she'd spoken the words, she'd still hoped she was wrong. She had stayed hopeful that her husband wouldn't truly work with murdering thieves who were terrorizing the area and stirring up trouble for their people, that he wouldn't truly steal from their neighbors whom they had been living at peace with for years. She had been clinging to the belief that he couldn't be responsible for such horrible deeds, that things were better than she'd thought, that all wasn't as desperate as she feared.

Since her talk with Marigold, she'd been trying to convince herself to cling to optimism. As she'd told herself that Fire Maker couldn't be all bad, she'd begun to hope that maybe it had just been a difficult season and that down the road, they truly would learn to respect each other, even if love never developed.

But he hadn't denied it. And if he hadn't denied it, she could only assume that it was true.

Lean Elk's daughter was dead. Noon Day Sun was dead. Four men at the fort were dead. Walks at Night's parents were dead. Many were wounded. And yet, it certainly seemed like Fire Maker was selfishly working with the enemy in order to increase his herd and build his wealth, clearly unconcerned about who might get hurt along the way.

His reckless actions could cause backlash from every direction. And, as their chief, that backlash was sure to fall on their people. If the settlers found out that they were involved in the raids, things would undoubtedly get ugly. If the army found out, they would regard them as a people at war. If the Comanche found out he was raiding and letting them take the blame for his non-violent attacks along with their own, they would surely attack with the full fury of wounded pride. There seemed to be danger on every side.

Niz looked out at her village, and a great sorrow came over her. What should she do with her speculations? If they were true, how could she best care for those she loved? What was the best path forward when every route seemed treacherous?

A part of her felt a responsibility to tell Ezra and the army. What Fire Maker was doing was wrong. He was involved. At the very least, if he had met with the Comanche, he knew how to find them. He had the ability to help end the violence. She'd told Ezra and Marigold that she wanted the Comanche stopped as much as they did, and it certainly was true. They were just as much of a danger to herself and to her people as they were to the settlers and soldiers. But if she told Ezra, the army would come.

If her husband still wouldn't help them apprehend the Comanche, the soldiers would be enraged. She doubted even Ezra

Taylor would be able to restrain the wrath of his men at that point, assuming he would even want to, and she wasn't so sure he would—or should. He had been charged with the responsibility of keeping the peace. Innocent people were dying; property was being stolen. Could she expect him to turn a blind eye?

And if the army came, what would happen to her people as a result? What would happen to Fire Maker's braves who would feel duty-bound to stand at his side? What would become of the widows and orphans such a skirmish would create? What would happen to Cloud Walking, Ever Flowering, Walks With Power, and her mother? What would happen to Strong Pine and Wise Hawk and Soaring Eagle? What would happen to White Bird and her children and all the people that Niz loved with every ounce of her being?

Besides, though she felt confident that Fire Maker was involved, she had no real proof. And he was her husband. How could she accuse him of something to those in charge without knowing beyond a shadow of a doubt that her speculations were correct? But if he was involved and she knew it and did nothing, then wasn't she more or less an accomplice?

Niz pressed her fist against her chest, truly in agony. She didn't know what to do. If only her father were still alive, he would know the right path forward. She could talk to him, confide in him, trust him. If only she could talk it out with Alex, go over all the pros and cons, figure it out together—he was always so good at helping her find solutions to her problems. But they were both gone. She considered going to Wise Hawk, but Fire Maker was her husband and the chief. How could she go behind his back to consult one of the elders? And what would Wise Hawk do if she did? He was a man of honor. A deep sigh came up from within; going to Wise Hawk was no option at all. The only other man she would trust enough to go to with such a serious predicament was Ezra, but she couldn't when he was the commanding officer at the fort. He was too closely connected. And thus, there were no options, nobody to turn to, no one she could trust to help her find a way forward.

The weight of the dilemma pressed down on her until it felt like it was crushing her.

Like a sweet scent on the wind, Marigold's words from their last conversation came back to her. *"Come unto me, all ye that labour and are heavy laden, and I will give you rest. Take my yoke upon you, and learn of me; for I am meek and lowly in heart: and ye shall find rest unto your souls. For my yoke is easy, and my burden is light."*

Oh, how she wanted to have someone to turn to, to learn from, to rest in. She was staggering under the load she carried. She was drawn to the hope found in those words, hope that there was someone bigger who was trustworthy and willing to step in and take over when things became too much.

But how could she turn to someone who allowed such suffering in her life? What if He allowed such suffering again? What if He didn't protect those she loved? What if He allowed them to be taken from her just as Alex and their son had been? And how could she turn her back on the religion of her people—people she loved so dearly? They wouldn't understand or congratulate her on her new faith. She'd be seen as a traitor, an outsider. Could she bear the pain of not belonging?

No, regardless of how compelling the words Marigold had shared were, it wasn't for her. And even if she did cry out to Him for help, He wouldn't listen to her anyway. She wasn't one of His followers.

This load was hers to carry. Hers and hers alone. And so carry it, she would. She'd find a way. There had to be a way.

Leaning down, she splashed water on her face, trying to wash away the fear and frustration she felt. Straightening, she pushed her long black hair over her shoulder. She gathered her laundered items and settled Walks at Night on her hip. Wading across the river, she started back to camp. Each step felt heavier than the last, the weight she carried pressing down on her until it was all she could do to stand under it. "Somehow, I'll find a way," she whispered to herself.

Nineteen

"**N**izhoni!"

Niz startled as her name was called through the brush-covered walls of her wickiup. Though she'd been sleeping, the desperation in the voice summoning her was enough to rouse her instantly.

"Nizhoni!" the caller cried out again.

"What's going on?" Fire Maker questioned groggily, opening his eyes as she stood up.

"I don't know," she answered. "Go back to sleep. I'll take care of it." She reached down and snagged Walks at Night. If only she could leave the sleeping child, but Fire Maker had grown increasingly angry and bitter over the past twenty-four hours since their conversation at the river. She didn't trust him to be alone with the little boy for even five minutes. It would be easier to deal with a cranky child than her regret if anything happened to him.

She ducked out the doorway with Walks at Night in one arm and his cradleboard in the other, just as the caller said her name once more. Panic seized her when she saw who it was.

"It's Ever Flowering," her brother-in-law said, his face etched with worry.

"What's wrong?" she asked, even as she started toward his wickiup.

"The fever, it's really high. She can't stop coughing, and now she's saying she can't breathe. You've got to help her, Nizhoni!"

"Have you gotten Mother?"

"No, I came for you first. I'll go there next."

"Yes, go get her. And take Walks at Night to Cloud Walking and ask her to watch him."

Walks With Power took the boy and his cradleboard and sprinted off through the village. Niz ran the last few yards to the couple's wickiup. Ducking through the door, her heart flopped when she saw her sister. The fire still burnt brightly in the middle of the dwelling. Walks With Power must have kept it stoked, likely trying to keep his wife warm despite her chills. Even from a distance, Niz could see Ever Flowering was soaking wet and pale. Dropping to her knees beside her, Niz laid her hand against the young woman's face.

"You're burning up!" Niz told her, fear filling her. Ever Flowering was so hot. Even if they could get the fever down and save her sister, could the baby growing within her survive?

"I'm fine," Ever Flowering whispered back, that small action clearly taking a great deal of effort. It sent her into a fit of coughing, and she covered her mouth with the blanket that had been drawn up around her shoulders as she shook beneath it. Niz cringed as she listened to the haunting, hollow coughs, each one hurting her heart as she watched the fit sap her sister's little remaining strength. When it finally passed and Ever Flowering sank back weakly, Niz's relief only lasted for a moment before her heart jumped into her throat. There was bright blood staining the blanket her sister had coughed into. She jumped to her feet, her eyes wild as Shy Fawn and Walks With Power entered the wickiup.

"It's consumption," she said, beginning to pace the small wickiup.

"Consumption?" her mother asked, shaking her head, unfamiliar with the word.

"The white plague," Niz explained dismally.

Shy Fawn gasped. Walks With Power spread his feet and crossed his arms over his chest, bracing as if for a physical attack. Niz pressed her lips together. If only it were a brute attack her strong brother-in-law could fight on behalf of his wife. He loved

Ever Flowering fiercely—there was no length he wouldn't go to save her. But the white plague was not something he could fight for her. No one could. With the realization of what it was that ailed her, they had all been reduced to helpless bystanders.

"I need to go for a doctor," Niz said as she realized it, pausing mid-step.

"No, Nizhoni. We'll get the medicine man," Shy Fawn protested. "We'll make her tea from the willow bark."

Niz shook her head. "It won't be enough, Mother. We've seen this before. Our medicine doesn't work on it. I'm going for a doctor."

Shy Fawn's face crumpled and she began to cry. "Fire Maker won't let you take a horse. You know that. And if you walk, it will take hours. What if . . ."

"So be it. I'm going. I don't know if the white medicine can help or not, but Mother, I have to try. It might be her only hope!"

"The doctor won't come here! You know he won't! They don't want to treat our people," Shy Fawn reasoned, crying in earnest. With the additional threat of the Comanche, along with the inherent dangers of walking so far alone through the wilderness, much of it at night, her mother was clearly as worried about Niz going as she was about Ever Flowering's condition.

Niz paced back and forth across the shelter a few more times. Her mother was right. The doctor was away from the fort last she knew, and even if he had returned, it was doubtful he would come. Suddenly, she faced her mother. "You're right, but I know someone who will. She's been helping with medicine nearly her whole life. I know she'll come and do whatever she can to help Ever Flowering."

"Don't go. I'll be fine," Ever Flowering whispered weakly from her mat, her breathing labored. Suddenly, another coughing fit seized her. Shy Fawn dropped down beside her secondborn, holding her up, trying to share her strength as the hollow coughs racked the young woman's body.

"I'll be back as soon as I can," Niz said, turning toward the doorway.

"It's too dangerous," Shy Fawn cried from the floor.

"My wife and child are dying!" Walks With Power choked out brokenly, stepping forward as he beat his fist against his heart. "If Nizhoni knows someone who can help her . . ." He turned toward Niz. "You're going for the doctor, and I'm going with you. We'll take my horses."

She nodded, relieved.

He went to Ever Flowering and crouched down beside her, pulling the blanket up to her chin and kissing her tenderly. "I'll be back with help as soon as I can, my love. Stay with us."

Ever Flowering nodded weakly, and Walks With Power kissed her again.

Tears stung Niz's eyes as she watched the tender exchange. Oh, to love and be loved so truly. That's why she had to go for help. She had to do whatever she could to save her sister, no matter the risk. Ever Flowering and the child she carried had to make it. She couldn't let them die.

"Mother, I'm going to send Cloud Walking for the medicine man. Do everything you can to get her fever down. Give her the willow bark tea and start cold compresses. We'll be back as soon as we can."

Shy Fawn looked up at Niz, her face lined with worry, tears running down her cheeks. She looked like she wanted to protest, but instead she stayed silent. Niz's heart hurt for her—she knew her mother must feel like she was choosing between the well-being of her children.

"I'll bring her back safe, Shy Fawn," Walks With Power promised solemnly. Shy Fawn nodded.

Walks With Power followed Niz out of the wickiup. "I'll get the horses while you talk to Cloud Walking."

"Take an extra," she instructed. "We'll need one for Marigold." With that, she ran through the village to Shy Fawn's wickiup. When she drew close, she was stunned to see Fire Maker sitting outside by the fire with Cloud Walking. They were sitting close together, and Fire Maker was talking in hushed tones. Filled with confusion and unease, she stopped. "What are you doing here?" she questioned.

Both Fire Maker and Cloud Walking glanced up quickly. Her husband's surprise morphed into a mocking smile. "You didn't come back. I was worried. I came to see if Cloud Walking had heard any news and found her distraught. I thought we could be a comfort to each other."

Niz glanced between him and Cloud Walking. Her sister was looking at the ground. Like a sickening bolt of lightning, fear ripped through Niz. Was Fire Maker trying to woo Cloud Walking? Were his attentions what kept her sister from saying yes to Strong Pine? The very thought nearly caused her to be ill.

While it was not unheard of among their people for a man to marry sisters to provide stability and assurance of a family line, it was rarely practiced. And especially not in their day and in their situation. For a brief moment, she wanted to scream at Fire Maker. He had no right! She was not barren, despite the blame he tried to place on her. She had carried life! How could he even think of bringing her little sister into the mix? He wasn't even a good husband to her; he certainly didn't need to ruin the life of her sister too.

But now was not the time. Ever Flowering was gravely ill. So she glared at Fire Maker and then turned her attention to her sister. "Cloud Walking, go get the medicine man and take him to Ever Flowering."

Cloud Walking stood, her gaze still on the ground, her face full of guilt. Closing her eyes and taking a deep breath, Niz gave herself a little shake and simply pushed past the girl, going in to get Walks at Night. He'd been laced into his cradleboard, and she was glad. Lifting it carefully, she settled the burden strap over her shoulders. Even if it was more complicated to take him, she wouldn't risk leaving her son in camp while she was gone. When she turned around, Cloud Walking was standing close behind her.

"I don't know why he's here. I didn't ask him to come. He just showed up," Cloud Walking whispered pleadingly.

"Why didn't you tell him to leave?" Niz hissed fiercely.

Cloud Walking finally met her eyes. The girl's face was clouded with confusion and despair. "Niz, he's the chief."

"I don't care who he is! You're my sister! And you know what he's like!" She felt like she was going to be sick and pressed her hand over her mouth.

"Niz . . . it's not like that," Cloud Walking started, glancing nervously at the door.

Niz drew a deep, shaky breath. "Listen. Now is not the time. Our sister is *sick*. Go get the medicine man and go straight to mother. Do not leave her side until I return, do you understand? Not once! That is an order."

Cloud Walking submissively dropped her head and nodded. It wasn't much, given the circumstances, but Niz would take it just the same. At least Cloud Walking would be safe with her mother until she could get back and try to make sense of the newest mess her husband seemed to be creating.

Impulsively, she pulled Cloud Walking into her arms and gave her a tight hug. Fire Maker would not come between them. She absolutely would not allow it; she would not let him use her sister to hurt her and have Cloud Walking hurt in the process. Cloud Walking hugged her back, and Niz took another deep, shaky breath.

Perhaps it had been nothing after all, at least on the part of Cloud Walking. Maybe it was an isolated incident, and Fire Maker had nothing to do with the reason her sister was putting off Strong Pine. It was possible she had jumped to conclusions. But Niz wasn't confident that was the case, and even if it were, she knew it had been a deliberate move on Fire Maker's part. Why else had he risen from his bed to go to her sister's fire when he knew both Shy Fawn and herself were occupied at Ever Flowering's? Why else had he sat so close and been so deep in conversation when it certainly wasn't his natural behavior? Whether he'd done so only to torment her, to cajole the teen into giving him Walks at Night, or to find private moments with Cloud Walking, she didn't know. Regardless, she was confident that, true to his nature, he was up to no good.

"Stay with mother," she whispered again, then gave her sister one last tight squeeze and left the wickiup with Walks at Night. Cloud Walking followed and immediately disappeared into the night to find the medicine man.

Fire Maker still sat by the fire, his handsome face taunting, a wicked glint in his eye. "Where do you think you're going?" he asked.

"For help."

"I didn't say you could leave."

"I didn't ask! I'm not your captive," she shot back, barely keeping her temper in check.

"Are you running back to your major?"

"I'm going to get someone who knows the white man's medicine. Ever Flowering is sick, Fire Maker! The wife of one of your strongest braves is," her voice broke, and tears stung her eyes. She blinked them back viciously, refusing to give into them. She raised her chin and forced her emotions to the background. "She's fighting for her life and the life of their unborn child. I'm not going to just sit by and watch it happen. I'll be back as soon as I can."

She didn't wait for his answer, afraid that if he said the wrong thing, she wouldn't be able to control her temper any longer. She was too unsteady, too overcome with fear and anger and worry. Right now she needed to get help for Ever Flowering. Everything else had to come second. Every other problem paled in comparison.

Finding her brother-in-law at the corral with three ready horses, they set off through the night. Walks With Power led, and she was glad he had come along. Though she knew the way, it would have taken her longer to navigate by the stars. Walks With Power was strong and smart, and at home in the forest, even in the dark of night. He kept a fast pace, and she focused on matching it.

As they rode, as she so often did, she tried to turn her mind off to all the swirling thoughts and worries that filled it. She tried to push them back, to press them down, to shut them behind locked doors, but she couldn't seem to do so. Fire Maker . . . Cloud Walking . . . her people . . . the Comanche . . . Walks at Night . . . Ever Flowering . . . Alex . . . their baby . . . Ezra . . . her mother . . . they all swirled around her mind in a confusing and painful tangle of fear and loss and grief and love.

She felt sick to her stomach and so distraught that she considered spilling what she had just seen to Walks With Power. Her brother-in-law was a good man, strong and brave. Perhaps she could tell him everything. She desperately needed to tell someone—to have somebody who could help. It was too much. She couldn't continue to carry it all on her own, not when more kept getting piled on top. The dilemma with Fire Maker, the Comanche, and the hunting rights had been bad enough, but with Ever Flowering so ill with what she now knew was consumption, and this new twisted piece of the puzzle with Fire Maker and Cloud Walking . . . Suddenly, Niz leaned down over the side of her horse as the contents of her stomach emptied.

Walks With Power drew his mount up quickly. "You okay?" he asked, his voice full of concern.

"I'm fine," she answered. But was she?

"Should we stop?"

She shook her head. "We need to get Marigold and get back to Ever Flowering before . . . before . . ."

Her brother-in-law nodded and instantly urged his horse on, the pace he kept even faster than before. She did her best to keep up and instinctively knew there was no chance of talking to him about all that troubled her when they were moving so quickly. And even if she could, it had been a terrible idea. The man was on the brink of losing his wife and unborn child. The last thing he needed was to be burdened with her problems as well. Niz sat taller on the horse's back and squared her shoulders. The troubles were hers to bear. She would figure out how to fix things. And the first thing she needed to do was to get help for Ever Flowering.

What had taken her six hours to walk, they covered in an hour and a half. Knowing they couldn't ride in together without the soldiers making a ruckus, she left Walks With Power in the safety of the forest and rode the last few miles by herself. She knew the soldiers had been on edge already when she left the fort. If the Comanche had yet to be caught, she imagined they would only be more so now. Seeing two natives racing toward the fort in the middle of the night would spark panic, and she certainly didn't want that. She needed to get in, get Marigold, and get back to Ever Flowering. When she drew close enough to the fort that she knew she would be seen, she lifted her hands in surrender. "I'm a friend!" she called through the night. "I'm a friend! I come in peace."

Even still, her hands shook. With as jumpy as everyone was, the possibility of being shot was high despite her proclamations. Shoot first, ask questions later was often the stance that was taken when fear was running rampant and danger was high. But Ever Flowering needed help, and Niz didn't have time to sneak into the fort and sneak back out with Marigold. Time was of the essence, and so it was a necessary risk.

The guards on duty called out to her to identify herself, and she did. Though they regarded her warily and questioned her thoroughly, they allowed her into the fort, and she hurriedly made her way down the familiar streets to Marigold's house. Niz knocked loudly and moments later Marigold opened the door, a wrapper pulled around her long white nightgown and her golden hair still in its long night braid. Her face revealed her shock. "Niz?"

"Marigold!" she cried, feeling unhinged. In a world that felt frightening and uncertain, Marigold felt peaceful and safe.

Marigold pulled her into a tight hug. "Niz, I didn't think I'd ever see you again!" she exclaimed. Suddenly, she held her at arm's length. "What is it? What's wrong? Something's happened."

"It's Ever Flowering."

"Your sister? What's wrong? Is it the baby?" Marigold's face was full of concern.

"She's sick. Really sick. I don't know if the doctor's back, but we need help."

"He's not. We haven't seen him yet."

"Then will you come see if there's anything you can do for her? I think it's consumption. It's bad. I don't know if..." Niz dropped her head, unable to finish her sentence.

"Oh, Niz," Marigold whispered sympathetically, tears springing into her blue eyes. "Of course I'll come. Give me a minute to change. Come, wait inside."

Niz stood in the cheery front room, Walks at Night sleeping on her back, while Marigold dressed. Looking around the familiar space for a long moment, she closed her eyes and breathed deeply. After the urgency of Ever Flowering's condition, the sickening fear of seeing Fire Maker with Cloud Walking, the rush through the middle of the night, and the worry and chaos that filled her, the stillness of the little house felt foreign. It was silent and peaceful. Simple joy seemed to hang in the air and fill the shadowy corners. There was something wonderful and sweet and calm about the homey cabin.

Opening her eyes again, she wandered around the room restlessly, stopping before the little wooden parlor table. On it lay Marigold's big, black leather Bible. Reaching out, she ran her fingertips over the gold gilt design on the cover before lying her palm on it. Whatever had stirred within her the day Marigold had ridden into camp for their second reading lesson, stirred again. A hint of something deep and eternal smoothed the troubled waters of her soul, and for one brief, fleeting moment, deep, deep peace settled in her heart like a hush.

"I'm ready," Marigold declared, opening her bedroom door, disrupting the holy moment.

Recalling their errand, Niz quickly turned toward her. Seeing her friend securing her shawl, doubt flickered across her heart. Ever Flowering was her beloved sister; risking her own safety to try to save her had been worth it. But now she realized that asking Marigold to travel back to her village with her was risking Marigold's safety too. She pressed her lips together, knowing she had to say something.

"Marigold, I'm so grateful you're willing to come," Niz started sincerely. "But you should know, I . . . I can't guarantee your safety. My brother-in-law, Walks With Power, is waiting for us at the edge of the forest with a horse for you. He's fierce and brave. He would do his best to protect us both if we encounter trouble, and I have my revolver and know how to use it, but . . . if we were outnumbered . . ." She shrugged, her face falling. "It's only fair to be honest with you. It could be dangerous."

"I'm coming," Marigold said firmly as she finished with her shawl. "You came to me for help, so I'm going to trust the good LORD to protect me and get me safely ho—" She stopped abruptly as she opened the front door.

Niz, following close behind, bumped into her. Looking up, Niz's heart seemed to stop. Ezra was standing on the porch. Her eyes meeting his, she instinctively took a step back. His gaze was intense; his eyes were shadowy. She hadn't seen or heard from him since she'd left in the middle of the night. That had been a week ago. Now, she couldn't make out his expression.

"LORD willing, we'll see to that, too, Ms. Langston," he said. He was breathing hard, as if he'd just run there.

"Well, I—I," Marigold stuttered, stumbling over her words. She paused and started again. "I'm on my way out to Niz's village with her. Her sister is sick. She came for help."

"We'll escort you."

"We?" Marigold questioned.

Ezra nodded down the road, and they saw Sergeant Green and another soldier leading four horses toward them. Marigold looked at Ezra and then back at Niz before giving a dainty shrug. "Wonderful. Thank you for the escort, Major Taylor. I know that will ease both of our minds. I just need to stop at the infirmary and gather a few supplies."

Nodding curtly, Ezra turned, leading the way off the porch. Guilt pressed down on Niz as she followed Marigold out the door. She knew information that Ezra needed to know, yet she didn't plan to share it. After meeting with the Comanche, she'd assured him she wasn't protecting them, that she wanted the raiders caught as much as he did, but now, she was withholding information that could lead him to them and potentially stop the raiding. Though her concern was for her people, she was effectively protecting the Comanche by hiding Fire Maker's involvement. Knowing that made it hard to breathe as she followed Ezra and Marigold off the porch.

Sergeant Green held Marigold's mount as she stepped up into the saddle, and Ezra paused at the bottom of the stairs, waiting for Niz. "May I give you a hand up?" he asked, his tone stiff.

"No, I can manage," she answered quickly. He didn't respond but took her horse's bridle and led it to the foot of the stairs. Using the steps, she pulled herself up onto the horse's bare back, the task a little trickier than normal with Walks at Night strapped to her. Once she was settled on the horse, Ezra handed her the reins without a word. He swung into his own saddle and led the way to the infirmary.

Once there, Marigold went inside to gather a few supplies while the rest of them waited silently in the dark. Niz sent a sideways glance at Ezra, but the bill of his cap kept his face covered in deep shadows. She couldn't make out his expression. Her hands began to shake a little, the strain of the night, her secret, his presence, and the sorrow of the stiffness between them taking its toll.

She imagined how angry he must have been when he returned from patrol to find she had disregarded his orders and left in the middle of the night; she assumed he was angry still. And although she understood why, the very idea made her sad. She wished there were some way she could explain, but what could she say? When she'd left, she'd known this was how it would be whenever she saw him next. It was how it had to be if she was going to figure out how to be satisfied with her life with Fire Maker, keep her people safe, give Ezra the freedom to move on, and allow him the gift of focusing on problems he could actually fix.

"My brother-in-law is waiting for us at the edge of the forest," she offered, knowing she couldn't make him understand or undo what she had done but still wanting to say something.

"I'm glad you didn't come alone."

She clasped her hands together, trying to still their shaking. "Major Taylor, my sister is very sick. I never would have come for Marigold if she weren't. I don't wish to put her in danger. I just . . . I don't know what to do. We're not sure if Ever Flowering will survive."

"I'm sure Ms. Langston will do all she can for her. And I'm just glad my private had the good sense to let me know you'd ridden in seeking her so we could escort you both." He paused. "It was good timing. We had just gotten back from patrol. Our horses were mostly still tacked up."

Niz pressed her lips together, feeling even guiltier that he had returned from patrol only to have to turn around and ride out again. A trip to her village would cost him and his men a sleepless night. He was consistently going above and beyond, sacrificing his own needs and comfort to help her, and in return, she was hiding secrets from him. She managed only a slight nod in reply. The silence stretched.

"Major, I . . . I think it's consumption," she finally said, her voice small, wishing with her whole heart that he could just be her friend again in that moment. She was scared. And out of everyone in the world, Ezra made her feel the safest. Some part of her needed to fill him in, at least a little. "I had to do something to help her, and the only thing I could think of was to get Marigold. So thank you . . . for coming."

"Niz." He waited until she looked at him. "No matter how much you want to, you may not be able to make this better." His face was still covered by the shadows of his cap, keeping his expression unreadable.

She shook her head. "Don't say that. I'll figure out a way to help her. I must."

"You can't control everything, Beautiful," he said softly.

Niz swallowed hard against the pain in her throat, her heart responding to his tenderness. She could feel the dam of her emotions beginning to crumble. Taking a deep breath, she raised her head and squared her shoulders. She wouldn't cry. She couldn't. Because if she started, how would she stop?

"You're wrong," she answered. "I have to. If I don't, who will? I need everyone I love to be okay."

Startled, she jumped as Ezra reached across the distance between them and took her hand. Glancing up at him quickly, she watched him bow his head.

"Father God, we come before You tonight and ask that You would heal Ever Flowering. Consumption is something we have no control over, but you're the Great Physician, so we ask that You heal her and make her well in Jesus' name. Please protect the child she carries and let her deliver a healthy baby in due time. In Jesus' name we pray, amen."

"Amen," Niz echoed. Though she didn't serve his God, somehow, Ezra's prayer was strangely comforting.

Marigold came out of the infirmary and Ezra quickly dismounted to pack the supplies she had collected into her saddlebags. When everyone was on horseback again, they set off with Niz leading the way.

Walks With Power was confused and wary when they first rode up, but Niz quickly explained that Marigold had come to help Ever Flowering and the soldiers were there to escort her. Understanding, he nodded and turned his horse, setting a fast pace as they covered the distance back to the village. They rode quickly and silently in single file, the terrain too difficult to navigate in the dark to risk spreading out.

If Niz had been conflicted during her ride to the fort, she was only more so on their way back to the village. The peace she'd felt in Marigold's home, especially when she'd laid her hand on the large Bible, the relief she'd felt at seeing her friend, the uncertainty, sorrow, and comfort of seeing Ezra, the fear that urged her to go faster and faster, the danger of taking soldiers back to her village when Fire Maker was working with the Comanche, it all circled through her thoughts over and over again as they rode west. Her stomach felt tied in knots, and she was thankful they were moving too fast to speak, even should they have wanted to—she felt too heavy and conflicted to be counted upon to string together words.

The eastern sky was just beginning to lighten at their backs when they reached the outskirts of camp. Throwing her leg over her horse's back and sliding down, hoping with all her heart that Ever Flowering was still alive, Niz grabbed Marigold's saddlebags. Leaving the horses with the men, she took Marigold's hand and hurried her toward her sister's wickiup. Summoning her courage, Niz drew Marigold inside the dwelling, trying to prepare herself for whatever they might find. As her eyes adjusted to the dim interior, Shy Fawn, Cloud Walking, the medicine man, and Ever Flowering came into focus.

"How is she?" Niz asked over the chanting of the medicine man.

"Alive, but just," her mother admitted, her cheeks still wet with tears. Niz wondered if she'd stopped crying since they'd left.

Motioning for Marigold to follow, Niz crossed to Ever Flowering and knelt down beside her. Shy Fawn and Cloud Walking backed up, making room for Marigold to do the same. Niz handed Walks at Night off to Cloud Walking, and when he woke and started fussing, the girl took him out of the wickiup. Niz nearly protested, thinking it best to keep them within eyesight, until she remembered Ezra was in camp. No matter if he was angry with her or not, he wouldn't let anything happen to her sister or son. She turned her attention back to the young woman who lay before her as Walks With Power entered the wickiup and squatted down beside Niz.

Marigold listened to Ever Flowering's heart and lungs, felt her forehead and picked up her arms and looked them over. "Has she been eating?" she asked.

"No," Niz admitted sadly. "We try to get her to eat, but she just won't. She says she's not hungry."

Marigold took that in with a nod. She moved Ever Flowering's wrist and then elbow. "Can you ask her if that hurts?"

Ever Flowering nodded weakly in reply.

Marigold sat back a little, with a grim expression on her lovely face.

"What is it?" Niz asked, watching her friend.

"Well, the fever, fatigue, difficulty breathing, painful joints, and bloody mucus definitely sound like consumption," Marigold said sadly. "And by looking at her arms, I can see she's just wasting away. Look at how her wrist bones stick out, poor dear." Marigold tucked Ever Flowering's thin arm back under the blanket where it would stay warm. "She's much thinner than she was the last time I was here, and that's not even been three weeks ago."

Niz translated what Marigold had said. Shy Fawn began crying harder, quiet moans escaping from between her lips. They all knew the seriousness of the White Plague. It had ripped through their village before, when Niz was very young. At their winter camps, they'd heard that it had done the same in other villages, wreaking havoc and leaving behind great heartache. As she listened to her mother mourn, the ache in Niz's heart grew. Still, she had to be strong. She had to ask the right questions, talk to Marigold, and help Ever Flowering however she could. "What can be done?"

Marigold looked at Niz with tears brimming in her blue eyes. She shook her head. "Not much. I'll give her laudanum for her cough, and a mixture of quinine for her fever, but they'll simply treat the symptoms. The only treatment that's proven to really help consumption is fresh air, rest, and good, nutritious food . . . and she already has all that. Try to encourage her to eat, but beyond that, I'm not sure there's much more that can be done."

Niz's heart sank. "Will she . . . ?" Closing her eyes, she gave a slight shake of her head; she couldn't bring herself to finish her question.

Marigold shrugged sadly. "I don't know. It's likely, Niz. Probable actually. She has a bad case of it. It's possible the pregnancy weakened her body, and she just can't fight it off like she normally could. I'm not sure. But I think your only hope now is to pray."

Nizhoni looked at the medicine man. "He's been chanting prayers all night."

Marigold wiped her eyes. "I see that. But is he praying to the God who can heal her?"

Niz just stared at her for a moment, the question sparking the same stirring within her that she'd felt earlier. As if he could sense the stirring and sought to drown it out, the medicine man suddenly grew louder, the wickiup full of the sound of his chants. With it filling her ears, Niz couldn't think straight.

She leaned toward Marigold to be heard. "Let's give her the medicines. Maybe they'll at least make her feel well enough to eat something, and we can begin to rebuild her strength."

Her friend nodded. "Yes, I think that's a good idea." Digging through her bag, Marigold produced the bottles and dispensed the medicine. When she was done, she handed them to Niz. "Keep these. You saw how much I gave her. Continue administering them as needed."

Niz nodded. "Thank you, Marigold. I can't tell you how much I appreciate it."

Already, Ever Flowering's breathing was growing easier.

"It's not a cure," Marigold warned, sorrow filling her eyes. "It's just masking the symptoms. Pray to Jesus, Niz. It's the only hope she has. I'll be praying too."

Understanding what Marigold hadn't come right out and said, Niz's throat began to ache. Ever Flowering was dying, along with the child within her. Short of a miracle, she had no hope.

Marigold reached out and squeezed her hand, her expression full of sympathy. "I wish I were a doctor . . . but even if I were, I don't think there's anything more that can be done. Unfortunately, there's very little known about consumption. We don't know how it spreads or why or even how to successfully treat it."

Niz nodded, absorbing that information. She wanted it to make sense, and it was frustrating that it wasn't going to. How did she protect her sister, her family, and her people from something she couldn't understand? But there was nothing more Marigold could do. As much as she didn't want it to be true, she trusted her.

"You'd better get back to the fort," she told her friend. She stood as Marigold did. "Major Taylor and his men have been up all night, and you nearly have been. Thank you so much for coming."

She embraced her for a long moment, wishing Marigold could stay and she could tell her everything that was weighing so heavily on her mind. If only they could have another night of staying up late talking, maybe together they could figure out what she should do. But what she'd said was true; the small party needed to get back to the fort. The soldiers had a job to do, and it wasn't safe—for anyone—for them to be at the village. Most importantly, Ever Flowering was sick. How could Niz think of anything else—speak of anything else—when her sister was fighting for her life?

Marigold hugged her back. "I wouldn't have dreamt of staying home when you needed me." As Niz drew back, Marigold searched her face. "Would you like to come out and say goodbye to the major, or would you like me to pass on your thanks?"

"I think I'm going to stay here with Ever Flowering," Niz said, dropping her eyes. If the worst was coming, she didn't want to spend another moment away from her sister. She felt both numb and full of sorrow, all at the same time. "Please tell him thank you for me. I truly appreciate all of you coming all this way in the middle of the night."

Marigold nodded, embraced Niz once more, then left the wickiup. Niz sat back down beside Walks With Power and started the painful task of telling them what Marigold had said.

"But her breathing is better," Shy Fawn protested, holding tightly to Ever Flowering's hand. "Don't you hear that it's better?"

"It's only the laudanum, Mother," Niz told her, wishing it truly were a sign of her sister's improvement. Her eyes were locked on Ever Flowering's beloved face as she thirstily drank in the sight of her, unsure how much longer she would have the opportunity to do so. Her anxiety built as the truth of that sank in. "It's only masking the symptoms. But while it's better, let's see if we can get her to eat and drink something."

Shy Fawn nodded and was getting up to brew a cup of tea when Fire Maker stalked into the wickiup. "Nizhoni, I need you outside."

Niz didn't take her eyes off Ever Flowering. "Not now."

"What do you mean, not now?" Fire Maker ground out. "I need you to translate for me. The soldiers are here."

"Fire Maker, I'll translate for you another time. I'm not translating today. I'm staying with my sister," she told him, swallowing hard. She could see with her own eyes what Marigold had been trying to tell her—Ever Flowering didn't have much time left. She was getting visibly weaker by the minute. They were out of options. Their hope had run out. There would be time for his greed later. For now, she would stay with her best friend until the end.

"I don't want you to translate another day. I want you to translate today," he countered rudely, his volume rising.

"Just go, my daughter. You don't want to make your husband angry. I'm sure you'll be able to come back to your sister soon," Shy Fawn whispered pleadingly.

Niz knew her mother was frightened for her, but she didn't respond to either of them. Reaching out, she picked up Ever Flowering's thin hand in her own and kissed the back of it. Tears began slipping down her cheeks.

For twenty years, Ever Flowering had been her best friend, her confidante, her accomplice, her other half. When she closed her eyes, she could still hear Ever Flowering's laughter echoing through the pine trees, just as it had when they were girls running barefoot along the river's edge, the hems of their dresses damp from dew, and their hands filled with wildflowers. They had woven necklaces from chokecherry stems and played at being grown women, tending pretend fires, bouncing pretend babies, and whispering secrets beneath the wide blue sky. In winter, they'd huddled close under shared blankets, giggling together and telling stories while the snow fell soft and silent outside.

They'd sat side by side, wide-eyed as they listened to their grandparents' stories, screamed together in delicious delight when their father chased them around their wickiup on hands and knees, talked over all the world's problems and dreamt about the future when they were young teens. Together, they had played, adventured, and explored, inseparable for years. Nizhoni had always been the braver one—climbing higher, singing louder, dreaming wilder. Ever Flowering had faithfully followed, conquering her fears just to be with Niz, their hearts tethered together like the strands of their mother's woven baskets—different, but forever bound.

"Woman, I'm not going to tell you again. Get out there and translate!" Fire Maker nearly yelled, his tone sounding dangerous. He reached for her arm and yanked her back roughly, pulling her away from Ever Flowering.

"Enough!" Walks With Power roared, jumping to his feet. "Your wife wants to sit with her sister, who is dying. Let her be!"

Niz closed her eyes, the tears coming faster. The simple courtesy of being stood up for proved to be her undoing. She heard Fire Maker and Walks With Power leave the wickiup, and there was shouting outside. Powerless to stop the tears, they continued to roll down her cheeks as she carefully moved back to her sister's side and reached for her hand again. Her mother came to sit beside her, putting her arm around Niz's back, holding her. When Walks

With Power returned, he was alone and breathing hard. Without a word, he sat down and tenderly took Ever Flowering's other hand in his.

Niz wiped the tears from her cheeks and took a shuddering breath. "Thank you," she said simply.

"It needed to be done. I've sat by too long. I won't sit silent any longer," he told her, his tone heavy.

"I'll be fine. Just . . . not today. I can't do it today," she whispered.

"You don't have to. The soldiers and the woman have left. Cloud Walking has brought Walks at Night in. Everyone is here. Stay with your sister."

Niz nodded, grateful her brother-in-law seemed to sense how much she needed everyone within eyesight. Quiet fell over the room other than the medicine man's chanting. They tried to convince Ever Flowering to eat and drink, but she was too weak. She refused it all. They sat by her side all day, praying to the spirits, hoping that against all odds, she would get better. As darkness fell, Ever Flowering slipped into a sleep they couldn't rouse her from. Still, her heart beat on, and though her breathing was ragged and labored, her chest continued to rise and fall.

Walks With Power had stretched out on the floor beside his wife, silent as he held her. Niz wasn't sure if he was still awake or not. Shy Fawn had cried herself to sleep. Cloud Walking's face was red and blotchy from the tears she'd shed. Sleeping on the other side of the room, she had Walks at Night on the mat beside her. Accepting the inevitable, the medicine man had gone. Niz still sat beside Ever Flowering, holding her hand.

In the silence, with everyone else asleep, her defenses were crumbling. Her grief, fear, and worry were rising up, choking her; tears stung her eyes, and she couldn't blink them back. Like a tidal wave on the horizon, she could see the emotions coming. Desperate for something else to focus on to keep them at bay, her eyes darted around the wickiup. She didn't want to leave Ever Flowering. There were no chores to be done. She hadn't thought to bring her sewing or her basket weaving when she'd retrieved the hides she slept on. Desperate, she shifted positions, looking for anything she might distract herself with. Something crinkled under her knee. Her letters from Raya and Mother Emaline. While she had been avoiding them for weeks, now her need for a distraction was greater than her fear of what was in them. With shaky hands, she reached between the hides and drew them out.

She sat staring at them for a long moment. If she didn't read them, she could imagine what was inside, writing the story the way she wanted it to go. If she read them, she would have to deal with the truth. Undoubtedly, they would stir up memories better left in the past. With a shaky breath, she put them down again, but then her eyes fell on Ever Flowering. The present was no better.

Lifting the top envelope from the stack, she quickly ripped it open, holding the pages up to the light of the fire. As she did, she caught her breath in wonder. She—Nizhoni Applewood—could read the words on the page. The scripted handwriting was more difficult to make out than the printed type in the books and newspapers Marigold had her practice with, but if she went slowly, she could figure it out. Recovering from her shock, she began to read.

My Nizhoni,

How accurately your parents named you. As I sit here thinking of you, all I can think of is how beautiful you are, beautiful in every way. It's not just that you have a beautiful face or figure, as other girls do. No, that's a common beauty. Your beauty is rare and special. Your beauty is like that of the mountains when the sun hits them after a rain, like the beauty of spring evenings and the first snow. You are beautiful like the river rushing over rocks and bubbling around bends, like a doe grazing amongst the morning fog, like the autumn brilliance of the aspens as they turn the mountainsides gold. Just like this beautiful world we live in, you are a work of art, my dear, crafted by the same Artist.

I know we've spoken of it in the past, and that it wasn't the right time, but you've been on my heart all day, and now I cannot sleep for thinking of you. So, I've risen from my bed and pulled a chair up close to the fire where my feet will be warm as I write (you know how I despise cold feet), and I'm going to write you about it once more.

There is a Creator, Niz, who created the whole earth; everything you see. He made the sun and the moon, the mountains and the deserts, the rivers and the seas. He made every plant and flower and tree, every animal, bird, and fish, and he made mankind. Not because He had to (He's beyond every power and spirit; He can do as He wills.) but because He wanted to. Look around you, Niz. He loves beauty. He loves creativity and new life and weathered old things that endure. He plants flowers no eye will ever see, feeds animals no heart will ever care for, sculpts formations no man will ever display in a garden, creates breathtaking views we'll never get the joy of appreciating, simply because He delights in making beautiful things. That same God fashioned you.

Your people, too, believe in a Creator, so I know this isn't a new concept. What's different is that I believe the Creator of the universe made a perfect world and put a man and woman there to commune with Him. Deceived by Satan, the man and woman sinned by doing that which God told them not to do. Through that one act, sin entered the world, and death and suffering began. The man and woman were shut out of the garden and separated from God because their sin could not commune with God's holiness. All these years later, humanity is still separated from God by sin. We have all fallen short of perfection; we have all done wrong things, thought wrong things, said wrong things. Those wrong things are sins, and they separate us from Him. But the LORD God had a plan to redeem us—and the world.

Many years after man was exiled from the garden, Father God sent His Son, Jesus Christ, to earth to redeem the brokenness of humanity. Jesus lived a perfect life and was unjustly crucified on a wooden cross. Satan thought he'd won that day by killing the Son of God, but what He didn't know was that Jesus was more powerful than the grave. It's hard to imagine, but three days later, Jesus rose again. He had paid the debt of our sin, overcome death, and was Resurrected by the power of the living God. Because of Jesus' work on the cross, every bad thing we've ever done, every wrong attitude we've had, every unkind word we've spoken, every sin we've committed, can be covered by the blood of Jesus and no longer separates us from God if we but believe that Jesus is the risen Christ, repent, and make Him our LORD and Savior.

There is indeed a Creator; Almighty God is His name. And not only did He create you and your people and all the people of the earth, He created You because He loves you and wants you to be with Him forever. The idea of eternity (time without bounds) without you was so devastating that Jesus willingly went to the cross. For you. For me. He willingly took on death and defeated it so that when our time here on earth is done, we will live forever with Him in the light of His perfection. The Bible says He will wipe away every tear from our eyes, and there will be no more pain or suffering. But we do not have to wait for death to experience the nearness of Jesus.

Before He left the earth to return to His Father in heaven after His resurrection, Jesus promised He would send us a Helper, another like Himself. He gave us the Holy Spirit, the third part of the Trinity, who is with us now, everywhere, and at all times. He is with me here in this cozy room at Atlas and Raya's, and He's there with you now in your village. With the Holy Spirit, we never face a day (or the challenges it might bring) alone. That is our hope, dear one. We have both the hope of eternal life with Jesus someday and life with the very Spirit of God today. He is a God full of love and mercy. He is kind and compassionate and unfailing. He cares about the widows, the orphans, the suffering, and the downtrodden. He is fully and completely good and trustworthy, and He is in the process of redeeming His creation, restoring it to the perfection it knew before the fall of man. His heart is only good—for you, for me, for the world.

You have suffered a grave loss, my dear. Your husband and your child were both ripped away from you. You have lost much. I know Chenoa said you have remarried, and I'm glad for you, truly. But

I also know you, and I know that you tend to avoid heartache. You try to bury it under for the sake of holding it all together for everyone around you. I know how much you love to be in control, and grief is messy and uncontrollable. So I may be going out on a limb here, but I'm guessing you've been running from it, afraid to face it. Niz, face it. Don't run anymore. Face it with Jesus. He's capable of holding you through the mess. Whatever challenges you're experiencing, whatever problem looms too big, He's capable of getting you through. Don't try to go it alone. There's no need. He went to the cross so that you wouldn't have to. He went to the cross so that He could be with you through this. Let Him. He will see you through.

For a moment after the fire, I wondered how I could serve a God that allowed such suffering. My heart was broken. I had lost not only my husband, but my three sons and unborn grandson as well. I essentially lost two of my daughters, who had lit up my world. My life felt like it was over. What hope could there still be? It felt as if everything good in my life was over. And then I realized, suffering happens. No one is immune. But amidst that fact of life, how could I not serve a God who offered hope and a future despite it? Without Jesus, that was the end of my family, the end of my sons, the end of my story. With Him, they lived on. My hope lived on. My story lived on. And I realized our tragedy was just as much why I believed in God as the happy times when everything was going wonderfully. It is the hope found in Jesus that gives my faith meaning, not the absence of difficulty or the presence of my comfort. It's that hope that I pray you will find too. The hope to go on. The hope that despite suffering and circumstances that seem hopeless, somehow, hope lives on.

My eyes are growing heavy, my dear, and the clock just struck three a.m. I pray you hear my heart through this letter, for it is my love for you that compels me to write it. You are strong and brave and clever and passionate, but I want you to know that if you ever find that you can't manage on your own, there is One who can help you and is oh, so eager to do so. He has loved you since before you were born, and His love stretches far beyond your years on this earth. He has plans for your life that are good, full of hope and a future. I love you, my daughter, and I am praying for you and your family tonight, that whatever trials you might face, that the God of heaven would lead you and guide you and make a way . . . even if there seems to be none.

I'll write again soon, because I have exciting news to share (though I'm guessing Raya already has) but I felt I couldn't wait to send this letter.

May the peace of God rest on you tonight, and may your sleep be sweet.

All my love,
Emaline

Peace. Nizhoni pressed the letter against her chest and looked around the dim wickiup, feeling panicky. If only peace didn't feel a million miles away. If only the letter had brought the distraction she'd hoped for rather than seeming as if her mother-in-law was in the room, speaking directly to the situation she currently found herself in. If only the letter had taken her away. Instead, the tidal wave of emotions was upon her, and there was nowhere left to hide. Her throat began to ache and tighten. Her eyes stung. She desperately tried to blink back her tears and push it all away, but her old tactics didn't work.

Niz could no longer hold off the emotions. They wouldn't be pressed down, her mind wouldn't be quieted. She couldn't stop the memories and the grief and the fear and the worry. They were crashing over her one after another after another. They were coming in violent waves, with all the ferocity she'd been so afraid of. The dam had broken; there was no putting it back together. Shaking, Niz sank down over her knees, her head in her hands, her forearms resting on the hides she knelt on, weeping silently, unable to hold it all together for one minute more.

Finally, after a year of being strong, of keeping loss at arm's length, with death breathing down her neck, she could no longer hide from her heartache. She grieved for her infant son, for Alex, for the dreams they'd dreamt and the love they had shared. She grieved for the family they'd been at the Applewoods, for the father she'd not given herself permission to mourn when she returned to the village, for what life with Fire Maker had become. Niz grieved for the hope of loving and being loved that had died in her heart. The raw truth of her situation rose up, and she faced it; every hard, unpleasant, anxiety-filled bit of it. She allowed herself to look at the future and admit she didn't know what was going to happen, nor did she have control over it. And that terrified her. With stark honesty, she looked through her tears at Ever Flowering, and her heart wrenched.

Ezra was right. This was beyond her control. Ever Flowering was dying, and she couldn't stop it.

She hadn't found a way. She was incapable of saving her sister or the baby that grew within her. The situation was completely out of her control.

The willow bark she had collected hadn't helped. All the times she'd convinced Ever Flowering to rest, slept beside her when Walks With Power was hunting, and encouraged her to eat—none of it had helped. Sending for the medicine man hadn't helped. Getting Marigold hadn't helped. Giving her laudanum and quinine hadn't helped. Sitting by her side hadn't helped. Nothing Niz had done had helped. She was completely and utterly powerless to save Ever Flowering, just as she had been powerless to save Alex, Luke, Will, and the child she carried.

Niz laid down, curling up beside Ever Flowering, the tears flowing, her heart breaking. The truth was like a searing knife to her heart. There was nothing more she could do. Short of a miracle, her beloved sister was dying. And she couldn't imagine life without her. But like a beacon of light, Marigold's words from earlier came back to her: *"Pray to Jesus, Niz. It's the only hope she has."*

Through teary eyes, Niz looked at her sister. She was desperate. The medicine man had chanted and prayed, and there had been no change. But what if Marigold was right? What if they hadn't been praying to the God that could heal her? What if Mother Emaline was correct? What if the God of heaven could make a way, even when there seemed to be none? "Jesus, Son of God, please heal my sister. You are her only hope," Niz whispered.

She watched, but nothing happened. Nothing changed. Ever Flowering did not wake up. Her breathing was still ragged, her form still deathly still. Feeling like her last hope had gone out, Niz wrapped her arms around herself, and for the first time since the days following the fire, she cried herself to sleep.

Suddenly, a very bright light filled her dreams. Out of the light, a man dressed in white walked into the wickiup. He knelt down and put his hand on Ever Flowering.

"Who are you?" Niz asked, afraid and yet not.

"I am the First and the Last, the Alpha and the Omega," the man said. "Your sister will live and not die, as will the child in her womb."

Suddenly, Niz opened her eyes. She sat up and looked for the man, but he was nowhere to be seen. Confused, she turned to Ever Flowering, but there was no change. Walks With Power, Shy Fawn, Cloud Walking, and Walks at Night were still sleeping. With a sinking heart, she realized it had only been a dream.

Ever Flowering was still sick and on death's door and there was nothing she could do about it. She couldn't save her sister. With a sinking heart, she looked around the room and realized she couldn't save any of them. She couldn't save them from sickness, from Fire Maker, from the army, from the Comanche, from the government, from life on a reservation. She couldn't keep them out of danger, couldn't keep their world good and happy, couldn't keep them from complication or pain.

No matter how much she wanted to find a way, no matter how many times she told herself she would, they were just empty promises. She'd been lying—even to herself. Despite all her drive and heart, she was incapable of holding it all together. She had come to the end of her abilities. She had nothing left. She didn't have things under control, and that realization was ripping her heart out.

If she wasn't in control, how could she protect the people she loved? And if she couldn't, who could?

"Come unto me, all ye that labour and are heavy laden, and I will give you rest. Take my yoke upon you, and learn of me; for I am meek and lowly in heart: and ye shall find rest unto your souls. For my yoke is easy, and my burden is light."

The words Marigold had spoken a week ago washed over her soul, only this time, she didn't hear her friend speaking them in her memory. Tonight, it was another voice who spoke, kind and gentle. It was the voice of the man from her dream. His words and tone were so compelling, and as it faded, like a leaf landing on a still pool, the words created a ripple. Like the wind stirring the leaves of the aspens, something stirred within her soul.

All around her, she felt the presence of someone mighty.

The medicine man had chanted and prayed. They'd tried their natural remedies. They'd tried the white man's medicines. She had tried everything she could think of, and at the end of herself, as she realized it was out of her control, the gentle voice, the promise of rest, the peace she'd felt when she'd laid her hand on Marigold's Bible, was left. It was still there when all else had faded away. It was still there when all the things she'd put her hope in—even herself—had proved futile.

Still, He remained.

Even in a room filled with sickness and sorrow, though Ever Flowering's condition was unchanged, when Niz felt overcome by her problems and alone with her pain, He remained.

Her thoughts turned to the fire. She felt the gripping grief she had refused to feel that day. She thought of the baby boy she had delivered. The Applewoods had served God, but Alex, his brothers, and his son, had perished. And yet, the tallest of the peaks, the blue of the sky, the rushing river, the promise of new life in Walks at Night, were still there. She could see it now. Despite the Applewoods' tragedy, God remained. Still, He was holding all things together. Still, in Him, they lived and moved and had their being. Just as Mother Emaline had said, the tragedy wasn't proof that He didn't exist. It was proof that He was their only hope.

Suddenly, she knew something innately, something she hadn't been able to grasp before: He was bigger than her worries, greater than the problems of man. His existence was not determined by how comfortable her life was.

She had refused to believe because He hadn't fit into her picture. He had let her father and her husband and her baby die. He had let her people get confined to a reservation, let the Applewood family get scattered by tragedy, let her make a terrible decision to marry a wicked man. She had assumed that a powerful God's plan would be the same as hers, and that if He wasn't carrying out her life as she'd planned it, then He clearly couldn't exist. But what she had failed to account for was that she was not God. God was not Nizhoni with a voice that boomed over the earth. He was God, and she was not. It had never been about her; it had always been about Him. It was His picture, His story, and she could participate or not—but either way, it didn't change the facts. He remained.

Regardless of what god or spirit man chose to worship, hardship came. No matter how strong the person, things existed that were beyond their control. In the stillness of the wickiup, she finally understood what Mother Emaline, Raya, Alex, Ezra, and Marigold had been trying to tell her all along—God was God. Regardless of what happened or didn't, He remained. And yet, even in His vastness, He was willing to enter into her story, broken, messy and all. He was able to carry the load that was crushing her, and in its place, He was offering her His light one.

She pushed herself up onto her knees and sank down over them, her hands clasped. "Father God . . . God of Abraham, Isaac, and Jacob, Jesus Christ, son of God," she whispered into the stillness, addressing Him the way she'd heard Him addressed when Raya used to read from the big family Bible. "You are God, and I am not. I can't do this on my own anymore. I don't have it under control. I can't find a way forward. I can't hold everything together for everyone—or anyone. But I believe You can." She paused to steady her shaky voice.

"You know what's best, even when I don't. I've been full of pride, thinking I could do it on my own, thinking I was brave enough, strong enough, clever enough. I was wrong. I can't even keep it all together for my family. But the Bible says You're holding it all together for all people everywhere, so let Your will be done, instead of mine. Help me be a part of Your story and forgive my pride for being offended when You weren't fitting into mine. You are God and I am not. So I submit myself . . . my plans . . . my spirit to You. Please take my heavy load. I can't carry it any longer, Jesus. It's crushing me, and I know now that You're the only one strong enough to carry it," she whispered, pouring out the truth that she desperately needed to share with somebody.

She'd heard the Scriptures read every night during her three years with the Applewoods. She'd listened to them talk about their faith. She'd had the head knowledge, but now, for the first time, the pieces were fitting together, the full picture was coming into view. The message of the gospel was becoming personal—it was meant for her. She believed in the God of the Scriptures.

She opened her eyes and looked at her sister lying still and unmoving before her. "Whatever happens with Ever Flowering, You will remain. I know that now. But if possible, please save my sister and her baby. We've tried everything else; now I'm asking You—please heal her. Make her well. I don't want to lose her," Niz whispered, beginning to cry again.

Lying down, curling up beside Ever Flowering, tears ran down her face like liquid prayers. And a deep peace settled over her as she drifted back to sleep.

Twenty

The next morning, Ever Flowering was no better but no worse. Around midday, she awakened. Though still very sick, she was able to eat and drink a little. Nizhoni gave her more laudanum and the mixture of quinine and Ever Flowering fell back asleep. Again that night, she woke up and ate and drank. Later, after everyone else was sleeping, Niz pulled out the rest of the unopened letters she'd put back between her hides the night before.

She'd done a lot of thinking throughout the day, and despite the grief Mother Emaline's letter had brought, she needed to read the rest of them. She was still scared to do so, frightened of the sorrow and longing they would likely stir up again. But Mother Emaline had been right—she couldn't keep running.

Marigold had told her Jesus had come to earth, taken on the form of a man, and gone to the cross so that He could be with them in their suffering. Marigold had said He wasn't far off and distant; He was there, helping them navigate the sorrow and the loss of living in a broken world. Since her prayer the night before, Niz had felt lighter, like a load had been lifted off her shoulders. Ever Flowering was still sick, she was still concerned about Cloud Walking, troubled over Fire Maker, worried about Walks at Night, anxious for her people, but there was a lightness—a relief. She knew she couldn't hold everything together anymore, nor was it her responsibility. There was someone else who was able to carry the load; she simply had to trust Him to do so.

When worries had come throughout the day, she had prayed about the problem. Mother Emaline had said the God of heaven could make a way when there seemed to be none. In desperation, she had clung to that and chose to believe it. When emotions had risen to the surface and she'd felt frightened by their intensity, she had shared her load with the One able to carry it.

Niz was trusting that Jesus wasn't far off and distant, unfeeling and unconcerned, but that He was there and that He cared. That while it wasn't all about her—she was only one piece of His very big story—that He still was deeply invested in and present in her pain.

Determined to trust Almighty God enough to stop running from the grief she was so afraid of, she opened the first of the remaining letters. One after another, she slowly made it through the stack of envelopes.

She learned that both women wrote just like they talked, and it made her cry as she missed them all the more because of it. Niz held her breath between letters as she read of Mother Emaline's sickness and their dire circumstances in Cincinnati, then smiled with joy as she learned of Raya's wedding. In the last letter, she read that Raya was expecting a child in the winter. Overcome, Niz clutched the unfinished letter to her chest, so full of happiness that it nearly hurt.

Tears ran down her cheeks as she remembered all the times she had dreamt with Raya about having little ones of their own. They had imagined how they would put their babies down for naps and then sit and sew, how the cousins would play together, and someday how their children would become the best of friends. Niz had promised to make Raya a cradleboard whenever the babies came so she could keep her hands free for her work, and Raya had clapped in delight. But year after year, Raya's womb had stayed empty.

During Niz's second year with the Applewoods, Raya had opened up about how much she wanted to have children and confessed how concerned she was that she seemed unable to do so. It was such a deep desire for her that Niz had almost been afraid to tell her sister-in-law when she had discovered she was with child. But she shouldn't have worried. Raya had rejoiced with her, putting aside her own longing to share in her excitement, just as she always did. Now, Niz felt great joy knowing Raya finally carried life within.

But when Niz wiped the tears from her eyes and saw Ever Flowering, her heart began to ache. It almost felt wrong to feel such joy over her sister-in-law's baby while her own sister lay on the brink of death. Her tears were happy and sad all at the same time.

She didn't understand how such joy could coexist with such sorrow, and so she did what she'd determined to do with all the emotions and dilemmas that felt too big for her. "Thank You, God, for Raya's joy, for the gift of a baby. Please keep her and the child safe and healthy. Thank You for letting me share this happiness with her. But You know my heart is heavy too. Help me make sense of both my joy and my sorrow. Please heal Ever Flowering and protect her baby," she whispered. "Let both of my sisters' joy be complete. And thank you for sending me Walks at Night, who has filled my arms and my heart. Help me trust you with all the rest."

Wiping the tears from her cheeks, Niz continued reading. In the last paragraph of the last letter, Raya shared that Chenoa had traveled to Idaho Territory and was happily settled with her new husband, Isaac Jones. They had just finished building their new sawmill and seemed very much in love. Raya shared that Chenoa seemed changed. She said their sister-in-law sounded somehow stronger, braver, and at peace—and that she was grateful to see it after they had all parted in the midst of so much heartache. Raya wrote that she longed to know how Niz was, too, and asked her to please find a way to send word back.

Niz folded the letter, determined to get some paper and send Raya a response before they left for their winter camp. No doubt the task would take her some time as her writing was still a work in progress, but she needed to let Raya know she was okay.

Slipping the letter back into its envelope, she impulsively kissed it before taking a deep, shaky breath. She'd done it. She'd read the letters she'd been incapable—and afraid—of reading. She'd conquered her fears. She'd done the hard thing.

The memories and grief had come, just as she feared they would. But she had faced them, and though her heart was filled with equal parts sorrow and joy, she was alright. That was something. And now she had the knowledge that her dear family members were safe and well, with love in their hearts and smiles on their faces once again.

As she slipped the letters back into their hiding place, this time opened and read, a smile filled her face. It felt freeing not to live in fear of opening letters that might make her face her pain. It was liberating to know she had been able to read them for herself. Though grief and loss swirled around her, freedom felt sweet.

~~~

The next day was much the same. Ever Flowering did not seem to improve, but she didn't get worse. They helped her sit up a few times to eat and drink, and she was able to do so. Slowly, her strength seemed to be returning. When there was still no marked difference the day after that, Shy Fawn and Cloud Walking moved back home to their own wickiup.

The braves were leaving on their second to last hunt of the year, and Walks With Power asked Niz to stay with Ever Flowering. Though she worried about what Fire Maker and his friends would do under the guise of splitting up to hunt, she was happy to stay with her sister. Her days were spent caring for Walks at Night and Ever Flowering, and as she did, she prayed unceasingly about what to do next. Soon she would have to return home to Fire Maker, face the dilemma with the army, and talk to Cloud Walking about what was going on. And she had no idea how to do any of it. But she prayed and trusted that God did. For the time being, she was sheltered from it all as she cared for Ever Flowering.

Three mornings after the men left to go hunting, there was a decided chill in the air when Niz woke. Leaving Walks at Night covered, she carefully got up and added wood to the fire. After spreading another blanket over Ever Flowering, she stepped out of the wickiup for a breath of fresh air. There was a subtle crunch as she did so, and she realized the first frost had come during the night. With her excitement growing, she turned and ducked back inside. Ever Flowering's eyes were open. "It's the first frost," Niz told her, her smile bright.

"The buffaloberries are ready," Ever Flowering said knowingly. "Your favorite."

"When Mother and Cloud Walking bring some back, I'll make us a dessert for our evening meal," Niz told her, happy they still had some sugar from the supplies they'd traded for in town.

"I'm feeling better. Go gather berries with the others."

Niz shook her head, swatting the very notion away as she came to kneel beside Ever Flowering. "No, I'll stay with you." She helped her sister sit up before giving her dried meat and a handful of dried berries.

"I'm serious, Niz. You've been so kind to stay and help me, but I'm feeling better . . . stronger. Go pick berries and enjoy the sunshine and fresh air. Leave me something to eat and drink. Maybe I'll even go outside for a bit to get some fresh air myself."

Niz wanted to continue to protest, but though her sister still seemed frail, she did indeed seem stronger than she had.

"Truly. I'll be fine," Ever Flowering assured her, reaching out and patting her hand. "Go."

Niz considered it as she straightened Ever Flowering's blankets and made her some willow bark tea. She hadn't given her sister laudanum or quinine in seventy-two hours, and still the fever had not returned, nor was her breathing labored.

She also had to remember that buffaloberries were an important part of their diet throughout the year; they needed as many hands gathering as possible. She mulled over her plans for the day as she went about her morning chores. When Walks at Night woke, she got him changed and sat him down with his breakfast.

"Get Blue Flower or Wise Hawk to check on me if it would make you feel better, but please go. You love gathering the buffaloberries," Ever Flowering encouraged from her mat.

Niz crouched down beside her. "Very well. I'll go. As long as you promise to eat and drink something every hour. I'll ask Blue Flower to stop in to check on you a few times throughout the day. And if you feel well enough, please, spend some time sitting in the sunshine."

"I will. Have fun, Sister." Ever Flowering paused and her face blossomed into a weak smile. "I'm sure Walks at Night will enjoy it too. Remember how much we loved it when we were little?"

"Mother always tried to make it into a competition to see which of us could fill more baskets," Niz remembered.

"But it never worked because we were too busy eating them as fast as we picked them," Ever Flowering finished.

Niz laughed. "That's true."

Ever Flowering shifted onto her side, wincing. "Bring some back to me tonight. They're always the sweetest right after the first frost."

Niz hurried to prop cushions up behind Ever Flowering to help her get comfortable. "Better?" she asked. Ever Flowering nodded.

Hearing women stirring outside, Niz knew they were likely getting ready to head out to gather. "I'll go talk to Blue Flower, and be back this afternoon, okay?"

"Have fun," Ever Flowering said, her voice weak but happy.

Niz watched her sister's slow blink and knew she would sleep again soon. Tucking the blanket up around the young woman's chin, Niz leaned down to kiss her forehead. As she pushed herself to her feet, she saw that Walks at Night was just finishing his breakfast. She held her hand out to him, and he shoved the last of his dried berries into his mouth and stood, toddling over to take her hand. Walking hand in hand back to their own wickiup, she talked to him as they went, telling him where they were going and what they were going to do. She knew he likely didn't understand, but she told him anyway. He liked being talked to and jabbered back, looking up at her with big, toothy grins, and squinting against the morning sun that hung behind her. Collecting her empty gathering baskets, she tucked them under her arm, took Walks at Night's hand again, and went to join the others.

Finding her mother and Cloud Walking among the women who had congregated, Niz gave them a report on Ever Flowering before leaving to ask Blue Flower to check in on her sister. The dear old woman readily agreed, and Niz rejoined the others as they set off.

Walking slower with her son in tow, she quickly fell to the back of the group. But she didn't mind. His wonder and glee at the world around them and everything they passed made her happy. To him, the world was new and fresh, full of excitement and wonder. He wasn't worried about anything, oblivious to the dangers of life, simply believing he would be taken care of. She thought about her new faith and prayed for help to be as trusting as her child. If only she could believe that God cared for her even more than she cared for her son. "Please help me," she whispered up toward the bright blue sky.

"That's wonderful Ever Flowering felt well enough to stay by herself today," Cloud Walking said, all smiles as she dropped back to walk with them. "Do you think she'll recover?"

Niz thought back to the dream she'd had and the kind assurance of the man's voice. "Yes, I do. A man in white appeared to me in a dream, Cloud Walking, and told me Ever Flowering would survive and so would the baby she carries. At the time, I wasn't sure I believed it, but now . . . I do."

"A man in white?"

"Jesus the Christ. The God Alex and his family served."

Cloud Walking gasped. "Nizhoni! You can't speak of the departed!"

Niz squinted up at the sky for a moment, trying to figure out how to best answer her sister. Finally, she shrugged. "I no longer believe Alex is dead, at least not the way I thought he was. And I'm not afraid to speak his name. Not anymore."

Another gasp. "What do you mean he's not dead?"

"I believe he's alive with Christ. Jesus died on the cross, but He defeated death and was resurrected . . . He came back to life. Now He lives, Cloud Walking, as do those who have put their faith in Him, as Alex did."

Cloud Walking stared at her, appearing stunned and frightened. "You believe that?"

Niz looked down at Walks at Night, walking so happily beside her, catching at the grasses with his free hand, not a care in the world. "Yes. I do."

"But you remarried! If Alex is alive, he'll be angry! And whose wife will you be?"

Niz shook her head. "It's not like that. He's still gone from this earth. Alex is alive with Christ in heaven. I'm still Fire Maker's wife." For better or worse.

Her sister looked at her skeptically. "I don't understand."

Niz started her story at the beginning, telling Cloud Walking about life with the Applewoods and their faith in their God. She shared how she felt after the fire, and how she'd been running from her grief, trying to hold it all back, desperate to stay in control. She told her of the stirring she felt when Marigold had been riding in, their conversation in her wickiup, the peace she'd experienced when she laid her hand on the Bible, what Marigold had said about praying to the wrong God, Mother Emaline's perfectly timed letter, the dream, and then the certainty she'd felt that above and beyond all else, God remained. She told her she believed Almighty God had saved their sister, and that He was making a way for all of them, even if it felt like there was no way forward.

Cloud Walking looked at her with wide eyes when she was done. "Nizhoni . . . our people won't like it if you believe in this new God. You'll be an outcast."

Niz was quiet for a long moment. "I've thought of that. But, Cloud Walking, Ever Flowering is getting better. When she was as good as dead, I prayed to Jesus, and now she is alive. I can't ignore that. I can't ignore my mother-in-law's letter that I read on the very night I most needed it, or the peace I felt when I touched His book, or the peace I feel now."

Cloud Walking looked at the ground, clearly in distress. "Maybe it was a coincidence. Maybe Ever Flowering would have gotten better either way."

"No." Niz had seen people die from the White Plague before. "Ever Flowering was on death's door. She was not going to get better on her own." She paused, sensing Cloud Walking's doubt. "You can think what you want, Sister, but I know what I saw . . . what I felt . . . what I feel even now . . . peace after so much worry. I felt like the weight of everything was crushing me . . . like I couldn't breathe. Now I can breathe again, even if circumstances are still the same."

"What has been causing you so much worry? Ever Flowering?" Cloud Walking asked, her brows drawn together in concern.

"Yes, that's certainly part of it. I've also been worried about you," Niz admitted.

"About me?" The teen sounded surprised.

Niz nodded. "Why do you not accept Strong Pine?"

Cloud Walking dropped her eyes to the ground as she walked, a blush rising in her cheeks. Finally, she looked up. "Nizhoni, it's . . . Sergeant Green!"

"What?" Niz asked, looking quickly at Cloud Walking and then up ahead when the girl pointed.

Sure enough, Sergeant Green was jogging toward them. Surprised, Niz quickly scanned the area where the group of women had arrived at the thicket of buffaloberries and were spreading out to gather them. No soldiers were in sight, but as she turned to the south, she saw Ezra and his patrol dismounting near a grove of aspens along the banks of the river.

"Hello!" Sergeant Green said, lifting his hand in greeting.

"Hello!" Cloud Walking replied in English, waving back.

Niz shot a nervous look at her sister before turning back toward the sergeant. She saw that he was smiling at Cloud Walking, his eyes trained on her.

"Hello, Sergeant Green. What a surprise to find you here." Niz tried to prop up a friendly smile.

"We're out on patrol. We were just riding by when we saw the women coming through the bushes." The man stopped awkwardly, still smiling at Cloud Walking.

"And you stopped to rest your horses?"

Her question drew the young man's attention back from her sister. "Oh, right. Major Taylor said we were stopping for a break. I saw Cloud Walking and thought I would come say hello." He paused. "What are you out here doing?"

Niz had only ever seen Sergeant Green as a serious young man, who was polite but professional. Now, his face was slightly flushed, his tone eager and inquisitive. For the first time, she noticed he likely wasn't more than twenty and was as much a schoolboy as he was a soldier. "We're gathering buffaloberries," she said, suddenly grim.

"Can I help? While we're here?" he questioned, looking between her and Cloud Walking. "I used to pick berries with my mother, so I know how. I could sure use a walk after so many hours in the saddle. And I would be nearby in case any trouble arises. The bears are probably out looking for berries this time of year too."

Niz gave him a knowing look and then turned to her sister. Translating his request to Cloud Walking, the teen quickly agreed, her eyes bright, her cheeks flushed. "My sister says you can help her pick berries, so you may. But Sergeant Green, you two cannot wander off. Cloud Walking must stay close to my mother at all times."

"I understand," he agreed quickly, smiling at Cloud Walking even as he answered. Cloud Walking shot Niz a happy smile, and the pair started off toward the thicket.

"Sergeant Green, I'm serious. I want to be able to see you both at all times!" Niz called after them. The young man lifted his hand in cheerful acknowledgement.

"Kids."

Niz turned expectantly, the voice familiar. Walks at Night turned too. Spotting his friend, he let go of Niz's hand and ran toward the major, giggling. Snagging him off the ground, Ezra tossed the boy lightly into the air, before settling him on his arm. "Hey, buddy."

"Buddy!" Walks at Night echoed, making them both laugh. He looked so pleased to be held by Ezra, and Niz couldn't blame him. Part of her wished she could run to their friend for a hug too. Seeing him brought both joy and relief. He was comfortable and safe and kind. But she was married, and she hoped by now he was courting Marigold. So, she didn't run to him; she smiled instead.

"I didn't expect to see you and your men here," she told him honestly.

"I didn't expect to see you either." In the light of day, even under the shadow of his cap, she could see his expression was friendly and open. He studied her for a moment, and then, seeming to remember himself, continued. "We were riding by on patrol when we saw you ladies coming. We needed a rest anyway, so I figure we'll take a break over there. With the Comanche still running loose, I reckon it makes sense to take our break nearby and keep an eye out for any trouble."

"You haven't caught them yet?" she asked casually, her heart starting to race. She'd hoped maybe they had. If so, she would have no reason to tell him about Fire Maker.

He shook his head, his smile fading. Walks at Night squirmed to get down, and Ezra set him on the ground. The boy toddled off, clearly spotting something he wanted to inspect. Niz kept her eyes on her son. "Are they continuing to raid?"

"Yes," he answered, seeming troubled. "Two more nonviolent raids, and another violent one. It still makes no sense. And we can't find them. We keep missing them. Even with extra patrols, it's a needle in a haystack with so much open land in these mountains. There's not many of them, and they're traveling light and smart. We find where they camped, we find where they've raided, but we can't find them. It's almost as if they have someone helping them evade us."

"There's a thousand places to hide out here and only one place to find them," she said distractedly, dropping her eyes to the ground as her thoughts spun. Her heart was conflicted; her mind confused. What was the right thing to do? If she told Ezra that Fire Maker was raiding and possibly working with the Comanche, she would be betraying her husband and putting her people in jeopardy. But if she didn't, she felt like she was betraying Ezra and was at least partly responsible for the raids. Helping him stop them felt like the right thing to do. But so did protecting her people and staying loyal to her husband. Her heart warred within itself.

"How's Ever Flowering?" Ezra asked, changing the subject, his voice suddenly full of concern. He seemed to be holding his breath as he waited for her answer.

"She's still sick, but she's alive! I think her strength is starting to return."

His relief was evident. "That's good news. I've been praying for her every day. I was worried about her . . . and about you. You seemed so burdened the last time I saw you. It's been difficult not to be able to get updates. But you seem good now . . . lighter maybe. I'm glad."

She turned her dark eyes up toward him, searching his face. Should she tell him what had transpired?

He looked away. "Anyway, I just wanted to come over and explain why we're here. Just continue as normal. We'll see to your safety and ride out when you're finished. You won't even know we're here."

"Except for him," she reminded dryly, pointing at the soldier who was now busily helping Cloud Walking fill her baskets with the bright, translucent red berries.

Ezra chuckled. "I'll go get him and tell him to rejoin the patrol."

Niz tipped her head and released a deep breath. "No, don't. I think I need to let my sister make up her own mind instead of intervening."

"That's unlike you. You haven't taken sick, too, have you?" he asked, reaching over as if he were going to lay his hand against her forehead to check her temperature.

She batted his hand away. "Excuse me?"

He laughed and held up his hands in surrender. "I'm only teasing." She made a face. "It's easier said than done when it's someone we love," he agreed.

"Yes, it is," she answered simply. There was a short silence as they both watched Walks at Night hit two pinecones together. Suddenly, she turned back toward him. "Hey, I wanted to tell you I read Mother Emaline and Raya's letters."

"Did you?" he asked, looking pleased.

She nodded. "They're both doing well. Raya remarried, and they're settled with her husband in Cincinnati. It sounds like they're very happy and have everything they need. Raya's new husband, a distant relative of Father Julius', sounds like a wonderful man, and . . . Raya's expecting!" she told him, barely able to contain her excitement. Her joy for her sister-in-law had continued to grow in the days since learning of her news.

"Niz, that's great. I'm so glad to hear it." She could tell he genuinely was, and that warmed her heart. She appreciated that they knew and cared about the same people.

"Yes, I'm truly happy for her. I need to go to town to send a letter back before we leave for our winter camp."

Ezra cringed. "Best not to venture off too far right now. I'll bring you a paper and pen and post your letter for you. I'm sure she'll be glad to receive it."

Niz glanced up at him, the dark cloud of reality rolling in to overshadow her joy. For a moment she'd forgotten about the trouble surrounding them, but his offer had brought it all back;

town was not a safe place for her to be at present. "Thank you. I would really appreciate that."

He met her eyes, his gaze steady. "Niz, I'm truly proud of you for learning to read. It's not an easy thing to do, but you did it. You learned faster than I thought possible, and now you're reading letters and going to write one of your own. That's quite an achievement."

Her answering smile was bright. His praise made her feel happy and accomplished. "Thank you," she said simply, enjoying the warmth in his hazel eyes. Giving herself a little shake, she added, "How's Marigold?"

He sent her a knowing look. "Ms. Langston is doing very well."

"Good. Please tell her I miss her." Ezra nodded. The quiet stretched for several moments. "Hey, I um, I'm sorry about how I left the fort . . . after you'd been so kind to me," she said cautiously. The conversation had been so pleasant; she didn't want to change its course, yet she felt she needed to apologize.

He was quiet, and when she glanced at him, she found he was studying her again. "I understand why you did, Niz."

"You do?" She'd expected him to still be at least a little angry.

"Yes, I do." He paused. "You forget that I know you . . . that I have for a long time."

Niz let that settle. It felt nice to be known—and to have the best believed about her intentions rather than the worst. There was something comforting about that.

"Well, I'm going to get back to my men and let you pick your berries," he said, easing back a step.

"Thank you, Major, for being willing to see to our safety today," she said, turning toward him. "You have no obligation to, and yet you are."

"Niz . . . I hope you know I'm still just me."

"I do," she answered, dropping her eyes as she nodded. She really did. But her heart needed him to be the major.

He studied her face and then nodded as well. "Good." He paused, glancing away for a moment. Suddenly, he jumped forward. "He just put a rock in his mouth."

Niz spun, instantly knowing who he meant. They reached Walks at Night at the same time. Ezra picked him up, and Niz pried his mouth open and dug out the rock with her finger, causing Walks at Night to screech in surprised anger.

"No, no! You can't eat rocks," she scolded, accepting her son, who now had crocodile tears welling up in his eyes. He cuddled into her arms, rubbing his face against her shoulder, seeking comfort as he started crying in earnest. He'd clearly been startled by their abrupt actions. She realized belatedly that it was a good thing he hadn't swallowed the rock in his surprise.

Ezra chuckled as he reached out and patted the boy's back. "There, there, little guy. You're okay."

Walks at Night cried harder.

"He'll stop crying when he tries the berries," she told Ezra over her son's head.

"True. They should be nice and sweet today. There was a frost last night."

"You know about buffaloberries?" she asked, surprised.

He laughed as he started backing toward his soldiers. "I've spent a lot of time in the woods, Niz."

"That's true, you have," she agreed, feeling embarrassed that she'd forgotten. He was right. He wasn't just the major. He was Ezra Taylor, the boy who had grown up roaming the mountains with Alex, getting into scrapes, and finding his way out.

Ezra's father had been a trapper and a mountain man, with a little log cabin just a mile upriver from the Applewoods. He'd frequently disappeared into the high mountains for extended periods of time, setting his traps and collecting his furs, leaving Ezra at home to help his mother. Ezra had been twelve when the woman had died. Lonely and drifting, he'd wandered downriver, and the Applewoods had welcomed him with open arms, happily absorbing him into their family full of boys.

Sharing a love for adventure, he and Alex had grown as thick as thieves. Whenever Ezra wasn't trapping with his father, the two of them were hiking, fishing, hunting, or exploring. Niz had heard the stories of them getting lost in the woods for days at a time and finding edible plants to survive on until they found their way back home. Ezra knew the land, the plants, the animals, and the rivers just as Alex had. She should have remembered.

"I'll bring you some berries," she offered.

For just a moment, a look of longing swept over his face. "I'd rather pick them with you." Niz's breath caught in surprise, and butterflies stirred within her at the intensity in his hazel eyes. But just as quickly, his expression changed, the lighthearted mirth of earlier back again. "Berries are always better when you pick them straight from the bush," he continued. "But if I were picking berries who would keep my men in line?"

She glanced over his shoulder as he gestured backward with his thumb, smiling as she noticed most of the soldiers were already stretched out for a nap. "Yeah, they look like they're a handful."

He sent her a playful grin. "They really are. Have fun today," he told her before turning and making his way back to his men.

Niz watched him for a moment, remembering the brief longing in his eyes and how her heart had felt at his words. She couldn't help wishing they could spend the day picking berries together, too. But honor and integrity were more valuable than updates, conversation, or fun. So instead, she went to join the women. Looking for Cloud Walking, she saw the teen and Sergeant Green picking berries not far from her mother, just as they'd been instructed.

Talking to the still-fussing Walks at Night as she walked, she went to pick beside Shy Fawn. Reaching the shrubs, she plucked one of the berries off the bush, popping it into her son's mouth when he opened it for her. His little mouth puckered as he made a terrible face, but then his eyes grew round as the tartness gave way to sweet. He reached for more, and she set him down with a laugh and showed him how to pick the bright berries and avoid the thorns.

"He reminds me of you and your sisters when you were little," Shy Fawn said with a chuckle.

"Ever Flowering and I were talking about that this morning. We always loved when the buffaloberries were ready. It was such fun to try to pick the sweetest ones. If you got it wrong, you paid for it with their tartness, but if you got it right, they were the best!"

"I remember once when my greedy little girls got impatient. You picked them before the frost," Shy Fawn said, smiling at the memory.

"Yes, and we paid for our mistake! I've never tasted anything so bitter!"

"Ah, but you learned." Shy Fawn paused. "Speaking of my girls . . . why does Cloud Walking pick berries with that soldier?"

Niz's laughter faded, apprehension rising up at the look on her mother's face. "He asked if he could pick with her. She said yes."

"And you agreed?"

"You said it yourself, Mother. She's not a little girl anymore. She's a woman. Cloud Walking should be allowed to choose for herself."

"I agree, but not him! Do you want her to leave her people like you did?" Shy Fawn accused, clearly aghast at the idea.

"No, Mother. I don't. Truly. But maybe it's not for us to decide. Maybe Cloud Walking must find her own path for her life."

Shy Fawn looked at her sharply. "That doesn't sound like my oldest daughter."

Niz shrugged in reply. Her mother was right. She'd always thought she'd known what was best for everyone, and she hadn't hesitated to tell them. But now, she knew the truth was that she could control very little, and sometimes even what she thought was best wasn't enough.

"Well, I agree. She does need to find her own path. So long as it's here with our people," Shy Fawn continued, a finality to her last sentence.

Niz gave her mother an amused look.

"What? I had one daughter who left our people to get married. I won't have another."

"Mother, they're not even talking. They're just picking berries. I don't think we have cause to worry yet," Niz reminded. "But even if we did, if it's what she really wanted, it wouldn't be the worst thing in the world."

"That's a matter of opinion," Shy Fawn answered grimly as she continued to fill her basket.

Niz nearly told her mother she could think of something far worse, but she held her tongue, not having anything but speculation to share about Fire Maker's intentions. Thinking as she worked, she filled half a basket full of berries as she wondered how much to share and when. In the end, she decided that if she talked to Cloud Walking and the girl confirmed his attention, she would tell her mother, but she wouldn't until then.

"Speaking of soldiers, you and the major had much to talk about," Shy Fawn commented casually.

"He filled me in on the trouble with the Comanche. I asked how Marigold was. He congratulated me on learning to read. We dug a rock out of Walks at Night's mouth."

"Hm."

Niz shot a sideways glance at her mother. The woman looked worried but said nothing more. Niz focused back on the berries as several minutes passed in silence. When she glanced over again, she found tears rolling down Shy Fawn's cheeks. Surprised and concerned, Niz put her hand on her mother's back. "Mama, what is it?"

Shy Fawn pressed her lips together, even as her fingers continued to fly, plucking the juicy fruit from the bush and dropping it into her basket. Repeating the process at lightning speed, she was filling two baskets to Niz's every one. Suddenly, she took a ragged breath. "I don't even know which of you girls to worry about more. Ever Flowering is sick. We nearly lost her. We may still. I can't imagine we can still hope for the baby . . ."

The woman's voice trailed off. After a moment, she wiped her eyes and continued. "You are married to a bad-tempered man who hurts you, and you seem to constantly be in danger, always braver, friendlier, and more daring than you should be. I love the fire that burns inside you, Nizhoni, but most of the white hairs on my head are from you!"

Niz winced in remorse. She knew that was likely true.

"And now your sister is off talking to that soldier, mooning over him, when she should be settling down with Strong Pine! What am I going to do with you girls? I'm frightened!"

Niz slipped her arm around her mother's shoulders and rested her head against Shy Fawn's. "I used to feel like that too. I felt like I had to control everything so I knew it would turn out well. I was so worried about all of you—about what would happen next—that the worry was consuming me. I couldn't breathe. It was choking me."

Shy Fawn nodded as if she could relate, and Niz cringed, sad that her sweet mother felt the same way. "And now?" the woman asked.

"Now I don't. Now I'm at peace," she told her.

"How?" Shy Fawn questioned doubtfully.

Niz began her story, telling it to Shy Fawn as she had Cloud Walking. She hadn't intended to tell either of them, but she didn't know how she couldn't. When she felt as light as she did after feeling so heavy, when she'd found rest for her soul, and relief from her fears, how could she keep it to herself?

But Shy Fawn stopped her halfway through her story, her face stormy. "Nizhoni!" she scolded. "You cannot speak of another god other than the Great Spirit. You'll anger him, and we'll all feel his wrath."

"Mother, you don't under—"

"That's enough!" Shy Fawn said severely. "I don't want to hear you speak of this again!"

"But Mother, Almighty God healed Ever Flowering!"

"I said that's enough!" Shy Fawn cried, her eyes wild with fear. "Don't say another word! And go call your sister. It's time she stopped passing the day with that soldier. That's what has caused you to betray your people and the Great Spirit—it's your time with the Applewoods, the major, and that woman who teaches you the words! If you had stayed with us in the village, none of this would be happening!"

"Mother," Niz started, wanting to help her understand. She'd been drowning before, but now she had life. She'd been weighed down and in despair, but now she had hope. She'd been running from things that felt too big and scary, but now she was standing firm to face them. Her new faith wasn't a bad thing—it had saved her!

"Go get your sister!" Shy Fawn said, her voice low and trembling.

Niz shut her mouth, her dark eyes troubled as she considered her mother. She knew that tone. She had gone too far. Shy Fawn was not going to hear anything else she said. Nodding, she picked up her son and went after Cloud Walking.

Drawing near, she heard that Cloud Walking and Sergeant Green were indeed talking, as her mother had said. It was stilted, but they were trying, finding a way despite the language barrier. He was teaching her sister the words for different emotions by using facial expressions, and Cloud Walking laughed as she repeated them, her pronunciation actually quite good.

"Mother wants you to come pick with her," Niz said, interrupting.

Cloud Walking looked up, seeming surprised to see her, as did Sergeant Green. "But the Sergeant and I have found a good spot here. There are many berries."

"Well, be that as it may, you need to come back. Mother's not asking; she's telling."

"I can't be bossed, Nizhoni. I'm not a child," Cloud Walking protested, her dark eyes flashing. Sergeant Green looked between them with a slight frown on his face. Though he couldn't understand what they were saying, he clearly knew what they were talking about.

Niz sent her sister a pointed look. "And yet you're acting childish. Go back and talk to Mother about it, not me. I'm just the messenger."

Cloud Walking turned to Sergeant Green as if she wanted to say something. Her eyes were dark and troubled. With a miserable sigh, she started back to their mother instead, her steps angry, her shoulders slumped with grave despair only known to girls Cloud Walking's age.

The sergeant turned to Niz, a protest building on his face. "We didn't go out of eyesight. I made sure we stayed where your mother could see her at all times."

"I know," Niz said, compassionately. The young man had been kind and polite every time she'd seen him. "It's not your fault. It's mine. I worried my mother with something I said. She's just gathering her chicks."

"Will you tell Cloud Walking I said goodbye, and that I enjoyed picking berries with her?"

"I'll tell her," Niz promised.

He hesitated. "I know it probably sounds silly, seeing as how we can't even communicate, but I like spending time with your sister."

It didn't sound silly to her. It had been the same way with her and Alex when he first visited her village. Thankfully, he was quick to learn their language, and she'd been motivated to learn English. "I know you do," she answered honestly.

"Do you think she might like spending time with me?" he asked shamelessly.

Niz laughed and shrugged. "Believe me when I say I have no idea what Cloud Walking is thinking. She's a bit of a mystery these days." She glanced at her mother, who was now in a heated discussion with Cloud Walking. "You'd better get back to the major, and I'd best get back to picking berries."

Sergeant Green nodded, but he looked disappointed.

Niz started to turn away and then stopped. "You've always been kind and respectful—to me, and now to Cloud Walking. Thank you for that. I think you're an admirable man, Sergeant Green."

He swept the cap off his head and held it in both hands. His face was serious again, as it had been every other time she'd seen him. "When I joined the army and they sent me out West, my pa said the Indians were savages. After seeing the aftermath of the raids that have been taking place, I almost wondered if it were true. But knowing you and your sister, seeing how you live in your village, how you stick together and how worried you were about your sister who was sick . . . having watched how you helped the soldiers who were wounded and taught Ms. Langston how to bake something decent to eat . . . Well, I don't see savages, I see people just like me. Truth be told, I suppose savages come in every size, shape, and color . . . I've seen some with white enough skin. But I suppose kindness, loyalty and good, honest people do too."

Niz smiled. "I like that, Sergeant Green. I agree. And I'm glad to know we've been able to help you see our people in a different light." She paused. "My people often see the white men as savages . . . they frequently take what doesn't belong to them, attack without being provoked, and treat us poorly. But you have shown my sister and I the truth of your words—that good men come in every color."

The serious young man gave her a slow nod of understanding. "I'm glad to be counted among them. I hope you consider me, the major, and Ms. Langston your friends. If you ever need anything, don't hesitate to come to anyone of us." He put his cap back on his head, tipped it to her, and started back toward his patrol.

"Oh, Sergeant Green, there is one thing. I asked the major, too, but he's got so much on his mind so in case he forgets, will you tell Ms. Langston I say hello? I miss her. And please, if she bakes you men something, tell her you enjoy it, even if she burns it or forgets the sugar."

Sergeant Green smiled. "Since you came to stay, she's been baking up a storm, and so far, all of it that I've tried has been edible. So thanks for that."

Niz beamed, glad that her friend was succeeding in her new skills.

"And as for saying hello, I doubt Major Taylor will forget. He's a man of his word. And he'll be over there for dinner when we get back, so he'll have the chance."

"Will he?" Niz asked, trying to sound casual.

"Yeah. Ms. Langston must really enjoy cooking now because he's there for dinner whenever we're not out on patrol. We used to be able to find him at home in the evenings, but anymore we know to go straight to her place if we need him. There's going to be a lot of broken hearts at the fort here soon. Anyway," Sergeant Green lifted his hand in farewell, "tell Cloud Walking I had a really good time with her."

Niz watched the young man leave, a myriad of emotions playing across her heart. Pursing her lips, she looked to where Ezra was lounging against the trunk of an aspen, his cap tipped over his face.

She'd encouraged him toward Marigold and Marigold toward him, and she would again in a heartbeat—she wanted them both to be happy. But something about finding out that Ezra joined her friend for dinner every night and that his men looked for him at her house before his own, made her sad. A hint of longing stirred in her heart. Maybe if things had been different . . .

But they weren't. So she would put on her bravest smile and be glad about the announcement Sergeant Green had insinuated was coming. After all, two of her favorite people, despite their individual heartaches, had been able to find a way to love again—that was something to celebrate.

Niz kissed Walks at Night's cheek and made her way back to her mother and sister and the berry picking. As she did, her thoughts returned to the conversation she'd just had. Though she wanted Cloud Walking to accept Strong Pine and settle down in the village, if her sister was determined to like the sergeant, at least Niz couldn't fault her choice. She got the feeling that Sergeant Green was one of the good ones.

Returning to the group, she found Cloud Walking not speaking to Shy Fawn, and thus Shy Fawn was not speaking to Niz. Steering clear of the drama, she busied herself picking berries, watching Walks at Night, and chatting with the women around them. Within an hour, Cloud Walking's mood had improved, and Shy Fawn couldn't resist her youngest daughter's gentle teasing, respectful questions, and charming smiles for long. Reluctantly, Shy Fawn began speaking to Cloud Walking and then to Niz until they were all—carefully—enjoying the day together once more.

The subject of the soldiers was not broached again until afternoon when the women were nearly ready to head home, having picked all the berries they would take from the patch. Niz sorted out a medium-sized basket full of the fruit, took a deep breath, and approached her mother. "I'm going to quickly deliver these to Major Taylor. Don't leave without me."

Shy Fawn looked at her sharply, and Niz could see the protest building on her face. She held up her hands. "It's a fair trade, Mother. They stopped their patrol to stay and watch out for us. We should at least give them a snack in return."

She watched as her reasoning hit home. Holding her hand up to shield her eyes, Shy Fawn looked out at the soldiers, where they still rested among the aspens. "Fine, but why does it have to be you?" she questioned.

Niz held out the basket. "Be my guest," she invited. After what Sergeant Green had shared earlier, and her dilemma about whether or not to tell Ezra about Fire Maker, she wasn't eager to face him again anyway.

Shy Fawn looked startled and didn't move to take the basket. "I don't know their words."

"You don't have to talk to them, Mother. You can just hand it to them. You know Major Taylor."

"I'll take it!" Cloud Walking offered, her face hopeful.

Shy Fawn's eyes narrowed. "You go, Nizhoni, but make it quick. Don't stay and talk."

Leaving Walks at Night with her mother so she could move faster, Niz hurried toward the group of soldiers, eager to be done with her errand and on her way home. Seeing her coming, Ezra stood and came to meet her. When he smiled, his dark hair tousled from his rest, his cap and jacket having been discarded, and his broad shoulders stretching his cotton shirt, she couldn't help noticing that Marigold was getting a very attractive husband. She held her basket out toward him. "In trade for your protection today."

Looking in the basket, his eyes lit up. "It's a good trade. We'll enjoy these." He popped a few into his mouth.

"Yes, well, I imagine getting a good meal while you're out on patrol is difficult. Hopefully these will help, though I'm sure you'll still be eager to get back to Marigold's cooking," she finished, unable to help herself.

He looked up, surprised. Then he smiled, amusement dancing in his hazel eyes. "Yeah, it's basically the same meal every night, but she's just about perfected it."

"I'm glad." She was. She wondered which dish had become her friend's specialty, but she wasn't going to ask. It felt too nosy.

Reaching into his pocket, he pulled out two cookies wrapped in a handkerchief. "She's sure got the hang of these too. You must be a good teacher. I still have two cookies left. Would you like one?"

Niz shook her head, her eyes narrowing just a little. She was happy for them, but he didn't have to rub it in. "I've had lots of berries."

He chuckled. "I should have guessed. They're sweet this year."

"I've got to go. We're headed home."

"What about your basket?"

"Keep it." It could be a wedding gift. She turned and started back toward her mother.

"I'll bring it back when I come for your letter," he answered. "Thanks for the berries."

She raised her hand in farewell and continued to where Shy Fawn, Cloud Walking, and Walks at Night were waiting to walk home together.

Twenty-One

T he next morning, the women went to a different patch of buffaloberries. They spent the entirety of the beautiful September day in the sunshine, gathering the pretty red berries and then laying them out to dry. Having gathered all they would take from that area too, they walked further the next day to the last patch they picked from every year. That evening, the braves returned from their hunt, and the following three days were full of processing animals and drying meat and berries.

With Ever Flowering getting stronger by the day and Walks With Power back in camp, Niz knew it was time to return to her own wickiup. She was reluctant to do so, worried about how things would go with Fire Maker. Still, he was her husband, and her place was with him. She determined she would move home that night. In less than three weeks' time they would leave for their winter camp, and she might as well make peace with him before then.

With her decision made, Niz continued to thinly slice elk meat and drape it over the drying rack, but in her heart she worried. Realizing her thoughts had become anxious again, she began to pray instead, asking for God's help in the situation.

Though she needed to face Fire Maker, she didn't know how to move forward. He was her husband, and she had made a commitment to him. Still, she had Walks at Night's safety to think about as well as her own. In addition, Fire Maker was protecting a band of raiders who were using violence against innocent people. If her suspicions were correct, he was profiting from the Comanche's presence and double-crossing the army.

Fire Maker had sold horses to Ezra on two occasions since she'd returned home able to read. As she'd been tending Ever Flowering, Niz had not been part of the negotiations. The men had found a way to make it work through signs, and Fire Maker had brought the bills of sale to her at Ever Flowering's for her to read and sign on his behalf. She'd done so without argument but had been appalled at how much he was charging for his horses. She understood making a profit, but the price he was charging was nearly robbery. Still, the army seemed desperate. With the raids continuing, they were getting increased pressure from the settlers as well as their superiors to increase patrols. To increase patrols, they needed more horses. And with the surrounding towns being small and remote, to acquire multiple horses, they had to pay Fire Maker's exorbitant prices.

With such a steep price increase, even from what he had charged the army before, Niz had to think one of two things was going on. Fire Maker was either using the army's desperation to line his pockets heavily, or he was no longer simply selling the horses he and his friends had raided for—she suspected he was now selling the horses the Comanche were stealing as well and giving the raiders a share of the profits. If she knew her husband, it was probably both.

Every few days, there were new horses in the corrals, and the new ones were usually the ones missing after the soldiers rode away. Niz wondered if the Comanche knew Fire Maker was raiding, too, and if he was being honest with them on the prices he was charging the army. She imagined he was likely double-timing them also, saving more than his agreed upon share of the profit, assuming they would never know the difference. If he was, she worried about what the Comanche would do to them if they found out.

If she told Ezra about Fire Maker, he would have to apprehend him. And she wasn't sure he could keep his enraged men from attacking the village in order to do so. The soldiers already disliked her husband with a passion, but if they found out he was helping the Comanche, she feared there would be a swift and lethal retribution. Even if her people survived the army's response to Fire Maker, what if the Comanche found out she'd exposed him? They would certainly be even more incensed by their lucrative deal being blown than they had been by Fire Maker supplying the army with horses in the first place, which had led to their initial attack. There was danger to her people on every side. The safest option seemed to be to keep her mouth shut. But still, that came with its own price. It might be safest for her people, but it continued to put innocent settlers in danger. She wrestled with the dilemma every minute of every day.

That night, she summoned her courage and returned to her wickiup as planned. Dread and anxiety filled her heart as she waited for Fire Maker, but he never came home. The next morning, she learned that Black Bear and Tall Peak had been out all night as well. Hunting, their wives had innocently said, but Niz didn't buy it.

Leaving Black Bear's wickiup with Walks at Night in tow, she wandered out to the corrals and stood looking out over the horses. Noticing an Appaloosa she hadn't seen before, she recognized that the herd continued to grow. Bowing her head, Niz prayed no one had been injured by whatever her husband and his friends had been up to during the night. She expected that when they returned, there would be more unfamiliar horses in the corrals. She could only hope they didn't come back with blood on their hands as well.

Sighing, she watched Walks at Night admire the horses before turning her attention to the landscape surrounding her. Tall and watchful, the pines stood along the back edge of the corrals, their needles whispering secrets in the breeze that only the mountains seemed to understand. Fluffy white clouds floated lazily across the vibrant blue sky. The smell of horses hung in the air. The temperature was crisp, but the sun was warm on her back, and squirrels were chattering in the trees. Despite her worries, peace began to settle over her; both creation and the Creator speaking to her troubled heart.

A group of young braves were busy tending the horses, and she watched, enjoying the rhythmic motion of their brushing. When they finished their chore, they secured the gate of the corral and put away their supplies, joking back and forth as they did so. Getting carried away, the joking turned to shoves, and White Bird's son, Lone Owl, ended up on the ground. The boy was quick to jump to his feet and grab hold of his brother, who had shoved him, grappling back and forth until the brother ended up in the big water trough they had just filled for the horses. The onlookers laughed heartily. Jumping over the side of the trough, the dripping boy took off after Lone Owl, who ran, laughing, out into the trees. The rest of the group ran along behind, whooping and hollering, to see what would happen next. Niz shook her head and looked back down at Walks at Night, a smile tugging up the corners of her lips.

"Are you going to be silly like that when you grow up?" she asked, seeing he, too, had been watching.

Jabbering away, Walks at Night set off on his short little legs, clearly wanting to follow after the big boys. With a laugh, she scooped him up. "Not yet, my son. Not yet. You've still got some years to grow before you can run off with the likes of them."

More at peace than she had been since returning home, Niz turned back toward the village, ready to start on the day's tasks.

Hours later, she was grinding amaranth seeds in her wickiup wondering again when Fire Maker would get home, worrying about what she should do once he did, and fretting over what he'd been doing while he was away, when there was a loud commotion in the village. Hurrying outside to see what the fuss was about, she saw two of the young braves from earlier stumbling through camp. Both were covered in blood. One looked to be staying upright only because his friend was keeping him that way.

"What happened?" she cried, pushing her way to the front of the gathering crowd. When she drew near, she gasped in horror as she saw jagged wounds slashed across the less injured boy's arm and terrible bloody gashes across Lone Owl's back. Both young braves looked ready to collapse. Her stomach churned at the sight, and she swallowed hard as she reached out for Lone Owl, taking his weight off his friend. "What happened, Cold Night?" she asked again, addressing the more alert of the two.

"A bear," Cold Night panted.

The growing crowd gasped. Two women came back with Cold Night's mother running between them. She cried out as she saw her son, and those gathered parted for her. The nine-year-old fell into her arms.

Niz turned. "Where is White Bird?" she asked. She knew her friend would want to be with her son as well, and the badly injured boy would need her for what was coming next.

"She's at the river. Tall Meadow went for her," a woman nearby said.

Niz's dress was covered with Lone Owl's blood, and his skin was slick with it. She was struggling to keep him upright. With a sinking heart, she remembered how he'd slept on her floor with his mother and brothers the night the Comanche had attacked. He'd been so full of life then. Now, he hovered on the brink of unconsciousness, no doubt battling shock as his young body tried to cope with the loss of blood.

"Cloud Walking, hurry, help me get him back to White Bird's wickiup. Soaring Eagle, go for the medicine man. Dressed In Furs, find my mother and ask her to watch Walks at Night. He's napping. And someone find White Bird!" she said, taking charge.

The women ran off to do her bidding, and Cloud Walking hurried to help Niz with Lone Owl.

"Where were you?" Niz asked Cold Night, seeing the boy was limping along with his mother's help, following his friend.

"A few miles downriver. We were fishing when the bear came out of nowhere. It attacked Lone Owl, and when I tried to help him, it turned on me. When the bear ran at the soldiers, I grabbed Lone Owl and got away as fast as I could. I knew the bear would be able to smell the blood, so I kept us moving. I didn't quit, Mother. I wanted to quit, but I didn't. I knew that bear would be back if we gave him time to find us. It was right not to quit, wasn't it, Mother? Lone Owl lost a lot of blood, but I figured I had to get him back to the village."

Cold Night's mother was crying, assuring her son through her tears that he'd done very well.

"The soldiers?" Cloud Walking questioned, her head coming up.

"Yeah. We didn't know they were nearby. We were just fishing. But then when the bear attacked and we started yelling, they must have heard us. Their horses came at a run. They shot at the bear and got him in the shoulder. He had a hold of me then, but he dropped me and stood up tall. He gave the loudest growl I've ever heard and rushed them, forgetting all about me and Lone Owl. So I grabbed Lone Owl and started running into the trees." His story made his mother cry harder.

Having reached White Bird's wickiup, Niz and Cloud Walking lowered the boy they carried onto a mat. Turning him onto his stomach, Niz crouched down, beginning to assess his injuries.

"Did the bear attack the soldiers?" Niz asked as she worked.

"I don't know. I didn't look back," Cold Night said, wincing as his mother began cleaning his wounds.

"Which soldier shot the bear?" Cloud Walking asked as she came back with water for Lone Owl. Glancing up from the injured boy, Niz shot her sister a sideways look. Cloud Walking looked pale. If she'd had any doubt that her sister was sweet on Sergeant Green, she didn't anymore.

"How am I supposed to know? They all look the same!" Cold Night retorted testily, clearly in pain.

Cloud Walking looked at Niz with wide eyes. "What if it was the sergeant?"

"They're trained soldiers, Cloud Walking, and there had to be several of them. They surely know how to handle a bear," Niz said quietly as she worked to stop Lone Owl's bleeding. She prayed she was right. It would be just like Ezra to jeopardize his own safety for the sake of two kids.

"All I know is that if they hadn't come along when they did, we would have been goners for sure," Cold Night told them before inhaling sharply as his mother began using sutures to close his wounds. He tried to pull away, but the woman held him firmly in place, clearly more worried about his injuries than his comfort.

"I can't get the bleeding to stop," Niz finally admitted, alarmed. She blew at hair that kept falling in her face before finally breaking down and using her blood-covered hand to push it behind her shoulder. She had to figure out how to stop Lone Owl from losing so much blood or they would lose Lone Owl.

"You're going to have to cauterize the wounds," Cold Night's mother suggested, her eyes never leaving her own son's sutures.

Niz pressed her lips together as her hands began to shake. She'd never cauterized a wound before, and there were so many of them. But she would do whatever it took to help the boy. "Cloud Walking, add wood to the fire. Get it good and hot."

Cloud Walking did as she was told while Niz packed the boy's wounds with more of the grasses she was accustomed to using. As she did, she prayed for Lone Owl and for wisdom to know how to help him. Seconds later, White Bird ducked into the wickiup, her eyes wild with fear, the medicine man and Soaring Eagle right behind her. Niz let out a deep sigh of relief as the boy's mother dropped to her knees beside her son, and the medicine man came to help. Niz was happy to let them take the lead and simply follow their orders as they worked together to save the boy. In time, they got Lone Owl's bleeding stopped, his injuries cleaned, sutured, and bandaged, and both young braves put to bed.

Leaving the boys in the capable hands of their mothers, Niz walked wearily to the river beside Cloud Walking to wash.

"Do you think they'll make it?" Cloud Walking asked somberly, kneeling at the water's edge and splashing it up over her arms.

"Cold Night will."

"And Lone Owl?"

"We'll see. The next few days will be telling. If he manages to recover from the loss of blood, I think he'll make it. Unless infection sets in . . ." Niz's words trailed off, sorrow filling her.

The boy's gruesome injuries had been difficult to deal with, as was the realization that it could have been any of them. A bear could have just as easily come out of the buffaloberry bushes while they were picking, as Sergeant Green had warned. Knowing it was always a possibility in the mountains where they lived made it no easier to deal with when it happened.

The boys had taken their bows and arrows for protection, but they were young and inexperienced and had been caught by surprise. In the heat of the moment, they likely hadn't had the presence of mind to use them—or else hadn't been able to get off a good shot. The same thing could happen to anyone. But what was most sobering was that she'd seen Lone Owl just that morning, being chased by his brother, yelling and laughing. As it had been with Leaping Water, it was difficult to comprehend—and accept—that a child could be so full of life one hour and fighting to stay alive the next. She thought of Walks at Night, and her heart constricted with fear; being a mother, loving another human being so much, was terrifying.

"Well, the poultice of yarrow and sagebrush you applied will help keep infections away," Cloud Walking pointed out. Niz nodded, hoping it would be enough. Though effective, there were still limitations. The teeth and claws of a bear were known for planting infections, and Lone Owl had sustained injuries from both. "And at least he has a better chance of living than he would have if the soldiers hadn't been nearby. The boys were lucky a patrol happened to be close and heard them yelling."

"That's very true." Niz washed her arms and hands, then started trying to get the blood out of her dress. "We're going to have to change and come back if we want to get these stains out."

Instead of heading back to her wickiup, though, Niz sat down on the riverbank, wrapping her arms around her knees and staring out over the high mountain valley. She needed a minute to collect herself before going back, finding Walks at Night, filling the village in on the young braves' tale, and starting dinner for Fire Maker—for whenever he returned. Cloud Walking sat down beside her. After several minutes of quiet, Niz turned to look at her sister.

"So, you're sure you're not interested in Sergeant Green?"

Cloud Walking had dismissed the idea as ridiculous, even after berry picking. Niz had suspected at the time that the teen was lying, possibly even to herself, but after the look on her sister's face earlier, she was now certain of it.

Cloud Walking blushed. "I thought I wasn't."

"And now?"

Cloud Walking leaned her head on Niz's shoulder with a sigh. "I don't know. All I know is that the possibility that he could have been hurt makes my stomach feel like it's tied in knots. I want to ride out and go find him, just so I can see for myself that he's okay."

Niz smiled sadly. "I understand."

"What do you think that means?"

Niz put her arm around Cloud Walking. "I think you'll know what it means when it's time," she told her, fighting the urge to express what she thought it meant and what should be done about it. "After all, you don't have to know how you feel right now. There's time."

"We'll be leaving for our winter camp soon."

Niz nodded, considering the peaks surrounding them. The tallest ones were already white with snow. "But we're not leaving today."

Cloud Walking was quiet for a moment before speaking. "Most of the time I think I'll accept Strong Pine. He's a good man."

"Yes, he does seem to be," Niz agreed. "What stops you?"

"I don't know. Every time I almost say yes, I just freeze . . . like I can't get the word out of my mouth. I start wondering if it's truly what I want, and what I should do, and if maybe there's something else waiting for me if I'm just brave enough to choose it."

"What else do you think is waiting for you?" Niz asked, forcing herself not to tell her sister it was just nerves and completely normal.

"I don't know. That's just it. I'm not sure what I'm waiting for." Cloud Walking paused. "Nizhoni, what if what I'm waiting for is Sergeant Green? It would mean leaving our village and our people . . . you and mother and Ever Flowering . . . it would mean living among his people, and that feels scary."

Niz bit her tongue. She knew what her mother would want her to say, but she couldn't say it. As difficult as it was, she knew her sister simply needed her listening ear, not her advice. "Well, that's something you're going to have to figure out. Take your time and make sure you mean whatever it is you decide. Marriage isn't something you want to rush into until you're certain."

Cloud Walking nodded. "Thanks, sister."

Niz smiled, inhaling deeply, thankful that at last, Cloud Walking had opened up to her. And it had happened when she wasn't trying to pry it out of her, wasn't offering advice, and wasn't stressed about what her sister would decide. "You're welcome."

She glanced back at the village, knowing she should get back. Spotting Fire Maker by the corrals, her heart plummeted. He'd returned.

"I'd better get dinner started," she said reluctantly.

Cloud Walking nodded and stood. "I'm sure mother's wondering where I am too."

"Hey, Cloud Walking, um, would you mind keeping Walks at Night with you tonight?"

"Because Fire Maker's back?" Cloud Walking's dark eyes were troubled.

Niz nodded honestly.

"Are you frightened about moving back home with him?"

"Yes," Niz admitted.

"You don't have to go home. You could stay with us too," Cloud Walking offered.

Niz took a deep breath and shook her head. "He's my husband. I need to face this. I can't run from it anymore."

Cloud Walking's expression was full of concern and sympathy, but she nodded. "We're not far away if you need us." She reached out and put her hand on Niz's shoulder. "If he starts being nasty, come stay with us. I'm going to have Walks With Power check on you later. If Fire Maker so much as lays a hand on you . . ."

Cloud Walking looked ready to fight at the thought of it, and Niz couldn't help but smile. Her baby sister really was like her. She was glad to hear Cloud Walking didn't know the full scope of what life with Fire Maker had been like. There were some things a little sister just didn't need to know.

"Thank you." Niz said, giving Cloud Walking a long hug before starting home.

As she walked, her steps were heavy. She hadn't been alone with her husband since she'd refused to translate for him; they'd barely spoken in the two weeks since. He'd been angry then, and if she knew him at all, she guessed he had only grown angrier with each day that passed, seeing her refusal and then absence as defiance. Though she knew it was the right thing to do to go home and face him, she was afraid of whatever punishment he had likely thought up to squelch her rebellion. But what she was even more afraid of was continuing on the way she had been—hiding at her sister's, denying reality, even to herself, pretending things were fine when they clearly weren't. She needed to face the truth. She needed to face Fire Maker.

Entering their wickiup, she started preparing their evening meal. When Fire Maker came in, he didn't say a word. He simply sat down by the fire and watched her. Niz tried her best to go about her business and not let his presence unnerve her, but her hands began to shake from the sheer strain of it. She prayed as she worked, praying that the God she now served could make a way where there certainly seemed to be none.

"Where were you last night?" she finally asked.

"Hunting," he answered with a mocking smile.

"Did you bring anything home that I need to see to?"

"No."

"You didn't have any luck, then?" she asked.

He smirked at her. "We did alright. We got what we went for."

Niz raised her head and looked at him squarely, meeting his eyes for the first time since he'd walked in the door. He was taunting her, challenging her to call him out. Instead, she dropped her eyes back down to the flatbread she was making. She was done talking to Fire Maker. She had just given him his last chance. It was time to go to Ezra.

What her husband was doing was wrong, and he clearly felt no remorse. She had hoped somehow things had changed. She had dared to dream that maybe he would come home miraculously repentant, or at the very least, simply done with raiding and ready to prepare for their coming move to the winter camp and all that entailed. But now it was clear that nothing had changed—and that it wouldn't change until someone changed it. The reality was that someone needed to be her.

Surely, if she went to Ezra and told him the truth about Fire Maker's actions, he could come up with a solution that would allow Fire Maker to answer for his crimes without their people paying the price. The Comanche could retaliate, but they would simply have to be ready. Their braves were strong. If they braced for an attack, they could likely defend their people without too much bloodshed. And it had come to a point that it was unavoidable. They were heading toward destruction no matter how one looked at it.

Fire Maker laughed low. "Too afraid to ask me any more of your questions?"

"I don't have any other questions," she responded truthfully. She already knew everything she needed to know. She'd talked to the Comanche, seen the horses, confronted her husband, and given him time to amend his ways. There was no doubt in her mind that Fire Maker was raiding. The evidence was all there; they were no longer simply speculations.

"Your hands are shaking," he observed, seeming pleased.

Niz didn't respond. She was fine letting him think she was scared. He would undoubtedly assume she was too frightened of him to do anything to stop him. But she wasn't. That had never been the problem. From the moment in the guardhouse when she realized he was raiding, it had always been that she was too frightened for her people and the consequences of his behavior that would fall on them. But now, what she was most frightened of was doing nothing. She would have to entrust her people to Almighty God while she did the right thing that was before her to do.

Fire Maker was just taking a breath, clearly getting ready to speak again when suddenly, for the second time that day, there was a commotion outside. They both looked toward the door. Seconds later, Black Bear stuck his head in their wickiup. "Fire Maker! There's a soldier approaching on horseback."

"Just one?" Fire Maker asked, a frown filling his face.

Black Bear nodded, and Fire Maker stood and quickly followed his friend. He turned back at the door. "Why don't you come? I'm sure you'll want to visit with your major, and he might need you to translate for him again."

Niz bit her tongue and took a deep, calming breath as she stood to follow. Her indignation wanted to remind Fire Maker that she was an honorable and faithful woman, but there was no point. Her protests wouldn't accomplish anything. He wasn't concerned with the truth, only with what served his interests. Deep down, she knew he already knew anyway.

When she stepped out into the early evening sunshine and shielded her eyes with her hand, she saw that it wasn't Ezra who was riding in. In fact, Niz didn't recognize the soldier. He was clearly in a hurry, though, and he looked agitated, even from a distance. When he drew near, he reined in his horse but stayed mounted.

"Fire Maker, Major Taylor sent me. He's located the band of Comanche that have been terrorizing the settlers as well as your people. He's been tracking them all day, and his mounts are tired. We've been on patrol for days. We were supposed to return home to the fort today, but then we picked up their trail. We've run out of supplies, and the fort is too far away to go for more. He knows you just returned from a hunt and have had a good season gathering berries and asks if you could loan him fifteen horses and send food for his men. He'll return the horses tomorrow once the raiders have been caught."

Niz did her best to translate as fast as the soldier was talking, and she could see the urgency of the situation in the young man's hurried words. When she finished, she waited breathlessly to see what Fire Maker would say.

Her heart raced as she tried to wrap her mind around this new bend in the road. Could it truly be that the nightmare of the raiding party was almost over? If so, she would no longer have to jump at noises in the night, worrying that they were sneaking back into camp, live in fear of the Comanche finding out Fire Maker was double-crossing them, or fret about their relations with their neighbors growing more troubled by the day. Finally, the raiders would be caught, and they could go in peace to their winter camp. Perhaps by the time they returned at the beginning of summer, they would again be able to go freely into town for supplies without fear of attack or arrest. After so much trouble, it was nearly over. She watched Fire Maker expectantly.

He stared at the soldier for a long moment and then tipped his head. "Who is this Major Taylor?" Fire Maker scoffed. "There are many white men roaming our lands, tearing up the earth with their plows, and killing our wild game. Many of them claim to be in charge. Why should I send my horses to some man who claims to be a major? Why should I take the meat I've hunted for my people and the berries I've picked to sustain us through the winter and give it to a man I don't know?"

Niz stared at her husband for a moment, too stunned to translate his words.

Fire Maker raised his brows at her in challenge. "Translate it," he said.

"Fire Maker, why act as if you don't know Major Taylor?" she whispered in dismay.

"Do I?" he challenged.

"Yes, you do! It's foolish to pretend as if you don't!" she cried. She pressed her fingertips against her forehead in despair, trying to get ahold of herself. "Fire Maker, he's asking for horses he'll return so he can capture our common enemies!"

Fire Maker's face darkened. "Nobody asked you! The soldier is here to talk to me. Now do your job and translate my answer."

Niz stared at him, seething with anger, frustration, and dismay. Here was a peaceful way out—for him, for their people. He could loan the soldiers the horses, send them a meal or two worth of food, the Comanche would be caught, their people would leave for their winter camp on good terms with the army, and their people and their hunting rights would be safe. And yet he was right—the soldier was asking him, not her.

"You didn't hunt the meat or gather the berries he's requesting. Why not consult your braves or the elders and let them help decide?" she whispered imploringly, desperate to convince him to change his answer.

"Do you dare to question me?" Fire Maker ground out, stepping close to her. His fingers dug into her flesh as his hand closed painfully around her arm. His eyes were burning, and his voice was hard. "Tell him."

Wincing, she turned slowly. Ashamed to be speaking the words, she translated Fire Maker's answer to the soldier. She watched the young man's face fill with outrage. Without another word, he spun his horse and rode back out of camp.

Fire Maker released her with a shove and laughed as he watched the soldier riding off toward the north. Turning toward Black Bear, he said, "As if I'd share our food and horses with the army!

For free! Surely they know me better than that." They both roared with laughter as if it were a great joke.

Fire Maker looped his arm around his friend's shoulders, and they went off together. Tall Peak fell into step beside them as they headed toward Black Bear's wickiup. There was little doubt they planned to celebrate their perceived victory over the army. Niz knew they would likely drink the night away until they were deeply intoxicated. There was a fifty-fifty chance Fire Maker would even make it home when they were through. It was just as likely he would pass out at Black Bear's.

Her heart sinking, she watched them go. Her husband had foolishly just squandered their best chance at peace. She felt the despair of it all the way through her body. Her stomach felt unwell, and her hands were shaking again. Any hope there had been of Ezra showing them compassion even after hearing of Fire Maker's treachery had surely just disappeared—or would once he heard his soldier's tale. This time, Fire Maker had gone too far.

Twenty-Two

"Nizhoni."

Niz turned shakily from watching Fire Maker leave with Tall Peak and Black Bear. Several of the braves were gathered behind her. Walks With Power was among them, as was Strong Pine. All of them had troubled eyes and solemn faces. She tipped her head and raised her eyebrows in question, unclear as to why they had stayed to talk to her. With Fire Maker in camp, it was him they should go to.

Walks With Power stepped forward. "We overheard that the major sent his soldier to Fire Maker, and that Fire Maker insulted him."

Niz nodded. That was certainly true. And she needed to figure out what she was going to do as a result. She had a premonition that her husband had just made a very grave mistake. Whatever the braves wanted, she hoped it would be fast, because she needed to think.

Walks With Power's brows drew together, his expression growing more troubled. "Nizhoni, the major's men have treated us well. When we were out on our hunts, we weren't hurt, nor did we miss anything as long as they were nearby. They've been like a wall to us, and to our people. Not only have they not taken from us, they've given us much without asking anything in return."

Niz couldn't hide her surprise. The braves had come to speak to her on behalf of the soldiers? Though what they said was true, she was shocked to hear them put words to it.

"They returned our horses that the Comanche had stolen," Stands Tall added.

"They defended our women and children when we were away and the Comanche came here to raid," Lean Elk said. "Though we suffered a great loss, if it weren't for them, we would have lost many more." The brave stopped talking, his face screwed up in pain. Niz's heart ached for him. She reached out and gently squeezed his arm, thinking of the darling daughter he had lost. No one knew better than Lean Elk how costly that raid had been. The men around him nodded their agreement.

"It's true that they've done much for us," Walks With Power continued. "They've seen to our women's safety, saved our young braves from a bear, and taught you to read so you can help our people. So, Sister, consider carefully what you will do." Her brother-in-law let out a deep sigh. "Because we believe Fire Maker's foolish actions are going to bring harm to our people. And he's so irrational that we can't even speak to him and make him see reason. No one can."

"You think the soldiers will retaliate." It was a statement more than a question.

"How can they not?" Lean Elk asked solemnly. "Fire Maker has repaid their good with disrespect. No one defies the army like he has and gets away with it."

Niz looked to where the soldier was still visible riding off toward the north. Turning, she spent a moment watching where Fire Maker had disappeared with Black Bear and Tall Peak. Finally, she turned back to the braves. They were saying what she knew in her heart. Something had to be done.

~~~

Ezra clenched his jaw as he listened to his soldier report what Fire Maker had said. He looked out over the high mountains trying to remain calm, but his blood began to boil.

He had been patient with Fire Maker for weeks, understanding that the mountain people had been wronged by the white man time and time again. He understood that they were angry. How could they not be when they were suddenly restricted as to where they could hunt, fish, travel, and live after being on the land for countless generations? The way the government had treated the natives was deplorable. And he had been determined to rewrite the story, as far as it depended on him.

But Fire Maker was maddening.

The man was unreasonable, selfish, and cruel. He seemed to be mean-hearted all around. Watching how he treated Niz had caused Ezra to see red, but that was only the beginning. Fire Maker's behavior with his wife was only confirmation of the kind of man he was. In business, as a person, and as a leader, he had shown his true nature time and time again, and now Ezra had seen enough.

Fire Maker spoke down to him every chance he got, ripped him off, and cheated the army. What was more, he suspected Fire Maker had been lying to him for weeks about the Comanche. He had refrained from taking action, trying to give him the benefit of the doubt, wanting to make peace, not war. But Fire Maker had insulted him, taunted him, disrespected him, spat on him, and ridiculed his men one too many times.

For weeks, Ezra's pleas to work together for the good of everyone had been laughed at. Now, when Ezra had asked only to borrow fresh horses and have a little bit of food for his men while they chased down the raiders who had targeted Fire Maker's people along with their own, Fire Maker had denied his request. And not only had he denied it, but he had refused to even acknowledge that he knew who Ezra was.

He and his men had spent weeks protecting Fire Maker's braves, his village, his people, and his wife, and still the man treated them with contempt and disrespect. Ezra filled with fury at the injustice of it.

He was the commanding officer of the local fort. He was a major in the United States Army. His men were trained soldiers who had risked their lives for Fire Maker's people. They had gone above and beyond, and the man had essentially spit in their faces again.

Behind him, his men were murmuring with anger and accusations. Their offense had been steadily building with each interaction they had with the chief. They took insults against their commanding officer personally, and Fire Maker had given them plenty of opportunities for insult. Added to that, their rage and horror had been increasing with each raided homestead they'd discovered. Ezra could relate; the raids had been terrible, the innocent victims heartbreaking, and their lack of success catching those responsible incredibly frustrating.

But that was about to end. He'd had his suspicions about Fire Maker's involvement in the raids; he had given him one last chance to disprove those suspicions and make his loyalties clear. And the chief couldn't have made them clearer. Now, he and his men would catch those responsible—*all* those responsible—and hold them accountable for their crimes. And Ezra meant to do so before the sun set again.

His soldiers grew louder as they discussed Fire Maker's slur, their volume rising as their conversations grew more heated. Ezra could tell their wrath was nearly beyond his ability to rein in, even should he want to. They now seemed as bent on Fire Maker's blood as they were on the Comanches'. To them, they were one and the same, cut from the same bad cloth. For once, he couldn't bring himself to disagree.

"What do you want to do, sir?" the messenger asked, having finished his report.

Ezra clenched and unclenched his jaw and opened and closed his fists, taking a moment to attempt to work out his frustration. He looked south toward Fire Maker's village—a village full of innocent people whose only crime was having a wicked scoundrel of a chief. Niz, Walks at Night, and their family were there.

But Fire Maker's terrible behavior could not be ignored any longer. It was too much.

Niz was a smart woman, he reasoned. If she had translated, then she knew what Fire Maker had said and would surely know the repercussions it would bring. He had to think she had gotten herself and her loved ones out of harm's way. And if her people elected to stay and stand with their chief, then they had made their choice. Fire Maker would pay for what he'd done, and if they stood with him, then they would pay, also.

Ezra's lips pressed together into a firm line. He turned his attention back to his men. They were angry, worn thin, and hungry for justice for a dozen victims. They were yearning for revenge. And so was he.

His attempt to give himself a moment to calm down had been unsuccessful. Instead, his thoughts had continued to spin, and his anger continued to grow.

Fire Maker had fought them every step of the way as they tried to apprehend the Comanche. Ezra figured the only reason a man like Fire Maker would do that would be if he was profiting off their presence. He'd had his suspicions for a while but had given him opportunity after opportunity to make a better choice for the sake of his people. Now, his chances had run out.

'Who is this Major Taylor?' Fire Maker had asked.

The answer was: the man the U.S. government had put in charge of keeping peace in the area. And keep peace he would—even if he had to use force to do so. His temper flaring, Ezra determined that Fire Maker would never forget his name again.

"Change course, men!" he yelled to be heard above the ruckus of thirty angry soldiers. "We'll deal with Fire Maker first and then the Comanche. All these weeks we have protected all Fire Maker has in vain. We've gone out of our way to make sure nothing of his was lost, and now this is how he's repaid us." His men roared with anger. "He's gone too far this time. We will not allow one thing to be left to Fire Maker come morning's light."

The soldiers shouted their approval.

Ezra ordered a third of his men to stay behind with the most fatigued horses and keep an eye on the Comanche, who had made camp on the other side of the ridge. Then he turned to the others.

All he had wanted were mounts to replace the weaker ones so they would be fresh if the Comanche tried to flee again—and dinner for his men. They would have left their tired horses with a few soldiers, apprehended the Comanche, returned Fire Maker's horses in the morning, and headed back to the fort. But even that had been too much to ask.

"Head out!" Ezra commanded, and his troops swung into their saddles, their weapons at hand. The ground shook with the thundering sound of hoofbeats as twenty angry soldiers started off toward Fire Maker's village.

~~~

Niz's brown eyes were troubled as she looked out at the tall peaks surrounding the village. She decided that she had three options. First, she could refrain from taking action and hope nothing would come of Fire Maker's insult. Ezra had shown restraint and a willingness to overlook his bad behavior in the past, perhaps he would again. Secondly, she could get her loved ones out of camp and leave Fire Maker to face whatever consequences might come as a result of his actions; after all, it wasn't as if he didn't deserve it. Lastly, she could respond to the braves' plea and figure out a way to intervene and stop whatever retaliation the army might have planned. The latter could be the most dangerous option of all. If she did the wrong thing, the soldiers were unwilling to be appeased, or her husband found out, the result could be disastrous. Her mind hummed, going over her options, trying to make a plan.

As she stood there, she realized there was someone else she needed to consult. In the past, she would have made a decision and gone forward with it, assuming she knew best. But that wasn't the case anymore. Now, she knew she didn't necessarily know what best was. Her understanding was limited. She had determined to submit her plans to the One who knew all things, so even with the braves watching her, she would seek to be led by His Spirit rather than her own.

"My understanding it limited," she prayed silently. "I only see in part. Please, LORD, show me what You would have me do. Give me wisdom. Help me know how to partner with You to protect the innocent."

There was no audible voice, no clear direction or startling revelation that came in answer. But as she looked out over her village again, there was a quiet plan that started taking shape within her.

"Lean Elk is right. No one defies the army like Fire Maker has and gets away with it," Walks With Power told her. "So, Sister, what are you going to do?"

Niz watched her brother-in-law for a long moment and then looked over the small group that had gathered. Inhaling deeply, she reminded herself that even though she was a woman, the braves standing before her were looking to her for wise leadership and guidance. They trusted her discernment. She didn't want to let them down. Though she wasn't certain the plan in her mind was from God, she had prayed for help, and the one idea was all she had. She would simply have to trust that it was enough. She gave them a decisive nod. "You're right. Something has to be done."

It was true that the army had been unfair, unkind, and dishonest to her people in the past. Some of the soldiers had been unbridled, violent men, full of hatred and greed. But that was some, not all. Her people had been living mostly at peace with those at the fort for many years now. And in the past several weeks, under the command of Ezra Taylor, the soldiers had been nothing but good to them. She would not allow them to be repaid for their kindness in such a way. And she would not allow her people to pay the price of her husband's folly.

"Go ready twenty of our horses, plus enough for you and me," she directed. "I'll gather food and bring it to you. Work quietly.

Don't let the others know what you are doing. Fire Maker cannot find out about this. Not yet."

The braves nodded in unison, relief written across their faces. "What you're doing is wise, Nizhoni," Lean Elk said. "I think grandfather would agree. If the major isn't too angry to receive your gift, perhaps our people and our village will be spared."

Niz nodded, encouraged by his words. The idea of having the support of one of their elders was reassuring. She prayed Lean Elk was right. She also prayed Ezra wouldn't be so furious over Fire Maker's slight that he would be unreachable. He'd always been a reasonable man, but even reasonable men had their limits. Niz just hoped he hadn't reached his.

Leaving the men to their task, she turned and hurried through the village. Ducking into her mother's wickiup, she started talking in hushed tones before the hide even swung closed behind her.

"I need your help. Both of you. We need to gather dried meat, berries, and nuts. Enough for three meals for thirty men. And we need to do it as fast as we can and quietly. No one can know what we're doing. Cloud Walking, get the meat. Mother, please gather the nuts. I'll gather the berries. Meet me back here once you have it," she instructed, swinging Walks at Night to her hip when he ran to her.

"Why?" Shy Fawn asked, clearly surprised to see her.

"There's no time to explain now. I'll tell you later," Niz promised, leaving again after giving Walks at Night a kiss and setting him down, leaving him where he would be safest.

Niz hurried as she worked. Time was of the essence. She knew it was likely that Ezra and his soldiers were growing angrier by the minute. While she hoped she was wrong, she had a feeling they wouldn't wait to take their revenge. They must be tired and hungry, and it was a dangerous combination when added together with anger, frustration, and offense. She had to reach them before they reached the village.

Once the food was gathered, she summoned the braves, and they helped her carry it to the horses and secure it. "Go on ahead," she told them. "I must fill in my mother and sister and speak to anyone who notices you riding out with the horses, so our plan isn't ruined. Once I have, I'll come behind you."

Walks With Power nodded as he jumped onto the back of his horse. "We'll do as you say. Your mount is tied to the corral, Nizhoni."

The braves rode out, each of them leading a line of horses behind them. Turning back to the village, she waited a few minutes, watching for anyone who noticed or remarked about their leaving. Thankfully, most people were inside their wickiups, involved in evening routines; the few who were out and about and took notice, she quickly approached and swore to secrecy. Though Fire Maker would find out, she didn't want him to until morning and only once he was sober. Otherwise, there was no telling what his foolishness might lead to in his drunken state.

Satisfied that they were in the clear, she stopped briefly to talk to her mother and sister and kiss her son goodbye before hurrying to her mount. As she pulled herself up onto the spotted horse's back, she thanked God that her people had been open and responsive to her taking leadership. She wasn't concerned that anyone she'd spoken to would go to Fire Maker. Whatever happened in the morning, at least she had the night to make things right with Ezra and the army.

Leaning low over the horse's neck, she set out at a gallop, hoping to keep the braves within sight. As she rode north, she prayed with all her might. She prayed that Ezra would be gracious and responsive, that Fire Maker would stay unaware of what was transpiring, and that her people and their village would remain unharmed. She prayed that she would know the right words to say when she saw Ezra and that he would hear her despite his certain anger.

As she closed the distance between herself and the braves, her apprehension grew as adrenaline pumped through her veins. Cresting a hill and starting down the other side, she saw what she had feared—the patrol was riding toward them at a gallop down the opposite slope. Her heart plummeted. It was true—they hadn't waited to respond to Fire Maker's slight. Panic coursed through her. Even from a distance, they seemed angry and set on retaliation. And while she understood it—had even expected it since seeing the rage fill the soldier's face as she'd translated—it was terrifying.

Ahead of her were twenty armed soldiers set on taking revenge on her husband, who happened to be their chief. Behind her lay a beloved village full of people she loved dearly. In between were only the braves—who she was catching up to as she could ride faster without having a line of horses behind her—and herself.

She had no doubt that if the army pressed on to the village, Fire Maker would call on his warriors to defend him. He would likely give no thought as to who might be hurt in the process or what would become of their village. Like usual, he was sure to only care about himself. And if they followed Fire Maker's command and tried to hold off the soldiers, innocent people would undoubtedly get hurt.

Niz thought of her mother and sisters at home with Walks at Night. She was sure by now they had moved Ever Flowering to Shy Fawn's wickiup and that they were waiting there together. Closing her eyes, she could picture them all sitting around the fire hard at work on projects, trying to keep their minds off what she had told them. For just a moment, she wondered if she should have told them to leave the village. They could have easily slipped away in the fading light and hidden in the forest until she returned for them. At least then they would have been safe regardless of whether or not Ezra and his soldiers accepted her gift and allowed it to appease their anger.

But just as quickly as the thought entered her mind, she dismissed it. It wasn't just her mother, sisters, and son whom she loved and cared about. The village was full of aunts and uncles, cousins, and friends. Each person in the village was valuable and loved. How could she protect her mother and sisters and leave the rest to their fate? Soaring Eagle, Wise Hawk, Blue Flower and all the others were also sitting around fires, working on projects, preparing food and eating it together. White Bird was surely busy nursing Lone Owl back to health, and Cold Night was likely being fussed over by his mother. Her heart hurt as their faces filled her mind. Failure was not an option. Drawing in a deep breath, renewed in her determination to stop the soldiers, Niz urged her horse to go faster.

She was still resolved to tell Ezra about Fire Maker but not like this, and not right now. When the soldiers' hearts were bent on revenge, they would be hard pressed to act with wisdom. Innocent people would get hurt if they entered the village now.

Niz was just seconds behind the braves when they met up with the patrol. With their hands in the air signifying they came in peace, she heard Walks With Power repeatedly shouting "Friend," in English, just as she'd taught him. The soldiers reined in their horses, their expressions a mix of anger, confusion, and unease. Several had their weapons raised, appearing worried and bad-humored. The mounts could also clearly feel the energy in the air as both the soldiers' and the braves' horses sidestepped nervously.

Even across the distance separating them, Niz could almost feel the soldiers' dark rage. Still, though they looked furious, they weren't shooting . . . yet. That was something.

As she quickly closed the gap between them, she scanned the group of men. They were all dressed alike in dark uniforms and dark blue caps, making distinguishing one from another difficult. Even still, she searched for the one she sought—the only one who could stop the coming bloodshed.

Spotting Ezra, her heart gave a wild kick. Pushing her reaction aside, she reined her horse toward him. In the fading light of evening, his expression was unreadable under the shadow of his cap as he called out to his men. Niz's heart was racing, and fear drummed a frighteningly fast beat within her. She still didn't know what she would say—what one could say in such a situation. How could she diffuse the anger of a man who was justifiably angry? He had been patient with her husband and had chosen to overlook his insults more than she ever would have thought possible. Now, he'd clearly been pushed too far.

Ezra Taylor was a good leader, and a good man, but he was still human. He undoubtedly had limits, just like anyone, and hungry, tired, and frustrated after weeks without success, those limits had clearly been reached. She wasn't sure that anything she said at this point could make amends for her husband's behavior.

But be that as it may, the time to try had come. Reaching him, she whispered a frantic prayer for help as she stopped her horse and quickly slid down from its back. Turning to face him, she dropped to her knees on the rocky soil, ignoring the way the sharp gravel bit into her shins as she did so. The reality was, in that moment, she wasn't talking to her friend. She was talking to an army major who was doing his job.

His horse pranced nervously beside her, but she didn't move—the situation was too grave to be frightened by an antsy horse. When Niz opened her mouth, heartfelt words started tumbling out. "On me, sir, let this guilt lie," she pleaded, head bent. "Please blame me. Let me take the fault for this offense against you. But please let me speak to you and hear me out."

She heard the creak of his saddle as Ezra swung down to the ground. The nervous horse quieted.

"You may speak," Ezra answered, his tone stiff. She didn't take her eyes from the ground to see what his expression might be. It didn't matter. She was pleading for the lives of her people. She would talk as long as he would listen.

"Please don't listen to Fire Maker or pay attention to what he said. He's foolish and unwise," she continued. Every other time she'd spoken of her husband to Ezra, she'd done her best to show respect; now, she would respectfully speak the truth. "He's true to his name—he foolishly makes fires where none are necessary, and now he risks burning our people. I was not in a position to speak when your soldier came, only to translate. But now we've hurried out to meet you with horses and food for your men. Please take this gift we've brought you, sir, and give it to the soldiers who follow you. Forgive me, please, for this insult against you."

The wind at her back stirred her hair, whipping long dark strands across her face, but she didn't bother to push it back. She kept her head bowed, unwilling to look up. The fact was that her husband had behaved terribly. She didn't blame the soldiers for being angry. Still, she wanted more for them—for Ezra—than revenge would get them. In that moment, she realized it wasn't just Fire Maker, herself, or her people she was contending for. It was the man in front of her.

Though he was very much Major Taylor in that moment, she knew Ezra. He was the man who had refused to take revenge on his Comanche captives, committed instead to doing the honorable thing by allowing justice to be served through the ruling law of the land. Though he was currently blinded by anger, she knew him well enough to know that if he succeeded in doing whatever was in his mind to do, he was going to regret it. And she respected him too much to stand by and let that happen. She cared about him too much to let him carry guilt for the rest of his life. She admired him too much to let him do something he would feel remorse for. She wouldn't let him continue down this path that would ultimately hurt him without putting up a fight—a fight for him, for his character, and for his heart. She couldn't. Not when she loved him. Her eyes stung with tears as she realized the truth.

She loved Ezra Taylor.

That was why she wanted him to be happy with Marigold, why she needed him to simply be the major, and why she was suddenly so filled with the desire to save him from himself. She loved him. And she was married.

Niz could never love him as anything more than a friend and would never let herself walk that slippery slope. That wasn't the way of honor. But she could love him enough to do whatever she could in that moment to keep his conscience clean and his heart free.

"Major, as God has held you back from spilling blood and taking your own revenge, may all your enemies prove to be as foolish as Fire Maker. You are building a solid reputation among your men and those in government, as well as among my people," she told him, every word sincere. "You fight the right battles, sir. You fight for justice, for peace, and to protect the innocent and vulnerable. You're a good man, sir. There's no hatred in you. You live your life and command your troops in a way that's good and right and pleasing to Almighty God. Because of that, I know you will continue to see victory and promotion in your life, and when you do, sir, what happens tonight will not cause you grief nor will it cause anyone to speak ill of you because you were responsible for the bloodshed of the innocent or took your own revenge. You won't have to carry the guilt of having attacked our village out of anger. As you leave Fire Maker—and your revenge—to God, He will extinguish your enemies." Out of words, Niz stopped. She didn't know what else to say.

Her head still bowed, she prayed her words had been the right ones and enough, and that Ezra would listen to reason and be reminded of the man he was—and wanted—to be. If only he would turn from his desire for revenge and turn the course of his men as well. For his own sake as well as theirs.

All was quiet for a long moment. The soldiers were still, watching and waiting to see what their commanding officer would do. The braves were silent, holding their breath, hoping their village and their people would be spared. Niz stayed on the ground, praying Ezra would make a choice he could live with.

Finally, she heard him release a deep sigh above her. "Praise God," he breathed. "Stand up, Niz." He held out his gloved hand and when she took it, he pulled her to her feet. When she lifted her eyes to his face, she saw deep relief etched across it. "Praise God He sent you out here to meet me, for your good sense, and for keeping me from bloodshed and revenge. I had decided to go after Fire Maker and make him pay for what he's done, but you're exactly right—revenge doesn't belong to me. And revenge on him would have put you . . . all of you," he added, his gaze sweeping over the braves, "in danger." He drug his hand across his face and then met her eyes again. "You're a wise woman, Niz. Thank you. Truly."

Her breath caught at the admiration she saw shining in Ezra's eyes. She could see she had succeeded in doing more than stopping him from attacking her village; she had succeeded in saving him from remorse. And she had earned his respect in the process. That knowledge unfurled like something warm and beautiful inside her heart, like a flower blooming in the summer sun.

Not trusting herself to speak, Niz caught her lip between her teeth and simply nodded in reply, hoping he somehow knew how sincerely grateful she was. Turning, she motioned to the braves to bring their gift. Jumping down from their horses, they began unloading the supplies.

"They've brought us food and horses as I requested," Ezra said, turning to his men. "Take it. We'll eat and go after the Comanche." There was murmuring among his men, and he held up a hand to silence them. "Rest assured, we will bring Fire Maker to justice, but it won't be tonight. We'll apprehend the Comanche first."

Seemingly satisfied, his men dismounted and accepted the baskets of food from the braves.

"Thank you, Major," Niz said softly as Ezra turned back to face her. That one command to his men had just saved her village and the lives of her people. The night would no longer hold bloodshed for her loved ones.

"Thank *you*," he answered. "Tonight, you've kept me from becoming the kind of man I can't stand. I was acting out of rage, and I was seeking revenge instead of justice." He clenched and unclenched his jaw. "And I would have lived with the guilt of it the rest of my days." Though his voice was gruff, his eyes seemed moist in the lengthening shadows. She clasped her hands together to keep herself from throwing her arms around him in a hug of gratitude and relief.

"Then we both have much to be thankful for," she answered sincerely. Seeing the braves had unloaded the food and handed over the horses' leads, she took a step back. "I hope you catch the Comanche, Major Taylor. And please be safe."

He nodded, his expression serious, his eyes shining. Niz pulled herself back up onto the back of her spotted horse before turning it and starting south toward the village. The braves fell in beside her, and when she looked back, Ezra and his men were riding off in the opposite direction through the twilight.

Turning forward again, she thanked God for what He had done. By giving her the right idea, the right words, and softening Ezra and the soldiers' hearts, He had diffused an incredibly volatile situation. He had worked on their behalf and answered her prayers. Just like Mother Emaline had said, He had made a way.

As she marveled over that, sadness began to seep in alongside her joy. Niz felt overjoyed that her people were safe and Ezra hadn't done anything he would regret, but there was an equal part of suffering; she was in love with Ezra Taylor. And even though he was wonderful and kind and honorable, she was married to Fire Maker. They were worlds apart, just as they had always been—and as they would always be.

The sting of that settled like an ache in her chest and a lump in her throat, but as they drew closer to their village, fear began to overshadow both the suffering and the joy. Ezra and the soldiers had only been half the problem. Just because an imminent attack by the army had been averted, the danger had not passed. Not for her. Now she had to face her husband. And that might be scarier still.

They arrived back at their village all too soon. When Niz slid off her horse's back, she found that her legs were weak upon hitting the ground. The stress of the evening's events, as well as her fear of facing Fire Maker, had taken its toll. Her hands were shaking as she handed her reins over to Walks With Power.

He looked up at her, his smile fading. "What's wrong, Nizhoni? The trip was a success."

Niz looked off toward Black Bear's wickiup. "Yes, it was."

Walks With Power watched her for a long moment and then nodded his head. He looked toward the wickiup too. "He's likely still drinking firewater with Black Bear and Tall Peak. Best not to talk to him until morning."

"That's what I was thinking too," she agreed. It would help to wait until her husband was sober, but even then, he would still be furious with her. She clasped her hands together, trying to still their shaking, and raised her chin. It had to be done. There was no way around it.

Having tied their horses to the corral, the other braves gathered around, ready to discuss their successful trip. After they had for several minutes, Niz looked seriously at each of them. "When I talk to Fire Maker, I can tell him I acted alone, and leave you out of it," she offered, knowing they would each face his wrath if he knew they had helped with what he would view as treason.

Lean Elk shook his head. "We rode with you; we will stand with you."

Niz squared her shoulders, trying to look stronger than she felt. "Are you certain? He won't be happy. And Fire Maker isn't quick to forgive. I don't blame you if you want to stay out of it."

"What kind of men would allow a wife to take the fall for something they'd been part of? Tell him we helped you and that you had our full support," Walks With Power said, reaching out and clasping her shoulder as a brother might. The men around him added their agreement.

Niz's chin fell against her chest, and she pressed her lips together as she nodded. Relief flooded her. Facing Fire Maker was less scary if he knew she had acted with the support of some of his braves. But more than that, she was touched by how honorable the men who stood before her were. They could have hidden behind anonymity and saved themselves from their chief's wrath. Instead, they were electing to face it with her. It was a weighty reminder of how most of the men in their village were—brave, honorable, and strong.

"In fact, don't tell him without us," Walks With Power continued.

"You don't have to be there," she protested. It wasn't going to be pretty.

"Yes, we do." Walks With Power's face was grim, and Niz realized he understood what could happen if she told Fire Maker the news by herself. She simply nodded, thankful beyond words. "We'll all come for the morning meal, and you can tell him then," he offered.

"Make plenty, because I always wake up hungry," Strong Pine added, sending her a playful smile.

Niz smiled back. "Are you sure you guys aren't just trying to get a free meal?" she teased, thankful Strong Pine had lightened the mood.

"Cooked by you, Sister?" Walks With Power asked with a grin. He squeezed her shoulder and then released her. "Always!" He started walking toward the corral with his horse and hers. "Sleep at Shy Fawn's tonight," he suggested as he went through the gate. "And tell Ever Flowering I'll be by for her as soon as I see to the horses."

Weighing her options as the braves dispersed, Niz decided to take her brother-in-law's advice. She went back to Shy Fawn's wickiup, ate the dinner they had saved for her, and played with Walks at Night. It was soon time to lay him down for the night, and with a grateful heart, she sang him to sleep as she smoothed the fine hair out of his face with a rhythmic motion. Her son would be safe as he slept. That was something to be thankful for, no matter what unpleasantness the morning held.

Once Walks at Night was sleeping, his young face peaceful and relaxed, Niz went back to the fire and sat up talking with her mother and sister. She told them about their meeting with the soldiers in hushed tones, not wanting to waken her son or for anyone passing by to overhear.

"Nizhoni, when Fire Maker finds out what you've done . . ." Tears welled up in Shy Fawn's brown eyes as Niz finished her tale.

"I know, Mother, but the braves will be with me when I tell him," Niz offered in consolation.

"They won't always be," Cloud Walking pointed out grimly.

"You shouldn't have gone," Shy Fawn scolded, wiping her eyes.

"Shouldn't have I?" Niz questioned incredulously. "What would you have had me do, Mother? Fire Maker has behaved terribly. Major Taylor and the soldiers were on their way here to take their revenge."

"You can't blame them," Cloud Walking added.

"But why did it have to be you? You should have let someone else go!"

"Who, Mother? He's my husband! I'm the wife of the chief! It had to be me. I had to try to make amends for my husband's foolishness. Should I have just sat back and hoped someone else would go in my place?"

Shy Fawn put her head in her hands. "Oh, I don't know. You saved our people from heartache by going, Nizhoni, but I fear you will pay the price with your own."

"I didn't save our people, Mother. It was Almighty God," Niz told her sincerely. "He's the One who gave me the words to speak. He's the One who made them ring true to Major Taylor. And He's the One who will be with me when I face my husband—tomorrow and in the days ahead."

"Nizhoni! I told you never to speak of your new God again!" Shy Fawn said severely.

"I can't not speak of him! I prayed tonight and—"

"That's enough!" Shy Fawn commanded, holding up a hand to silence her daughter.

Niz stopped, but her eyes flashed. How could she not speak of the One who had saved their village and their people? They were all sitting safely around their fires, with whole homes and hearts because God had moved Ezra to relent. They had watched Ever Flowering stand up and walk home with her husband earlier because God had healed her. How could Niz stay quiet about that? Yet she held too much respect for her mother to continue speaking. She would be silent for now . . . but not forever. And in the meantime, she would pray that her mother's heart would be softened.

Cloud Walking graciously asked for help on the fringe of her new leggings, and Shy Fawn leaned over to assist her. The conversation moved on, and soon they all settled down for the night. Fears about the next morning tried to arise inside of Niz, but she closed her mind to them, choosing to pray instead. When she was done praying, she kept her mind silent, knowing nothing good would be accomplished by spending her night worrying. Instead, she would get a good night's sleep and trust that the same God that had undoubtedly changed the heart of a major could handle her husband.

Twenty-Three

N iz woke while it was still dark. Her mind instantly started spinning, going over the events of the night before and worrying about the day ahead until she knew there was no way she could sleep again. Quietly, she stood and left her mother's wickiup. Ducking out into the crisp morning air, she saw that the sky in the east was just beginning to lighten. After glancing around the quiet village, she decided to go for a walk in hopes of quieting her troubled heart.

Full of apprehension, she wove her way through the wickiups and ended up walking along the river—a place that always quieted her mind and brought her comfort.

Water was life to her people. They cherished it and respected it. They knew how to find it, and they shaped their lives around it. Without it, they knew they wouldn't last long. Because of that, she had always loved to walk along the riverbanks, watching how the water rushed around bends and splashed against rocks. It was so steady, so sure, so determined. When obstacles found their way into the river, be it boulders or fallen trees, the water simply went around them, continuing along its course on the other side. As she watched it again in the early morning light, she wished she could be so graceful and determined, so undisturbed by the obstacles of life.

Though she was thankful for how the situation the night before had ended, she was frightened about facing Fire Maker and worried about what their future held. Her husband was a difficult man. He was arrogant and cruel, harsh and selfish. She didn't trust his reactions or his judgment. His braves were right—no one could reason with him, least of all her. Yet, she couldn't help hoping that somehow, someway, he would be reasonable and understand why they had done what they'd done. If he didn't, there would be no persuading him. And her mother and Cloud Walking were right. The braves would only be with her for so long before she would face him alone. The very thought of it made her feel shaky. "Almighty God, please help me," she whispered into the stillness of the morning.

If she knew her husband at all, she felt sure he was counting her trespasses. Her refusal to translate when Ever Flowering was sick had been two weeks ago, yet she had no doubt it had not been forgotten, nor had she been forgiven. Added to that was the time she'd spent away, which he would undoubtedly see as her neglecting her duties to him, and now this latest indiscretion, which would certainly make him angriest of all. He would see it as betrayal and blatant defiance. To a man who fed off being in control, thinking of how he would respond filled her with a sinking dread.

Still, she would not go back and change what she'd done, even if she could. She wasn't the kind of woman who could sit on her hands and watch suffering happen. She couldn't stand by and watch someone be mistreated, nor remain silent when something had to be said. If Fire Maker had wanted a wife who would be timid, quiet, and afraid, he'd married the wrong girl. She simply couldn't do it. Though she would continually strive to act with as much grace and wisdom as possible, she would not sit by and let him hurt others. Where that left them, she didn't know. Their marriage, their life together, building a family—it all felt completely impossible.

She'd given up on love, camaraderie, or even civility within their marriage. All she dared to hope for was safety—for herself, Walks at Night, and their people. And even that felt unattainable with Fire Maker at the helm.

Sitting down on the bank of the river, she took a deep, steadying breath and wrapped her arms around her knees. Despite her inner turmoil, she couldn't help but notice the beauty spread out before her. The pale morning sky was baby blue, and blushing hues of gold over the eastern mountains announced the rising sun. The few wispy clouds suddenly bloomed rosy as the first sunrays touched them, and Nizhoni watched in wonder as the blinding, golden orb appeared over the ridge.

No matter how many times she'd watched the sunrise, it always felt new. Each morning it whispered of fresh hope and new possibilities, and she basked in its ability to shatter the heavy clouds of discouragement that had gathered during the midnight hours. Delighted by the beauty, a smile touched her lips as the robins, thrushes, and mountain bluebirds began their morning songs. A light breeze ruffled her hair as it danced over the golden grasses of autumn and swirled through the changing leaves of the aspens.

Breathing deeply, she filled her lungs with the scent of the river, moist soil, and pungent pines. Slowly, her heart quieted within her. As it did, peace settled. And this time, it wasn't simply the momentary peace that came from a beautiful view; it was that alongside the peace she had only known since the night she'd cried out to Jesus Christ the Son of God. She breathed deeply of that peace in the stillness of the morning, letting it soak all the way through her into the deepest places of her heart. It was a peace that was full and complete and went beyond her circumstances. Though she didn't know how things would end up, she knew it would be okay in the end.

Niz watched as a doe and her fawn came down to the river to drink, their eyes big and gentle, their ears large and pointed. Squirrels scampered through the boughs of the pines. The rust-colored breast of a robin caught her attention as it lighted on a nearby branch, and she watched as it sang its cheerful song. The distant haunting bugle of an elk carried on the still morning air, and she closed her eyes, picturing the majestic bull. As the sights and sounds of the mountains and the peace of God soaked in, she began to feel refreshed. The tension drained out of her shoulders, and her thoughts quieted. Finally, when the golden magic of the sunrise had given way to clear blue skies, she rolled her shoulders and pushed herself to her feet with one last deep breath.

"If you're God in nature, you're God in the village," she whispered. She was thankful she wasn't going back to camp alone.

She considered the changing leaves as she walked back to the village, realizing they were likely just a week away from the peak of their color. It was time to gather acorns and the last of the berries. Just after the mountainsides flamed gold, they would start packing supplies and disassembling their camp. They would head to lower elevations very soon. But first, she had breakfast to make and a conversation to have. Then, somehow over the next few days, she would need to figure out a way to talk to Ezra and tell him what Fire Maker had been doing. Whatever the price, she needed to tell the truth before they left the area.

Her thoughts roaming, she looked off to the north. She wondered if the soldiers had apprehended the raiders yet and how long they would be away from the fort. She prayed Ezra was safe and that God would give him wisdom and strength for whatever the day held. He would catch the Comanche; she was sure of it. He was a good leader and a good soldier—he would be victorious. She hoped those qualities would also enable him to deal with Fire Maker without putting her people in jeopardy. Either way, though, Fire Maker needed to come to justice, and she trusted Ezra to bring it about.

The horses in the corrals caught her eye, and she wondered when he might return the mounts they'd loaned him. Whenever he did, she was worried about how Fire Maker would respond. She hoped no one would get hurt and that she could find a chance to talk to Ezra then. If she couldn't, she would need to find a way to visit the fort.

If she did have to visit the fort, at least she could stop and see Marigold. The very idea of it made her smile. Niz wanted to tell her friend that she now followed Jesus and fill her in on what all had been happening since the last time they'd spoken.

Anticipating the news Marigold would have to share, Niz wondered if her friend and Ezra had married yet. She truly hoped so. They were both beautiful people, and she wanted each of them to be loved and have someone to love in return. Picturing them together, happy and complete, she smiled, even as she steeled herself against the bittersweet ache that filled her. Painful or not, they were perfect for each other. Ezra likely hadn't been at the fort much in the week since she'd talked to him while picking berries, but she hoped he'd made time to marry Marigold when he had been.

The village was waking up. As she walked between wickiups, Niz smiled and greeted friends and family. Fires were being stoked, and sleepy-eyed children were beginning to play. When she arrived at her own wickiup, she found Fire Maker snoring loudly inside. Her anxiety began to build again at the sight of him, and she moved back outside to light a fire and prepare their breakfast. There was no use waking him before it was necessary.

The meal was nearly ready when the braves arrived. When they greeted her and she looked up and saw that Wise Hawk was with them, standing between Lean Elk and Walks With Power, her throat felt thick and tears stung her eyes. She stood to welcome him, honored that he would come.

"I see you're surprised to see me, Nizhoni," he said, his old, weathered face gentle. "My grandson told me about what you did last night, and although I was not there, I will stand with you. You did a good thing to lend our support to the soldiers as they chase down our common enemies—and to soothe their anger. By doing so, you have made our lands safer and saved our people much heartache."

"Thank you, Wise Hawk," she said, taking his wrinkled hand and kissing the back of it with feeling. Her own grandfather had been gone many years, but Wise Hawk had often filled that void. She remembered sitting at his feet, listening to his stories as a wide-eyed child. He had taught Soaring Eagle, Ever Flowering, and herself how to use a bow and arrow, navigate by the stars, and rescued them once when they were caught in a snowstorm. That he would now come to be a part of a hard conversation, lending his presence and his wisdom, filled Niz with emotion.

Leaving Strong Pine and another of the younger braves to get Wise Hawk settled in a place of honor around the fire, Lean Elk and Walks With Power stepped close to Niz.

"Even Fire Maker cannot argue with Wise Hawk. When he sees he is here, he will have to hear us out," Lean Elk told her.

"I can't believe he came," Niz said, her throat aching with emotion.

Lean Elk smiled kindly. "When I told him what you had done after Fire Maker sent the soldier away empty-handed, he was impressed. He says you are quite a woman and an asset to our people. He's lived many years and seen many things. He says you saved lives last night with your quick thinking."

"Lives that Fire Maker put in jeopardy," Walks With Power added darkly.

"Well, I'm grateful and honored that he's here," Niz told them sincerely. She glanced back at the elder who was now sitting near the fire, his face stoic as he waited for the meal to begin. She was truly moved by his praise that Lean Elk had shared, as well as by his attendance. While the braves' presence felt like safety, Wise Hawk's felt like a gift. Glancing past him to the fire as she blinked back tears, she noticed her flatbread was smoking.

"My bread!" she exclaimed, rushing to the fire. Flipping it, she found she had caught it just in time. The golden-brown crust was just on the verge of turning dark. She breathed a sigh of relief; she'd put too much effort into grinding the amaranth seeds and mixing the dough, just to let it burn. When the bread had finished cooking, she ducked into the wickiup to waken Fire Maker.

She said his name, but he didn't stir. Knowing he was likely still sleeping off the alcohol he had consumed the night before, she squatted down on her heels and gently shook his arm. With a groan, he pushed her away, nearly knocking her over.

"Fire Maker, some of your braves have come to share the morning meal with you. Wise Hawk is here too," she said, trying again.

She watched her husband blink heavily. When he sat up, he swore and held his hand to his head, squinting against the bright light streaming in through the doorway. Realizing he was likely battling a headache, Niz cringed. An aching head would not improve his disposition.

"I have breakfast ready," she told him with a smile, hoping the promise of food would help.

He reached out and pushed her away again, this time knocking her off-balance and making her fall. "I've told you not to wake me. I'll wake up when I'm ready. You're trying to make me feel lazy, but I won't let you."

Caught off-guard by his accusation, she found her feet again and dusted off her hands. "Fire Maker, I'm not trying to make you feel lazy."

"Yes, you are, and I'm not going to let you guilt-trip me," he said, laying back down on his sleeping mat.

Her frustration growing, Niz took a deep breath. She had expected a confrontation outside, but she hadn't anticipated one just trying to get him out of the wickiup. "I promise I'm not trying to guilt-trip you. It's just that the br—"

"Yes, you are," he interrupted. "You always are. You're always trying to make it seem like I'm in the wrong. You're always trying to make me look bad. But I'm your husband, and I'll sleep as long as I want to. I'll tell you when I'm ready to eat, you don't tell me. Do you understand? Don't try to tell me when to wake up!"

Niz grimaced, knowing those gathered outside could hear every one of his loudly spoken words. She was embarrassed for him and for herself. "Fire Maker, some of your braves and Wise Hawk are here to share the morning meal with you. They're waiting outside," she repeated, realizing he must not have heard her the first time.

He sat up again. "What are they doing here?" he growled, continuing to hold his head.

"We need to speak to you."

"We?" he asked suspiciously. He looked up at her and narrowed his eyes. "What have you done, Nizhoni?"

"Why don't you come on out for breakfast, and we'll tell you?"

"If you've turned my friends against me . . ." Fire Maker let his threat dangle.

Niz held his gaze for a long moment. A hundred replies went through her mind, but she pressed her lips together, keeping every one of them back. They wouldn't accomplish anything, and she would have her moment to speak. Instead, she started to stand. As she did, he grabbed her wrist, holding it painfully tight.

She winced. "Please let go of me."

He didn't. His eyes were full of threats.

Twisting her hand free, Niz stood. "Join us outside. I have breakfast ready," she repeated.

Finishing the final preparations on the meal, Niz served it as soon as Fire Maker took his place near the fire. He looked around at the braves who sat there, his expression wary. "Go ahead and spit it out," he said, addressing them.

They looked at Niz, and she cleared her throat. Fire Maker turned his attention to her, his eyebrows raising. He was obviously surprised that she would be leading the conversation.

She cleared her throat again, trying to summon her courage. Though she would rather not be the one to speak, she knew she needed to do so. It was her responsibility. It had been her directions the braves had followed, her decision to defy Fire Maker and take the supplies to Ezra, and she who had spoken to him and presented what they brought. The braves had gone along with and supported her decision, but she had taken the lead. Now she must do so again.

"Fire Maker, we took twenty horses and food to the soldiers," she said, deciding being direct would be best. As she finished, she watched rage twist his handsome face until he was barely recognizable.

"You did what?" he demanded.

"We took enough dried meat, berries, and nuts for three meals for the patrol. We supplied twenty horses, which they will return," she explained quietly. "They were chasing our common enemy, Fire Maker. They did not ask our men to ride with them, only for fresh mounts and a little food to sustain them on their way. So we rode out yesterday evening and took it to them."

"After you heard me say I would not supply them with anything?" Fire Maker thundered. The braves looked back and forth between themselves, seeming uneasy. Niz wasn't. She'd been yelled at by him before. She sat still, her back straight, her gaze unwavering.

"It was not wise to say so," Wise Hawk said solemnly, entering the conversation, his face stoic.

Fire Maker's rage was like a palpable force as he turned on him. "No one asked you, old man!" he bellowed.

The braves and Niz gasped, shocked that he would speak to their elder with such disrespect. It was unheard of among their people. Elders were gravely honored, just as they had been for generations. More than ever before, Niz saw clearly how wicked her husband really was. If he dared to yell at Wise Hawk and speak to him with such insolence, then there truly must not be anything good within him, not even deep down. She wasn't sure if she felt more shock, sadness, or embarrassment for him—he had just demonstrated the depth of his harshness to them all.

Wise Hawk, however, did not react. Not even a muscle in his wizened face moved. "Your wife has done a good thing."

"My wife has defied me!" Fire Maker hissed back. "She has betrayed and disobeyed me. She deserves to be beaten, not praised! So, don't you dare stick up for her ol—"

"Fire Maker, we took the supplies and rode out in the direction the messenger had gone," Niz interrupted, diverting her husband's wrath away from the elder before Fire Maker could disrespect him further. "We met the patrol along the way. The soldiers were coming here to confront you—and anyone who stood with you."

A look of surprise replaced the anger that had filled his face. "Wait. So, let me get this straight. They were coming here to attack us, and yet you're trying to make it sound like I'm the one to blame?" He laughed, looking at her as if she were crazy. When he turned to his braves, clearly expecting them to agree, they only stared into the fire, seeming uncomfortable.

"You insulted the soldiers, and they were determined to have their revenge," Niz continued, saving the men from their discomfort. "If you would have survived the night, you would have been apprehended."

"You have such little faith in our warriors?" he scoffed. "You don't think we're man enough to hold off a small patrol? Those pathetic soldiers are nothing more than dogs!" Laughing, he reached over and hit Walks With Power's arm with the back of his hand. "What do you make of that? She doesn't think we can hold off a few soldiers who are so incompetent they don't even know how to track."

"We would not have stood with you," Walks With Power said, his eyes flashing.

Fire Maker jerked back as if he'd been struck, and fury filled his face again. "You dare to say such a thing to me—your leader?"

"You are no leader!" Walks With Power shot back. "You only lead us toward foolishness and death! The soldiers have been better to us than you have been. They have protected what we hold dear—our wives, our children, our people, our village. The only thing you hold dear is yourself!"

Fire Maker looked from Walks With Power to Niz. His eyes narrowed, and hatred shone from them. "You did this," he said, jabbing his finger toward her. "You turned my braves against me. You are working with that major, working against me, against our people. You are trying to weaken us by stealing our horses and our food, by causing trouble within our camp."

"I've spoken the truth," Niz answered quietly. "I was trying to protect our people. The soldiers will return the horses. We've had a good year of hunting and gathering. We can spare the food. Our people will not go hungry. And we have escaped bloodshed and the soldiers' revenge. They have graciously overlooked your bad behavior." She watched Fire Maker's face turn red and his hands clench into fists. She instinctively leaned back, trying to distance herself from him.

"*My* bad beh—" Suddenly, Fire Maker stopped, his angry face contorting. He clutched his chest, making groaning noises, before one of his hands flew to his head. He gripped it, crying out as if he were in agony.

Niz stood quickly, unsure of what was happening. "Something's wrong!"

She had expected him to be furious, but she hadn't expected this. Suddenly, the left side of his face began to droop, and his strong left arm fell limply to his side. The braves clamored to their feet, seeming uneasy and fearful. They watched, wide-eyed.

"Fire Maker? Fire Maker, can you hear me?" Niz asked, going down onto her knees beside him. He didn't seem to be focused on anything. His expression was confused, and drool began to run from his mouth. Suddenly, his eyes closed, and he slumped over. Catching him, struggling to hold him up, she looked to Strong Pine, who was closest. "Help me get him inside! Walks With Power, go after the medicine man!"

The braves jumped into action. Pushing her out of the way, Strong Pine, Lean Elk, and the others carried Fire Maker into the wickiup. Walks With Power raced off through the village. Niz stood and watched, feeling like everything was spinning. Her heart was racing, and alarm, concern, shock, and confusion were crashing through her in a cloudy swirl of emotion. In the midst of it all, suddenly Wise Hawk was beside her. He reached out and took her hand. His touch was gentle. "Sit with me. We will wait for the medicine man together."

"I should go in and help my husband," she told him, her voice shaky.

"Sit down, Nizhoni," he said kindly. "The braves are with him. They will see to Fire Maker." She nodded submissively and helped him sit again before taking the spot beside him. He lifted his head and looked out toward the far peaks. "I've seen this before, my girl. When the face goes slack, there is nothing one can do but wait. Now, only time will tell if his spirit will come back to him."

"There's nothing that can be done for him?" she asked in dismay. Fire Maker was so young and seemed so strong and healthy.

Wise Hawk patted her hand. "We will wait together."

Twenty-Four

O ver the next week and a half, life in the village went on as normal, even while it stood still inside Niz's wickiup. Outside, the women were gathering acorns and berries. The braves went hunting one last time. She heard the harvest was good; a plentiful end to a plentiful year. Cloud Walking reported that a small delegation of soldiers had brought back the horses. Through it all, Niz stayed in the wickiup with Fire Maker.

Holding his head and shoulders in her lap, she spooned water and broth into his mouth by the hour, trying to keep him hydrated despite his unconscious state. Though his heart continued to beat, his condition did not change. Not once in ten days did he open his eyes, move his fingers, or speak a word. His face stayed slack, his facial muscles drooped on his left side, and he remained unresponsive.

Wise Hawk came to sit with her daily, and they passed hours together in silence. Her mother, Cloud Walking, and Ever Flowering came too, stopping in just to see her and tell her about what was going on in the village. They brought Walks at Night with them when they came, and Niz held and cuddled him as long as he would let her, enjoying every chance to see her sweet son. When they left, they would take him back home with them, and she would resume her silent, lonely hours. She told herself it wouldn't last forever and that as hard as it was, it was for the best—she knew how much Walks at Night's presence had bothered Fire Maker, and she didn't want to add any stress to him if he was somehow aware of his surroundings.

But the days crawled by. Other friends and family stopped in, but despite their visits, they were the loneliest ten days of her life. She missed her son. She missed her people and the tasks that gave her purpose.

The one bright spot was that Ever Flowering was feeling the baby move, and when Niz laid her hand against Ever Flowering's swollen abdomen at her sister's urging, Niz felt it also. After being so worried the child had not survived the high fevers and Ever Flowering's weakened condition, Niz cried tears of joy.

While time seemed to stand still in an endless cycle of silence, spooning broth, and watching for any sign of life from her husband, Niz experienced a range of emotions. She felt guilty that a part of her was relieved. Sometimes, as ashamed as she was to admit it, even to herself, she nearly hoped he wouldn't wake up at all. When she faced that truth, she wept, crying out to God to make her heart pure.

Life with Fire Maker had been difficult, but she refused to give up hope—or give up on him. For better or worse, he was her husband. She had committed her life and her loyalty to him, and she would not rescind that now. And so she spent her days living in the tension. Hour after hour, she came to the same conclusion—though her husband hadn't been trustworthy, she believed Almighty God was. Thus, she would hope and pray for Fire Maker's healing, believing that if God brought her husband back from the state he was in, He could bring him back a changed man.

But it wasn't to be. On the tenth day, Fire Maker died. When his breathing stopped, Niz simply closed her eyes and sat there in silence. She had already cried all her tears; she didn't think she had any left. Unmoving, she stayed where she was, feeling sad about how things could have been and weren't, grieved by what their marriage had become, and thankful that it was over. Finally, she was free of the burdens she had carried since becoming Fire Maker's wife. Sorrow flooded her as she reflected on the potential he had wasted and the end he had come to. His last conscious moments had been filled with greed, foolishness, and anger, and that was what brought her the most sorrow of all.

Wise Hawk, who had been sitting with her, went to alert the others. Starting into motion, she set to work preparing the corpse, following the traditions of her people. She straightened Fire Maker's limbs, placed his bow and knife beside him, and wrapped him tightly in his hides and blankets.

With her immediate tasks completed, she stayed in the privacy of her wickiup and allowed herself to sit with her grief. She had decided in the long days of silence that whatever happened, she wouldn't do what she had done before. She wouldn't push down her emotions in fear of them, bury them under, keep herself busy to escape them, or refuse to give them space. She would face them, feel them, pray through them, and then, and only then, she would move on.

Hours after Fire Maker had breathed his last breath, she pushed herself to her feet and left the wickiup, finally feeling ready to do so. Stepping out into the fresh air and October sunshine, she took a deep, deep breath. The mountainsides were ablaze with bright splashes of brilliant gold. The blue sky seemed thinner somehow, and there was a decided chill in the air, even though it was mid-afternoon. Pulling a blanket around her shoulders, she started off toward her mother's wickiup. Having had hours—and ten days—to process, she was eager to be back with Walks at Night and her friends and family. The wickiup had been too empty, too silent, and too still, and she was craving noise and people.

When she reached her mother's wickiup, only Cloud Walking was outside. Niz watched the girl stand, her face full of concern. "Nizhoni! Wise Hawk told us the news. Mother said to give you time, but I brought Walks at Night back for his nap so I would be here whenever you came. Are you okay?"

Niz nodded as tears stung her eyes for the first time since Fire Maker died. This time, she didn't try to blink them back. Instead, she walked blindly into her younger sister's arms. Cloud Walking held her tight as she cried out all the tears she hadn't realized she had left.

Later, when Walks at Night woke from his nap, she took him for a walk, seeking solace in his company, the comfort of the mountains, and the chance to stretch her legs. She'd been cooped up for a long time. Getting out of her wickiup and away from the village brought perspective she desperately needed.

Ever Flowering and her mother were there when they got back, having returned from gathering acorns. More tears came, and Ever Flowering looped her arm through Niz's and led her down to the river, where they sat arm in arm while Niz shared every thought that filled her. Ever Flowering listened and helped her process, guiding her through her grief as she debriefed.

"I don't know how to feel," Niz admitted. "I'm sad . . . and I'm relieved. Can I be both? Is that wrong?"

"You can be both, Nizhoni. Grief is rarely only one thing—it comes tangled," Ever Flowering told her thoughtfully, her eyes gentle. "It's like the sky holding both sun and storm. Both are real. It doesn't have to be one or the other; both emotions can be true at the same time. You don't have to choose between them."

Absorbing her sister's words, Niz laid her head against Ever Flowering's shoulder, letting her imagery settle. Though Fire Maker hadn't been a good husband, he was the second one Niz had lost in just over a year. It was a confusing and uncomfortable mix of grief and loss and awkwardness as she dealt with that and the reality that she'd loved her first and regretted her second. And now they were both gone.

As Niz shared that struggle, Ever Flowering didn't scold her for speaking their names, nor seem shocked by her range of emotions. She just let her talk, reminding her of what was true and pointing her toward better days ahead. Encouraged and relieved, Niz thanked God once more for saving Ever Flowering; she couldn't imagine life without her.

When the shadows gathered, they stood and went back to Shy Fawn's wickiup together. Walks With Power joined them for their evening meal and said the council had decided that with Fire Maker's passing, they would leave for their winter camp in five days' time. Niz was glad—a change of scenery would be good. At their winter camp, she would figure out life for herself and her son. By the time the snow melted and the trees began to leaf out again, surely she would have found a new rhythm. That night, she slept beside Walks at Night in her mother's wickiup.

The next day, they laid Fire Maker to rest, extended on a scaffold in a high cleft of the mountain, as was customary for their people. They mourned together, singing their songs of grief. When they returned to the village, her wickiup was burnt according to their traditions, along with Fire Maker's personal belongings. Though her people were taking care that Fire Maker's spirit did not return, Niz didn't feel any fear. She didn't speak his name before them, nor share her new beliefs due to her mother's pleading, but she felt unendingly grateful for the hope and peace she had found in Jesus that freed her from the superstitions that had kept her bound in fear and anxiety.

With her husband buried and her wickiup burnt, Nizhoni and Walks at Night moved in with Shy Fawn and Cloud Walking. That night, Niz tossed and turned, feeling sad and unsettled even as she slept. When she woke the next morning, she still felt tired. With their move to the winter camp only three days away, there was much to be done, and Niz was thankful to have work to keep her hands—and mind—busy. When darkness fell, she sang Walks at Night to sleep before holding him close, thinking of all that had happened and wondering about what came next.

"What's on your mind?" Cloud Walking asked, scooting her sleeping mat closer.

Niz rolled onto her back, turning her face to look at her younger sister, surprised she was still awake. The hour was late.

"I can't sleep," Cloud Walking offered. "I could tell you weren't either . . . you weren't snoring."

Niz hit her sister with a cushion. "I don't snore." Cloud Walking giggled quietly and returned the blow, which Niz blocked with her elbow. "Cloud Walking! That almost hit Walks at Night!" she scolded.

"You started it!" Cloud Walking said, hitting her with the cushion again.

Niz caught it and wrestled it out of her sister's grip. Victorious, she put the cushion behind her head and laid on it with great satisfaction. They may be grown up now, but she could still win a pillow fight.

Cloud Walking rolled her eyes before laying her head in the crook of her arm as she looked at Niz. "Back to my original question. What's keeping you awake?"

Niz let out a small sigh. "The future."

"What about it?" Cloud Walking asked.

"What comes next, I guess . . . I have a few hides, a few baskets . . . Fire Maker's horses . . . a small son . . ."

"Just be glad our people aren't like other tribes we've heard about—no one expects you to join your husband in the afterlife. Our people will take care of you and Walks at Night."

"Yes, I am thankful for that," Niz agreed sincerely.

"Then what is it?"

Niz stared at the ceiling of the wickiup for a long time. Finally, she let out a deep sigh. "I'm twenty-one."

There were a few seconds of silence. "And?" Cloud Walking prompted. "I already knew that. I'm your sister, remember?"

Niz made a face at the teenager. "And . . . I've already buried two husbands. Two! What if people think I'm cursed?"

"What if you are?"

Niz reached over and swatted Cloud Walking. "That's not helpful."

"No, I'm serious. Who cares? Maybe our people would say it's a curse, but from where I'm sitting, it sure looks like a blessing. You told me yourself you didn't see a way forward, but you didn't see a way out. Now you're free."

"I didn't mean for Fire Maker to die."

"Well, maybe you don't get to choose the way out. Maybe you only get to be thankful that there was one."

"I feel guilty for being thankful."

Cloud Walking was quiet for a moment. When she spoke, her dark eyes were serious. "Did you pray for your God to strike Fire Maker down?"

"No!" Niz exclaimed, forgetting for a moment to speak quietly. "Of course not!"

"Right." Cloud Walking looked satisfied. "Nizhoni, you were married to a wicked man. You prayed to your God for help, and He helped you in the way He saw fit. He saved our people from the pain of a foolish chief. You shouldn't feel guilty about thanking your God for an answered prayer."

Niz let that settle, processing what her little sister had said.

"When Ever Flowering was sick, you prayed for healing, right?"

"Yes."

"But you told me that you trusted your God with the outcome because you believe He's sovereign, right?"

Niz nodded. Cloud Walking had been listening after all.

"And when she didn't die, you thanked Him for healing her, didn't you?"

"Yes, of course."

"Right, because it would be rude not to. Well, I think this is the same. You serve a powerful God, Nizhoni. You prayed; He answered your prayer according to His sovereignty, and you're thankful. If He had healed Fire Maker and changed his heart, you would have been thankful for that too."

Cloud Walking made it sound so simple and straightforward. Niz took a deep breath, and as she did, peace flowed in like a calming wave. Cloud Walking was right. She would have been thankful either way. Almighty God had answered her prayer. Who was she to disagree with how He'd answered it? Or to feel guilty as if He'd chosen wrongly? Maybe it really was enough to simply be thankful for an answered prayer and trust His sovereignty.

Niz turned her head to look at her sister again, noticing the lovely contours of Cloud Walking's face, the kindness of her eyes, the quickness of her smile. "When did you get so wise, little sister?"

"Little? I'm taller than you now," Cloud Walking quipped.

Niz made a face. "Okay, let me rephrase that. When did you get so wise, *younger* sister?"

The teen smiled broadly.

Niz turned to look up at the ceiling again. "It's just that I wonder . . . I mean, not that I want to even think about this yet of course, but . . . like I said, I'm twenty-one . . ."

"And?"

"And . . . what if I want to marry again someday but everyone thinks I'm cursed? Do I live the rest of my life alone? Life with Fire Maker was difficult, yes, but I know what it's like to have a wonderful marriage, too. And perhaps someday I won't want to live alone anymore. What if I want to marry and hopefully have more children—siblings for Walks at Night—but no one will have me?"

Cloud Walking laughed, earning herself a scowl from Niz. "That's what you're worried about?"

"Maybe."

"Trust me, that won't even cross Ezra's mind. In fact, if he knew about Fire Maker, I'd bet he'd be here tomorrow to whisk you away."

Niz gasped. "Cloud Walking! I wasn't talking about Ezra!"

The teen rolled her eyes. "But you should be."

"No, I shouldn't!" Niz protested.

"Give me one good reason," Cloud Walking challenged as only a younger sister could.

Niz glared at her. "I could give you several, but the main one is, I think he's taken."

"What?" Cloud Walking looked doubtful.

"It's true," Niz told her miserably. "I encouraged Marigold and Ezra to marry. When we were berry picking, Sergeant Green said they would wed soon, and that was nearly three weeks ago. I'm sure they have by now."

"Why would you do that?"

"They're perfect for each other, and I wanted them both to be happy."

"Well, that was dumb."

Niz narrowed her eyes at the young woman lying beside her. "How was I supposed to know I would be a widow just a month later?"

"You need to learn to mind your own business sometimes. You don't have to control everything. If two people are meant to be together, they'll find their way to each other with or without you."

Niz's first instinct was to be offended, and she didn't try to hide it. But then, as she thought about it, she realized her sister was right. She'd learned a lot since she'd tried to push Marigold and Ezra together, namely that she didn't always know best or have the ability to make everything work out. In her mind, encouraging them toward each other had been the right thing to do; in actuality, her attempts to control the narrative might have cost her the gift of loving and being loved. The ache in her chest grew.

"What about you? Who do you love?" she asked, trying to shift the conversation.

"That is not up for discussion. Like I said, sometimes you need to learn to mind your own business," Cloud Walking said, and suddenly, like a flash of lightning, she yanked the cushion out from under Niz's head. Niz's eyes widened in surprise as her head thumped against the ground. When she looked over, she saw Cloud Walking placing the cushion under her own head and grinning. She glared, and Cloud Walking put her finger to her lips and pointed at Walks at Night. "Don't wake the baby."

Her head sore, Niz stuck her tongue out at her sister.

"Wow. That was mature," Cloud Walking said dryly. Suddenly, they both started laughing. Remembering themselves, Cloud Walking glanced timidly back at Shy Fawn as Niz clamped a hand over her own mouth and checked on Walks at Night.

"Go to sleep, girls," Shy Fawn scolded drowsily from her own sleeping mat, and Niz was so close to breaking out in another spurt of laughter that she had to turn away so she couldn't see her sister. Still dangerously on the edge, she stayed facing away so long she fell asleep before she could trust herself to talk to Cloud Walking again. But for the first night in many nights, she went to sleep lighthearted and happy.

~~~

The next morning, Walks at Night woke early and was ready to play. He played with the fringe on Niz's dress, fingered the beadwork, tapped her forehead, tried to look in her shut eyes, and finally wrapped her dark hair around his sticky little fingers, accidentally pulling it as he unwound it. Resigning herself to the fact that he wasn't going to sleep again no matter how tired she was, Niz stood to her feet and scooped him up. Wrapping a blanket around them both, she stepped out into the still morning.

The sun was just beginning to lighten the eastern sky, and the air was cold. A skiff of snow had fallen during the night, turning the ground white. It would undoubtedly be gone as soon as the sun touched it, but for now, the world was clean and fresh and still. Walks at Night cuddled in close, seeming perfectly happy to stay in her arms where he was warm, now that they were up.

Niz couldn't hold back a sleepy smile. "I'm happy with that too," she told him, pressing a kiss against his cheek. She'd missed him.

When he pointed and started babbling about water, she carried him down to the river. Standing on its bank, snuggled into the blanket together, they watched the sun come up. Squinting against the brightness, Walks at Night pointed in awe and babbled as the sun appeared over the eastern mountains.

"Sun," she told him. "That's the sun."

"Sun," he repeated.

"Good," she praised with a big smile and another kiss on his little cold cheek. His answering grin was proud and toothy. She pointed to a bluebird in a nearby tree. "Bird."

He jumped up and down in her arms with excitement and did his best to mimic her once more.

"You grew up so much in ten days," she said sadly. It had only been a week and a half that he'd been out of her care, but it felt like he'd changed greatly in that short time. His baby babbling now had recognizable sounds and a few clear words.

Walks at Night pointed at the river, she named it, and he tried hard to repeat it. They continued the game for several minutes until he pointed toward the east and excitedly said, "Horse!"

"No, the horses are back over there in the corral," she corrected, turning so she could point out the animals that were barely visible on the other side of the village.

He immediately swiveled in her arms. "Horse!" he said again.

Niz shook her head, getting ready to correct him once more but stopped as she caught sight of a lone horse and rider approaching. Recognizing the dark blue uniform of a soldier, she started walking toward the rider, hoping to intercept him and ask what he wanted before he awakened the camp. When she saw that it was Ezra, her heart began to race. Frustrated by her traitorous reaction, she focused on taking deep breaths, knowing she had to compose herself by the time he dismounted.

She hadn't seen Ezra since delivering the food and horses to him, but much had happened since. There were a dozen reasons she should turn around and go back to the safety of the village, where she could hide her true feelings in the presence and accountability of others. Yet her moccasined feet continued moving forward, going out further into the mountain meadow to meet him, curious about his reason for coming.

Noting that he was alone, she wondered where the soldiers were that he typically rode with. Why had he come and especially at such an early hour? She certainly hoped all was well and that his visit wasn't an indication of trouble.

In her arms, Walks at Night was a lively, jumping expression of excitement as he too had recognized his friend. Niz tried to calm him as she tried to calm her heart—and was completely unsuccessful at both.

For the first time since she had met Ezra, she was available. She could run to him and hug him just as her son surely would. But Sergeant Green's words came back to stop her. No matter how much she no longer wanted it to be true, it sounded like Ezra's heart now belonged to one of her dearest friends. For many years he had honored his friend by keeping his distance, and now she would honor hers. They just weren't meant to be.

Niz watched as Ezra reined in his horse not far from them and stepped down out of the saddle. With the rising sun behind him, she couldn't make out his expression. Walks at Night was excitedly reaching his arms out toward him, but she kept a firm grip on her son, needing the security of holding him. With her arms around Walks at Night, she could hold herself together.

Reaching them, Ezra tousled the boys' hair with a smile. "Hey, little guy," he said fondly.

Walks at Night began to jabber wildly and incoherently with only a few words like horse and river standing out amongst the rest of his one-year-old dialect. Niz smiled, keeping her eyes on her son, forcing herself to laugh casually. "I think he's happy to see you."

Ezra didn't respond, and she glanced up at him cautiously. When she met his hazel eyes, there was nothing casual about the moment. Her breath caught at the intensity of his gaze.

"Some of my men came across some of your braves last night. Walks With Power was with them. He managed to get across that Fire Maker had died. Is that true?" Niz nodded, not trusting herself to speak, feeling altogether too emotional. He winced. "I'm so sorry you're going through this again."

Looking up into his handsome face, her eyes filled with tears. Ezra felt like the safety of home, the warmth of a roaring fire on a frozen winter night, and the comfort of being known and deeply loved. Before she could stop herself, she was walking into his open arms, and he was wrapping them around her, holding her and Walks at Night tight against his solid chest.

"Ezra, he was working with the Comanche," she said, the words spilling out. "He was raiding homesteads, stealing horses that he sold to you. After the Comanche raided our village, I think he started selling you the horses the Comanche had stolen, too, charging you those crazy prices and splitting the profits with them. I wanted to tell you. I know I should have told you. I was going to. I had made up my mind. But then your soldier rode in, and Fire Maker was so rude, and you were so angry."

"I know," he murmured against her hair, resting his head against the top of hers.

"You know?" she asked, surprised.

"We caught the Comanche. I'd had my suspicions, and then they ended up telling us everything about their deal with Fire Maker. We had to take them over the mountains to stand trial. We were going to arrest Fire Maker when we returned the horses and take him too, but when we arrived, Cloud Walking said he was ill."

"So, you decided to wait to see what would happen," she finished, understanding.

"I didn't want to start trouble with your people if there was no need. And then, when I heard last night . . . but the soldiers weren't sure they had understood Walks With Power correctly. I was supposed to be leading a patrol this morning. I thought about sending Sergeant Green to find out what had happened for sure, but . . . I had to know if . . ."

Niz wiped her eyes and stepped back out of Ezra's arms. She held Walks at Night tighter, trying to make up for the warmth she'd lost by stepping away. Antsy, the boy started fussing.

"Marigold must have been sad to see you heading out on patrol again so soon after returning from your trip over the mountains," she said cautiously, quickly counting days up in her head as she tried to quiet her son. Ezra must have only just returned.

His amused smile made her heart leap. "Marigold?"

"Ms. Langston . . . I'm sure . . . but . . ." Niz paused, seeing him shake his head, his smile growing by the second.

"Ms. Langston left to join her father at Ft. Sidney just before we caught the Comanche. I saw her off and made her promise to write . . . to both of us."

"But . . . Sergeant Green said you went to her house for dinner every night you weren't on patrol."

He sent her a pointed look. "She knew how taxing the extra patrols were, so she offered to cook dinners for us officers since you had taught her so well. She was trying to ease the burden."

"He said there were going to be a lot of broken hearts at the fort . . ." Niz argued, confused, pressing her hand to her forehead. What exactly had Sergeant Green said? Had she read into it?

"Probably because she was leaving soon."

"But . . . you were perfect for each other!" Niz protested, trying to comprehend what he was saying.

Ezra shook his head, amusement brightening his hazel eyes. "Stop. You can't control who I love, Beautiful." He smiled as she frowned. Reaching out, he ran his hand over her dark hair. "So I rode out here this morning to ask you a question."

She lifted her chin. "What's that?"

"After all these years, are you finally not married?"

Her breath caught in surprise, and she could feel her eyes shining at him. "No, Ezra, I'm not married."

She watched with delight as he let out the breath he'd been holding. "Good. Then for heaven's sake, will you marry me, Nizhoni?" Her eyes widened and he reached out and cupped his warm hand to her face. "I know it's too soon. I really do. But you're leaving for your winter camp, and I had to ask before you go. If you want to take the winter to get your bearings, fine. I'll still be here waiting for you when you come back. I just can't let you go without asking." He brushed his thumb over her cheek.

"I can't risk some other guy swooping in over the winter and stealing you away yet again, because I really want to be your husband and love you the way you deserve to be loved every day for the rest of our lives." His eyes began to dance with amusement. "Which if your record holds might be short-lived . . . but even if it is, I would die a happy man if I got to spend even one day married to you."

Her mouth fell open in shock, and she let out a cry of disbelief. "Ezra! How could you joke about a thing like that? That's the most insensitive, rude—"

He laughed as he gathered her into his arms. "So, what do you say, Beautiful?" he asked, interrupting her scolding. "Will you marry me?"

Tipping her head back, she looked up into his ruggedly handsome face, studied his hazel eyes, took in his masculine features, and reveled in how tenderly he held her. She remembered what it had felt like to kiss him, and her heart began to drum.

"Can you please just say yes already?" a familiar voice requested from behind her. Niz jumped and Ezra laughed, releasing her as she whirled around. "I don't need to speak English fluently to know he's asking you to marry him," her sister continued.

"Cloud Walking! Are you spying on me?" Niz demanded.

"It's not spying if I can't understand what's being said!" Cloud Walking argued. "And I just came for Walks at Night. I thought you two might like a moment alone."

"Oh." Niz looked to where her son was reaching for the ground, for his aunt, for anything other than where he was. She'd been so intent on Ezra, she hadn't noticed. Ezra reached out and ruffled the boy's hair as Niz handed him to Cloud Walking.

"I told you he would come today," Cloud Walking said jubilantly. "I was right, wasn't I?"

"How did you know?" Nizhoni asked, narrowing her eyes.

"Because we're leaving for our winter camp the day after tomorrow, and you're not coming with us," Cloud Walking answered nonchalantly.

"*What?*"

"Your place is here, Sister. We all know it . . . well, everyone but Mother. Walks With Power went out searching for the soldiers yesterday. He knew if the major learned Fire Maker had died, he would come for you, just as he has."

Niz's eyebrows furrowed together as a frown filled her face. "But . . . my place is with our people . . . I learned to read . . . Ever Flowering . . ."

"Nizhoni, you don't follow the beliefs of our people, you're in love with a major in the United States Army, and you sleep with a cushion under your head," Cloud Walking said with a laugh. "You belong with Ezra Taylor." She held up her hand to stop Niz's protest. "Ever Flowering is so much better. If they need someone to read something, they'll know where you are. Our people will be back next summer, and we'll come visit the village often."

"We?" Niz asked, raising an eyebrow in question.

Cloud Walking smiled and shrugged. "I belong with Sergeant Green just like you belong with the major. I accepted his proposal when he came to return the horses. We're getting married tomorrow—just before our people leave."

"*What*?" Niz questioned again in disbelief.

Cloud Walking shrugged. "I realized I love Sergeant Green, and I want to make my life with him. That's why I couldn't bring myself to marry Strong Pine. He's a good, good man, but he's not my man. Sergeant Green is."

"How do you know? You can't even talk to him!" Their mother was going to be so mad.

"I can speak some English!" Cloud Walking argued. "I've been practicing. Ever since I had to sit at the major's kitchen table and listen to you repeat the same words over and over—a—a—apple, b—b—bear, c—c—cat. What? I could see the pictures in the book too." Cloud Walking sent her a sassy look. "Anyway, I love Sergeant Green—Samuel. And I want to learn more about this Jesus Christ you follow . . . this God who answers prayers, leads His followers in love, and brings peace. I want that too. I'm also going to need you to teach me more English, because I definitely need some lessons. Maybe we could work out a trade." Cloud Walking grinned. "But there will be time for that later. Right now, you've got someone waiting." She pointed at Ezra. Turning, the teen galloped like a horse back toward the village, drawing peals of laughter from Walks at Night.

Shocked, Niz stared after her sister for a long moment. A lot truly had changed in ten days, much more than just her son. When she'd felt like she'd been out of it, secluded away in her wickiup, she really had been. A great deal of life had been going on outside the hide hanging over her door. But thinking back on the feeling, praying, and surrendering she had walked through, she realized plenty had been going on inside it too.

She startled as gentle arms slid around her shoulders and stomach as Ezra drew her back against the warmth of his chest. He rested the side of his face against hers. "What was that about?" he asked.

Despite his thick uniform, she could clearly feel his muscles and the strength of his arms that held her, but it made her feel safe, not frightened. There was no fear in her that he would treat her as Fire Maker had. She knew Ezra Taylor. She'd known him when he was just Alex's best friend, the soldier in command, a one-year-old's buddy, and her concerned friend. She had seen him when he was angry, frustrated, and insulted, and observed how he responded when confronted with wisdom when he was acting out of emotion. His reactions were safe, his character was admirable, and the way he treated others was patient, compassionate, and kind. Without even trying, he had proven over and over again that he was a man worthy of her trust. She believed his soldiers, the braves, Marigold, and Mother Emaline would all agree.

Niz snuggled back into the comfort of his arms as she shrugged. "She's marrying Sergeant Green and wants to hear more about Jesus."

"Aw, yes. Tomorrow's the big day, right?" he asked, kissing her temple. He followed it by dropping his head and pressing a kiss against the line of her jaw, making her shiver.

"You knew?" she accused, fighting his distraction.

She felt him smile. "You still haven't answered my question, Beautiful. Do you mind if we finish that before we move on? I've been waiting a very, very long time."

Not able to hold back a smile of her own, she turned in his arms. He was right—she could think about Cloud Walking's news later.

Refocusing, she looked up at Ezra and felt her heart filling with so much love that it ached. Could it truly be that the man who had loved her for years, who had been a true friend to Alex, to her people, and to her, who spoke in poetry about her, and pinned up pictures in his office of the most important men in her life, the man who had filled her empty arms with a son and brought beads to her mother—the man whom she had fallen deeply in love with—wanted her to be his wife? And there was finally no reason why she couldn't say yes and spend the rest of her life loving him and being loved by him in return?

This was hope. This was joy. This was a thousand answered prayers for Jesus to somehow work out something that seemed impossible; a future only an all-knowing God could put together; a happy ending—and beginning—where there had literally been no way. After the heavy burden she had carried and finally surrendered—a burden full of grief, loss, broken dreams, hard things, pain, and suffering—this was the sweetest trade she'd ever made.

Grief for joy, loss for new beginnings, broken dreams for a rosy future, hard things for comfort, pain for healing, suffering for love.

It wasn't a fair trade. She knew that. And her heart filled with thankfulness for the love of God that had always been giving her better than she deserved, making a way where she had none, and redeeming her from impossible situations. Tears gathered in her eyes, and she didn't blink them away. The moment almost felt holy as the magnitude of the love of God crashed over her.

She took a deep breath. "I want to live in the mountains."

He nodded his agreement. "This is home. For both of us."

"Walks at Night—"

"Is our son. He'll be our oldest, but hopefully not our last."

She tilted her head, watching his face for his reaction. "Could we call Walks at Night by his given name—Alex?"

"Are you asking if I like the name? Or if it's okay to talk about and remember your first husband?"

She lifted her shoulders and let them fall. "Maybe a little of both."

"I've actually spent a lot of time pondering this. Here's what I think. Do I wish things had gone differently, and I had found you first? Certainly. But Alex was like a brother to me, and I'll always miss him. He's a part of both of our pasts, and actually, I'm glad that we share his memory. I'm not threatened by that. I know if he could choose anyone else to be with you, honestly, it would be me. And he would threaten me within an inch of my life that I had better treat you right." Niz laughed, even as her eyes filled with tears. "And so that's exactly what I'm going to do, Beautiful. I'm going to love you like he would want you to be loved—the way I want you to be loved. He was our past, but we are the present and the future, and I'm confident in us. So, absolutely, let's call our son by his given name, and when we do, let's do so in honor of a man who meant the world to both of us. Don't be afraid to say Alex's name around me. We'll remember him together."

She nodded as he reached out and tenderly wiped away the few tears that had slipped down her cheeks. His gentleness was like rain to her parched heart. She leaned into his hand.

"So?" he asked, gently prodding. "An answer would be good because I'd really like to kiss you . . ."

"One last thing."

"Name it," he said, his gaze dropping to her lips.

"You must promise that before we settle down here in the mountains that you'll take me away. Take me up to the Black Hills or down to the desert, but wherever else we go, you have to promise that you'll take me to the Pacific so we can explore the shores and watch for a spouting whale together." Raising her chin, she met Ezra's hazel eyes that were now full of both wonder and love, and said the words she could no longer hold back. "What I want with my whole heart is to be your wife and to take this journey of life by your side, because I think you, Ezra Taylor, are going to be my greatest adventure."

Ezra leaned down and pressed his lips against hers, the strength of his love and the fullness of his joy coming through his kiss. Her heart seemed to race and stop all at the same time.

And yet, as much as she loved it, as much as she never wanted it to end, she knew that the man in front of her was a very good gift from a perfect God—a God who heard her prayers, answered them, and had a plan that was truly best, even when she didn't understand what best was. That knowledge made her heart drum to a new rhythm—a rhythm of true and perfect love.

The End

A Note From Ann

Dear Reader,

As I finished this book tonight (currently 2:45 a.m.), I just sat here for a moment unsure of what to say or how to process it. I needed a minute. I can't believe this series is over. It's been ten years in the making, and these characters have come to feel like friends.

This story was a challenging one to write. It took a ton of research to write the cultural setting of this book, and while I absolutely loved traveling to western Colorado, combing through museums, and doing online research on the vibrant and beautiful culture of Native American tribes in the area, it was a lot to wrap my head around. I never named the tribe I imagined Niz belonging to because I don't pretend to know the beautiful intricacies of it. Though I did my best to learn and bring historical accuracy into this work of fiction, I'm sure I'm still seeing through my lens, and my picture is incomplete. I never want to dishonor a group of people through an incomplete picture, so Niz's tribe will remain a work of fiction with roots in real and beautiful indigenous people groups. Please realize this decision was made with the intention of honoring and respecting. I look forward to heaven one day, where every tribe, tongue, and people will be represented, where we can learn firsthand about the different people groups God loves with a full, complete, unhindered perspective.

One of my favorite things to do when writing a book is to stand in the setting where it takes place and spend a moment just seeing, smelling, breathing, and listening. The beauty of a story isn't found on a page; it's found in a human experience. That includes mine as an author, yours as a reader, and hopefully, if I was successful in wrapping them in flesh, the characters'. Like most of our lives, there were elements of Niz's experience that were beautiful and heartwarming, and there were elements that were difficult to write, difficult to insert myself into, and likely difficult to read too. But the reality is, life comes with both. Joy often exists alongside suffering, love alongside loss, good alongside hard. And we walk the uncomfortable road of living in that tension. Like Niz, sometimes we find ourselves in circumstances that we never thought we would be in, where things feel dark and uncertain, where we can't see a way out and we don't feel like we can continue on. And in that place, our hope is Jesus. I pray you felt that hope while reading this book.

I've known for years that Niz's story was going to be a fictional retelling of the Biblical story of Abigail. When I started diving into Scripture to really learn about the heart of the story, I realized it was going to be a difficult road. The first challenge was that the main character was married to another man for most of the story. How do you write a God-honoring love story when one of the characters is married and there's no redemption in that marriage? I realized that to do so, love had to look a whole lot deeper than a cute and cozy relationship based on chemistry, attraction, and all the popular tropes. It had to look like the true meaning of the word, which is better characterized by words like selflessness, sacrifice, patience, kindness and long-suffering. Secondly, it's not fun to retell a story about a character who is described as evil in his dealings, harsh, and badly behaved. Though we know Nabal in the biblical story is made in the image of God, we see no sign of redemption in his life, no redeeming glimmer of good in him. In this book, as Niz walks this road with Fire Maker, I realized a harsh, evil, badly behaved man is not going to be a loving, caring husband—or even simply indifferent and neutral. He's going to deal with his wife in accordance with the condition of his heart, and that is difficult to witness.

Writing Niz's story with an emotionally and physically abusive husband was painful. I wanted someone to step in and save her; I wanted her to go for help. We see those things begin to happen in the end, but ultimately, we see the LORD come to her defense. He gives her beauty for ashes. He gives her freedom. He wraps her in love. Though justice will always come, it doesn't always play out the same way. Circumstances, people, and plans are different. So, if you're looking to the LORD for justice, waiting for Him to come to your defense, seek Him for His specific plan for your life and ask how you can actively partner with Him in it.

As I wrote this book, I began to realize that this wasn't a story of a woman and a man. Instead, it was a story of a Defender. As heroic, gentle, and easy to like as Ezra is, he's not the hero of this story. And even though Nizhoni is a peacemaking truth speaker who seeks to help her people, she isn't either. The LORD God Almighty is the hero of this story. It's all about Him.

When Niz realized that she wanted God to be a version of herself with a big megaphone, I found myself in that. How easy is it to want things to work out like we think they should? It's so natural to slip into patterns of control, thinking we know best, trying to work everything out to fit this plan we think will keep life happy and good for everyone we love. We just want everyone and everything to be okay. To make that happen, it's easy to think everyone needs to act as we think they should—including God. And when He doesn't move according to (our) plan, it's tempting to accuse Him of not being good or not being powerful. But the reality is, we're not God. He's not me with a giant speaker. He's not you with a megaphone either. He is Sovereign. His ways are above our ways; His thoughts are above our thoughts.

If we want to be followers of Jesus, we have to understand that this is His story that we get the incredible opportunity to be part of. This is all about Him and His plan to redeem the world. He is the God of restoration, redemption, and resurrection, and He is always working in that direction. His goodness—and existence—is not dependent on our comfort level or His willingness to play by our rules. Though He is intricately invested in our lives because of His great love for us, He is God and we are not. We don't have all the answers. Our version of what best is, is often flawed. This Christian walk is about surrender. Surrender is where we put our faith into practice; faith that He is good even when life is hard, faith that His ways are best even when we don't see it, faith that He is trustworthy even when things aren't going according to our plan. Following Jesus isn't just saying we believe He exists (the enemy believes that) it's submitting to the Lordship of Jesus, and making Him the Lord of our lives—wherever that takes us and however that looks. As Niz bends her knee to surrender control of her life to Jesus, we see Him take over and do things only He can do—things she never could have accomplished. How many times does He do the same in our lives? I know I've seen it time and time again in my own. When there seems to be no way, He makes one.

One thing I really loved about Niz's character (taken straight from Abigail's), is that she's a strong woman who doesn't shrink back. She's a woman of intelligence, beauty, and discernment who has a voice and uses it. Though she wrestles with heartbreaking realities, Niz stays faithful, self-controlled, and strong as she deals with a difficult person. She makes peace and diffuses dangerous situations, but she tells the truth. She doesn't run from conflict when conflict is necessary, but she bravely faces it with wisdom. I think sometimes we believe being godly means keeping the peace by being quiet or not speaking up, but in this story, we see a woman walk the fine line of being respectful and wise while also refusing to stay silent in the face of injustice. She was strong, and she didn't hide it. She embraced it, and God used it. If you've ever been told you're too much—too loud, too outspoken, too joyful, too fiery, too honest—know that you were created to be strong. The challenge isn't to suppress that part of you; it's submitting it to Jesus and letting it accomplish the good purpose He created it for. You're likely still in the process of refinement, as we all are, but you're not too much—you were wonderfully made.

As I wrap this up, I want to leave you with this lesson I learned from the story of Abigail: There's so much power in reminding someone of who they truly are (as Niz reminded Ezra of who he was when he'd forgotten in the face of revenge). Don't hesitate to do so. Drenched in love and wisdom, remind them of who God made them to be. Maybe you need to remind yourself of your true identity too. And most importantly, remember the truth of who God is. He is trustworthy. He is good. He is in the process of redeeming. He is faithful. When you keep that in mind and trust Him to work things out, there will always prove to be a way forward in the end.

Honestly, I can't believe this series is over. After so many years, these characters have found a place in my heart. Thank you for following me through these books, and for allowing me to share these stories with you. I pray you found yourself entertained by these strong women, encouraged by the themes, and inspired to lean into Jesus even a little bit more.

I love to hear from my readers, so always feel free to send me an email or reach out on social media! And I look forward to meeting you again as we lean into the grace and redemption of Jesus in the pages of fiction.

May the LORD bless you and keep you and cause His face to shine upon you,

WANT MORE?

WE HAVE TWO WAYS YOU CAN EXPERIENCE MORE OF THE MOUNTAIN REDEMPTION SERIES TODAY!

1. FREE BONUS SHORT STORY

We know Mother Emaline from her role as Raya, Chenoa, and Nizhoni's beloved mother-in-law. But while we've seen her unwavering faith and the impact she's had on her daughters-in-law, where did her faith come from and what were her years like before tragedy struck?

There was a time when Emaline's own life was filled with the rosy hues of love and coming of age - yet even then, storm clouds were brewing on the horizon. A family secret, a desperate situation, and a stranger at a ball collide in a perfect storm that promises to solidify her faith and her future - or break her in the process. To get Emaline's short story absolutely FREE and start reading today visit:

https://anngoering.com/mountain-redemption-series

2. Q&A WITH THE AUTHOR

Go behind the scenes with Ann A. Goering, as she discusses the inspiration and research process behind the Mountain Redemption Series, pronunciations of names, and her writing process. Hear her expand on the Biblical themes woven throughout the books, the purpose behind her storytelling, and how it applies to you (her beloved reader!).

If you enjoyed the books, you won't want to miss this video Q&A with the author! To watch it visit:

https://anngoering.com/mountain-redemption-series-qa-with-the-author

AUTHOR BIO

Ann Goering is an award-winning journalist and author of Christian fiction.

Goering is passionate about helping women encounter Jesus, experience transformative hope, and live a life deeply rooted in the Word of God. She's worked alongside an international Christian ministry for the past 15 years, as well as serving at her local church, and leading groups of women into encounters with Jesus through small groups and Bible studies.

She believes so much in the power of stories to illustrate spiritual principles, grow faith, and increase empathy, so wherever she is, you'll find her sharing stories that reveal the beauty of Jesus amidst everyday life.

Goering loves entrepreneurship, travel, rodeos, interior design, deep friendships, and good hair days, but her absolute favorites are the people in her life.

She's a Midwest girl soaking up the sunshine in the American Southwest, living on chicken molé and sweet tea, homeschooling her three best friends (aka daughters) with the only guy she's ever kissed.

CONNECT WITH ANN!

Website: www.anngoering.com
Facebook: www.facebook.com/AuthorAnnGoering
Instagram: www.instagram.com/ann.goering
Email: ann@anngoering.com

Love *To the Beat of a Fool's Drum*?
Please consider taking a moment to leave a review!
It truly means so much to the author – and your words mean more to future readers than ours ever could. From the bottom of our hearts, we truly hope reading *To The Beat of a Fool's Drum* has been a 5-star experience!